THE CARETAKER

WINDY PRASERT

Middleton

ISBN 978-1-7336832-0-3

Library of Congress Control Number 2019904421

Cover and design by Damonza
Edited by Shaylin Gandhi, Kim Chance, and Dahlia
Borroughs

Printed and bound in the United States of America
This edition published in 2019 by Middleton Publications

Visit www.WindyPrasert.com

For Paul, Collin, and Mikaela

THE CARETAKER

Windy Prasert

Middleton
PUBLICATIONS

PART I - THE CARETAKER

More than mere fantasy, Rick's soul recognized it all, a familiar, yet unknown place lulling him home. There and gone in a flash, the vision lingered like the tail-end of a dream.

And in that moment, Rick Holliday very nearly knew . . . something.

1

GHOST HUNTERS

Matt fussed with his hair in a compact mirror before staring soberly into the lens. "Are you recording?"

Rob pressed a button on his camera. "I am now."

Matt's eyes darted as his voice lowered. "We're here at Serenity Grove, the oldest cemetery in Hood Valley, where locals say some serious hauntings have been going on." With a set jaw, Matt awaited the crack of a twig or a sudden chill in the air. "Legend has it there's one ghost here who's particularly angry."

Rob forced back a groan. He'd filmed this display a hundred times in cemeteries all over Oregon. The set-up was always the same: the crew entered a graveyard under cover of darkness—sometimes with permission, usually without. The camera rolled while Matt crept around ancient tombstones, following rumors of hauntings and murmurs of sightings. That they'd never found anything of substance didn't matter; careful editing took care of that.

Crooking a finger, Matt shuffled toward the rear of the

cemetery. "We're headed to the spot where people experience their greatest terror, where tales say an old man
haunts the living. And folks, this guy is scary." Drawing
out the tension, he cocked his head, attentive to the
darkness.

Walking alongside the sound girl, Rob flicked the light
on his power cap. Not too much; in this business, the
darker, the better. There was also the small matter of the
caretaker who lived on-site. The three ghost hunters had
quietly trespassed around the old stone cottage on their
way in. But, as Matt always said, it was easier to ask
forgiveness than permission—at least once the episode
aired.

"We're getting close," Matt teased. "Let's see what the
EMF shows us." He thrust the meter at the camera. The
needle hovered in the yellow zone. "Look at this, folks.
We're picking something up. Let's see if we can get a
stronger reading further into the heart of the old man's
lair."

Taking the cue, Rob zoomed closer—the tension-
building shot—and threw a thumbs-up.

"We're about to enter the nest, folks," Matt whispered,
"and I can feel the spirit nearby. I've got goosebumps.
Check this out."

Rob pulled the shot back as Matt rubbed his arms,
careful not to reveal baby-smooth skin.

Six more months, he thought. *After that, I can talk to
Hank, try to get on the morning show, or maybe that afternoon talk show no one watches. I'm over this ghost-
hunting shit.*

Matt edged onward as if an attack were imminent,
whipping his head left and right before halting beneath a

large, crooked elm. Rob recognized the dead tree from the photos at their prep meeting. Lifeless and barren, the gnarled tree seemed to have died trying to grow away from itself. Matt had nearly leaped from his chair at photos of the grave beyond—a simple cross leaning askew, with a paint-chipped name scrawled across the weathered wood:

Herbert Casper
June 2, 1935
June 11, 1998

No *beloved father*, no *loving husband.* The surrounding grass had turned a muddy brown, and even Rob had to admit the pictures looked creepy as hell. Here, under a full moon, it was enough to spook just about anyone. Rob reminded himself he'd spent too much time in the editing room creating spooky scenes from nothing to be bothered by a dead tree.

Matt knelt, holding the EMF machine over the grave. A hidden button enabled him to ramp up the drama, and Rob made sure to film at an angle that would hide its subtle deployment.

The needle jumped. "Guys, we've got a reading! Herbert Casper, we're here to talk. Tell us why you're so . . . so very angry."

Rob fought the urge to check his watch, knowing they'd have to film similar scenes two, if not three times, before the night was over. There'd be a shot of Matt running toward a shimmering figure that the camera would barely miss. Matt would assure his audience that the spirit *had* been there and the crew *had* seen it. Creaks, rustlings, and distant moans would be added later to match Matt's reaction to the silence.

I could start asking around the union on Monday.

"Herbert Casper, show yourself!" Matt shouted as he crossed onto the dead man's grave.

Even in the warmth of a September evening, a sudden chill made the hairs on Rob's arms jump to attention. Rattling branches breached the quiet. The dip in temperature would have been easy to dismiss had Rob not also spotted a shift in Matt's demeanor. Even the sound girl skimmed a hand over her bare arm.

Something brushed Rob's leg, and his heart rate accelerated. As a trained cameraman, nothing could distract him from a clean shot, but he looked down anyway.

Nothing but his own two legs.

He'd unbalanced the camera. Rob cursed under his breath and tried to shake off the ominous change in the air. Maybe he was coming down with something—Melanie had seemed sniffly when he'd left for work. He rolled his shoulders back to quell the iciness creeping into his bones, which helped for roughly three seconds.

A voice pierced the darkness, seemingly from every direction at once.

". . . the hell off my grave, you little shit!"

The sound girl dropped the boom and sprinted back toward the gate. *So much for cheap labor*, Rob thought, even as he resisted the impulse to join her.

Matt's brows drew together as he whimpered with a mousy squeak. "Mr. Casper?" Gone was the familiar bravado that made him the perfect host for cheap television.

Rob thought for one incredulous moment that Matt might even cry. He hoped he could get *that* on tape.

". . . said get off! You're not robbing my grave, not tonight!" The words rose and fell from the oddly disembodied voice.

Matt was beginning to look like a man who'd just filled his Pampers. "I, uh, we're not robbing, we're . . . Rob, are you getting this?"

"Yeah." Rob knew Matt must be out of his element to address him directly on film. Matt liked to be the sole star of the show, giving the illusion that he was the lone wolf in a spooky graveyard.

A high-pitched screech filled the air as a menacing laugh swarmed. The voice, dark and foreboding, turned Rob's blood to ice.

"Get out before I shove my fists up both your asses!"

Rob didn't need to be told twice.

"I'm out, man." Rob turned to run, but a body slammed into him. He crashed to the ground, and the camera went flying. Later, the footage would show a grainy image of Matt sprinting away while the EMF machine lay in a shattered mess. Matt, the brave ghost hunter, the self-appointed Seeker of Souls, was apparently as heroic as a titmouse when up against the real thing.

Which made Rob realize they *were* up against the real thing. He grabbed the camera as the old man's ghost howled.

". . . asshole, I said move before you piss all over the place!"

Rob ran faster than he had in his life.

ALL HAD FALLEN SILENT IN THE HEART OF THE CEMETERY as eerie, unnatural moonlight bathed the old man's grave. A lonely owl called while the receding taillights of a van lit the darkness beyond the gate.

A cloud drifted across the moon, plunging the cemetery into smoky obscurity. Sparks of electricity pawed at the edge of the wind as in the moments preceding a storm.

Thick fog poured in, and two translucent figures stepped from the veil that divides the worlds. They approached the old man's cross while the breeze rattled the tall weeds beyond the grave. Two women drifted in and out of focus, solidifying and melting. The first sported a tan jumpsuit beneath a frilly apron. Aqua Net feathered hair hovered above her shoulders as her ghostly white expression alternated between profound loss and desperate longing. She gazed at an unseen, distant point, her apron unmoved by the strengthening wind.

A girl far younger stood at her side, her thick, shock-blonde hair tied in a lacy bow. Severely cut bangs curled under her brow, while a cropped denim jacket covered a faded *Frankie Say Relax* tee. Peering at the ground, she bent, scooped up an object, and turned it over in her hands.

The woman in the apron ran a hand faintly over the cracked grave marker. "We saw that, Herb. You're not supposed to do that when they've got cameras."

Wild laughter slashed through the fog as an elderly man in suspenders swung from the gnarled elm. He hung upside-down from the lowest branch, holding his fedora in place. "Hush up, woman. I have every right to protect my property however I see fit. And don't call me Herb."

The teen rolled her eyes. "Oh, my God. You know they weren't, like, robbing your grave. They never are."

Herbert dropped from the branch, landing in a crumpled heap as the crack of shattering limbs filled the air. "Not anymore, they're not." Grabbing his legs, he forced his bones back into place and ran into the fog, the echo of his laughter fading with him.

The women stared into the mist left in his wake. The young girl tossed the orange, Nerf-topped microphone from one hand to the other before flinging it over her shoulder. "We should tell Rick. Oh, my God, he's gonna have a total cow when he finds out. You were supposed to hide this thing."

"I did! I can't watch Herb's every move, you know."

Silence wedged between them as their faces shimmered in the low light. They remained for an eternity—or perhaps mere seconds. Time had stopped on their side, a place that was neither here nor there, everywhere and nowhere. A coyote howled across the valley, calling to its mates, its family, its brethren.

The woman in the apron turned to the girl. "Bellbottoms seem to have made a comeback. That girl with the long stick was wearing them."

The teen crinkled her nose. "As if. There's no way those were bell-bottoms. They weren't wide enough."

The older woman raised her chin. "I know bellbottoms when I see them, dear. They were all the rage when I was alive."

"I was, like, the queen of bell-bottoms, and I'm telling you, they were wider." The teen snorted and pulled a long string of gum between her lips as she moved down the path.

Apron-woman scrambled to follow. "If those weren't bell-bottoms, maybe I'm out of touch."

"No duh. You've been dead for thirty-five years. How could you be in touch with Liver fashion?"

The moon illuminated the lonely path as the women merged with the fog, and the night took them. A black cat strolled across the old man's grave and sprayed the worn cross before scampering into the nearby wood.

In the distance, a wild man's laughter echoed.

2

THE CARETAKER

Gravel crunched beneath Rick's boots as he approached the cemetery gate, wound the chain through, and set the padlock in place. As he passed tombstones by the dozens, golden sunlight fell away from the Serenity Grove sign and the granite marking the loss of generations. Trees rustled in the breeze, whispering that darkness would soon fall.

He detoured onto a footpath, skirting the lonely mounds of leaves that dotted the expansive cemetery. In another week, the rest would abandon their trees. For now, Rick took in their brilliant colors, reminders of another season come and gone.

Though barely thirty, he walked with an old man's hunch, bent and full of effort. His back ached, and his limbs tired quickly as if his body had flown ahead in time. Meandering alongside the cattails of Barlow Pond, he caught the soft splash of stocked trout breaking the surface. As the western hills darkened, he could imagine the houses gone, the pavement disintegrated—nothing left but a small cabin in the woods where he could finally be alone. Just him and his dwindling shadow.

He thought about that a lot.

His cottage came into view, its harsh lights solidifying the darkness. Beneath a steeply pitched roof, stone walls gave the quaint house the appearance of having been plucked from a Victorian painting. Only the most curious visitors ever spotted the cottage hidden behind the tall hedge, most choosing to hastily return to the living world after fulfilling their obligations to the dead. Flower beds lined the gravel path where thick shrubbery obscured the humble abode during the day. As dusk settled in, solar lights flickered to life, illuminating the door. He stopped at the white picket fence where a wooden box with the word *Comments* on the side was nailed to the gatepost. Lifting the lid, Rick removed a single card, peeked at it, and shoved it into his pocket.

A weight pressed against his leg. Bending with an audible creak, Rick scratched the black cat winding between his boots. "Hey there, B-Benson. How's my boy today?"

With a flick of his tail, the cat sprang across the path into the encroaching darkness. Rick longed for that freedom, to leap away, returning only as he pleased for food and the occasional pat on the head.

Hell, he could live without the pat.

A noise made Rick instinctively step behind the hedge. Peering through the shrubbery, he spied a woman at the cemetery entrance. She tugged at the iron bars, clanging the chain.

He frowned. Daytime visitors usually ambled to their

beloved one's resting place, stayed a short time, then scurried back to the gate, desperate to get out.

He'd never seen anyone desperate to get *in*.

The woman ran a hand across the chain as if looking for a way to remove it.

I could let her in.

She wouldn't stay long—they never did. A quick visit would gratify her. She likely wouldn't return for months, maybe even years, having made her mandatory visit to whomever she felt accountable. No one ever came to remember someone or to feel close to them. Visits were payments and little more.

The woman buried her face in her hands.

I should let her in.

Familiar angst gnawed. Opening the gate would guarantee some clumsy interaction. They'd both stand awkwardly at the gate, and she'd probably thank him while he fumbled with his keys. He'd have to acknowledge her, and nothing panicked Rick more than the notion of speaking to strangers.

Or anyone, really.

The woman scanned the sign displaying the cemetery hours as she ran a hand through a mane of long, blonde hair. When she finally returned to her car with slumped shoulders, Rick breathed a long, slow sigh of relief. The car sputtered to life and backed onto Main Street, disappearing into the darkness.

Alone again, he slipped down the cottage path. Hidden from the world, he felt at ease. But a thought occurred as he opened the door to his special place, his center, his refuge.

Who was she trying to visit, anyway?

The scent of apples from inside chased the question from Rick's mind. Lighting a fire, he built a comfortable blaze and settled into his chair. Before long, the fire's warmth wrapped around him like flickering arms, and he caught himself drifting off. With a shake of his head, he forced himself upright and glanced at his watch—five after seven. The fire crackled in the darkened room, and he switched on the lamp with a sigh.

He was as prepared as any living man could be for the hours that lay ahead.

"Right," he said to the empty room. "Let's get s-s-started."

VOICES WAFTED IN WHILE SOFT MURMURS TRAVELED OVER a vast chasm. The whispers grew louder, closing the distance between time and space. Shapes formed while the temperature dipped, and lights flickered as the chatter increased. Though the windows were shut tight, the fire danced like a wind had broken through, and the wooden floor groaned, burdened with an unseen weight.

"I thought s-s-so." Rick settled back with the dread he always felt at the onset of the gatherings. With a flash of light, the room's occupancy increased from one to three.

Rick knew he was in for a long night from their body language. They stood as far apart as the walls would allow —not that walls could confine them. Tension circled the two glaring women. Wearing one of her more outlandish aprons with broad frills and oversized pockets, Madge stood rigidly at the fire. Rick thought he could topple her with the tap of a finger if he could touch her.

Beside a basket of apples, Stephanie folded her arms, the cheap plastic of her pink jelly shoes striking the floor in measured beats. As if pulling against elastic, her head swiveled, and she glanced at Madge, who turned at the same moment. They both doggedly twisted away.

Rick bided his time until someone spoke. He didn't have long to wait.

"I am *so* not talking to her," Stephanie spat as she fell onto one of the couches. She twisted her head so severely that Rick mused if she were alive, she'd have a headache later.

Immobile by the fire, Madge's expression morphed from obstinate to wounded. "I thought she would appreciate it. I wouldn't have done it had I known she'd react like *this*." With a quivering chin, she smoothed her apron.

Rick glanced at his latest book find on the coffee table: *Don't Sit There—Ten Ways to Prepare Company for the Ghost in Your House*. All day, he'd looked forward to curling up with it, but the way things were going, that wasn't likely.

"What h-h-hap—"

"She painted my room! She snuck in while I was out and painted it! And she got stupid orange paint on my Michael Jackson poster." Stephanie's expression darkened. "My *Thriller* poster, Rick."

He should have seen this coming.

The most surprising thing Rick had learned about life after death was how utterly boring it was. The residents were trapped behind the iron gates, unable to leave the confines of the cemetery. They had another place to go, another plane of existence, though Rick knew little of it. Tidbits he'd picked up over the years gave a fuzzy image of a dimension where each had a space they guarded with their very deaths. Yet even the most extraordinary place couldn't bring relief from being caged for years, even decades. Nothing ever changed; they died, and time stopped. Gone were the usual time-wasters the living took for granted. There were no more trips to the mall, the grocery store, or the park. They were stuck with the books they'd died with, the latest albums in their collections only as new as the year they'd passed from one world to the Next.

Once, Rick had tried to read a book alongside Madge, but that only brought on a lengthy discussion with a thousand questions Rick had struggled to answer.

"What on earth does it mean to be all that and a bag of chips?" she'd asked, peering over his shoulder.

Grappling for an analogy, Rick had answered, "It m-means they're special, I g-guess."

Madge scrunched her face. "But what does a bag of chips have to do with it?"

"Maybe they're, like, special chips," Stephanie offered, a strand of blonde twirled around a finger, "like those new Cool Ranch Doritos."

Madge's smile grew distant. "Remember Twinkies? I used to put them in my children's lunches. You should try one, Rick. They're delicious."

What had happened next taught Rick the importance of releasing information cautiously. "They stopped m-m-making them."

For three long months, Madge had wandered the cemetery, dabbing her eyes with her apron until Rick had shown her a newspaper article promising the return of Twinkies. When they did, he bought an entire case, only to be overcome with guilt at her anguish for having forgotten how they tasted.

Yet Madge's boredom was far more calamitous than her nostalgia. From morning to night, her living days had consisted of cleaning, cooking, and caring for her family. She'd been happy as a housewife. Unlike most women of her era, the age of Aquarius hadn't sparked a desire for independence. The women's liberation movement had brushed against the doorstep of her life, and she'd swept it right back. She'd had no interest in leaving her aprons behind, throwing her beret to the sky, or her bra to the fire. Through and through, Madge was the epitome of the Happy Homemaker. Now, trapped in a world where dust never settled, no one was ever hungry, and beds never needed to be made, Madge was a soul without a purpose. She needed something to do, some task to fill her days, no matter how mundane.

And every now and then, Madge lost it.

Sometimes it was little things: organizing the closet, rearranging the furniture in their common room, pulling blankets apart, and crocheting them again. But those banal tasks weren't always enough to satisfy Madge's increasingly restless spirit.

Once, Rick had been rudely awoken to find Herbert beside his bed, screaming a string of swear words so foul that Rick learned three new ones that night.

"Dammit, Rick, that woman is at it again. Someone needs to put a stop to this."

Rubbing the sleep away, Rick wasn't sure what he could do to stop anything from happening in a dimension he couldn't reach. "What is it n-n-now, Herb?"

"She took my rocking chair apart and turned it into a . .

." Panting, Herbert tore his fedora from his head, crushing it in his hands.

"Into wh-what?"

Hurling the hat to the floor, Herbert savagely stomped it into the hardwood. When he could inflict no further damage, he spat on it. "She turned it into a damn knick-knack shelf."

Madge was a housewife without a house to wife.

Several months had passed since her last episode. Now it seemed she'd gone off the deep end again, diving into another home-improvement project that would bring months of bitter squabbling.

"C-Can't you p-p-paint it back?" Rick asked, and, reading the answer on Stephanie's face, he felt for them both.

"She used the last of the pink paint that time she went crazy over Easter."

"I did not go crazy," Madge protested as she wrung her hands. "In my day, Easter was a big deal."

"You painted my Rubik's Cube! Oh, my God, what am I supposed to do with a pink Rubik's Cube? I was, like, so close to finally solving it, too."

A tense quiet fell, and like with most things that turned their world upside-down, there were no words of wisdom Rick could impart, no solutions he could offer. His problem-solving skills were limited to pruning shrubs, measuring headstones, and ensuring Livers didn't trample the flowers. All he could do now was hope this latest disagreement didn't last as long as the Pink Easter Feud of 2010.

At least Madge's restless nature would be satiated for now.

He hoped.

———

Tensions gradually eased as Madge ran a finger over the dusty mantel, leaving it eerily undisturbed while Stephanie lay on her back singing what she still thought was Michael Jackson's latest hit.

"Wh-Where's Herbert?"

Stephanie tugged at her gum. "He's having a heart attack. Again."

"You know how much he likes to relive it, dear," Madge said in a painfully obvious effort.

"I g-guess if he'd r-r-rather have another heart attack than b-be at the meeting, he must not have anything to s-s-say."

A distant howl suddenly crossed the worlds, growing louder as it sped closer, ending abruptly in a distinctive *pop*. As if geared up for a fight, the elderly man appeared beside the basket of apples with one thumb tucked behind his suspenders and a crooked fedora atop his head.

"I've got plenty to say, and I'll be damned if I'll let you keep me from saying it, Rick." Practically spitting the words, Herbert shook a stack of papers and leaned against the wall. "I have a list of complaints."

Madge smoothed her hands over her apron. "When have you not had a list?"

"If he did his job properly, I wouldn't have to make one."

The old man had a thousand ideas about what he thought the caretaker's job entailed and wasted no time verbally assaulting Rick when he felt he wasn't performing. Though

Herbert's otherworldly demands were often impossible to fulfill, that didn't stop him from making them. Daily.

"Sit down and stop being dramatic." Madge moved to the empty couch, her eyes flickering toward the teen. "Stephanie, dear, you know gum isn't allowed in the meetings."

"Oh, my God," the girl groaned, spitting the wad into her hand. "This isn't church."

"Dammit, I've got things to say!" Herbert shouted, shaking his papers with increasing vigor.

Frustrated with yet another late start, Rick cleared his throat. "You'll have a chance to s-state your c-c-complaints. S-S-Sit down, Herb."

The old man plopped heavily into a creaky chair. "Don't call me Herb."

Rick pushed away thoughts of his warm bed. "Let's s-start the meeting."

"Don't you mean Herb's Complaint Hour?" Stephanie quipped, spraying a wet raspberry in the old man's direction.

Rick pressed on. "At the last m-meeting, Herbert again expressed his c-concerns about g-grave robbers and asked for more s-s-security—"

"You should be patrolling the grounds at night, jackass. That's when they strike. Caught a whole group of them just the other night." Herbert leaned back with a satisfied smirk.

With her hands folded neatly in her lap, Madge turned to the old man. "They weren't grave robbers, and you know it. You shouldn't have used the microphone on them."

Herbert reached into his back pocket and retrieved the object in question, twirling it like a baton. "Like always, Rick, I had to do your job for you."

"Herb, in the t-ten years I've been caretaker, no one's tried to d-d-dig you up yet." Rick turned toward Madge, cocking a thumb toward the orange Nerf-topped device. "I thought you w-were gonna lock that thing up."

"I've told you, we can't lock the closet. It's common property."

"If you stopped using that thing on Livers, they'd, like, stop coming around." Stephanie flopped onto her stomach, one leg waving in the air.

"You need to take our concerns more seriously. You're supposed to be working for us, and you haven't been up to the job." Herbert glared beneath bushy eyebrows as he tapped a finger on the arm of the chair.

"If I feel there's a c-credible threat, I'll b-beef up s-security. Heck, I'll hire a man to s-stand guard over your grave twenty-four hours a d-day."

"Go ahead and mock me, but mark my words; you'll regret not listening to me." Seething, Herbert settled back in the chair.

Ignoring his hateful glances, Rick went on. "At the last m-m-meeting, we all agreed that the c-current level of security is s-s-sufficient."

"And at every meeting for the last twenty-one years," Madge added.

Herbert waved their chuckles away with a sneer.

"In Old News, Herbert said he b-b-believes that the cat has been spraying his t-tombstone."

"I caught the little hairball in the act! Backed his ass up

to it and shook his tail like a middle finger right at my name."

"Well, n-no one else has seen him do it, s-s-so with no other witness, B-Benson stays."

Herbert sank deeper.

Desperate to get the meeting moving, Rick turned to Madge. "Last week, you announced you'd be s-starting a cooking c-c-class. How's that going?"

Madge stiffly retied her apron strings. "I held classes every afternoon at two, and neither of them showed up."

"Oh, my God. You're the only one who still eats, and there's, like, no point. Food drops right through us."

"It's the thought that counts," Madge retorted, her voice shaky, and turned to the fire as she fanned the air. "Can't you turn down the heat in here, Rick?"

Herbert huffed. "There she goes with her imaginary hot flashes again."

Shrugging, Madge deliberately fanned harder.

"Halloween is c-c-coming up, and I'll be patrolling the g-grounds again. Although last year we only had a m-minor issue with some kids teepeeing the g-gate."

"I bet they were gr—"

"Like, seriously, don't even say it."

Exasperated with Herbert and the snail's pace of the meeting, Rick rubbed his temples. "We s-s-still haven't heard from S-Sister Athena about a seance this year."

Here was a bit of news Rick was pleased to report. For the past five Halloweens, Sister Athena and her new-age followers had come to the cemetery hoping to contact some long-departed spirit, leaving behind a mess of beads and burnt incense. Rick couldn't fathom how her followers fell for the notion that ghosts spent eternity wandering aimlessly, waiting for someone with The Gift to rescue them from their ethereal nightmare.

The reality was rather mundane, with far more painting and hat-crushing than any Liver could suspect.

Madge brightened. "If she does come, I hope she wears the cape she wore that first year. Livers seem to be getting awfully lazy with fashion these days."

"She looked super ace last year," Stephanie piped in. "All those beads and that long dress—so bitchin'. I would have looked totally rad in that dress."

Rick pressed on. "The c-cat came up m-missing but showed up the next d-d-day."

"To spray on my tombstone!"

Dread crept up Rick's spine as he gathered every ounce of strength for what came next. "Time for New B-Business."

All eyes turned to Herbert, and with a raised brow, Madge waved a hand. "You could always have another heart attack, and we could avoid all of this."

"I keep telling you that if that little pissant took care of these things, I wouldn't have to keep bringing them up."

"Let's g-get it over with, Herb."

Time halted while Herbert listed his usual litany of complaints. The cat. The lack of security. The overgrown shrubbery Rick insisted on pruning, making Herbert's grave even more attractive to those waiting for the chance to dig him up. "Why don't you just put up a sign with flashing lights and a neon arrow pointing to my body, saying, 'Dig me up, motherf—'"

"Herb, please!" Madge paled, nodding toward Stephanie. "There's a *child* here."

"Oh, my God, stop calling me that! I'd be nearly fifty if I were still a Liver."

Madge's face crumpled. "Still . . . you were practically a baby when you died. Why is it so hot in here?"

Already a quarter past eleven, Rick gave up on the book and now only wanted to go to bed. They'd be here until midnight again if he didn't steer the meeting back on track. He held up the card from the comment box. "We g-g-got one today."

Conversation ground to a halt as even Herbert leaned forward in anticipation of a duty Rick hadn't been warned of when he'd accepted the position. Much of his caretaker training had been strictly on-the-job.

Several months had passed after his arrival before Rick had first heard the now-familiar *creak-slam* of the wooden comment box lid. Thinking little of it, he'd glanced up briefly from his book: *Angry Spirits—Channeling Your Ghost's Rage on Moving Day*.

The residents had gathered in a tight circle at the hearth as heavy rain beat against the windows. Even Herbert had shown up, standing shoulder-to-shoulder with Serge, the caretaker Rick had replaced. They stared so intensely that Rick began to worry that he'd missed something vital.

"Aren't you going to get that?" Serge appeared hopeful yet wary.

"G-Get what?"

Rick's worry increased as they wrung hands and chewed nails. Was the cottage on fire? Was *he* on fire? Was someone actually digging Herbert out of the ground?

Serge stepped forward with a nervous smile. "Someone left a comment."

Rick tried to make a connection that seemed evident to

everyone but him. No one had left a comment before. Knowing that human nature was to complain rather than compliment, he'd taken the lack of comments as a positive sign. Now he wasn't so sure. "I d-d-don't—"

"Oh, my God," Stephanie wailed, "would you just go get it? We're dying here."

"Pun intended, asshole," Herbert snickered, though with less malice than usual. That alone was telling.

Darkened skies warned against heading out into the downpour, yet the sight of the residents clustered at the fire told Rick he'd better get out there, storm or no storm. Minutes later, he shook the rain from his hair as he warmed his hands at the fire. He pulled the card from his pocket with numbed fingers, nearly feeding it to the flames. Gasps, shrieks, and a foul sentiment from Herbert regarding where Rick kept his head reverberated as he caught the card just before it hit the blaze.

Rick opened the card and read aloud. "'I put f-fresh marigolds in my sister's vase. Please tell the grounds k-keeper to take c-care of them.'" No one moved—not a soul, dead or alive, uttered a sound as Rick fumbled to grasp the enormity of what had been written.

Stephanie slid an arm over Madge's shoulder. "I'm sure she'll come back. She was probably only here for a minute. It's, like, pouring out there." The pity in her voice suggested that even she knew she was grasping.

"I missed her. She hasn't been here for twenty years, and I missed her."

For the first time, Rick realized that not one of the residents had had a visitor in the months since his arrival. Livers had come and gone, leaving flowers on the graves of souls who'd already moved on, quietly whispering remembrances before returning quickly to their cars. One man showed up once a month like clockwork, shoulders hunched, and placed a miniature American flag at a marker inscribed *Cherished Son* before shuffling back through the gate. Yet none of the ethereal beings who still inhabited Serenity Grove had been visited. Not one of them seemed to have been remembered.

Though Madge's sister never returned, Rick came to expect a brief visit from Stephanie's friend, Tracy, each birthday, leaving a card thanking Rick for keeping the grounds well-manicured. On those days, the cemetery was filled with joy as the residents gathered around Stephanie's tombstone and listened to the friend tell tales of family reunions, turmoil with former classmates, and one year, the best news of all.

"Rachael Johnson is so fat now. She's gained, like, a hundred pounds."

That night, they'd all gathered beneath the stars and congratulated Stephanie on the joyful news that her high school adversary had become a cow.

Comment cards brought a slice of the living world into the land of the dead, and even the most mundane comments fired hours of discussion. They brought more joy than the Livers who'd left them could ever know, and sometimes, as it was for Madge on that stormy day, they brought anguish and heartache. After that, Rick never hesitated to rush to the comment box when he heard the telltale *creak-slam*. Armageddon couldn't have kept him away.

Rick held up the latest card for all to see, and a hush blanketed the room. "'The cemetery is t-t-too creepy at night. C-C-Can you d-do something about that?'"

It was Stephanie who broke the silence in a voice

rimmed with sarcasm. "Why not let Madge paint the whole freaking cemetery like she paints everything else?"

Tensions renewed, Madge and Stephanie argued while Herbert insisted on rehashing his complaints. Rick sank deeper into his chair, wondering for the thousandth time if it was all worth it.

As the night wore on and hostilities grew, he thought about the outside world and what it had put him through.

It was worth it.

3

WISH YOU WERE HERE

Working at the rear of the cemetery, Rick imagined that no town existed a few hundred yards from where he raked. That he was secluded, far from civilization alone with the chill that signaled the onset of autumn. As a brisk draft swept up the canyon wall, he savored the fresh scent of the rapids below. The distant hills called, and his rake halted while his imaginary cabin floated forward. A smile touched his lips as the recurring fantasy of solitude began to carry him away.

"Hmm, Hmm, da-da- daaaa . . . "

Reality crashed in, wrenching Rick from the daydream. The spirit of a long-dead teenage girl materialized. She regarded two closely planted tombstones, weathered by the battering of more than fifty seasons. Rick predicted what was coming.

Wait for it . . .

"Oh, my God, I dedicate this song to the Smyths! This one's for you!" Stephanie rounded the couple's shared grave with swinging arms and a voice badly out of tune. She warbled out the lyrics to her favorite Debbie Gibson tune with the soulful crooning that only a teenager can muster. Circling the tombstones, her feet pumped like an over-caffeinated aerobics instructor.

If there was one thing Rick could say about Stephanie, it was that she was one hard-core song dedicator. Shortly after his arrival ten years earlier, with his nose buried in a book on the paranormal, he was snickering over a passage claiming ghosts were the result of global warming. The dead could rest in peace if we all just recycled more. Early on, Rick had already surmised that no living person knew a thing about life after death.

His heart had skipped a beat when the teen popped up in a mismatch of layered skirts and an off-the-shoulder tee. "I w-w-wish you guys would knock."

She tossed her hair with a snort. "We can't knock, dork." In a swirl of skirts, she'd plopped onto the coffee table with a puzzled expression before tilting her head in a way that made Rick wonder if he were covered in the remnants of his tuna sandwich. He instinctively wiped a hand across his mouth.

"W-W-What are you s-staring at?"

"I can't figure out your song."

He could think of no response to *that*.

"You don't really look like a song kind of guy, but, like, everyone has a song. I just need to figure yours out." Crossing one leg over the other, she'd continued staring unabashedly, each passing second increasing his discomfort. "How old are you? Fifty? Sixty?"

"I'm th-th-thirty. I've told you a hundred t-times."

"You seem older." For days afterward, she'd followed

Rick's every move, desperate to pin a song to him. She'd interrogated him about everything from his favorite foods to what kind of animal he would transform into for a day. "Something about a guy puttering around a cemetery, kind of creepy—"

"Hey," Rick protested, though even he couldn't deny the accuracy of her assessment.

After a week, even Madge had piped in, peering with an intensity that made Rick feel like a bearded woman at the circus. "I've never known her to be stumped by anyone. Rick, dear, you are an anomaly."

There's the understatement of the century.

In the end, Stephanie had given up, though she'd claimed she was still thinking it over.

Now, ten years later, she danced among the dead, and Rick remained songless. "There's love in your eyes!" The cheap, plastic headphones buried in her hair did little to muffle the blasting tune. Rick recognized the familiar song and where it was on the cassette: side one, track two. He knew every song, along with each accompanying dance move. For more money than he'd ever spent on a single item, he'd bought an original Debbie Gibson album and played it on the phonograph on the anniversary of Stephanie's deathday. And her birthday. And Easter, Christmas, Sean McFadden Day—every occasion she felt warranted slipping the vinyl from its sleeve. When it wasn't a special occasion, she donned her headphones and played the cassette so often that Rick knew every word.

She danced circles around him, snapping her fingers to the beat. "Did you know she wrote every song herself? Wait, let me get my hat!" In a flash, she was gone, leaving Rick alone with the ringing echo of sudden silence. He sighed as he resumed raking a pile of freshly fallen leaves, mindlessly separating the brightest colors into a mound. Methodically, he scraped the ground, savoring the moment.

Seconds later, Stephanie returned, and the brown bowler atop her head fought to contain her enormous hair. She kicked through the pile of leaves, but they remained untouched. Resuming her ghostly dance, the forever-teen snapped, dipped, and swiveled her hips in a series of distinctly eighties moves. With a flick of her wrist, she tossed the headphones aside, then flipped the switch on a ghetto blaster she'd placed on the grass.

"Looove, it's only a dreeeam . . ."

". . . as any d-d-dream may s-s-seem . . ." Catching himself, Rick blushed. It was bound to happen when you heard anything forty thousand times.

"If you had a television, we could watch MTV. They play this song, like, fifty times a day." After the song ended, she waltzed to the boom box and flipped the switch. Rick soaked in the quiet. Stephanie swept around the grave of the long-departed couple and planted herself at his side. "What day is it?"

As Rick pulled a brightly colored leaf from the pile, he hesitantly replied, "S-S-Sunday." Just as he knew every word Debbie Gibson ever sang, Stephanie's penchant for song dedications, and that she would have married Jack Tripper had she lived, Rick knew precisely what her next words would be. Predictability could have been Stephanie's middle name.

"Oh, I used to love Sundays! I'd get all bundled up in my quilt and watch Jerry Lewis movies all day long. Do they still play those on channel twelve? Or Bob Hope, or, oh, my God, Elvis movies were the best." Stephanie skipped to Rick's other side, giggling like the seventeen-year-old she would always be. "At night, we'd all watch *Family Ties*. Oh, my God, I had the hugest crush on Alex, even though he was kind of a doofus, but, like, in a hot way, you know? But I really loved Jack from *Three's Company*. I kind of always thought he and Janet would get together, even though they were like brother and sister. I totally would have married him. Or John-Boy—so dreamy with that mole-thing on his face. At least, I think it was a mole. Do you think they called him John-Man later? Whatever. But you know who I didn't love?"

He knew. Dear God, he knew.

"I so did *not* like Fonzie. All my friends were, like, 'Oh, my God, Fonzie is so hot, Fonzie is so cool, Fonzie, Fonzie, Fonzie.' But I was like, whatever. I don't like guys who ride motorcycles. They're so loud. Why do guys like loud things?" A squirrel hopped across the path, stopping at Stephanie's feet, and she bent, allowing it to run up to her shoulder. Though Rick didn't fully understand how it worked, he had a vague notion that animals could cross between worlds. In the dead world, where the squirrel was now, they disappeared from living eyes. Aside from people like Rick, at least.

"Friday nights were the best because we got to watch *Webster*, even though my sister hated it. She said it was just like *Diff'rent Strokes*, and I was like, oh, my God, it's so *not* like *Diff'rent Strokes*. I mean, on *Diff'rent Strokes,* there were *two* boys. We wanted to watch *Dallas*, but Dad said we were too young to stay up that late, so we had to watch the stupid *Dukes of Hazzard*, which was dumb because no one I knew was watching that show." Racing down her other arm, the squirrel returned to the living world and scurried up a nearby tree, scattering leaves in its wake.

Stephanie's words barely registered as Rick raked long slow rows in the grass. He watched longingly as a flock of geese flew overhead, the air filled with nasal honks. He liked the idea of a mass exodus, a gathering of birds who all instinctively decided to get out of Dodge. Did they know they'd be returning in the spring, or did they merely allow instinct to take over each year? Did they consider the north their home or the south? Which was the refuge, and which was the—

"Who's that?"

Following Stephanie's gaze, Rick spotted a woman leaving the cemetery. Her head down, she carried herself as if her shoulders were being pressed from above. It wasn't the solemn, reverent walk of the typical visitor who tiptoed through. Instead, she walked like a woman in the fresh throes of mourning.

He frowned. There had been no burials in over a year; little Maddie had been the last. Madge and Stephanie had carried the toddler everywhere, racing through the grave-yard as she'd laughed through endless rounds of peek-a-boo. Rick wished he could have told Maddie's grieving parents how happy and pain-free she'd been during those three days before moving on to her Next.

Maddie's parents had walked with the same weight this woman now carried.

"Maybe she's, like, passing through."

It was possible. Livers—kids, mostly—occasionally cut through the cemetery. But Rick knew this was no random shortcut and that this was not a woman trying to shave a few blocks from her trek home.

And then, he recognized her; she was the woman who'd desperately tried to get in after hours.

She got in, but it doesn't look like it did her much good.

Rick and Stephanie stood side-by-side as the woman reached the open gate, stopped, and turned. Rick felt exposed, as if caught in the act of spying. The woman stared into the cemetery, her gaze landing near the cottage as her blonde hair lifted in the breeze.

"'Wish You Were Here,'" Stephanie whispered. "That's her song."

VISIONS OF THE STRANGE WOMAN FLITTED THROUGH Rick's head until an unexpected phone call brought everything to a screeching halt. His daydreams vaporized, and Rick raced to the shed, gathering an assortment of tools. As the last of the light waned, he reached a spot of untouched ground—a quiet plot near the gate.

With three days to prepare, Rick grabbed a shovel and began to dig.

4

NEW GIRL

The residents argued bitterly during the three days leading to the new arrival. As Rick roped off the freshly dug plot, Madge and Stephanie appeared at his side, embroiled in a bitter dispute.

"Everyone comes to the cottage straightaway," Madge said. "It makes sense to introduce her to the meetings at the same time."

Stephanie folded her arms like a wounded child. "Sure. Like, who doesn't want to die, and the first thing they get to do is go to a meeting. So lame." In two long strides, the teen was toe-to-toe with Rick. "There should just be one of us to greet her, and it makes sense that it should be me."

"Rick, you can't let Stephanie meet her alone. She'll scare her off with her . . ."

Stephanie glared. "My what?"

Madge waved a hand. "Excessive bounciness."

The young teen's eyes narrowed. "So, I'm bouncy. So what? Like, where's she gonna run off to anyway? It's not like she can leave. You're just jealous that I'm still young and you're old. Like Rick."

"I'm not old . . ." Rick mumbled.

With her lips pressed so taut they turned white, Madge straightened. "I was in my forties when I died, which is still very young, and Rick can't be more than forty-five, fifty at most."

"I'm thirty. How m-many times—"

"Old, old, OLD!" Stephanie hopped in place, a tantrum in full swing.

When Rick thought it couldn't get worse, the only other person more childish than Stephanie darted from behind a nearby elm. "I'll show her around. I may be old, but I'm agile." Herbert swung his hips with an obscene leer, eliciting a groan from Stephanie and a scolding from Madge.

As the dead argued, Rick disappeared into his cottage with a sigh.

IN THE END, RICK DECIDED A MEETING WAS BEST. LEAVING the new girl alone with any of them would be a recipe for disaster.

Blackened windows reflected the fire as night fell, and a tense quiet tightened the air, compressing Rick's every breath. As the caretaker, he was the man in charge, a fact that should have given him some confidence.

It didn't, and he wasn't the only one who was restless.

With a bag of brightly colored yarn at her feet, Madge crocheted the world's longest scarf while Stephanie stared at the door, her knees bouncing as she sat on her hands.

Even Herbert impatiently tap-tap-tapped yellowed finger-nails on the arms of a chair.

Despite being the largest cemetery in Hood Valley, burials at Serenity Grove were a rarity. The small town barely registered on a map, and many families preferred to inter loved ones in the newer, more modern cemeteries closer to the city. Rick had only buried four in the decade of his employment, and none had stayed long, moving on to wherever their Next was. Of the three current residents, all had been entombed long before Rick's arrival.

"Oh, my God," Stephanie said, startling Madge into dropping the crochet hook with a metallic clink. "Where is she?"

Herbert chuckled from the corner. "Maybe she saw Rick and decided she'd be better off staying in her coffin."

Madge made a show of turning away as she fanned herself. "Don't be ridiculous, Herb. You know she can't do that. Rick, is it necessary to have the fire going?"

Herbert sprinted from his chair so fast that he was in front of Madge before she registered his charge. "Hey." He displayed a stiff middle finger, wagging it inches from Madge's eyes. She let out a surprised squeal as he leaned in close with a devious smile. "Don't call me Herb."

Scurrying to the opposite end of the couch, Madge brushed her apron as if to rid herself of any lingering Herbert traces.

Suspense always accompanied a new arrival, but this time, the tension was amplified. Nearly five hours had passed since the funeral, and their latest resident was late. Frank had arrived as the last car had driven somberly away, and little Maddie had appeared the moment her casket was lowered into the ground, running circles around her mourners while she sang nursery rhymes. The new girl should have arrived hours ago, but there'd been no sign of her.

"Let's just s-s-start the m-m-meeting."

Never one to miss an opportunity to complain, Herbert insisted the cat was still spraying his grave and nagged Rick to install motion-activated lights. Rick allowed Herbert's demands to wash over him as his gaze drifted to the darkened windows. The full moon rose while he listened for any sign of their missing resident.

After a twenty-minute tirade—short even by the old man's standards—Rick reached into his pocket, extracted a comment card, and cleared his throat to a suddenly quieted room. "'Th-Thank you for the lovely f-f-funeral. She would have l-l-loved it.'"

Stephanie halted her bouncing knees. "Oh, my God, did you hear what her mourners said? That she was too young to die? What if she's, like, my age? Wouldn't that be totally rad?"

Madge pursed her lips. "Dear, it's never *rad* when someone dies young. You, of all people, should know that."

"I'm tired of hanging around all you old fuddy-duddies. It's time we had someone too young to die around here for a change."

"I'll thank you to refrain from referring to me as a 'fuddy-duddy.'" Madge turned to Rick. "How old is she, anyway? What did her obituary say?"

"She j-just turned t-twenty-two."

Stephanie shrieked. "Twenty-two! Oh, my God, she really was too young to die!"

Rick glanced at his watch. "She should have b-b-been

here by now. She was b-buried at eleven, and it's already b-been five hours—"

Even as the words left his lips, a voice called from beyond the door.

"Hello? Is someone there? I can't . . . can't knock or anything . . ." Shaky and high-pitched, the voice sounded panicked. "I keep trying, but my knuckles won't make a sound. It's like my hand wants to go right through . . ." Words dwindled to muffled sobs as the crackle of the fire amplified.

"C-C-Come on in," Rick called.

"I can't! I'm trying, but . . ." A low howl floated through the door.

"For crying out loud, doesn't she know how to walk through doors yet?" Herbert tapped his fingers impatiently.

Madge threw a scowl in Herbert's direction, then faced the door."Just walk through, dear!"

The sobs on the other side intensified as Rick tentatively rose from his chair and opened the door. In the darkness stood a girl, her alabaster skin etched with tears, giving her the appearance of a cracked porcelain doll. Yet, with the piercings in her nose, eyebrow, and bottom lip, the resemblance ended there. Every stitch of her clothing was black, from her leather jacket to her heeled boots. Impossibly blue hair, the shade of the deep waters around coral reefs, fell loose around her shoulders.

Stephanie gawked. "Whoa."

Composing herself with a painted-on smile, Madge ran

her eyes over the girl as she hurried to the door. "You must be our new resident." She extended a hand.

The girl cringed as if Madge's outstretched hand were a snake coiled to strike. "You can . . . see me?"

Madge stepped aside, allowing a full view of the others. "Yes, dear, we can all see you."

A fresh tear fell with a relieved smile, transforming the girl into something extraordinarily beautiful. "Oh, wow. No one could see me before . . . it was . . . wow, this is good, this is great." With an unsteady hand, she swiped her tears.

"Come in, dear." Madge flashed Rick a guarded look as she led the girl to one of the couches.

The new resident cautiously sat, glancing nervously at the others. "Where am I?"

"Serenity Grove," Madge answered with a hostess's smile.

"The cemetery?"

An uncomfortable silence stilled the air. *She's been in the cemetery all day*, Rick thought. *How could she not have recognized it?*

"Why don't we all introduce ourselves?" Madge patted the girls' knee, looking as worried as Rick felt. The girl winced at her touch, strands of cobalt glinting in the firelight.

Rick cleared his throat. "She hasn't h-h-had her intake yet. She was s-s-supposed to be here right after the—"

"I'm Madge!" She cut off Rick's words with a warning glare. "Now, let's see, I died in 1984, so that's . . . how many living years is that? Well, it's over thirty. And this is our Stephanie. Introduce yourself, dear."

Unlike Madge, Stephanie didn't appear the least bit

alarmed. With a palm to her chest, she scooted to the edge of her seat. "Oh, my God. Okay. So, I'm Stephanie, but you can call me Stephy. Everyone used to. I've been here since 1987, and, oh, my God, we have so much to talk about!" She resumed bouncing, her hands flying. "Oh, and my living age was seventeen. I have so many questions. Like, did you have a boyfriend, and what's school like now, and are there still preps and jocks and—"

"Stephanie," Madge cut in, "there'll be plenty of time for girl talk when we get to the common room. Rick?"

The teen tucked her steepled hands beneath her chin as all eyes turned to the caretaker.

Put on the spot, Rick's cheeks burned. *Say something. Say anything. You're the caretaker.* "Uh . . . I'm Rick. I b-b-buried you."

Madge lowered her head with a groan as the new girl blinked, her expression a mixture of revulsion and disbelief.

Unable to contain herself, Stephanie stood, pumping her legs like a marathon runner waiting for the starting shot. "Is *Who's the Boss* still on? Did Tony and Angela get married? Some people say I look like an older Stephanie from *Full House*. I don't think so, but, like, we do have the same name and hair—"

"Do you mean *Fuller House*? That show on Netflix?"

Madge blinked. "What is a Net Flick, dear?"

"Oh, my God," Stephanie blurted, and the new girl jerked. "Please tell me you have a Betamax player. I still have a rental of *Mannequin*—"

"We should g-g-get on with the intake," Rick interrupted. "We're d-doing this c-c-completely out of order."

"Order-Schmorder, asshole," Herbert pouted. "Isn't anyone gonna introduce me?"

Madge waved a dismissive hand. "That's Herb."

"It's Herbert, dammit."

Avoiding his scowl, Madge turned to the girl at her side. "And your name is?"

A croak escaped the girl's lips, her body rigid. "Taylor."

Rick felt a pressing need to take over. "I think we've s-s-stretched this out l-long enough. I have an intake to d-do. T-Time for you all to scoot. Except for you, Taylor. You s-stay here."

Madge retreated to a corner while Stephanie stood at the fire, a long string of gum dangling from her teeth as she stared longingly at the new arrival.

"Hold on there, Rick." Herbert crumpled papers in his bony fingers. "What about my list?"

"Dismissed. M-Meeting adjourned."

Muttering a string of curses, Herbert pointed at Taylor with narrowed eyes. "Don't ever call me Herb," he spat before a mist carried him away.

"We'll see you soon, dear." Madge disappeared, leaving a dim outline in her wake.

"Don't, like, take forever. I have so much to ask!" Stephanie waved as she, too, dissipated, leaving Rick and Taylor alone.

The room fell silent, and Taylor turned. "What's happening?"

With the others gone, the crackle of the fire softened, warming the room with a soft glow. Rick dreaded the intake, but it had to be done. After removing a folder from the filing cabinet, he sat across from the shaky girl. "We have s-some things to g-go over—"

"I'm really dead, aren't I?" Her drained expression begged for any other truth, and when Rick remained silent, she covered her face and sobbed.

He held back a groan. He didn't deal well with crying girls—or crying anyone. "L-Look, I, uh, just have a few questions, and th-th-then you can—"

"All those other people . . . they're dead too?"

Fidgeting, Rick wished he was better at these things. "Well, yeah, they're all d-dead too. I j-just have a few—"

"How long have you been dead?"

Rick felt heat rise to his cheeks. The last thing he wanted was to get into *this*. "I'm not, uh, I'm n-n-not d-d-dead."

A painful grimace twisted her lips. "Then why can you see me? I tried to talk to my brother when he was out there at the . . . at the . . . and he acted like he couldn't even hear me." Her breath hitched.

Rick glanced around the room as if his eyes would land on some magical object that would save him. "I'm s-s-sort of different."

Pulling her hands from her face, Taylor stumbled toward a box of tissues. Her fingers flew through, and the box remained untouched. Another swipe, then another. She thrust her hand forward repeatedly, taking shallow, stunted breaths. "Why can't I grab it?"

"S-Sit down, T-T-Taylor," Rick said gently, and then louder, "C-Can we get a hankie up here?"

Madge instantaneously appeared, throwing a handker-chief onto the table. "Don't be long, dear," she said and whirled away with a wink. Taylor stared wide-eyed at the spot where Madge was and then wasn't, her mouth moving soundlessly.

"You can just g-grab that."

While her eyes darted, Taylor carefully plucked up the handkerchief as if it were a filthy rag.

"You c-can't really affect the living world, and s-since those are my tissues, you can't touch them. It doesn't work that way with everything, a-and like I said, it's hard t-t-to explain—"

"So, I can't talk to my brother, or my parents, or anyone except all those dead people I don't even know?"

As a Liver, Rick wasn't the best at teaching *Dead 101*. "It's c-complicated."

A fresh wave shook her. "So, will I just be here forever? Do I have to go sit in my . . . coff . . . coff—"

"The others can g-g-go over that once we're d-d-done. We really should f-f-finish." Rick picked up the file, his frustration rising as his speech worsened. "Most of this I can g-get f-f-from your obitu . . . from the newspaper, b-b-but there's some stuff I need from you. Wh-Wh-Who was your worst enemy?"

"Huh?"

"Maybe someone f-f-from school or work? A n-neighbor?"

"I don't think I have . . . had one."

Rick ticked a box. "Who were y-y-you c-closest to?"

Taylor sniffled, and her face dropped. "My dog, Buster."

"I mean like a p-p-person, s-someone who could v-v-visit your . . . v-v-visit you here at the . . . where w-we are."

A honk sliced the air as she blew into the handkerchief. "My brother, I guess. Why do you need to know all of this?"

Beyond uncomfortable, Rick prayed for the end and longed for his bed. "I n-n-need to know what kind of people I might be d-dealing with now that you're . . . h-here. Sometimes p-people like to d-d-do things—"

"For heaven's sake, Rick, you're just awful at this." Rushing to Taylor's side, Madge gave him a disapproving frown. "Land sakes. If she weren't already dead, she'd kill herself after talking with you."

Rick only shrugged, too spent to defend himself.

Madge gently pulled the handkerchief from Taylor's hands. "Your old life is over, that's true, but you have a new life here with us. We're your family now. It's not easy at first, but you'll see, it's not so bad here."

Wary hope crept into Taylor's pale face. "Really?"

"Really. First, you'll never see the inside of that coffin. There are precautions against that, so get that out of your head right now, okay?"

"Okay." Though still visibly on guard, Taylor's shoulders relaxed.

"Second, you won't be here forever. How long you're here depends on a lot of things, but this is just one part of your existence. I've seen people stay for fifty years or more while others move on after just a few days."

"Move on," Taylor repeated, nearly breathless, "to where?"

"The afterlife."

Horror-stricken, Taylor pulled back. "*This* isn't the

afterlife? I mean, I'm d . . . not alive anymore, so how is this not the afterlife?" Her eyes darted upward as though the afterlife itself would fall through the ceiling.

"No, dear, this is more of a . . ."

"A holding p-place?" Rick offered as Madge shot a look that made it clear he should stop talking.

"Like purgatory?" Taylor clutched her shirt with a gasp.

"No, dear. It's more like the place you go between the life you knew and the Next." Madge's brow furrowed, and it seemed to Rick that even she thought it sounded a bit like purgatory. "Regardless, you can spend as much time up here as you want, or you can come down below with us . . ."

"You mean . . . H . . . H . . ."

"Goodness, no, dear!"

Rick couldn't hide his smirk. *Not so easy, is it?*

"It's not really below us, like underground. We just think of it that way because, well, you have to think of it as *somewhere*."

Stephanie bounced in from the kitchen. "I always thought it was, like, next door."

"How can it possibly be next door? Next door to what? Dear, the living world is all around us. We have nowhere to go but down, so it must be down."

"Like a basement? Oh, my God, no wonder you're always painting everything. Who wants to live in a creepy old basement?"

"Bullshit," Herbert crowed as his form materialized. "It's in Canada. Why do you think it's always snowing?"

While Madge defended her position, Stephanie

complained that no one was listening, and the room filled with chattering female voices until Taylor silenced them.

"I need to get out of here." Her boots clicked on the wooden floor as she rushed across the room, inexplicably snapping her fingers. "What time is it?"

Stephanie pointed to the clock, and Taylor rested a hand against her forehead while she paced. "I'm too late."

Madge and Rick shared worried glances while Stephanie took a tentative step forward. "Like, I know it's hard at first—"

Taylor wheeled. "It's not hard! It's . . . I need to go." She spun on her heel and reached for the door.

"T-Taylor, wait. Let's t-t-talk this through—"

"I'm not talking to you!" Grabbing for the doorknob, Taylor grunted as her hand passed through. Again and again, she failed to open the door. "How do I get out of this place?" Then, closing her eyes, she leaned forward and fell through, disappearing. Choked sobs echoed through the wood.

Rick and the others stared in silence. The fire died down, its embers glowing orange as the windows rattled against a sudden wind.

Stephanie appeared at Rick's side. "How long do you think before she figures it out?"

Having no answer, Rick shook his head. He only knew he wasn't looking forward to the moment when Taylor realized she couldn't leave.

5

MOONEY

R ick swore at the grating alarm. Getting out of bed seemed a ridiculous idea. He'd slept little, searching until daybreak with Madge and Stephanie for the new girl. All they'd found was a discarded soda can and a sun-washed photograph, a remembrance of a resident long gone.

"How c-can you t-t-two see?" Rick followed the women, little more than darkened shades, through the vast, moonlit cemetery. "I k-k-keep running into t-tombstones."

"It's not as dark for us. It's like, um, I don't know—"

"Like Alaska in the summertime," Madge broke in, the outline of her body swimming in the darkness. "Nighttime is brighter for us."

Rick had wanted to delve further into this new revelation but left it for another day, straining to hear any sign of the missing resident. He finally stumbled into bed as the birds began their morning song.

Just five more minutes. Smashing the snooze button, he tucked his quilt tightly around his ears. He nearly allowed his eyes to drift closed again until he remembered that today the sod would be delivered. If he missed it, another week would pass before he could top off Taylor's grave. Rick didn't think she could handle staring at the mound of dirt concealing her cold body for that long.

The clock flashed a quarter to eight, and Rick came fully awake. The sod guy always arrived early.

Shoot.

The smooth, polished floor froze his bones as he slipped into a pair of wool socks and grabbed his robe. Racing to the bathroom, he quickly ran a brush over his teeth, threw on yesterday's flannel, and hurried out the door. He fumbled for the gate key and came up short, remembering with an ever-sinking gut that he'd left it on the hook.

"Shoot!" A crow startled into flight as Rick sprinted back toward the cottage. Cursing himself, he prayed he hadn't missed the delivery.

Halfway there, he stopped in his tracks. With a groan, he turned toward a rectangle of freshly turned soil, where Taylor sat on the slab of granite embedded with her photo.

"Hey, T-T-Taylor," Rick said, musing at his absurdly chipper tone, "whatcha d-d-doin' there?"

Chin in hand, Taylor's brown eyes remained fixed on the dirt. "Just sitting here, being dead." She wasn't crying —there was that, at least—but Rick doubted she'd accepted her fate overnight, either.

Before he'd come to Serenity Grove, Rick hadn't thought much about death. You lived, you died, and you came to an end. Maybe you went to heaven, perhaps the other place, but you sure didn't stay here. Ghosts were a fantasy, spirits little more than stories to tell around a campfire.

In truth, the dead remained unchanged, with the same failings they'd carried in life—still struggling, forever human.

"I uh, I'm g-g-going to finish up here t-today," he stammered. "Just w-waiting on the delivery—"

"They left." Taylor's gaze remained unflinching, and she shuddered. "I tried to stop them, but they didn't hear me. They just drove away with my grass."

The temperature dipped with a growing cloud cover, and the last maple leaf cascaded down to settle on the soil that covered Taylor's body. What must it be like, staring at your own grave?

"Hey, look at m-m-me."

Lifting her pale, drained face, she said nothing.

"We're g-going to get you t-taken care of today. D-Don't go anywhere."

With a laugh more like a muffled sob, she returned her chin to her palm. "I *was* going to jog to Disneyland, but I guess that can wait."

An hour later, Rick backed his truck to Taylor's grave. Eight fresh rolls of sod bounced in the bed. He hopped out and began unrolling the grass. Peeking sideways, he saw Taylor still atop her granite, and as her hair fluttered around her pale face, she nearly smiled. Not *entirely*, but after the last twenty-four hours, Rick would gladly take a nearly.

As the bare earth disappeared, Taylor's shoulders began to relax, and her brows unfurled. What had started as a gruesome lack of foresight seemed to have turned into an exercise in healing—the covering of a wound, a bandage on her soul.

Rick hoped it stuck.

"Hi, kitty. What's your name?" Black paws rested on Taylor's arm as the cat stood on its hind legs, reaching. She ran her fingers behind his ears.

"That's B-B-Benson."

A quiet stillness fell, broken only by the cry of a distant falcon. Rick wondered if the others knew Taylor was here or if they'd already tried to approach her. Maybe they were allowing her to settle on her own, though he didn't think their curiosities could keep them away for long. Perhaps they were watching now, hidden behind nearby graves, peeking around trees.

After a while, Taylor broke the silence. "Rick?"

"Yeah?" Another strip of sod rolled over her bones.

"Why can Benson see me? How come I can touch him?"

Rick stood, cracking his aching back. "Animals are d-different. I think they can live in b-both worlds at once. S-S-Sort of, anyway."

Taylor's gaze lost focus, staring toward an unseen horizon. "If my dog Buster were buried here, we'd be together forever, right?"

Rick parted his lips without a clue as to what he would say. Thankfully, Stephanie saved him, appearing in a misty cloud.

So, they *were* watching.

"Animals skip this part. They, like, I don't know, go somewhere else."

Taylor's face fell. "Why?"

Benson rolled onto his back, lifting his paws as

Stephanie ran her fingers over his belly. "Madge says they don't have stuff to work out before they move on, like us."

As if a switch had been flicked, the temporary upswing in Taylor's mood reversed. Once again, she morphed into the gloomy girl she'd been on arrival. "I miss Buster. I wish someone would bring him to visit."

With the final strip of sod laid over Taylor's grave, Rick spread his arms to showcase his work. "All d-done."

Staring at the grass, Taylor struggled to lift the corners of her mouth. "Thanks," she managed.

Stephanie stole a quick glance at Rick and quietly slipped away, leaving a silent mist in her wake.

Murkiness pasted to Taylor like glue, and she seemed to take no notice of Stephanie's departure. It would take months for the grass to fill in and hide the unnatural outline of the casket beneath. But with time no more than a memory for her, how long would it really take for the traces of her burial to disappear?

Tossing his tools into the truck, Rick climbed in. The old engine sputtered to life, and he paused before throwing it into gear.

I should say something to make her feel better. Something . . . wise.

But one look at her face told him that they'd both be better off if he kept quiet. So he drove away, leaving Taylor alone atop the tombstone etched with her own name.

NOVEMBER WAS JUST AROUND THE CORNER, THE AIR already crisp, and with his rake in hand, Rick dove into his daily routine. He allowed Taylor and her dead problems to drain from his mind as he hummed an old Andrews Sisters tune, and the world drifted away within the lyrics of a fence and wide-open country.

He could walk from sunup to sundown and still not cover every inch of the land in his charge. Ten acres had been devoted to orchards, where the sweet scent of apples, pears, and cherries ripened the air. At the northernmost edge, the property overlooked a deep gorge, with Barlow River flowing far below. Rick spent many a quiet afternoon at the canyon rim, the silence broken only by the desperate call of sparrows. A dense wood covered the eastern quarter, untouched for eons and overgrown with lush ferns and brilliant moss-covered boulders. The air was colder there, the leafy canopy impenetrable by sunlight. Even in the heat of summer, Rick wrapped himself in a thick flannel when the need to disappear within the cave-like woodland became too strong to ignore.

Many of the graves covered the southwestern end of the property. Unlike most small-town cemeteries, the tombs were spread far apart, each carefully placed within view of a tree, meadow, or the snow-capped mountain. A small family plot could take up the space of an entire city block, with benches and flowering shrubbery sprinkled throughout. Serenity Grove was all about comfort—if not in life, then at least afterward.

Cocooned in the oldest corner of the cemetery, Rick hummed as he raked, tarrying far from the road. For a decade, he'd watched over the dead at Serenity Grove, and they'd been the best years of his life. Sure, there were minor annoyances—Herbert chief among them—yet even

Herbert and his constant whining couldn't outweigh Rick's content.

As he reached Herbert's grave, the man himself appeared with crossed arms and a sour twist on his lips. "I told you that damn cat was spraying my grave." A crooked finger pointed.

Rick shrugged. "What am I s-supposed to see, Herb?"

The old man scratched a fingernail along the wooden cross, yet the paint remained unshaved. "Are you blind? Look at this yellow streak! I know cat spray when I see it."

Over the years, Rick had offered to clean up the cross, and Herbert had flatly refused, saying that graves were like houses—the shittier they looked, the less likely they were to be robbed.

"That's not c-cat spray, Herb. The p-paint is yellowing. If you'd let me use p-p-proper outdoor paint on it—"

"Don't mess with my cross. Graves are like houses. The shittier they look—"

"I know." Rick swerved toward the cottage, leaving the old man behind. "Good thing, t-t-too. Every day, the town grave robbers line up around the b-block, waiting for a chance to d-d-dig you up."

"You can bet your britches that I'll be bringing this up at the meeting!" Herbert howled louder than the wind.

Rick smiled as he walked away. *I know you will, old man.*

HERBERT HELD THE MEETING UP FOR TWENTY MINUTES, claiming an aneurysm. That was a new one. Herbert had declared broken ribs, bear attacks, and strokes. Once, he arrived headless, communicating only with his middle finger. If nothing else, the old man kept things lively.

"Right," Rick began, "how are you getting along d-down . . . on the other side, T-Taylor?"

Indigo bangs hid the girl's eyes. "Okay, I guess."

"She hasn't come down yet," Madge whispered.

Rick knew Taylor was anything but okay.

In the week since her arrival, she'd spent her days moping atop her tombstone, desperate to catch the attention of passing Livers. She waved, danced, and yelled as they shuffled by, oblivious.

Stephanie had made it her mission to acclimate Taylor to the cemetery. Though she'd failed at every attempt, Rick had to give the teen credit for trying. Stephanie had asked Taylor about her life in the outside world, her favorite foods, and her song. Taylor only stared at the gate with dead eyes, her focus elsewhere, until Stephanie finally poofed away, defeated. Granite had become Taylor's permanent throne. After a while, the others gave up trying to convince her to go up, down, or anywhere else. She seemed to prefer to dwell close to the living, invisible to them.

And then there had been the incident with her brother.

Three days after Taylor's burial, a Trans Am parked at the gate, and a young man entered the graveyard. When Taylor spotted him, all hell broke loose.

"Mooney! You're here!" She leaped from her granite and raced toward the gate, her face swallowed up by a gaping smile. She pounced, her arms poised to wrap around his neck. Instead, she fell through, tripped over her feet, and sprawled clumsily to the gravel.

Oblivious, Mooney walked on, curiously sweeping a hand over his jacket as if brushing away an insect.

"Mooney! Hey, Mooney! It's me!" Taylor flapped her arms like an eagle, and when that didn't work, she held her hair up like the wings of a cobalt airplane.

Mooney strolled on as Rick and the others spied from the comment box. "Someone should stop her," Stephanie suggested.

Taylor waved and flapped like a mad woman. "Mooney!"

"Yes, someone should," Madge answered, yet no one moved.

Unaware of the ghost at his side, Mooney reached Taylor's grave and pulled his collar around his ears before shoving his hands deep into his pockets. Rick had seen it all before. Mooney might show up again in a week, then in a month, then once a year before he stopped coming altogether. As it was with all Livers, Mooney would move on. Every visit was the same: the mourner would perform the same ritual, staring levelly at the tombstone, perhaps laying a memento at its base before quietly leaving.

But that wasn't how Mooney rolled.

He dropped to his knees, and grievous, anguished wails poured through the cemetery. Taylor's desperate dance halted as she watched her brother fall to pieces.

"Taylor, what the hell? How can this be happening?" he moaned. "I wish I could talk to you."

"I'm right here, Mooney! Look!" She resumed the flapping, the waving, the jumping.

"You guys—" Stephanie began.

"I think not, dear." The group fell back into silent, watchful horror.

Mooney kicked at the ground, wrinkling the turf that hadn't quite set. He stomped over Taylor's grave, ripping the sod to shreds. "Why you?" And in a dramatic move that Rick didn't think people did in real life, Mooney shook his fist at the sky.

Taylor blinked. "Knock it off, okay? You're stomping on my head."

Mooney twisted his foot into the green mat. A strip of sod moved left and right until it finally tore in half.

"Hey, don't do that. Rick just planted that grass."

Rick couldn't help the groan that escaped, knowing it would take all day to repair the damage.

"Why'd you have to be so stupid?"

"Hey, that's not fair. Don't call me stupid—"

"I guess you know what happened with Mom and Dad."

Taylor seemed to have lost the breath she no longer had. "I don't! Please, you have to tell me!"

He answered by lifting his face and unleashing a string of swear words that caused even Herbert to raise a brow. After kicking the sod one final time, Mooney ground his heel into the mud and turned toward the cottage.

Following his retreat, Taylor scampered in an absurd circle. "Mooney, if you'd just pay attention . . . would you stop walking?"

And suddenly, he did stop, spraying gravel. Could he have heard Taylor's pleas? If he had, it would be a first. Without the aid of an amplifier, no amount of screaming could be heard by a Liver. Other cemeteries had bullhorns, elaborate speaker systems, even PAs. But the only tool at Taylor's immediate disposal was her own voice, and every being in the cemetery, both living and dead, held their collective breaths.

Inches from his ear, she screamed as loud as her lungs could allow. "Mooooney!"

Reaching into his pocket, Mooney brought out a cell phone, swiped it, and held it to his ear. "Bro! Yeah, I'm just now leaving. Uh-huh. I'll be there in ten minutes. Man, it's creepy here. I keep feeling like someone's watching me. I . . . oh, I'll call you back."

Rick cringed as Mooney's eyes landed on him.

With his anguish gone and features composed, Mooney replaced his phone and approached casually as the others scattered. Taylor remained behind at the path, looking more crushed than ever.

Smiling as if he were waltzing into a business meeting, Mooney stopped at the comment box. "Sorry about that. I didn't think anyone was here."

Rick stared at the ground, and Mooney leaned close enough for Rick to catch the scent of his aftershave. "Do you ever, I don't know, see ghosts in this place? I mean, it's kinda creepy here, right?" He glanced around with a shudder.

"Uh, y-y-you know it's . . . n-n-not really . . . I n-n-need to g-g-get the . . ." Turning in a circle, Rick could think of nowhere to escape to and stared dumbly at Taylor's brother.

"Alright, then." Mooney turned on a muddy heel, and as he passed through the gate, a chuckling Herbert sank below ground while the rest scattered to the other side.

With the roar of her brother's engine, Taylor collapsed.

Taylor was anything but okay, but Rick could do no more than move forward and hope for the best.

"S-S-Since this is your first official m-meeting, we should g-g-go over the rules."

Taylor shrugged.

"Right. First, we g-go over old b-business, then new b-business. That's where the c-c-comment box comes in. You can also bring up any c-concerns you've had d-d-during the week."

"Why can't I just tell you?" With arms pressed tight over her chest, Taylor's ever-shifting mood darkened. "Why do I have to wait for these meetings?"

"Because, dear," Madge cut in, "we don't just go around blurting things out. We're not heathens."

The truth was slightly more complicated. Rick remembered when a spark of brilliance had hit a year into the job. Madge and Stephanie had appeared on the stone path as Rick had stood before the cottage. He noted the flaking paint and made the mistake of thinking out loud. "Needs re-p-p-painting." Two hours later, he sat helplessly on a tree stump as the women argued whether Rick should repaint the dwelling white, off-white, or cream.

"Like, what's the difference?" Stephanie asked, her foot tapping on the stone path.

"All the difference in the world, dear. This is white." Madge pointed to a hydrangea in bloom before caressing the frilly lace that edged her apron. "This is off-white. See?"

Plopping on the grass, Stephanie groaned. "Oh, my God, Madge, those are, like, the same color. He should paint it cream. Rick—"

"You c-can argue about it at the m-m-meeting." Rick surprised himself with his unusually firm tone.

"What meeting? Since when do we have meetings?"

"Since n-n-now," he stammered, and with that, the Friday meetings were born.

In the end, the meetings made things easier, although not necessarily *easy*. It didn't mean they left him alone the rest of the week, but at least their issues could be addressed all at once.

Madge's voice shattered the quiet. "Taylor, dear, since this is your first meeting, why don't you go first?"

Stephanie snorted. "It might cut into Herb's complaint hour."

Herbert stepped from the shadows, his fedora forever crooked on his thinned hair, and shook a fresh stack of papers. "I'll be damned if you refuse my God-given right to bring up every one of these. Number one. I have irrefutable proof that my coffin is sinking by a quarter-inch a year. That proves you don't know how to dig a proper hole. Number two—"

"Herb, I didn't even b-bury you. That was the last c-c-caretaker."

"Number *two*—"

"Why can you see me?" Taylor's eyes bored into Rick, her breath coming in short bursts.

"I . . . what d-do you m-mean?"

Sweeping her bangs aside, she leaned forward, pointing her body like a missile. "Just what I said. Why can you see me? Hear me? You're not dead, right? So why you and not my brother?" Her eyes blazed.

Rick recoiled. How could he possibly begin to answer?

"Rick is different," Madge jumped in. "He can

communicate with us in ways that most living people can't."

Taylor's wrath turned on Madge. "I know *that*. What I want to know is why? Why him? Why not your children? Or Stephanie's parents, or Herbert's . . . whoever?"

"I had people."

Fiery tears welling, Taylor swiveled back to Rick. "What's so damn special about you?"

"Dear, that's quite enough out of you. It's not ladylike—"

"She's right. She d-d-deserves to know why a n-n-nobody like me has b-been given a gift that m-maybe he doesn't d-d-deserve."

Unblinking, Taylor folded her arms once again.

It wasn't just the memories, though remembering was painful enough. Rick had difficulty fully understanding the complexities of the so-called gift that often seemed more like a curse. "When I was t-ten-years-old, I d-d-drowned. I was revived, b-but I guess this was a lingering effect." He peeked at Taylor, hoping that was enough to satisfy her.

It wasn't. "So, you died and came back with this special power. It still doesn't make sense. Why you?" The fire hadn't left her eyes.

Stephanie patted Taylor's leg. "Like, this isn't really fair—"

"You're right. It's not fair." Shaking off Stephanie's hand, Taylor crossed the room and planted herself in front of Rick. "It's not fair that this guy who can't even talk properly gets to talk to whoever he wants."

In a flash, Madge grabbed Taylor by the arm and spun her sharply. "Now, you listen here, Missy. Life is unfair, and yes, death is unfair too. You're not the only person who left loved ones behind, who lost something. But if you insist on throwing these fits, moping around, and screaming at the living, please do us all a favor and do it where we can't hear you. Quite frankly, dear, we are all sick to our own deaths of it." With a swivel, Madge sauntered back to her seat, folded her hands in her lap, and pursed her thin lips.

For a moment, no one spoke. Taylor remained stiff until her shoulders drooped, and she covered her face with unsteady hands. With deep, convulsing breaths, she returned to the couch as a breeze rattled the windows, the tension faded, and the crackling fire filled the silent void. The stillness made Rick want to wave his hands just to make the air move.

"Aw, hell, is that thing crying again?" Herbert tossed his papers in the air, sheets cascading to the floor.

"I'm sorry," Taylor croaked. "I shouldn't have said all that. I guess no one ever tells you that it doesn't end when it ends, you know?"

The other dearly departed shifted uncomfortably as if they felt her sentiment in their cores. A sorrowful hush stilled them, then crept into Rick's bones and settled there, kindling an ache in his heart. Taylor was difficult. Hell, at times, they all were.

How difficult would he be when his clock stopped ticking?

"When I first died," Madge said, nearly in a whisper, "I tried to hop the gate. I spent all night out there. I tried climbing over it and digging underneath. I wasn't even able to make a hole." She held up her index finger. "That's how I broke this nail."

Stephanie gazed at the windows. "Oh, my God. I

climbed the tallest tree in the cemetery—that oak behind Barlow Pond—and screamed at the top of my lungs, hoping someone would rescue me."

Taylor nodded, and a flicker of a smile touched her lips. The world lightened a bit, and her half-smile reminded Rick of the calm after a storm, the first call of a sparrow signaling the worst had come and gone.

Madge smiled. "Herbert broke his TV the first night he was here. He tried to climb into it to get to the other side."

Taylor glanced at the sulking ghost in the corner. "You have TVs here? How?"

"Oh, my God, that reminds me." Stephanie bounced in place. "You haven't brought your television yet. Do you have one of those computaters? I so want to go on the line to that Net Flick thing. Like, you haven't moved in at all." Stephanie's bird-like squeal bounced off the walls.

Taylor turned to Rick, who shrugged. "I d-don't know. They never told me how it's d-done."

"You're telling me we could have been watching Walker, Texas Ranger all this time?" Herbert yelled, throwing himself back into his chair. "Well, stop wasting time and tell her how to unpack her damn stuff."

"Oh, my God, this is so exciting."

Madge sat beside Taylor. "There's really nothing to it. You just summon your things."

"Summon them? How?"

"Just envision the item where you want it, and it will appear."

Stephanie hopped from one foot to the other. "How big is your television? Is Cheers still on? Did Sam and Diane ever get married?"

"I don't own a TV."

The silence lasted all of three seconds, broken by Stephanie's gut-wrenching wail. "Oh, my God, you guys, why do we have such bad luck with televisions? First, Madge's grandkids broke hers, which wasn't much of a loss. It was just an old black-and-white. But then Herb breaks his, then Frank gives his away right before he dies. Are we just, like, cursed to never have a television again?"

"I don't get it. How can Madge's grandkids break her TV . . . here?"

As Stephanie collapsed onto the couch, Madge turned hesitantly back to Taylor. "You can summon anything you own, but it's only a replica. The real thing is still in the living world. If it breaks there, it breaks here, and vice-versa. When my grandchildren broke the knob off my TV, the knob fell off here too." She shot a concerned glance at Stephanie, now rocking on the floor. "Our Steph never owned a TV."

Hope surfaced. "Can I summon my dog, Buster?"

Even Stephanie, in her near-catatonic state, stared, horrified. Rick had wondered aloud the same when he'd first arrived, but they'd promptly admonished him. He hoped they'd go easier on Taylor.

"Dear, you can't replicate a living being. Would you want to be summoned here if you were still alive?"

Taylor's face flushed. "I guess not."

"In any case," Madge continued, "since you can't take it to the afterlife, your things stay here or in the living world until they break. A lot ends up in the closet. We tend to acquire a lot of knick-knacks."

Taylor's face lightened ever so slightly. "Stephanie, I have a laptop and a Netflix account."

Stephanie rose to her elbows. "Really? You have the Net Flick?"

"And I haven't heard of *Who's the Boss*, but we have *The Walking Dead*. I don't know if that's the same, but it's pretty awesome."

Stephanie leaned forward with interest. "What's that?"

"Zombie apocalypse."

Laying a hand on her chest, Madge appeared unnerved. "Goodness, that doesn't sound pleasant at all."

"And I have Facebook and Twitter. Maybe we can look up people you knew."

Stephanie sat upright. "I don't know what those are, but I . . . okay, what are those?"

Taylor smiled fully then, and her entire being softened, filling Rick with such relief that he found it impossible not to beam in return.

"You post things on your wall, and you look at other people's walls, and sometimes they share memes and links to other stuff. Oh, and you can tweet."

Once again, silence prevailed. Even Herbert leaned close, the floor around him littered with paper.

Stephanie looked as if her head would explode, sending lace and hairspray to the corners of the earth. "Did you guys get any of that?"

"Something about bird calls and walls," Madge offered, fanning her reddened face. "Like the bulletin board at the corner store, I think . . . Rick?"

He shifted uncomfortably. "I don't have F-F-Facebook or Twitter or I-Instagram—"

"Instant what?"

"Sounds like some sort of new telegram service."

Herbert pointed an accusing finger at Rick. "What in the hell happened to Western Union?"

"So, all I do is imagine it in my head, and then it appears?"

"That's right. Just imagine it in your room."

"Wait!" Stephanie shouted, "she hasn't even built her room."

"Oh, yes," Madge said, "you should do that first. Otherwise, all your stuff ends up in the closet, and that thing goes on forever."

A slow smile spread across Stephanie's face. "This is gonna be so tripendicular."

Taylor's face fell. "I don't . . . I'm not ready to take a step like that. Moving in, I mean. I need to get out of here." The invisible switch that governed Taylor's ever-shifting mood flipped. Gone was the smile that lit the atmosphere. Gone was the girl standing at the precipice, ready to jump into the new life she'd been unwillingly plunged into.

And, as quick as a deer, Taylor too was gone, through the door in a haze as the outline of her ethereal body clung to the chilly air.

6

A DYING GIRL'S FINAL WORDS

Rick woke early to a freshly cleansed sky, the sun shining through a blue so rich he could almost brush his fingers against it. Drifting past the dormant peach grove beyond Barlow Pond—where Herbert had once pretended to drown when Rick was new and naive—Rick followed a narrow path lined with wild ferns and moss-covered rocks. Fallen pine needles covered the forest floor as he wove within the embrace of the dense woodland.

In a hidden clearing surrounded by lavender, an unmarked grave overlooked the canyon. Wild clovers and crabgrass covered the vacant, bodiless mound. Surrounded by former caretakers, an unadorned headstone lay at the head of the secluded clearing chosen for men of his type; by nature, caretakers were solitary, both in life and afterward.

Death cured little.

As his eyes roamed over his predecessor's tombstones, Rick wondered, had a Taylor been thrust upon them? A

Herbert? Had the dead in their care been at peace, settled into their Nexts? Or had the caretakers who'd come before also been unwillingly dragged into petty disagreements, emotional outbursts, and cursed with ill-tempered residents?

A pair of falcons cried overhead, their wings spread wide as they drifted on a current, and Rick's mind wandered back to Serge's final day. The caretaker Rick had replaced had done what he could to prepare him for the complexities of taking care. He'd warned of the old miser, the emotional teen, and the restless housewife. But Serge had gone on to his Next less than a year after Rick's arrival, and though Rick had known it was selfish, he'd wished for more time.

As the hours had crept closer to Serge's final day, Rick couldn't hide his dismay. "I c-c-c . . ." His throat tightened with every syllable. If he could have, he'd have grasped Serge by the arm and somehow prevented him from moving on. There was no way he'd be able to perform solo. He was too fragmented, too inadequate.

Too wrong.

"S-S-Serge, I c-c—"

"You can because they're broken, too. They're still here for a reason."

All these years later, Rick still questioned Serge's faith in him. Perhaps he'd merely been gracious. After all, who else was there to care for this band of ghostly misfits?

It dawned then that everything didn't have to begin and end with him. He hadn't been hired to patch their broken souls and wasn't responsible for their eternal happiness. Herbert and Taylor weren't his burdens. Flowers, rain, and overgrown grass—those were his responsibilities.

Madge will help Taylor adjust. She's good at things like that.

Like the easy flick of a switch, Rick relinquished responsibility for his blue-haired dilemma and rested on the cold, hard grass as a flock of barn swallows flitted from tree to tree. The river below lifted a mist up the canyon wall, coating him with a filmy dew. As he lay back against the epitaphless tombstone rising from the ground, Rick allowed his eyes to drift closed.

Rick slumbered, one of the few living men to sleep atop his own grave.

SUNDAY MORNINGS BROUGHT A QUIET UNLIKE ANY OTHER. On the cusp of winter, the cemetery was the last place the townspeople ventured as they prepared for the inevitable snow and ice ahead. During the three previous seasons, Rick had longed for those chilly months and the seclusion they would bring. Now, eager to prepare for winter's looming fros, he grabbed his clippers and plunged into the biting cold. Darkened skies threatened rain, glazing the air with a crisp, clean scent. A breeze caught him, and he pulled his flannel closer.

He jolted to a stop; Taylor was slouched atop her tombstone. *Not again.* Rick trudged toward her grave, the weight of each step growing as if he were wading through water in iron boots.

Stephanie lay on the lawn nearby and picked at the grass as one leg swung in the air. The silence roared—even the birds seemed to have taken refuge elsewhere.

After a moment, Stephanie spoke. "So, can I ask you a

question? You don't have to answer if it's too personal or whatever."

Taylor pulled her chin from her palm, her face drawn. "Go for it, I guess."

Stephanie plucked a blade of grass. "Did it hurt? When you died?"

Rick groaned. At times, Stephanie's enduring youth was a blessing, sweetening an otherwise grim, shadowy world. In other ways, like now, her innocence was a cross they all had to bear.

Taylor's brow took a downward turn. Her hair crested the breeze like an ocean wave as if each strand mirrored her sorrow. "I felt pressure. When my head hit the steering wheel, I saw a bright flash, like when you look at a light and close your eyes, but the afterimage is still there. I was aware of the pain but not feeling it. It's hard to describe."

"Like the memory of pain," Madge said, stepping forward.

Taylor nodded, her arms tightening around her chest. "I broke my leg when I was little, and I remember how much it hurt, but I don't feel it now. That's how it was when the crash happened. The pain was there but in the distance." She cocked her head toward Madge. "How did you die?"

Madge brushed her arms, shifting. "I . . . it was a stroke."

Taylor turned to Stephanie, her mood curiously lightened. "How about you? How did it happen?"

Stephanie sat up, tucking her knees beneath. "It was an accident. Like, I was at a party, and there was this guy, Billy, who I'd totally had a crush on forever. I was waiting in his car, and it was cold in the garage. I noticed the keys were in the ignition, so I turned on the heat. I remember wondering what was taking Billy so long, and the next thing I knew, I was here, watching my sister being carried through the gate while they put me in the ground. I guess I died of stupidity. I didn't even know you could die of that until I went and did it."

Rick realized he'd never investigated their deaths. They all had files and had all been through intakes. That he'd never bothered to read them brought a lump to his throat.

Taylor slid from her tombstone onto the cold grass. "I died texting and driving. That's pretty stupid. Stupider, actually."

Madge stepped forward. "What's texting, dear? Is it some birds-and-bees thing the kids are doing now?"

Taylor blinked. "You type a message to someone on your phone, and it shows up on theirs."

"Like Western Union?" Herb sprang from a nearby oak, challenging Rick with an accusing scowl. "I thought you said they got rid of it for that Instant Gram service."

"I understand," Madge said, though her face suggested she was far from it.

Ignoring them both, Taylor went on. "Anyway, the last message I sent was, *'O-M-G, I lol'd so hard I peed my pants.'*" Crimson spread into the hollows of her cheeks.

Here we go again, Rick thought and prepared for Taylor's familiar rush of tears.

Madge glanced at the others, perplexed. "What does it mean to be loling? Surely *that* must be some sex thing the kids are doing. It sounds like it, anyway."

"Don't you get it? Those are the words that will immortalize me forever! That's how everyone will remember me—the girl who died peeing her pants." A fresh stream of wails broke, and Taylor sank back against her tombstone.

Stephanie knelt and rested a hand on the sobbing girl's shoulder, her expression grim yet sincere. She seemed to have instantly matured, the seventeen-year-old discharged by the seasoned middle-aged woman she would have grown into. Rick hoped she could finally get through the shambles that Taylor had become to the person at the core.

Stephanie leaned forward and whispered, "So . . . was it, like, a lot of pee?"

Her sobs reduced to a trickle, and Taylor met Stephanie's gaze. "I didn't really pee. It's just something you say."

"Ew." Stephanie recoiled. "I wouldn't want anyone thinking I peed my pants."

"Well, dear, I'm sure no one thought she did," Madge interjected, with a palm cupped to her lips. "You didn't, did you? It happens to everyone, especially when you get older—"

"No!" Taylor leaned back against her tombstone, her eyes drifting shut, and Rick knew exactly how this would end. Taylor would throw a tantrum, scamper away, and the others would be doomed to spend the winter tiptoeing around the oversensitive, freshly dead girl.

Herbert spat on a nearby shrub. "If this texting thing makes you pee all over yourself, why are the kids even doing it? Sounds illegal, if you ask me."

"It totally sounds grody." Stephanie wiped imagined urine from her legs. "I wouldn't want to do it, no matter how nice it feels." Large, pink roses flamed on her cheeks. "Does it, though? Feel nice, I mean?"

A slow smile lifted Taylor's lips as she began to

chuckle in a way that sounded like a bird choking on a berry. *This is it.* Rick wondered what happened to residents who went over the edge and never came back.

Taylor's sudden, sharp laughter echoed as she fell to her side. Stephanie turned to Madge, who looked more confused than ever.

Herbert cocked a thumb in Taylor's direction. "This girl is screwy. I better not catch her texting on my grave. I have enough problems with that damn cat." With a final glare, the old man disappeared into a cloud.

"Yes, Rick, maybe we should have a rule about texting around the cemetery." Madge spun into her own ghostly mist.

Creeping to Taylor's side, Stephanie laughed along with her, moved by a joke she didn't understand.

Rick headed to the tool shed with his clippers in hand as the two young women behind him laughed so hard he thought that if they were still alive, they'd both be peeing their pants.

7

SO MUCH FOR SOLITUDE

Rick struggled to focus as the weekly meeting droned on. Stephanie inundated Taylor with a litany of questions. How she'd gotten her hair so blue, if she'd had it done at Supercuts, and if her piercings were some sort of punishment. Earlier, Rick had overheard Madge whisper, "No one would do that to themselves on purpose."

Stephanie seemed particularly interested in selfies. "Like, you don't have to wait for your film to come back from the Foto Hut or anything?"

"You just post your picture from your phone."

"But, like, where does the picture go . . .."

Taylor pulled her cell phone from her back pocket, and the others fell into quiet amazement. "The battery's dead, but it's all in here."

Madge straightened. "We have loads of batteries in the closet. What size do you need? Nine-volt, or maybe some double-As?"

Stephanie reached forward and gently stroked the

black screen as if it were alive. "It's, like, made of glass or something, you guys."

Herbert squinted. "Bullshit. That's just a damn calculator. I've seen those newfangled cellular phones, and they're as big as walkie-talkies."

With a shrug, Taylor tossed the phone onto the coffee table. "There's a calculator on it."

"On it?" Stephanie asked. "Like, inside? How does it fit?"

"It's an app," Taylor said, spiritless.

"Appetizer . . ." Madge mumbled, shaking her head.

"Now this nut job wants us to believe she's got food in her magic calculator. I demand more security around here, Rick. I trust her about as much as I trusted Nixon."

As the dead bickered, Rick's mind drifted back to his imagined cabin. Time withered, and he could almost taste the crispness in the air, see the tiny dwelling surrounded by trees—

"Oh, my God, why? Like, we can't even taste it, and the apple cider runs all over the floor." Stephanie's tattered voice pulled Rick from his daydream. He'd missed something vital, and he stiffened.

Madge dabbed at her forehead with a handkerchief. "Some of us have nice memories of Thanksgiving. Maybe instead of being a party pooper, you could try to appreciate the work I do. Goodness, it must be a hundred degrees in here." She swiped the kerchief along her outstretched neck.

"Could you please turn the heat down so Mrs. I-Died-During-Menopause can be more comfortable? Gag me." With an eye-roll, Stephanie leaned close to Taylor. "Madge gets kind of insane around the holidays."

Madge's voice cracked as she fanned the air. "I can't help when I died, and I do not get insane."

"You so do! Last year you threw an entire turkey at the wall when Herb made it dance across the table. It was epic."

"No one appreciates the trouble I go to."

Anxious to avoid another derailed meeting, Rick changed the subject. "T-T-Taylor, how are y-you adjusting? You seem b-b-better this week," he lied.

Taylor shrugged. "There's still a lot I don't understand."

"L-Like what?"

Leaning back, she crossed her arms, though her expression softened. "Well, how'd you find out you could, you know, talk to us?"

"Oh, what a story that is. Rick—"

His face flushed. "We d-don't need to hear this."

"But it's a good story, let me tell it," Madge begged.

Knowing the battle was already lost, Rick sank. "If anyone's t-t-telling the story, it'll be me. You're just gonna t-tell it—"

"Truthfully? We wouldn't want that, would we?"

So often, Rick felt like the sole source of entertainment for the dead in his charge, but his concentration was flagging, and he knew his stutter would turn the story into an hour-long tale. "Fine, t-tell it."

"Yay! Madge tells it so well!"

Rick raised a brow. "How many t-times has she t-t-told it?"

"Never mind that, dear." With a dismissive wave, Madge turned to Taylor. "He came here a week after the last caretaker died, and he had no idea."

"About what?"

Madge smiled. "Anything."

BEFORE HE'D SPOTTED THE HAND-PRINTED *CARETAKER Wanted* sign, Rick Holliday had expected that he'd live in the cramped storage room behind Shorty's forever—gas attendant by day, voracious reader by night. He'd had no plans to improve his lot in life, no desire for a better-paying job. If nothing else, Rick was a man highly skilled at standing still. As he'd backed his truck to the cemetery gates, he'd had no grasp of what a caretaker did. And yet, the notice had stirred something in him, awoken a foreign curiosity.

As he climbed from his truck, he spotted a teenage girl sunbathing on the grass. With one leg crossed casually over the other, she looked like a girl enjoying a lovely day at the park rather than lying in a graveyard. She spotted Rick and waved. Rick hesitantly reciprocated with a forced half-smile.

He regretted it immediately.

The girl sat up with such apparent surprise that he glanced behind, sure she must have intended her wave for someone else. Yet not another soul was around, and when he turned back, neither was the girl.

Gone. Vanished. Disappeared.

Brushing the raised hairs on his arms, Rick walked toward the cottage. A sheet of paper had been taped to the door—'Inquire Inside'—and when Rick creaked the door open, an elderly man stared.

As if he'd been waiting.

The brief interview diverted into a tour of the grounds as Sandy Barlow pointed out the orchards, Barlow Pond, and the tool shed. He hadn't questioned Rick about his skills, nor had he asked for a resume. The man had merely gone over a caretaker's duties, how to behave around mourners, and the tricky lock on the gate. Rick had the impression that he'd had the job the second they'd shaken hands.

In truth, the job had been his the instant he'd returned Stephanie's wave.

A week later, Rick entered the cottage with a thrill. Boxes covered every surface, were piled in corners, and cluttered on tables. Most had belonged to Serge, packed hurriedly by the former caretaker's sister before she'd flown out the door, stopping only long enough to blurt, "Do what you want with these things. This place creeps me out." Since the brief interview the week before, Rick's every waking hour had been spent counting the days and thinking back to the trees, the vast expanse of land, and the cottage.

His cottage, now.

After stammering through an awkward conversation with a vacuum salesman asking for directions, Rick carried his boxes in from the truck. A black cat wound between his boots, and he knelt, scratching between its ears. "Hey there, b-boy, where'd you come from? Go on now; time to get home. It's darn near d-dark."

Inside, Rick skirted nervously around Serge's boxes like square-shaped grenades. He couldn't shake his ghoulish awareness of Serge's belongings, watching his every move. Rick spent much of that first day folding flannels, dusting furniture, and washing the sheets Serge's sister hadn't bothered to pack. Compared to Shorty's, the cottage felt as grand as a mansion, and with shelving to finally display his books, Rick began to whistle.

He was going to like it here.

A sudden rattle from the kitchen stilled him. After several attempted break-ins at Shorty's, Rick was on alert. Wiping dusty hands on his jeans, he crept from the bedroom, grabbing the only weapon he could find—a small table lamp with a kitten on the shade. Gripping the kitten-lamp high overhead, he slunk into the kitchen, whipping his head in every direction. The rattle came again, pots and pans crashing. Rick cautiously moved to the cupboard and opened it, yet nothing seemed out of place. He closed the sideboard and lowered the lamp to the counter.

A noise from behind startled him, and he spun.

Purring near the open window, the black feline he'd spotted earlier blinked.

Rick laughed, feeling all kinds of ridiculous. "Spooked me, boy." He rubbed beneath the cat's chin, and the cat's tail sprang up like a dagger. "Did you belong to Serge?"

The cat thumped his head softly against Rick's arm, and he wondered how long it had been since the cat had been fed. It had to have been weeks, though a quick glance told him the cat hadn't been starving. Still, nothing beat a can of . . . whatever cats liked.

"Hungry, boy?"

The cat perked his ears, dropped from the counter, and raised a paw.

Rick fished in the cupboards and found a dusty can of tuna. After scooping condensed fish into a bowl, he made a mental note to pick up a few more tins on his next trip into town. "I don't know what Serge called you, but you look like a Benson to me." He rinsed the empty can, tossed it into the garbage, and smiled, pleased with the name.

Over the days that followed, Rick settled into his new routine. He scoured the grounds, memorized the layout, and spent an entire afternoon exploring the tool shed. To his delight, he found a riding lawn mower, practically unused. Pushing the mower into the sunshine, he remembered the vast expanse of lawn he'd spotted the day before just over the north hill.

It didn't look like it needed mowing, though.

Ten minutes later, Rick clipped along at a whopping eight miles per hour. As he marked hills, groves, and meadows, he was overwhelmed with the surety of everything falling into place. He imagined quiet days and peaceful nights. No co-workers, no hovering boss, no commute.

No people. He could finally, thankfully, be alone.

His smile faltered when he spotted a woman waving energetically at the edge of the grassy hill. Rick tentatively waved back, his mood darkening.

So much for solitude.

As he inched closer, something about the woman put his hair on end. Dressed in green polyester slacks, a paisley blouse, and a bright orange apron, she looked plucked straight from a seventies sitcom. She waved Rick over. He grudgingly cranked the mower in her direction. Feeling suddenly idiotic riding the slow-moving man-toy, he was just beginning to wonder if he should walk the rest of the way when he blinked.

The woman had popped out of existence.

Rick stared at the spot where she should have been, rubbed his eyes, and looked again.

Gone. Vanished. Disappeared.

He killed the mower, and the sudden silence was deafening. Rick inspected the hedge where she'd stood only a moment before, and an eerie chill slithered up his spine. Maybe she'd simply walked away—though he'd been staring directly at her. Perhaps she'd stepped behind a tree —though there were no trees nearby. A hundred explanations ran through his mind, yet the one glaring answer that made the most sense was one he couldn't entertain. He'd watched that ghost hunter show and found it comical. Poor acting and convenient timing when the camera happened to move away just as a ghost appeared. All that supernatural hocus-pocus was little more than cheap entertainment for the masses. Rick hadn't believed in ghosts before, and he wasn't about to start now.

Rick cranked the key, and the mower jerked to life. He glanced around while riding back to the shed—no woman, no shimmering figure. And then, thinking back to the interview, Rick recalled something Sandy Barlow had said as they'd walked along the edge of the woods.

Visitors like to do their grieving in peace, so just leave 'em be.

That explained it. Rick had spotted a mourner who had probably become overwhelmed and left. Satisfied, he gave it no more thought, though a nagging sense of having missed something fluttered in the recesses of his mind.

The following days passed without incident, and with Rick's belongings safely tucked away, he found the sight of Serge's boxes too much to bear. He carried them to the attic and stacked them in a dark corner to gather dust. He didn't like the waxy slick the boxes left on his palms, obsessively washing up to his elbows each time he came down. With the reminders of the old caretaker finally gone, his new life sank in fully, and he beamed.

The antique phonograph in the corner beckoned, and he flipped through a stack of vintage albums until he found the perfect record. He slid the vinyl from its sleeve, and as crackly music filled the air, Rick began to sing. Grabbing a broom, he danced, holding it tenderly, as he'd seen real men do with real women in the old black-and-whites. Halfway through, he returned the broom to its spot, kicked off his boots, and headed toward the bathroom.

Grabbing a washcloth, he turned on the shower. Steam clouded the mirror, and as Rick hopped under the hot water, he caught himself humming a different tune—something about a fence and wide-open country. He decided he'd find the box of his old cassettes; the former caretaker had left behind a perfectly good stereo. It must be worth something with that 8-track player . . .

As warm water cascaded over his body, he fumbled for the shampoo bottle. When he opened his eyes, his heart took a nosedive.

"You arrogant shit." A fully clothed man stood inches away, a perfectly dry fedora atop his balding head. "Aren't you ever gonna introduce yourself? You've been ignoring us for three days."

Frozen, Rick could only gawk in the scalding water, and when he parted his lips, he managed only a mousy squeak.

This isn't happening, no one is here—

"Well, jackass?"

His muscles unlocked, and Rick scrambled back. He

found his voice wrapped in a scream as his legs tangled in the plastic curtain. Scurrying from the bathroom, stark naked and soaking wet, he raced toward the front door. But as his palm wrapped around the knob, a throat cleared behind him.

He turned to see five sets of staring eyes.

The old man from the shower glowered as Rick gaped at the small crowd. The woman who'd waved gasped, fanning her reddened face with her apron while the sunbathing teen gawked.

"Ace!"

Releasing her apron, the woman threw a hand over the girl's eyes. "Goodness, you should really put something on. There's a *child* here." The teen's limbs flailed as the woman fought to shield her from the sight of Rick's nude, dripping body.

Rick's mind exploded while all logic shattered. A squeal—perhaps his own—resounded, and he grabbed a throw pillow from the nearest unoccupied chair. Instinct told him to run, yet his legs refused to budge. "What d-d-do you want? How d-d-did you g-get in here?"

A middle-aged man who seemed vaguely familiar waved with a crooked, embarrassed smile. Where had Rick seen him before? Seemingly of its own volition, his head turned, and his eyes landed on the mantel, where a framed picture he'd meant to put away remained. It was a photo of someone he'd never met—never *should* meet—as the subject was currently dead. Buried. Not a hundred yards from here.

Rick's legs wobbled.

The old man from the shower cocked a thumb in

Rick's direction. "What's wrong with this idiot? Hasn't he seen dead people before?"

As Rick's legs failed him, the world faded to black, and he was out before his head hit the floor.

RICK SQUIRMED AMID STEPHANIE'S GIGGLES. "IT WASN'T exactly f-fair. No one warned m-me."

The others roared with laughter, holding their stomachs and rolling on couches as Rick sulked. Even Herbert crowed from the corner. "The little chicken-shit was so scared I thought he was gonna drop a load right there on the rug." Laughing wickedly, Herbert aimed a long, pointed finger, and Rick instinctively moved his hands to his crotch to cover up the memory.

"You should have read the instructions Serge left in his boxes. Why did you think they were sitting here in the living room?"

"I don't know! They were his p-p-personal belongings. Just . . . let's d-d-drop it." Wishing the meeting would end, Rick wondered who had the tougher time: Livers who waltzed through life oblivious or men like him.

"So, how did you end up getting him to listen?" Taylor asked.

"It took a few days, but eventually, he calmed down. We had to keep showing ourselves to prove we were real."

"Oh, my God, he convinced himself he was hallucinating." Stephanie laughed so hard she lost her voice and resorted to waving her arms breathlessly.

"I don't understand. Hadn't you seen dead people before? Didn't you say you got this way as a kid?"

Thoroughly flustered, Rick glanced away, unable to meet their stares. "They d-don't exactly introduce themselves at the grocery store. Can we get on with the m-meeting?"

"Anyway," Madge continued, ignoring Rick, "he finally agreed to talk with us as long as we promised never to pop up in the shower again."

Stephanie's laughter abruptly died as she glanced guiltily away. Rick wondered briefly what that look meant but decided he'd had enough embarrassment for one evening.

Some things were better left unknown.

8

TAKE IT OR LEAVE IT

Another day brought another round of the same duties Rick had performed for a decade. He swept through his morning chores early and, at precisely one o'clock, headed to the cottage for lunch. He passed the basket of fragrant apples on the way to his favorite chair. The sweet, crisp scent coated his tongue, and he grabbed his worn copy of *When Ghosts Disappear —The New Alien Abduction Phenomenon.*

Rick methodically washed the dishes in the same order he repeated every day. Plate, glass, butter knife. After sweeping a rag across the counter in the same counter-clockwise motion, he folded the towel into the same rectangular shape. A man of routine, Rick crawled beneath the covers at the same time each night and rose at the same hour every morning. He ate the same foods, read the same books, and thought the same thoughts.

The caretaker left the cottage and resumed his work, humming the same tune and taking the same steps through the graveyard that he'd walked without fail for the last 3,650 days.

Midway through his rounds, he paused to take in the view where a row of hedges obscured an old stone bench —a spot that had become his secret hideaway. A deep gorge led to the river below. Across the canyon, farms dotted green hills. Lines had been drawn across the landscape where crops would be planted in the spring and sheep grazed in fields enclosed by wooden fences. It was the best-kept secret in town, that view, and Rick took a moment every day to enjoy his private spot, rain or shine.

And then, though the nearest grove was half a mile away, the scent of fresh apples suddenly flooded in, sharp and sweet. Peering over the hedge, Rick spotted movement.

A woman was headed straight for him.

Scrunching low, Rick peered through a gap in the hedge as the visitor stopped at the foot of a grave several feet away. After a moment, he recognized her as the "Wish You Were Here" girl, though now that she was close, something else about her seemed oddly familiar. Long, blonde hair cascaded down her back in symmetrical waves, and her skin was the color of silky cream, aside from a row of tiny freckles dotted across her nose. A pink floral dress reached her ankles, and Rick could barely make out a pair of flat, shiny white shoes as she pulled a sweater tight. Studying her profile, Rick was sure the woman hadn't come to little Maddie's funeral. He would have remembered that haunting gaze, the unseen weight upon her shoulders. And yet, there was something—

"Hello, Grandfather."

Her voice made his heart flutter and his head light.

Then, with no reasonable explanation, he flattened his body to the ground.

What's next, Peeping Tom? A hidden camera in the bushes? Rick knew he must look preposterous, and, twisting his head, he glimpsed a way out. He could crouch-hobble to the left, crawl behind the old oak and sneak across the path to the dense stand of pines that edged Barlow Pond.

Yet something tugged at his sensibilities, and he peeked again through the hole in the hedge. The woman's eyes had a depth most Livers didn't possess, a sadness that gave her the appearance of a kicked puppy. She seemed somehow separated as if she existed in a protective bubble only she could inhabit. Her eyes mirrored how Rick had felt for as long as he could remember. Leaving now was impossible.

Wait. Watch.

The woman laid a thin blanket tenderly on the grass, and as she smoothed the edges, Rick realized it was Frank's grave she stood over—a resident who'd moved on only a month before. More than a resident, Frank had been Rick's friend, the only person—living or dead—who Rick had felt a genuine connection with. A kind, gentle soul, Frank's eyes had been permanently etched from a lifetime of smiling. Frank never interrupted and never tried to finish his sentences. Over time, Rick found that his stutter lessened in Frank's company. As much as Rick longed for solitude, he hadn't minded when Frank joined him on his morning rounds, reminiscing about his living days between morsels of quiet. Often, they'd ended up on the same bench where Rick now hid, savoring the view, tranquil in their unspoken companionship.

Frank had often talked of his granddaughter, crowing over her accomplishments. What was her name again? Mindy? Mandy? It started with an M. Maureen—

"It's me, Emily."

Ah, yes, Emily. How could he have forgotten the name he'd heard a thousand times? No wonder she seemed so familiar—she was the spitting image of Frank. Rick slapped his forehead, throwing him off balance and sprawling toward the hedge. He dug his boots into the dirt to keep from smashing into the shrubbery.

Emily looked up. "Hello? Is someone there?"

Cursing himself for his awkward position, Rick prayed she wouldn't investigate. *What's worse than a creeper? A cemetery creeper, that's what.* Quietly, he inched his way to the gap and released a sigh. She hadn't left the blanket. Glancing around, he saw no way to escape now that she'd been alerted. He'd have to settle in and wait.

Emily ran a pale hand across the tombstone. "Why haven't you come to see me?"

That grabbed his attention. Residents were bound to the cemetery. Rick had once watched as Herbert had run after a group of kids and smacked into the emptiness between the open gates. An invisible force had thrown him back on his tired old ass, preventing him from taking even a single step beyond. Once buried, the residents couldn't leave until it was time to move on. And after that . . . no one knew.

"Is it the job?" Caressing the marble, Emily ran her thumb over the lettering. "I tried, but I couldn't do it. It just wasn't right for me." Her words were cotton, and her voice sang soft, lyrical notes. She brought a hand to her face and brushed a stray hair aside—a simple movement Rick found strangely captivating.

"I'm happy now, and I think . . . well, I *thought* you'd be happy for me." She pulled two apples from her handbag, gently placing one at the base of Frank's headstone. "From our spot. One for you, one for me. Just like you used to say." Taking a bite, she lifted her chin to the sky.

Rick raised his chin in unison, savoring the scent that drifted through the hedge. How long he'd been crouched behind the shrubs, he didn't know and didn't care. Time was irrelevant. It was as if the meaning of life itself were compacted into this one moment.

The rustle of the blanket brought him back.

A pang shot through Rick's chest as Emily tucked her belongings back into her bag. He absentmindedly rubbed the spot with his palm. Emily studied her grandfather's headstone for so long that Rick wondered if she would stand there forever. He wouldn't mind if she did. He could just make out her shape beneath the long dress coated in tiny flowers in a pattern that was far too aged for her yet suited her all the same.

"Please come back. I miss you so much." She rose, folded the blanket, and trudged toward the gate, that same invisible weight slowing her steps. Had she been at Frank's funeral? It was likely, though five years had passed. Rick tended to wade through funerals with his head down, praying no one would take an interest in him. Maybe she *had* been there. If he could just get a better look—

"Oh, my God, who's that?" a voice whispered close.

Startled, Rick chomped down hard on his tongue.

Stephanie smirked. "She's cute. Is she the girl from the other day?"

"I d-don't know," he lied, tasting blood.

"Then, like, why were you spying on her?"

Nearly losing his balance again, Rick stood with a burning face. "I wasn't s-s-spying, I was—"

"He was choking the old chicken. This is what he does all damn day when he should be patrolling the grounds."

"That's . . . Herb, y-y-you just . . . I would n-n-n, I would n-never—"

"You should talk to her."

Emily moved closer to the gate, each step tugging at Rick's chest. "Why w-w-would I want t-to d-d-do that?" he said as he massaged his ribcage.

Herbert snickered. "Cuz she's a hot tamale!"

"I d-don't . . . she . . . I d-d-don't . . . you know what? F-Forget this." Stomping away, Rick tried to calm the stampede inside him.

"Where ya goin', me young laddie?" Herbert cackled.

Stumbling over his feet, Rick tried to escape them—all of them, everyone in the universe. Shame slid over his skin. He *had* felt perverted, spying on Frank's granddaughter. Why had he done it? He could have gone on with his business, clipping, trimming, and wandering artfully away as he did when any visitor entered the cemetery. Never before had he stayed.

Watched.

Herbert materialized in Rick's path with his signature rude gesture. "I know where he's goin'. Go on, boy, it's only nat-u-ral!"

Rick looked toward the gate in time to watch as Emily tripped over flat ground, her arms flailing wildly for purchase before she climbed into a small, battered Honda.

Tightening his jacket, Rick hurried to the cottage and

slammed the door. He shook off his coat and fell into his chair, overwhelmed with an awkward shame he didn't understand. He grabbed his book, *Cooking for Vegan Spirits*, and stared at the wall.

After a long while, his nerves began to settle, and he remembered something Emily had said.

Why haven't you come to see me?

She could have spoken Mandarin, and it would have made more sense. Frank had been gone for a month, but he'd been buried at Serenity Grove for five years, and Rick was sure Emily had never visited in all that time. The master of avoidance, Rick was skilled at recognizing faces, learning patterns, and knowing when to remain concealed.

Her haunted face was one he would have remembered.

CREAK-SLAM.

Silence whooshed as Rick cocked his head, every muscle tensed. He knew that noise. Leaping from his chair, he took two steps toward the door before regaining his senses.

It could have been anyone. Count to a hundred.

"One, two, three . . ." At twelve, he tiptoed to the door and peered through the tiny opening—no one. Stepping into the cold, he snaked along the narrow stone path and laid a hand atop the comment box. With his palm burned with hesitation. A storm was brewing in the shifting wind, the clouds scudding high above as if someone had lifted the earth's canopy, and the hairs on his arms rose as a low rumble echoed from the west. He opened the box.

A letter sat inside with a single word scrawled across the front in perfect cursive.

Grandfather.

A burst of wind lifted his chin in time to catch a glimpse of Emily as she passed through the iron gate. Tearing the letter from the box, Rick softly lowered the lid. Beyond the iron gates, the same Honda from earlier reversed onto Main Street and sputtered away, backfiring as it rounded the corner. Indifferent to the bitter cold, Rick gazed after the car before hurrying back to the cottage, the envelope gripped tightly between his fingers.

Inside, the perfume of apples permeated the room. The temperature had surely risen twenty degrees; an inferno crept beneath Rick's flannel. Turning the envelope over, he examined the lettering. Mourners never left envelopes in the comment box. They abandoned cards, scraps of paper, and once, a power bill with a note that read, "The earth is precious; conserve energy." Rick wasn't sure how a grave-yard could conserve energy more than it already did, so he'd chucked the bill.

He ran a thumb under the flap, and a folded sheet tumbled out. The letter was handwritten—a simple detail that made it inexplicably more endearing.

Dear Grandfather . . .

That Peeping Tom feeling shot forward as if Rick were snooping on someone's private diary. These were *her* words, *her* thoughts. Her very essence was on these lines. But the letter wasn't addressed to him—what right did he have to read it? He folded the paper and shoved it back into the envelope.

It wasn't his letter to read. He both accepted this and mourned it at once.

But . . . but.

If Emily had intended the letter for Frank, why not place it on his grave? People had done *that* before. Several times a year, Rick scooped up the soggy remains of drenched paper, trinkets, and prized heirlooms and dumped them into a box marked with the name of the dearly departed. Mourners often returned to retrieve their offerings once they'd gotten past their initial grief.

But . . . but.

If she meant this for Frank, she would have left it for him. She wants someone to read this. Mimicking Herbert and his never-ending list of demands, Rick shook the envelope.

"She wants *me* to read it," he said, vaguely aware of his unsteady breath.

Removing the letter, he opened it fully.

Dear Grandfather,

It's been a while since I've felt you. I miss you so much, and things aren't the same now that you're no longer here. I know you've been gone for a few years, but it always felt like you were still here. But now, you're truly gone, and I can't understand why. Well, I think I do, but you know I wasn't happy. At least, I thought you knew.

Robert hired me back at the bookstore. I offered to start at the bottom stocking shelves again, but my replacement had quit the week before, and he was happy to bring me back as manager. When I walked into that bookstore again, I thought it would feel like a failure, that I'd given up my dream and yours. Instead, it felt like going home. In that way, I've never regretted my decision.

This morning, I gathered the best apples from the cellar and made your favorite pie. I put it on your . . . well, I don't like calling it what it is, so let's say I put it where you're resting. I hope you like it.

I'll be visiting every week until your return. Sundays are my days off, so if you want to make your presence known, I'll be here.

I love you.

Signed,

Your Em

P.S. I still have Boo.

DRAWN TO THE APPLES ON THE TABLE, RICK ALLOWED HIS feet to carry him close. He grabbed one from the basket— red, round, and smooth. Unlike waxy store-bought apples, these had come from the grove in the cemetery, untouched by modern chemicals. He bathed in the tart, sweet perfume as he drifted back to the not-so-distant past.

Back to the many walks he'd taken with Frank.

This orchard reminds me of the apple grove behind my house, Frank had often said, where he and Emily had plucked fruit from ripened trees. After Emily's father died, Frank had stepped into his son's role. Together, they'd survived the loss of a father and son, and even in death, Emily had kept Frank going.

In the end, the others had looked forward to Frank's regular Emily updates. Aside from Rick, who led a singular, dull life, Emily had become the residents' sole connection to the living world, and in their own deaths, they'd lived through her.

Because, while the others had remained year after maddening year locked behind the iron gate, Frank had been different. He'd had one ability no other resident had.

Unlike the rest, Frank had not been bound.

IT HAD FINALLY REACHED THE END OF A LONG, HOT summer, and an argument had broken out. For once, Herbert wasn't the instigator.

"I'm just saying, it seems weird."

Madge fanned her reddened face with her apron, avoiding Stephanie's gaze. "I don't know how your daffodils ended up on my grave. Are you sure they were yours?"

Stephanie rolled her eyes with a huff. "Tracy puts daffodils on my grave every year. Like, everyone knows that. Besides, no one's visited you in forever."

Madge blew into a handkerchief. "I don't know how they got there, and even if I did, how is it my fault? Isn't anyone curious to know if I had a visitor after all these years? And I missed it!"

Herbert swung from the chandelier. "This is exactly why I keep saying you need to set up cameras. First, it's daffodils. Next, they're digging—"

"Herbert, please come down from there," Frank said in an even, calm voice.

Herbert landed in a heap of tangled limbs. "You'll see."

Frank flashed Stephanie a gentle smile. "I know you don't believe Madge had anything to do with it. She couldn't have picked up your flowers if she'd wanted to. Her hand would've gone right through."

Stephanie dropped her eyes. "I guess so."

Frank turned to Madge. "It wasn't anyone you knew. Just a couple of kids cutting through on their way to school. They grabbed Stephanie's flowers and dumped them on your grave." He rested a hand on her leg. "I'm sorry."

A soft "Oh," was all Madge could muster.

"If you s-saw it," Rick asked, "why didn't you say s-s-something sooner?"

The others turned to Frank, all with seemingly the same question.

"I didn't see it exactly, not in the way you're thinking. Not as it happened." Frank's usual light, cheerful disposition faded. "I saw it just now. They dropped the flowers, cut through the hay field, and now, I can see them in class. The taller one is making eyes at a cheerleader."

Silent astonishment filled every corner, every pocket of air.

"But that was, like, days ago. How are you seeing it now?"

A memory sparked. Rick had acquired a sizable collection of books on the supernatural—hauntings, paranormal activity, new-age theology—and most of it was hogwash. But this . . . "Are you t-talking about astral p-p-projection?"

"I think so, though this was the first time I traveled to someone else."

Stephanie shook her head. "What's he talking about?"

Rick turned this new revelation over. "It means he can p-project into someone else's head and read their m-m-memories." A few living people claimed to possess the power of projection. He'd never heard of the dead having the ability. Then again, Barnes and Noble didn't have a *How Dead Stuff Works* section.

Madge waved a hand at her face. "I've heard about this, but I didn't think it was real. Heavens, it's like an oven in here."

"I don't get it. Projecting where? Like outside the cemetery?"

Shuffling to the window, Frank gazed into the fall evening as the sun hovered over the western hills. "The first time it happened, I thought I was dreaming. Then I realized I couldn't be dreaming because I hadn't slept since I died. So, I knew it had to be real."

"Is it like p-p-possession?" Rick asked, unsure if he really wanted to know.

Frank smiled faintly. "I can't affect them, but I think they know I'm there. Before now, I only visited one person."

"Emily," Madge said, nearly whispering.

"Yes, Emily. I just have to think about her, and wherever she is, I pop into her mind."

Stephanie grabbed her head with her hands.

"Don't worry, I can't do it with you folks here."

"That's like . . ." Stephanie let out a breath, still clearly troubled.

"I know. It's very . . . intrusive. I felt the same way the first time. Like I was invading the most private part of her. I had access to her thoughts, feelings, even her memories. Turns out, that girl has been carrying an awful lot on her shoulders." Frank moved to the fire, his back bent as if he carried the same burden. "Before I died, she was just starting on her degree. Becoming a librarian was all Em had ever talked about. She always had her nose in a book, and by the time she started high school, she had so many that she had to store them at my house. Then, I invaded her mind. I can't think of any other way to put it. At first, it happened beyond my control. I found out things about my Em that even she hasn't figured out yet. The first thing I learned was the hardest."

His hand rose, wiped something away, then lowered again. "Emily didn't know she was doing it for me. *Wanted* it for me. She really thought it was her dream. That was the worst part. After she got her degree, they hired her at the library right here in town, and when I visited her, my worst fears were confirmed."

"What fears?" Stephanie asked.

Frank stared silently at the wall.

"She hated it," Madge offered.

Frank nodded. "She knew the very first day. Words can't describe how I felt, discovering I'd unknowingly set her on a path she never wanted. These last five years have been . . . well, they haven't been easy. You think you want to know. You think you want to get inside their minds and find all the answers you've been seeking. All the questions, the what-ifs."

He gazed at Madge with a secret knowledge that it seemed only they shared, neither able to look away.

"On this side, it's better not to know when it's too late to mend."

A MONTH AFTER THE MEETING, FRANK FOUND RICK AT their usual afternoon spot. Plunking down on the stone bench, Frank leaned back and placed his hands behind his head. "My Em quit." His smile went on for miles.

When Emily returned to her job at the bookstore later that week, Madge made an apple crumb pie. Though Frank had long lost his sense of taste, he'd said it was the best apple pie he wished he'd ever eaten. A day later, Frank received his papers—with no unfinished business, there was nothing to keep him any longer.

Now, Frank's words—or warning—echoed. There had been a message in Frank's story, though Rick couldn't fathom what it was.

Lifting the envelope flap, Rick removed the letter again.

Grandfather . . .

Emily could never know the truth—that, in the end, Frank had been proud. Reading through a second time, Rick's heart broke for a woman he'd never met. As he mouthed each word, he took note of her perfect penmanship and the funny way she dotted her i's—the tail lifting faintly off the page.

When he reached the end a third time, his breath caught.

"Pie."

The letter slid from his fingers. Storm clouds churned in the east as Rick burst into the frosty air. He raced toward Frank's grave as a raindrop splashed in his eye. "Dammit." He sprinted and spotted a small, white object at the base of Frank's headstone. Another drop landed on his head with a splat as he skidded to a halt on the slick grass.

Any second now, the skies would open up. Snatching the pie, he ran as if his life depended on it.

Halfway down the path, the sky unleashed. Rain pummeled the cheesecloth as Rick picked up speed.

Thunder crashed as he grappled with the doorknob, and for one heart-stopping moment, the pie nearly toppled from his hands, but he managed to wrench the door open and hurry inside. The scent of apples was suffocating. Rick set the pie beside the basket of red fruit as rain slapped the windows. The fire crackled through a fresh wave of thunder.

Rick lifted the cheesecloth, praying the crust wouldn't break off. Bit by tantalizing bit, the pie came into view, revealing a brown lattice top. The smell of cinnamon replaced the sickly sweet apple scent. Loaded to the hilt, the lattice dome had been piped closed with a braided edge. Rick breathed deeply, his hands on the ceramic plate. Astonishingly, it was still warm. He marveled at her effort, baking a pie for a man long dead. This pie mattered as much as it would have had she made it for a living person. She—

"Oh, my God, that looks so yummy."

Startled, Rick took an involuntary step back and smashed his elbow against the door frame.

Stephanie bent close to the pie. "I bet that smells delish."

"D-Doggonit, stop s-s-sneaking up on me." Rick felt caught in the act of . . . something. "Someone left it over there, on the g-g-grave—"

"You should talk to her next time she comes around."

"I'm n-not . . . why would I . . . g-g-get out of my house."

With an artful twirl, Stephanie grinned and transformed into smoke.

Rick's heart thumped as wildly as the thunder outside. He examined every inch, every braid of crust, every grain of sugar of the delicate pastry.

"To hell with this." He draped the cheesecloth over the pie, hung his jacket, and settled into his chair. Embarrassment clung like a second skin as he glowered at the white cloth. Emily's letter clawed into his thoughts—her sadness, her anguish that Frank's spirit had abandoned her.

It doesn't matter what she thinks happened. It has nothing to do with me. People come here trying to contact their dead relatives instead of moving on as they should. Frank's grandkid is no different. Rising, he went to the window, following the rivers of rain that etched the glass.

"It's not my problem," he firmly told the pie and fell back into his armchair as if he'd been poured in. "I'm a caretaker, not a therapist."

With his feet settled on the coffee table, he grabbed his newest book, *Contacting the Dead Through Social Media.* He read the first sentence, then again. And again. From the table, the pie mocked him.

Over the next three hours, he read the first sentence a hundred and twenty-two times, but the only thing on his mind was Emily.

———

By five o'clock, Rick had fully memorized the sentence, *the dead are all around us; one must only know their Twitter handle to contact them.* The pie beckoned as he sauntered into the kitchen. He opened the oven, threw in a frozen meal, and set the timer.

The pie stared at him from inches away. "Just waiting for my dinner," he informed it, settling his chin into his palm as he watched.

Emily's letter gnawed. Once a resident received their papers, they were given twenty-four hours to contact their chosen Liver before ascending to whatever lay in store. Frank must have visited Emily. Wouldn't she have known? Or had Frank been diverted and said his goodbye to someone else instead? It made no sense.

Madge materialized in the opposite chair. "She's as lovely as Frank described."

Rick jumped, this time, thankfully, without injury. "You g-guys have got to stop d-d-doing that."

"What did her letter say?"

Rick hesitated. "I d-d-didn't read it."

"Sure, you did. Stephy and I watched you from the bedroom, and we saw Emily deliver it."

"You had n-n-no right—"

"And," she interrupted, "we watched you run like a bull in Spain to save that pie. So, come on. What did it say?"

Rick prepared to protest. He'd say that it wasn't right that they spied on him all the damn time. He was tired, he could say, of having no privacy. He'd never signed up for this constant surveillance when he took the job.

Instead, he sighed and picked up the letter.

WHEN HE FINISHED, THE REMAINING RESIDENTS HAD gathered, huddled together while they hung on Rick's every word. Even Herbert seemed oddly attentive.

"Oh, my God, it's so sad. Emily thinks he's mad at her. She doesn't know."

"But she wouldn't know, would she? No living person knows what happens after we die." Madge glanced at Rick. "Present company excluded."

He could only shrug.

"Why?" Taylor asked.

"For the same reason that we don't know what happens when we move on to the afterlife. We're not meant to."

"But why?"

"Dear, if we knew everything that would happen next, there'd be no point in living. We'd always look to the future while the present whittles away." Sadness drifted behind her eyes.

"It's just . . . didn't Frank give her a final message?" Stephanie asked. "He always said he would."

Her shoulders stiff, Taylor turned to Rick. "You have to tell her."

"No, dear," Madge jumped in. "He can't do that."

"Why not?"

Yeah, Rick thought, for once in agreement with Taylor. *Why not?*

"Number one, it would be interfering. Frank made his decision, and he had a reason. We can't upset that."

"Upset it? She's already upset! She thinks he's left her, and he's disappointed." Taylor rolled onto her back with a decidedly Stephanie-ish flop, her cerulean strands fanned like a halo.

"For reals, like, Frank couldn't have wanted this."

"Regardless, it's how he left it, and there's the simple fact that she would never believe Rick."

Rick's budding hope withered. She was right. How could he ever convince Emily of the truth without coming off as a complete nut job?

"Eh, it's hogwash," Herbert pulled off his socks and rubbed his fingers between wrinkled toes. "You females are always overly emotional. She probably didn't even notice Frank was there. I say leave it alone. If she wants to wallow in self-pity, let her."

Taylor glared at the old man.

"As much as I hate to agree with Herb, he's right." Gravely, Madge turned to Rick. "You must leave it, dear."

He wasn't sure he'd ever have told Emily the truth in the first place, but the knowledge that he never could somehow felt like a betrayal to both Emily and Frank. "Right. M-M-Meeting adjourned."

They stared. "Like, we weren't having a meeting."

"N-No. Right." Embarrassed, Rick fell back in his chair. "G-Get the hell out then, I guess."

Murmurs rose as they prepared to leave. "He's probably gonna . . ." After Herbert gestured rudely, the others groaned, and in a flash, all but Taylor disappeared.

Indecision carved her face, and she edged forward as if to speak before wafting through the door. An unnatural hush fell over the room. As Rick's exhaustion settled in, the oven timer rang.

"For crying out loud." Rick glared at the pie as he passed through the kitchen. After the potatoes were salted and the vegetables buttered, Rick moved to the table, ogling the pie as he chewed. Unable to finish, Rick tossed the dinner into the garbage. Images of Emily flashed as he mindlessly fished in a drawer for a serving knife. Long, slender legs hidden behind a skirt danced at the corners of his mind as he grabbed a dessert plate from the cabinet. How did she get her hair so shiny? Did she ever put it in a ponytail or up in a bun?

No. A bun wouldn't look right on her. Rick pulled a tub of ice cream from the freezer. *It's perfect just the way it is, loose, just kind of falling over her shoulders . . .*

The serving knife hovered above the pie. Rick looked around, afraid of being caught in this act of . . . what was it, anyway?

Resigned and emptied of the will to deny himself any longer, Rick cut into the pie. "Frank, if ever we should meet again, this one's for you."

In this realm, no pie was better.

9

YOUR EM

For the first time in ten years, Rick deviated from his routine.

The sky darkened as he strolled the grounds, a chill sweeping the trees. White mist poured in, hovering eerily hollow above the ground. Rick tried to focus on the work ahead. That he'd left his clippers on the bench never entered his mind. He searched for tree branches that hung low and heavy, like the oak that shaded Frank's tombstone, where the two of them had spent hours talking about Frank's granddaughter.

Emily, was it?

He shook his head as if to dislodge the image of her willowy body. "Stop it," he muttered as he diverted toward the towering oak. In a hundred steps, he'd be there, beneath Frank's tree.

Where *she* might show up.

Rick told himself he was taking in the scenery. Winter had its own beauty, even when the leaves were down and the skies painted gray. Every few steps, he glanced behind,

sure he heard soft footfalls on the crisp grass. Circling the
hedge to the bench often missed by visitors, Rick plopped
down, pulled a bottle of chocolate milk from his coat, and
peered over the shrubbery to the vacant path beyond. Half
an hour passed. Then an hour. He should get back to the
cottage—it was the perfect day for a fire and a good ghost
story—but even as he shivered, he told himself the fresh
air was good for him. As his teeth chattered behind his
lips, he convinced himself he was not frozen to the bone.

He most assuredly was not waiting.

SUNDAY ARRIVED UNUSUALLY WARM FOR MID-NOVEMBER
—another perfect day for landscaping. Rick saw no use in
letting a sunny day go to waste, so, with his hedge trimmers in hand, he headed toward a certain grave, whistling
indifferently. Cool and nonchalant. Just an average guy
strolling through a cemetery. Whenever he glanced back,
the path remained empty, and he shook off a peculiar
disappointment.

Good. I don't need any interruptions. Still, Rick
couldn't keep his gaze from returning to the path. Across
from Frank's grave, an azalea grabbed Rick's attention.
Running his fingers over the large, white flowers, he
dusted the leathery leaves and studied each stalk while
stealing peeks at the deserted walkway.

Then his breath stopped, and his already overworked
heart raced. Emily's Honda was parked at the gate, the tick
of the engine echoing. Climbing out, she plucked the
snagged sleeve of her sweater from the door. Though it

had to be nearly sixty degrees, a purple scarf was wound around her neck.

Taylor waved from atop a nearby headstone, yet Emily walked on, oblivious.

Instinctively, Rick crouched. Catching himself, he sprang upright, gripping the hedge trimmers in one hand while the other rested on his hip. He casually tapped his foot.

I look about as laid-back as a knife-wielding male prostitute. As Emily approached, Rick dropped his hand and spoke to the bush. "You're looking lovely today."

No. Stop that.

A rubber band tightened around Rick's heart when Emily looked in his direction. *Relax. You're just working.* He suddenly wished he were anywhere else and berated himself for coming out in the first place. What had he been thinking? As he turned back to the path, his nerves jabbed; she was less than ten feet away. Sky-blue eyes landed on his. Emily smiled politely.

Rick swallowed rising bile. *She's looking at you. She's looking at you. She's looking . . .*

Coolly tipping a hat he wasn't wearing, Rick smiled in a way that felt broken and returned his hand to his hip. "Nicedayforawalk." He groaned.

Emily's widening smile sent Rick's insides quivering. The way her lips tilted upward—he'd never seen a smile like it. No. Of every person who'd ever lived, none had been blessed with a smile as stunning as hers.

She smiled. At me.

A stupid grin creased his face as she turned off the path, and his brain screamed for him to move. *Stop star-*

ing! Work, trim something! He aimlessly chopped an entire branch from the azalea.

At Frank's tombstone, Emily pulled a mason jar from her bag and rested it on the granite slab. "I know you're still angry with me. I made you some apple cider last night. I need to tell you . . ."

A semi-truck roared down Main Street. Rick leaned in, desperate to hear, and stumbled into the bush, making a racket loud enough to wake the dead.

Emily turned and grinned. Rick's lips convulsed into what he hoped was a reciprocating smile. He worked the hedge trimmer with tingling limbs and numb toes, relieved when she finally turned back to the tombstone.

Herbert appeared with a scowl and pointed at Rick's feet—where more than half the bush now lay in shreds.

"What the hell are you doing? You've destroyed resident property!" Herbert hopped within the decimated bush. "Are you even listening, asshole?"

Rick strained to hear, but the old man's raving swept Emily's words away. She stood and caressed the tombstone, and their eyes locked.

The world fell apart, and Rick felt he could see past those eyes to the hills beyond. As he hacked through Herbert's midsection, the perpetually grumpy ghost unleashed a string of curses that would make the devil himself blush. But Herbert was a thousand miles, dimensions, universes away. Rick's throat shrank to the size of a straw as Emily lifted her hand and wriggled her fingertips. After stepping on her own foot, she limped toward the gate.

Sliced in two, Herbert lay on the ground, leaning on his elbows. "Dammit, Rick, look what you did to me. You've cut me in half, you son-of-a-bitch!" He brought his hands to his neck, pulled, and his head toppled onto the grass with a sickening noise, like a kiss in reverse.

Appearing from a thin cloud, Madge waved toward Herbert's scattered body parts. "Pull yourself together, Herb."

Herbert tore off a leg and threw it at an unflinching Madge. "Don't call me Herb, dammit!"

Madge followed Rick's gaze, ignoring Herbert's squalling as she stepped over his detached skull. "She has his eyes, don't you think?"

As Emily turned from the main path toward the cottage, she dug into her bag. She tripped, scattering papers, pens, and packets of gum. She scooped up her belongings—along with a decent amount of gravel—into her bag. Rick heard the familiar *creak-slam* as she placed another envelope in the comment box.

"Rick?"

With a herculean effort, he turned. "Yeah."

"Never mind." Madge frowned at the disembodied head on the grass. "Get up, Herb."

"How can you stand there while I'm lying here mangled because of him? He's desecrated the dead! This is a federal offense! It's . . ." Herbert's face scrunched. "It's necrophilia!"

"Goodness, Herb," Madge said, "necrophilia is . . . well, it's not this."

Herbert's voice trailed off as he pulled his torso through the grass. "I'll be damned if it ain't necro-something."

As Emily reversed her car onto Main Street, Rick was sure he saw movement inside her vehicle.

Something that looked just a bit like the wave of a hand.

———————————

EVENTUALLY, HERBERT PULLED HIS LIMBS TOGETHER AND disappeared in a fit. Rick went to work gathering the butchered remains of the azalea. He'd done a number on the bush, and an uneven mess remained. Herbert had been right; Rick had destroyed resident property. What little that had survived would have to be dug up and replaced in the spring.

Rick's mood worsened as he returned to the cottage. He'd behaved like a schoolboy with a crush. Sure, Emily was pretty, beautiful even, and Madge had been right—she had Frank's eyes. His mouth, too. And there was the way her hairline grew down just a little in the center of her forehead, shaping her face into a perfect heart—

"Stop it!" A startled crow took flight. Rick realized he hadn't put the tools away. Diverting toward the shed, he spoke aloud as Madge and Stephanie appeared.

"I don't need this." Unaware of the women walking at his side, he strode within the tunnel of his thoughts. Stephanie giggled, and Madge elbowed her.

"She'll stop coming eventually. Stop bringing these pies and ciders and letters and . . ." He trailed off, the hedge trimmers slipping from his fingers. *The comment box.* Hurrying along the path, he opened the lid and . . . stopped. He wanted to grab the letter, rip it open for all to see, and read her beautiful, perfect handwriting until the sun set.

But this time, his stubborn side won.

Removing the letter, he sauntered inside and was immediately assaulted by the sweet aroma of apples. After casually tossing the letter beside the fruit basket, he moved to the living room. He needlessly stoked the fire, straightened stacks of books, and checked for cracks along smooth walls. The letter meant nothing. It wasn't eating away at him, bite by bite. Shame swept in. What was wrong with him? He liked—no, *loved* his life, just the way it was. He'd never so much as given a girl a second glance, let alone felt . . . whatever it was that had inexplicably overtaken his good sense.

And yet, no one had waved at him before. None had smiled and acknowledged him so candidly. Emily hadn't looked away when he came into view, hadn't suddenly become captivated by the cover of a trashy magazine at the checkout line. She'd seen him—really seen him—and still, she'd smiled, waved.

She's polite. That's all, nothing more. Rick's hand hovered over the letter, then stilled.

I should open it.

I should toss it in the wastebasket.

Indecisive, he moved to his chair and stewed.

———

IN THE DAYS THAT FOLLOWED, RICK WANDERED THE ROOMS in his cottage, eating only when his stomach ached. Showering became a memory of something he used to do. He reorganized books, threw out everything in the fridge, and scrubbed an imagined stain on the rug.

Even while he busied himself with mundane tasks, the letter whispered. As he sulked before the fire, he was dimly aware that he must resemble a male version of Taylor, ever morose. He fixed her gaze on the basket of apples, blinking only when his vision wavered. The sweet, heavy aroma made him nauseous. Images of Emily swam in his mind—blonde hair cascading, soft curls bouncing.

So she'd smiled at him—lots of people smiled before he opened his yap, and their friendly smiles invariably shifted to confused discomfort. Then again, Emily had waved. He had to admit *that* never happened. Still, it meant nothing. A smile was only a smile, a wave just a wave.

Then why was he so miserable? Why did he want more?

Tuesday morning, he found himself on the path that passed Frank's grave. He told himself he wouldn't look, yet his head turned toward the fabric-topped jar. Bending close, he spotted two apple slices and a cinnamon stick inside. *I'm not picking that up,* he told himself as he lifted the jar.

You like her.

You could care less.

She'd tied the fabric with raffia, the center kissed with a tiny bow. A jar like this was made to be displayed on a kitchen shelf, an adornment to brighten a room. What else did she make? Did everything she made look as tantalizing as this—

"Why haven't you read it?"

Rick nearly dropped the jar, and after getting hold of it again, he gripped the cider tightly with both hands. "What's it g-gonna take to get you g-g-guys to knock that off?"

Madge tied her apron strings with a smirk. "You need to read the letter."

A hot blush crept to Rick's cheeks. "What l-l-letter?" he said, knowing the lie was useless. The residents were a twenty-four-hour surveillance system that he could never deactivate. "It's not for me. It's for F-Frank."

"As caretaker of this cemetery, it's your job to read it. If Frank were still with us, you'd be reading it *to* him."

In a last-ditch effort, Rick threw a defiant glare. "Well, F-F-Frank's not here, so what's the p-p-point?"

"The point is that she left it in the caretaker's box, so the caretaker needs to read it."

He scrambled for an excuse, any escape, and came up empty.

"Oh, my God, just read it," Stephanie's disembodied voice said while her legs protruded from behind a nearby monument. "Like, at least get it out of your system, so you'll stop being so grumpy."

For once, reason replaced stubbornness. They were right. It was Rick's job to read whatever ended up in that box. *Dammit.* Why couldn't Emily put her letters on Frank's grave like everyone else?

With the choice taken from him, Rick started on the path toward the cottage.

He had to fight to keep from sprinting.

THE TWO WOMEN SQUEEZED TOGETHER ON THE COUCH AS Rick ran his fingers over the parchment and the indents her pen had made.

Emily's pen, in Emily's hand.

Grandfather,

I left you some apple cider. I added cinnamon just the way you like. I think it's the same way you used to make it . . . or pretty close, anyway.

I went out to the house yesterday. You probably know Mom put it up for sale last year, but no one seems interested. Well, they do, until the buyers come inside with that awful agent that Mom hired, and then they all say they get a weird feeling and leave. Mom thinks I'm doing something to creep them out, but you know her.

I wanted to see if I could get a feeling. It used to be strongest in the kitchen, where we spent so much time together. But now, there's no sense of you there. It's just an ordinary, empty kitchen.

Maybe I'm crazy, but deep down, I know that you were always with me even after you left, and no one could have convinced me that you weren't there.

Until now.

I miss you and wish you'd come back. Robert changed my schedule, so I'm off at noon on Wednesdays. I'll pop by around one o'clock. I hope you'll be there.

I love you.

Signed,

Your Em

P.S. You should warm the cider before drinking it. I already added sugar, so you don't need to add any more :)

As Rick gingerly returned the letter to the envelope, the women remained huddled in rapt attention.

"S-Satisfied? I read it. N-Now you can all go b-back to whichever d-d-direction it is that you go when you're not b-bugging me to death." His voice was jagged and rough, but even as the words fell, he regretted them. He was just so . . . he didn't know, except that he wanted to be alone. He ran a finger along the envelope's edge, oblivious to the action and how it made his skin tingle.

"Oh, my God, don't you see it?"

Rick flipped the envelope over and examined the back. "S-See what?"

Madge flashed Rick a look he wasn't sure he liked. "That letter wasn't meant for Frank."

His mind raced. "What are you t-talking about? The letter is addressed to her g-grandfather, it s-starts out '*G-Grandfather,*' and she goes on about how her g-grandfather isn't, I don't know, haunting his old h-h-house." Rick tossed the letter on the table, a move which proved just how little he cared, though his fingers somehow felt empty with the envelope no longer clutched between them. As he rubbed his temples, the twinge of a headache burrowed beneath his skull. "As f-f-far as I know, Emily only has one g-grandfather b-b-buried here." The apples clawed at his throat.

"Dear, it might have started as a letter to Frank, but it ended as a message to you. The last part. It's clearly meant—"

"Everybody out!" he shouted, standing abruptly. "Just . . . leave me alone f-f-for a while."

"Rick . . ."

His pulse raced, his skin alight. The sting behind his eyes alarmed him, and he lowered his voice. "P-Please."

In a flash, they did just that.

Alone now, Rick suddenly found the cottage too quiet. He deliberately looked away from the jar, desperate to clear his mind. He yearned for utter nothingness, yet no matter how hard he tried, his mind kept wandering back to the letter.

"To hell with it." He grabbed the envelope and ripped the paper out. "They're wrong, that's all. Just wrong." He reread the last few lines.

I'll pop by around one o'clock. I hope you'll be there.

And then . . .

P.S. You should warm the cider before drinking it. I already added sugar, so you don't need to add any more :)

His finger traced the words again and again until they stopped making sense. After Rick set the letter back on the table, a war broke out in his mind. Holding the jar like an injured bird, he turned it over, apple slices bobbing until he finally opened the top and carefully set the checkered fabric aside. He poured the cider into a mug, and when the microwave dinged, he carried the jar to his chair with baby steps.

Like a man lingering at the rim of a canyon, Rick hesitated, the scent of warm apples wafting. After an eternity, he took a sip and allowed the liquid to roll on his tongue. He took another sip, then another, and for the first time, Rick finally understood the term *comfort food*.

He'd never felt more comforted in his life.

A KNOT IN HIS STOMACH GREETED HIM THE FOLLOWING morning, twisting from inside. As he tiptoed to the cold, dead fireplace, he spotted the calendar on the wall. *Wednesday*. His stomach wrenched. He lit the fire and sank into his chair. This time, with no hesitation, Rick removed the letter.

I'll pop by around one o'clock. I hope you'll be there.

Rick Holliday was both excited and filled with dread.

R ick devoured the letter twice more, his eyes hurrying down the page. When he could read no more, he found himself in the kitchen, unsure where to go. There was work to be done, but another glance at the calendar sent his stomach lurching. He wanted to hide in the darkness of his cottage and curl up in a corner.

He didn't want to see her.

He needed to see her.

Imagination took over, racing with invented scenarios. With perfect clarity, Rick saw himself strutting along the path, bold and fearless, the sun shining on him in all the right spots.

There she stands, a sudden breeze lifting her hair, whipping behind her in long streaks of gold. She smiles, hopeful, and reaches a hand toward me. Rick, *she whispers, her voice a sultry purr.* I've been waiting for you.

I chuckle as if her blatant want means little. Sauntering to her side, I wrap a strong arm around her waist.

She gasps, her eyes fluttering. Yes, *she whispers, burning with desire.* This is what I've waited for. *Her eyes drift closed while her lips pucker.* Kiss me, Rick. Kiss me now.

My lips curve with a self-assured smirk. I lean in, watching as her mouth inches forward, waiting, wanting . . .

"Oh, my God, you guys, I think he's having a stroke." From inches away, Stephanie waved a frantic hand in Rick's face.

Rick caught himself leaning forward, his lips pursed to the air. "What are you d-d-doing?" He crashed into a dining chair, his arms flailing.

"What are *you* doing?"

Swiping a hand across his mouth, Rick's stomach ached as he wondered how much she'd seen.

"He does look rather flushed," Madge remarked, peering into his eyes.

Turning away awkwardly, Rick thought that if an airplane suddenly fell from the sky and obliterated him, it wouldn't be the worst thing.

"Oh, my God, that's right, Emily's coming today. Emily, Emily, Emily comes today," Stephanie sang.

Rick's face felt hot enough to melt butter. "Just . . . out of m-m-my house."

Herbert leaped onto the couch. "Are you gonna watch her from the window?" He laughed, displaying his favorite rude gesture.

"Rick," Madge said, "you should talk to her."

Unsure what to do with his hands, Rick shoved them into his pockets, then pulled them out again. Running twitchy fingers through his hair, he blew out a long breath.

It was impossible to meet the residents' eyes, yet he was suddenly exhausted from the constant fight; in his mind and the nosy dead.

Finally, Rick said the most honest thing he could. "G-G-Girls like her and g-guys like m-m-me—"

"Are not as different as you think," With a wink, Madge disappeared.

Herbert dropped from the ceiling and humped the floor lamp. "Emileee, oh Emileee, your love is so shocking to meee—"

Hurling a copy of *Selfies with Ghosts*, Rick watched as the book sailed through Herbert's ghostly form. As the old man disappeared, his cackle stretched on forever.

Alone now, Rick's mind began to drift. *Maybe Madge is right. Maybe we're not so different*, Rick thought, as the tension in his back lessened. "M-M-Maybe . . ."

But maybe we are.

Floating into the kitchen, Rick stared at the clock, tried to remember how clocks worked, then returned to the living room. He fell into his chair, forgot why he'd sat down, and walked into the bathroom. As he examined his reflection, he tilted his head, bounced on his feet, and flashed a half-smile.

"Hey, what are you doing here?"

It's a graveyard, stupid. Why else would she be here? He tried again.

"Hi, I noticed you standing there. Are you lost?" He raised his palms to his sides, questioning.

Even worse.

With a hand on his hip, he lifted his chin. "I see you like apples—me too. Although if I have too many, I get diarrhea . . ."

With a groan, he glared at his reflection. "You're a fool."

———————

D ARKNESS SWARMED AS R ICK'S EYES CREPT OPEN. THE fire had burned to embers, and the wind had picked up, battering tree limbs against the house. His heart sank as he bolted from the chair with a quick glance at his watch—ten after five. Racing to the kitchen, he peered out the window into the night, then trudged back to the living room. He fell into his chair with a heavy thud and stared into the darkness.

There was no denying it. He could pretend to the others but no longer to himself, and for the first time since Frank had left, Rick felt like crying.

"Dammit."

A drop of rain hit the window. Rick wondered idly if he should bother to rebuild the dying fire. Another drop. *Plink*. Rain zigzagged down the glass.

"I wonder . . ." Rick sprinted to the door. He wrenched it open and nearly stepped on something foreign. He pinwheeled his arms to keep from falling into the cold.

At the doorstep was a plate covered with a red-and-white checkered cloth. Rick swept up the offering and almost went back inside before he thought better of it and tip-toed down the wet, cold path. Creaking the comment box lid open, Rick found two envelopes inside. Numb fingers plucked up both, and he raced toward the cottage.

A gust battered the house as he fought to keep his balance, fearing he'd drop the letters. Or worse, the cloth-covered plate.

Once inside, he set the plate and envelopes on the dining table.

In her perfect handwriting, Emily had written *Grandfather* across the front of the first envelope. But it was on the other that his eye lingered.

Caretaker.

His throat was suddenly drier than parched dirt, and Rick stumbled to the kitchen on wobbly legs. After downing half a bottle of chocolate milk in one gulp, he allowed the cloth to slide from the plate, exposing a mound of cookies that smelled of brown sugar and apples.

Rick lifted the second letter, handling it like an explosive. It could be a complaint or an admonishment. It could be anything, and reading it could change everything. Fear coursed as he envisioned all possible scenarios, the least of which resulted in unemployment—the worst, humiliation.

Luckily for Rick, a lifetime of degradation had prepared him for the worst.

He opened the envelope.

Dear Caretaker,

Hello! My name is Emily, and I've been here a few times recently to visit my grandfather, Frank Bennett. First, I need to apologize for leaving the pie and the jar of cider (I noticed you had cleaned them up). I guess I wasn't thinking that I was littering. It was silly of me to leave food out in the open like that, attracting animals and gosh knows what else!

I also wanted to tell you what a joy it is to come here. I guess that might be a strange thing to say about a graveyard, but I don't think many people really appreciate what a beautiful place this is. You clearly take great care to keep it well-maintained! I noticed that awful azalea bush is finally gone. Grandfather hated azaleas, so I know he appreciates it!

Anyway, thanks again for cleaning up the messes I thoughtlessly left behind. I promise I won't leave any more food lying around! So please accept this batch of applesauce cookies I baked as my most sincere apology.

I hope you like apples . . . I use them a lot in my cooking! I hope to be able to say hi the next time I'm around. I plan on being there on Sunday, the usual time.

I wish I knew your name so I could call you more than 'Caretaker.' In the meantime, I'll just call you CT :)

See you on Sunday!

Signed,

Your Em

P.S. The cookies go great with hot chocolate! I left a packet underneath :)

Rick read again from beginning to end, vaguely aware of his own ridiculous smile. He returned to the dining table and found a single packet of hot chocolate mix at the bottom of the plate. Two minutes later, he savored the largest in the batch with a hot cup of cocoa.

He couldn't have stopped smiling if he'd tried.

11

A COOKIE SAYS A THOUSAND WORDS

S aturday arrived with an icy chill. After crawling out of bed, Rick bundled into his robe and flicked on the radio, his breath forming a cloud as the forecast predicted snow and possible ice. He knew the crisp blue sky outside foretold the coming freeze, and a single word came to mind.

Flowers.

If anyone had bothered to ask, he'd have told them that his top priority as caretaker wasn't what most people imagined. It wasn't digging holes, or—contrary to what Herbert expected—chasing after grave robbers. It wasn't popping out from behind tombstones to make ominous one-liners about wicked things afoot.

It all came down to flowers.

Visitors expected them. They even planted them. They complained when they withered and died. For Rick, his flower responsibilities were doubled. The residents expected them. They demanded that he plant them. They also complained when they withered and died.

The most important thing about graveyards: never, ever let anything die.

Hurrying to the shed, Rick tossed a dozen flower pots into a wheelbarrow and plunged into the freezing cold. A thin blanket of clouds invaded the horizon as he crossed the cemetery. He stopped at each delicate flower and carefully placed upturned pots over every blossom. With each step, the air grew colder, and judging by the warning in the overcast sky, he suspected the snow would begin long before nightfall.

As he rounded the bend, a familiar voice froze him.

"I wish you would come back."

Rick knew that voice—had memorized it as though it were his own—even with the added crack. Cautiously, he peered around a tall bush and spied Emily kneeling at Frank's tombstone.

What day is it? WHAT DAY IS IT? This wasn't her scheduled visitation day, so why was she here? Shredded by indecision, Rick's left foot sought the safety of the cottage while his right remained stubbornly rooted to the path. He wasn't ready. A lifetime or two was needed to prepare for an Emily visit. Yet his need to escape was overshadowed by his need to wait. Watch.

Listen.

"I don't know what to do," Emily whispered. "I'm happy at the bookstore, and I hoped you'd be happy for me." She released a long, uneven sigh.

Rick's stomach twisted. *You're wrong about Frank.*

He lived in a world where he was privy to truths that most Livers were unaware of. Though he pored over books of hauntings and ghosts, Rick scoffed at claims that the information within was Authentic and Verified through Years of Intensive Research. Whether he wanted to or not, Rick knew the reality of death. Still, he'd had no issue keeping that knowledge secret, allowing the Livers of the world to go on speculating, inventing, and guessing—quite erroneously—at what may lie ahead. Aside from a momentary desire to ease the suffering of little Maddie's grieving parents, the world's incorrect assumptions of death had never bothered Rick before. Nor had it been reason enough to correct their false knowledge.

Until now.

As Emily pulled another aromatic apple from her bag, the scent reached Rick even from across the path, and he found her pain nearly unbearable. She cradled something before placing it on Frank's tombstone, but from Rick's angle, it was impossible to tell what it was.

"Please come back. I can quit, try to go back to my old job. Just send me a sign." Her body shook with the cold, and Rick suddenly wished he could bring her back to the cottage, bundle her up at the fire, and warm her bones.

If only there were some way she could know . . . oof!

"Oh! I'm so sorry!"

Their bodies crashed together, and after she stepped back, Emily brushed her fingers lightly against Rick's hand. Feeling dangerously faint, visions of Emily carrying Rick's limp body to the cottage flitted.

"It's alright! Flowers! Cold!" He thrust an upturned flowerpot at her as if that would explain everything.

"Are you hurt?"

Fiercely aware of her proximity, Rick resisted the urge to fan himself in a decidedly Madge-like manner. "I was working! Not standing here. See?" He pointed to the flower pots, wishing he would stop. Just. Stop. In a concerted effort to do precisely that, he blurted, "I put pots over the flowers!"

Stop now . . .

And then he turned, stumbled over his foot, and plunged headlong into his worst nightmare. As he fell, Rick recklessly reached out to gain his footing and grabbed two soft, fleshy orbs. Emily stumbled back before crashing to the ground.

"Sorry! I'm sorry!" For a million years, Rick would feel the fire in his cheeks. He bent clumsily to the gravel, opened his arms, and grabbed her around the waist. As he lifted her light frame, he realized, horror-stricken, that he was practically groping her—again—and dropped her back to the gravel with a thud. "I don't know how . . . would you like a blanket?"

Surely *this* was grounds for termination. Possibly jail time.

"It's okay." Emily stood and brushed the dusty gravel from her dress, tucking a stray hair behind her ear. Her eyes locked on his, her lips widened, and she giggled nervously. The music of her laughter forced Rick's heart into his throat, and he couldn't have hidden his smile if he'd tried. She glanced away, making his grin even more impossible to wipe away. Every movement, every nuance was mystical. A more ideal human couldn't exist. Her perfectly upturned nose, the flawless complexion of her skin, that one wisp of hair wonderfully out of place—the universe seemed unfairly balanced in her favor.

Discomfort swallowed him as the silence stretched. He had to say something. "I better go—"

"Cookie?" Reaching into her seemingly bottomless bag, Emily removed half a cookie wrapped sloppily in plastic. She smiled in an uneven, shaky way.

Through sheer force of will, Rick pulled his eyes from hers and took the treat, turning it over in his fingers. Buckets of saliva filled his mouth. *She ate some of this. Her mouth was on this.*

"This is my favorite kind." It could have been chocolate chip, or it could have been pressed kale—it made no difference. At that moment, it *was* his favorite cookie. He became mildly aware of his goofy grin—intensely aware of hers.

The residents gathered, circling a hole where an azalea had once lived. "Did she just give him a half-eaten cookie?"

"Oh, my God, it's sweet. But it'll be years before they work up the nerve just to, like, shake hands."

Emily finally broke the spell. "I guess I should go. I came today because I have to work tomorrow." She wound a curl of hair around her finger.

"That looks relaxing . . ." Had he said that out loud? Surely not.

A smile the width of the Grand Canyon exploded onto her lips. No, not just her lips. When Emily smiled, her entire essence came along for the ride. "Do you want to try it?" she asked, holding her hair out to him.

Oh, God . . .

With a wrinkled forehead, she stepped back. "No, of course not. That was dumb." She bit her lip as her cheeks reddened.

"Neither of those idiots knows how to talk to people."

"It is rather awkward."

Rick stepped forward. "It wasn't dumb. I'd like . . . I probably shouldn't . . . this is my favorite cookie."

Her smile returned tenfold. "I hope you like it."

"I will! Watch!" Rick unwrapped the plastic and shoved the half-cookie into his gaping mouth. "Shee? It'th dewithous."

"I'm glad." She twisted her foot into the gravel. "I should get going. There's supposed to be a storm coming."

Rick forgot how to chew, and his knees threatened to buckle. The very idea that she would leave him alone on this path was the worst kind of cruelty. "You bether get thomewhere thafe." Crumbs spilled over his flannel.

Emily turned toward the path, and three steps away, she stumbled, then turned back, her fingertips fluttering. Rick's heart sank with each step while cookie remnants dissolved to mush in his bulging cheeks. He watched, mesmerized, as Emily passed beyond the gate and climbed into her car.

Herbert cackled and disappeared into the mist as Madge and Stephanie sidled next to Rick. "What kind of cookie was it?" Madge asked.

"Huh?"

"The cookie. What kind was it?"

Rick swallowed hard as Emily's car disappeared onto Main Street. "Oh. Yeah, it is. Warm out. Wait." As he floated toward Frank's tombstone, the first snowflakes began to fall. An old stuffed ghost with the word *BOO!* stitched across its chest rested against the granite. Snow came down in large flakes, and Rick grabbed the toy, tucked it safely under his arm, and stumbled back to the path, forgetting the wheelbarrow and the plants he'd set out to save.

And Taylor, unseen by any of them, stepped from behind a tree and shuffled dismally into the heart of the cemetery.

12

AFTERLIFE

nowflakes rained in frozen droplets, a sure indication that the night was growing colder, and as the wind picked up, ice pellets hit the window like gravel. Rick added more wood to the fire for no reason than to keep his hands busy.

"I'll be c-cutting down the old elm over by the walnut g-g-grove."

"What? You can't do that!" Herbert dropped from the chandelier. "My grave has a perfect view of that elm!"

"It's an eyesore."

"Exactly! It's dead! It's ugly! It's just the deterrent I need to keep the damn robbers away!"

"Visitors have c-c-complained." Rick eyed the apples on the table, as fresh as the day he'd brought them in from the orchard, and he wondered why they hadn't rotted. How long ago had that been? A month? Two?

He knew that bringing the Boo inside had been a bad idea. Emily had known a storm was coming—she'd said as much—yet she'd left it anyway. But he couldn't leave it in a coming snowstorm, could he? He'd wanted to protect it, keep it safe. He didn't fully understand why—he just knew it seemed necessary.

"Rick!"

Herbert's screech snapped Rick back to the present. "Huh?"

"Are you listening to me, asswipe? I said I'll make your life miserable! I'll follow you everywhere you go! If you cut down that tree, I . . . I'll haunt you!"

Madge snickered. "I think we all know who you'll be haunting when the time comes, and it certainly won't be Rick."

"Oh, my God, like, for real. Poor Travis."

Taylor's brows bent. "What does he mean, he'll be haunting someone? How can he do that? I thought we couldn't leave this place."

"It's not a haunting in the way you're thinking," Madge said. "Before you go to the afterlife, you're gifted with one last contact with a living person. But instead of contacting a loved one, as most do, our Herb plans to contact his worst enemy."

"That asshole will be sitting in a pile of his own dung once I'm done with him." The old man cackled, the elm apparently forgotten.

"Why is that so funny? It sounds cruel."

Stephanie rolled to her back, crossed one leg over the other, and pulled a long string of gum from her teeth. "From, like, the day he got here, all he's talked about is getting back at Travis." She tucked the gum back into her mouth with a snap.

"Who's Travis?"

"Herb's boss."

"It's Herbert, dammit. Why can't you assholes get that straight?" With an easy flick of the wrist, he turned the chair around and sat backward. "Travis had no respect for his elders."

"But why do you want to haunt him?" Taylor asked, shaking her head. "Why waste your last contact on someone like that instead of a family member or a friend?"

"Because for Herb," Madge answered, "retribution is far more important than forgiveness. That's probably why he'll never get the chance."

"If ever someone deserved to be haunted, it's that hooligan."

Madge turned to Taylor. "Before Herb died, his boss retired and was replaced by his younger son. Travis made changes the older employees found difficult to keep up with."

"Bamboozled, more like," Herbert spat.

"As you can imagine, their personalities didn't exactly mesh."

Stephanie rolled her eyes. "Like, who could mesh with *him*?"

"He was trying to edge us out, send us into early retirement, and replace us with inexperienced idiots willing to work for peanuts. You don't know what it's like out there now. Damn computers do everything but wipe your ass."

"It did seem they were being set up to fail," Madge agreed.

"He had me pushing a damn cart from one end of the room to the other all day. Sometimes there wasn't even anything on it, but that pissant made me walk across the room again. Asshole did it just to demean me."

"One by one, the others caved and took early retirement. Except, of course, for our Herb."

Herbert lifted his feet to the table. "It tore that little shit up."

"The more stubborn Herb became, the more his new boss had it out for him, and soon no one was allowed to put anything on Herb's cart. He had to push an empty cart all day until Travis found a new task to put him in his place."

"What did they make him do?"

Hiding a smile, Madge cleared her throat. "He had to refill the . . . feminine products in the ladies' restrooms."

Taylor's jaw dropped. "They made you stock the tampon machines?"

"In every damned women's shitter in that building." Fishing a handkerchief from his back pocket, the old man spat into it.

"But Herb got his revenge," Stephanie said with a smirk.

"That's true. You've had your retribution. There's no need to waste your last—"

"Hush up, woman. What I did was petty. I'm not even close to done with him."

"What did he do?"

"Travis hung a cowbell from the ceiling that he rang at the end of the workday. I don't have to tell you that the bell wasn't appreciated by the other workers."

"Let me tell this part. It's my favorite!" Stephanie jumped in, giggling as Madge swept a conciliatory hand toward the teen.

"So, Herb, oh, my God, he took a sanitary napkin from his cart, and when everyone went to lunch, Herb wrapped it around the . . . what's it called again, the long thing in the middle that makes the dingy sound?"

"The clapper."

"Oh yeah. Herbert wrapped it around the clapper, taped it in place, and waited."

With a snort, Herbert brought his feet down and leaned forward, listening intently to the telling of his own story.

"So, like, everyone came back from lunch, and Herb went on as usual. He waited all afternoon, making sure he'd be back in the mailroom at five o'clock when Travis would ring the bell. Herb puttered around the room, dusting his cart, cleaning the coffee machines—just killing time, you know? But he was watching that clock. So was Travis, waiting for the clock to strike five, and when the time finally came, Travis grabbed the rope, and when he pulled . . . nothing happened."

Herbert roared from his seat. "You should have seen his face! He pulled that damn bell, and all anyone heard was a thump, like someone punching a pillow. He pulled harder every time, and no one heard anything but that soft thud. Finally, that jerkwad looked up, and when he saw that sanitary napkin, he darn near turned purple." Herbert stood, rested his hands on his hips, and emulated his mortal enemy. "'Who did this?' that idiot screamed, like a whiny little girl, panting like he just ran up twenty flights of stairs." Unable to go on, Herbert fell back into the chair.

Stephanie picked up the story. "Travis reached up and yanked the sanitary napkin from the clapper, and that's when everyone saw what *else* Herb had done."

Even Rick, morose though he was, let out a chuckle.

"In bright red marker, Herb had written TRAVIS on the back of the napkin," Madge finished.

"He was waving that damn napkin in the air, asking, 'Who's responsible for this? Who?' with his own name printed on it for all to see."

Rick interrupted. "B-B-But it was Herb's undoing, that little t-trick of his."

"It was worth it." Herbert smiled.

"Why was it his undoing?"

Madge smirked. "Because Herb laughed himself into a massive heart attack and died right there on the mailroom floor."

"Worth it!"

"And he's p-p-planned on haunting T-Travis ever since," Rick added, "though I agree w-with everyone else. I think the m-man has suffered enough. He did have an employee d-d-die on him, after all."

Gathering himself from the floor, Herbert's laughter died down. "That little shit hasn't begun to suffer." With a smile more wicked than even the devil could manage, the old codger disappeared into another realm.

———————

WITH HERBERT'S EXIT, THE MEETING ABRUPTLY ENDED, and Rick stood at the window, watching the snow pile up outside. As the others disappeared, Madge joined him at the window. "Rick, can we talk?"

Sensing this had something to do with the one subject he wanted to avoid, his body tensed. "I need to b-bring in some wood for the f—"

"Sit down."

Rick sighed and sat.

"It's about Emily."

His fingers tingled. Rick tried on his best I-could-care-less face. "What about h-h-her?" He felt like a cat on catnip.

"You like her."

Running a hand through ragged hair, he leaped from his chair. "I . . . she's . . . I need to g-g-get the f-firewood."

"And it's clear she's smitten with you, too."

He glanced down, suddenly captivated by his hands. "I d-d-don't know what you're . . . you women are always t-trying to read into things." Shocked to hear an undeniably Herbert-like phrase from his own mouth, Rick gave up the fight. A quick glance at Madge's hopeful face filled him with apprehension. "Why d-do you think that?"

"Do you really think she brought all that food for her dead grandfather? And don't forget the letters, dear. I doubt she felt it necessary to give Frank her visitation schedule. She wanted to be sure *you* would know when she was coming."

Rick thought over the letters Emily had left and tried to think of any hidden messages she might have worked in. He supposed if he wanted to, he could find all manner of clues in his favor.

Still.

"You like her, and she likes you. She's left you letters, food, and practically hand-fed you a used cookie just this afternoon."

"Oh, my God, Rick. Just, like, talk to Emily," Stephanie said as she materialized beside Madge. "But, you know, try to keep from manhandling her."

As if he were a marionette manipulated by an unseen puppeteer, his gaze settled on the Boo leaning against the basket of apples. Rick imagined what it would be like to talk to Emily as a normal man might—to take her on a real date, maybe even touch her hair, her arm, her lips . . .

His mind suddenly reversed, showing him how it would sound when she laughed at his audacity. *Date me? YOU want to take ME on a date? Ha! I was just nice because I felt sorry for you—*

"I g-gotta get the f-f-f . . . wood." Rick grabbed his coat and hurried into the snow. By the time he returned with an armload of logs and frost in his hair, the women had gone.

"Good," he muttered. "Mind your own business." Though he wouldn't admit it even to himself, he'd secretly hoped they'd still be there, still trying to talk him into . . . something. Stacking wood at the hearth, Rick snapped off the lights, and it took every ounce of energy to avoid looking at the basket on the table.

As he pulled back the covers on his bed, he resolved to toss out the apples in the morning, then drifted into an uneasy sleep.

13

THE GHOST AT THE WINDOW

Rick awoke to over a foot of snow, but thankfully no ice. Still, so much had drifted against the door that he had to use the garbage can lid to clear a path to the shed. After gathering an armful of firewood, he took inventory in the cellar. There was no more inclement weather in the forecast, but the menial tasks kept his mind busy, and he went about them with gusto.

The morning news had reported hundreds of outages. Had Emily lost power? He remembered what she'd said yesterday—she'd come on Saturday because she had work today. Did she know how to drive in the snow? That little car of hers didn't look like it could handle slick roads. Did she know how to turn into a skid? How to pump the brakes and leave a cushion between her car and the next? What if some idiot came careening out of a side street and . . .

Racing to the phone, Rick picked up the receiver and placed his finger on the dial pad before he realized he didn't even know her number.

"Dammit." Sprinting through the kitchen, he grabbed the phone book and began flipping through, abruptly stopping when he reached *Al's Goat Rental*.

Even if he could find her number, what would he have said? *Hi, this is Rick. I know we only had one conversation, and I ate half of your cookie, but could you promise me you won't drive in the snow today? I'd really hate for something to happen before we get a chance to see how this thing plays out.*

Right.

Tossing the phone book aside, Rick sat in his chair. The fire crackled along with his brain. The others seemed convinced Emily liked him, but how could he be sure? What assurances could anyone offer that he wouldn't be rejected? Humiliated? People, he'd learned, were born cruel.

Niceness was a learned trait.

He liked his life just fine, thank you very much, and he wasn't as lonely as most people thought. He was happy on his own. Content.

Safe.

As he stared into the fire, Rick made a resolute decision: he would keep his distance. He'd keep track of Emily's visits and make sure he was conveniently in town —at the grocery store, the hardware store, anywhere but here—eliminating any possibility that they could bump into one another, both figuratively and literally. Eventually, she'd give up on Frank, as all Livers did once they got on top of their grief, and he'd never have to deal with her again.

As he made the decision rock solid, his heart plummeted.

THE SNOW HUNG ON STUBBORNLY IN THE FOLLOWING DAYS, and Rick made it through by keeping busy with hardly a thought of Emily—aside from every few minutes. He threw the apples out a dozen times between Sunday and Wednesday, each time diving into the trash to rescue them.

With the cemetery covered in snow, Rick was bound to the cottage, and his potential distractions were drastically cut. He organized his books according to size and color, then arranged them back alphabetically. The counters sparkled, the cans in the pantry faced forward, and the tool shed gleamed. He refinished a table and retiled the bathroom floor, and even the windows had needed washing—twice. Dragging a rug to the panes had been a necessity so he could scrub by the light of the sun. Perfectly reasonable. He certainly wasn't looking for *her*.

When Wednesday arrived, and the snow finally began to melt, Rick's breakfast lurched as Emily's Honda pulled up to the gate. From the window, he watched as she climbed out of the car wearing a long, powder-blue dress cloaked by a heavy parka. When she popped the trunk and leaned inside, Rick craned his neck to see, but the lid blocked his view.

"Whatcha doing?" Stephanie broke his concentration.

Rick tensed and drew a hand across his moist forehead. "C-C-Cleaning the rug."

"Uh-huh."

The trunk lid slammed, and there she was—beautiful Emily, with her long, loose hair, heaving a large, glass punchbowl through the gate.

"What's she carrying?"

Rick's pulse took another leap as Emily veered off the main path and headed straight for the cottage. "Get down!" Rick dove to the floor, praying he hadn't been spotted. Mindlessly, he grabbed at Stephanie's white, fingerless glove and tried to pull her from the window, but his hand passed through hers with ease.

"She can't see *me*, dork."

Embarrassed and desperate at once, Rick muttered under his breath. "T-Tell me what happens."

"She's at the gate. Now she's opening it . . . oh, my God, she's gonna drop that punchbowl . . . nope, she's got it. She's walking toward the door, and now she's setting the punchbowl down and leaving a note on it. Wait, she's picking the note back up. She's going back to the comment box and putting the note inside. Now she's, uh, looking back toward the cottage, just, like, standing there."

"What d-do you mean she's just s-standing there?" Rick unbuttoned his flannel as the temperature rose.

"Just what I said. She's standing there, looking around." Stephanie giggled. "I think she's looking for you."

Rick's heart raced at Stephanie's hunch and how ridiculous he must look crouched on the floor of his own cottage, employing a ghost to spy for him. As far as compromising moments went, this had to be at the top of the list.

"She's heading into the cemetery. You can get up now, weirdo."

Not entirely trusting the teen, Rick peeked out the window, and when he found the path empty, he hurried to the door. With one more quick glance down the walkway, he creaked the door open, grabbed the punchbowl, and carried it to the table.

"Oh, my God, what is it? Take the cover off!"

"I bet it's some sort of fruit thing," Taylor said, appearing beside Stephanie. "Or something with apples, anyway."

Madge wafted in from the kitchen. "It's got to be an ice cream float. It looks white."

Hesitation stilled Rick. "Sh-Shouldn't we wait for Herbert? We d-don't want to leave him out of my p-p-personal life, do we?"

The old man's disembodied head floated through the wall. "My money's on eggnog. Better have rum in it."

Rick groaned and began to pull the cloth away.

"Wait!" Stephanie cried, sending a startling pain rushing through Rick's shoulder. "The comment box! She left a note!"

Rick no longer bothered trying to appear dignified or uninterested. They all knew—there was no use hiding it. After peeking out the window, he sprinted to the box and slipped a hand inside. Hoping Emily wouldn't spot him, he hurried back inside with the letter.

Three dead women and one eternally grumpy old man stared. There was no time for decorum, no time to pretend. After tearing open the envelope, Rick pulled out a short note and held his breath.

"Oh, my God, read it!"

"Out loud, dear."

Rick mused at their anxious expressions. But his curiosity—his need—was a thousand times stronger than theirs could ever be.

After a moment's hesitation, he read aloud.

Dear CT,

I feel silly still calling you that, but I never did learn your name. I hope you fared well in the snowstorm. I was worried about you all alone out there!

I brought you some eggnog—it's my grandfather's recipe, and even people who say they don't like eggnog love it. I hope you do too!

I didn't put any rum in it—I'm not one for alcohol— and it should keep for a couple of days. I hope you like it, and I hope to see you again soon!

Signed,

Your Em

P.S. I know I said I'd stop leaving messes behind, and then I went and left my Boo. I guess I was a little preoccupied and forgot my promise. I'll be picking up Boo today, and I promise, from now on, no more messes!

"WELL," MADGE SAID WHEN RICK FINISHED, "THERE'S your opening. Go talk to her."

"No."

"Oh, for Heaven's sake, why not? Never has there been a more perfect setup. What do you want? A hand-written invitation?" She pointed at the letter in Rick's hand. "Well, there it is."

Rick glanced at Emily's Boo leaning against the basket. Surely she knew by now that he'd taken it. "I c-c-can't." There was no way he wasn't going to come off as a total creeper now. With a groan, he nodded toward the table.

"What's he looking at?" Taylor asked.

Madge followed Rick's gaze. "Her Boo. She's probably already noticed he took it from Frank's grave."

"So?"

"It's a bit of a faux pas for a caretaker to remove trinkets. It's frowned upon."

Silence filled the room as Rick's hope drained away.

"What's wrong with you guys? She won't care that he took it!"

Tense quiet rang in Rick's ears, Taylor's shouts echoing within his skull. He wanted to shout, too. Sure, he'd removed objects left by visitors before and set them aside until they returned to retrieve them. But he hadn't put it in a box or set it aside. Emily's Boo was prominently displayed on the table like a shrine. If she came to the door . . . he didn't want to think about how it would look.

"Now that I think of it," Madge said with a spark in her eye, "it's actually very thoughtful that you brought it inside. You know, so it wouldn't get snowed on."

Rick pulled his gaze from the table. "I what?"

"Who leaves a stuffed toy out in the open with a storm on the horizon? You took it to keep it safe. It was actually quite kind of you, and I'm sure that once you return it to her—*right now*—she'll be quite grateful." Madge hurried to the door.

"Oh! Yes," Stephanie jumped in, following Madge. "But you should, like, return it now before she asks about it."

The women waited at the door, and Rick was hit with an odd sense of having been granted permission. Whether by the ghosts who took it upon themselves to guide his hand or by the universe in all its infinite wisdom, he didn't know. But with no time to ponder, he ran with it. "Right." Clenching his fists, he took a deep breath and turned.

Madge stopped him as his hand found the doorknob. "Rick . . . your coat."

"Right." He grabbed his jacket and reached again for the knob.

"Rick . . ." Taylor said.

"What?" Now that he'd made up his mind, he was desperate to catch Emily before his courage fled. "What n-n-now?"

Sheepishly, Taylor pointed toward the kitchen. "The Boo?"

An exasperated grunt spilled out as he raced to the kitchen and grabbed the stuffed toy.

After one final pause, Rick stepped into the cold.

14

BOO

A s he peered around the hedge, Rick regretted everything.

Emily frantically dug through the snow, her hands red and frozen. Sniffling, she searched in vain for the Boo that Rick held in his hands.

Guilt froze his blood. His gut filled not with butterflies but a flock of angry, pecking crows. Nausea curdled in his stomach. *You shouldn't have taken it. You should have let her find it in the snow.* It would have been ruined, but he'd be in the clear. Had he really thought she'd be grateful for his transgression? That he'd even entertained the idea was preposterous. He envisioned how he must look—the creepy, stammering cemetery man holding a stuffed toy like a prize. She'd either laugh in his face or run for the hills.

Fool.

There was still a chance to salvage what little pride remained, so he started on the path to the cottage, hoping he could make it back without being spotted. She'd search a while longer, realize her mistake, and leave, and Rick would place her Boo in a *Frank* box, as he'd done with the trinkets other grieving Livers left behind. He'd finally be able to forget about her and the delusion that her entrance into his life had brought. People like Rick were meant for a singular existence, and people like her—

"Why did I leave it?"

Emily's quiet sobs halted Rick's steps. Why *had* she left it, knowing a storm was on the way? But he knew why. She'd left it for the same reason other Livers had in their desperate grief.

Hope.

Hope that her grandfather would return. Hope that her offering would appease him. Hope that somewhere, there still existed someone to leave it for. She'd wrapped five years of hope into her Boo, and now all hope was lost.

Only it wasn't.

As the Boo weighed heavy in his hand, Rick knew he could not withhold her hope. Would she laugh at his longing? Maybe. Would she snatch her hope back and run from the mad caretaker? Probably. But as he watched her claw through the frozen snow, his wish faded in the face of hers. Inevitable rejection suddenly paled in comparison to her pain, and that was okay. He would live. He'd already lived through worse.

With more mettle than he imagined possible, he took a deep breath and turned back toward Frank's grave. Emily looked up as Rick's boots chewed the gravel, her eyes moving first to his face and then to his hand.

"I, uh, brought this inside. The snow . . . the weather was bad . . ." As he shifted from one foot to the other, he fell silent. She wouldn't believe him. Worse, she likely read the truth in his condemned eyes. Searching his face, she rocked forward on her heels as if to get a closer look, her breath seeping through the space between them. The cold formed a fog, penetrating his skin. She looked for . . . what? A sign of who he was, who he'd been, who Future Rick may be? He felt like a car accident, stared at with eyes that just couldn't look away, no matter how horrifying the scene.

Rick closed his eyes, unable to face her. *Drop it. Walk back to the house. No, run. Lock the door and stay inside forever.*

And then, as he prepared to lay the Boo gently on the ground, his body was covered with a foreign softness. His arms were pinned to his sides, and his nose inexplicably tickled. Creaking one eye open, he lifted the lid halfway. Emily's hair was inexplicably attached to his face, her body pressed against his. His cheeks were wet, and he wondered briefly if the moisture was her tears.

Hope flooded back tenfold.

"What in Sam Hill are you doing, asshole?" Herbert's crass voice screeched. "Hug her back, fool!"

But Rick's body had turned to stone.

After a lifetime, Emily pulled away, disconnecting their two forms. The force of her grip had been so strong that he should have felt lighter. Instead, an enormous, crushing weight fell. A flush crept across Emily's cheeks, and her chin quivered. "I'm so sorry. I . . . shouldn't have done that." She curled her hands around her body as if to stop her insides from spilling onto the gravel.

Unable to move, Rick struggled to breathe, and he fully understood the meaning of being scared stiff.

"Oh, my God!" Stephanie yelled. "What are you waiting for?"

Emily looked right, left, everywhere but at Rick as her face grew redder. Even the tips of her ears seemed to have caught fire. "I should go. Thank you for . . ." Gently, she took the Boo, and though Rick couldn't bear to look, he heard soft footfalls as Emily stepped onto the main path.

A tight group of dead souls stood a few feet away, with expressions ranging from utter disappointment to downright horror. Taylor looked as if she were about to cry; Stephanie *was* crying. Herbert merely shook his head.

Even Herbert is disgusted with you.

Unwilling to read the contents of his heart written on their faces, Rick traced Emily's path as she inched toward the gate—toward the end of something that had almost begun.

It's all for the best. It wouldn't have worked out anyway—we're too different. Rick's stomach lurched, rose, and flopped. It had been a pleasant but unrealistic fantasy. As Emily edged another few feet further, Rick accepted, quite calmly, that he'd never be the hero in anyone's story. There would never be a grand romance, no tale of soulmates found, and he was surprisingly okay with that. His destiny, after all, had always been singular. Stephanie's sobs reached his ears as if even the residents knew the truth as he did. As if they'd just witnessed the end of a long, torturous battle.

But . . . whose battle had been lost?

Something stirred, and the scene replayed. Emily should have been horrified. She should have run screaming from the lunatic who'd swiped her Boo. Instead, she'd thrown herself into his arms and thanked him with an embrace. And he'd returned the gesture with a chill.

Who had been defeated?

Rick's stomach settled, he unclenched his fists, and out of nowhere, a movie began in his mind.

An empty rocking chair on an old, rickety porch appeared. Beside it, Rick rocked gently in a matching chair as the sun set in the west. A gentle breeze moved in the tall grass as water trickled from an ambling brook, traveling from one unknown place to another. With a creak, an unseen weight settled into the empty rocker, a hand took his, and their fingers intertwined. No longer empty, the rocker swayed, and her smile made the world explode.

More than mere fantasy, Rick's soul recognized it all, a familiar yet unknown place lulling him home. There and gone in a flash, the vision lingered like the tail-end of a dream.

And in that moment, Rick Holliday very nearly knew . . . something.

Emily was far up the path—she'd almost reached the gate. Freed from the stony grip of a lifetime of fear, Rick took a step forward. Then another.

And then he ran with all his might.

"Emily!"

Though he quickly closed the distance between them, Emily stopped yet remained facing the iron bars. Coming to a halt, Rick placed a hand on her shoulder and gently turned her, and when he looked into those sky-blue eyes, he couldn't ignore that they were now the dull gray of pain.

I caused that, he thought. And then; *I can fix it.*

"My name is Rick," he said, with more conviction than

he'd ever announced, and then, he stepped forward and wrapped his hope around her.

Emily hesitated only a moment before she entwined her arms around his neck, pressed her body close, and sighed. It was as if they were two people who'd spotted one another across a crowded room after a lifetime of searching. It was . . . relief.

Distantly, cheers rose as Rick and Emily remained locked in their embrace for an age. He was utterly unaware of how frozen his limbs were. All that existed in the entire universe was Emily. Forever and a day passed before she gently pulled away, and they stood together on the path, each staring into the other's soul. Tiny flecks of brown danced in her blue eyes. How long would it take to count them?

"Your name is Rick. I like it."

He stared in silence, lost in a world no one else could penetrate.

Well . . . maybe one person.

"Yeah, boy, take her inside. Or don't you know what to do with a real girl?"

Without so much as a glance, Madge calmly thrust out an arm and pushed Herbert violently to the ground. "Ask her out, dear. Offer to take her to dinner."

Emily awkwardly turned on a heel as a pink hue blossomed on her cheeks. "I guess I'll see you on Sunday?"

Rick had never asked a girl on a date before. But then again, he reasoned, he'd never hugged one either. Maybe it was time to try more new things. "How about you see me on Friday?" He felt silly being nervous now; he'd just smothered her body with his own, after all. "I mean, would you like to dinner with me?"

You're blowing it already.

"Smooth move, Ex-Lax," Stephanie ribbed.

Emily's smile widened. "I would love to dinner with you, CT . . . Rick," she corrected, covering her grin with a hand as delicate as a fairy's wing.

Rick's heart knocked lightly against his ribcage at the sound of his name on her lips. "I lock up at six o'clock."

"I'll be here," she said and kissed his cheek before turning toward the gate.

Rick smoothed his hand over the moisture where her kiss lingered. As he watched her go, each step threatened to shred him. She opened her car door and wriggled her fingertips, and he had to resist the urge to run after her.

"Six o'clock!" Rick called, waving back.

"I'm looking forward to dinnering!"

As she drove away, Rick felt for the first time in his life that he was truly alone.

And didn't want to be.

The women gathered around, gushing over the impending date. Their voices melded before falling away to an incomprehensible whisper.

Rick tried to hold onto the lingering touch of her lips on his cheek as he walked back to the cottage, smiling from ear to ear.

For the first time in all his days, Rick Holliday had a date.

15

THE PROM QUEEN AND THE UNDERTAKER COWBOY

He was a wreck.

Rick had never been on a date; had never expected to be on one. With one peck on the cheek and a couple of clumsy embraces, his carefully planned life had taken a wild detour, and for once, he had no idea where it might lead.

Wearing his usual attire—jeans, a flannel, and work boots—he grabbed his collar, took a whiff, and scurried from his chair with a cringe. Panic set in as he riffled through a drawer, tossing aside one flannel after another—a hole here, a tear there. Until now, his clothes had seemed perfectly fine, but now, he saw a wardrobe more befitting a homeless man.

A pile of unwashed shirts grabbed his attention, and he held one up to the light. It looked . . . okay. After a quick sniff, he decided it wasn't too bad. He buttoned the shirt and smoothed out the wrinkles. He spotted a half-empty bottle of cologne in the medicine cabinet a former caretaker had left behind. Not entirely sure where he was supposed to apply it, he poured some into a cupped palm and splashed beneath his arms before patting the crotch of his jeans.

Madge poked her head from the shower curtain. "Heavens, Rick, you're joking, right?"

Cologne splashed over his shirt. Great. Now he smelled like a used car salesman. "I'm d-dressing, for crying out loud."

With a dismissive wave, Madge stepped from the tub. "Don't be silly. I've watched you dress hundreds of times."

"What d-do you mean, you've—"

"Honestly, though, you're not thinking of wearing that?"

"What's w-wrong with it?" he muttered, annoyed that his protest had been derailed, yet filled with a new worry as he stared into the mirror.

"You don't want her to think you don't care enough to put on a clean shirt." Madge gave him a long, scrutinizing look and shook her head. "You're a mess."

"Yeah," Stephanie agreed from the doorway, "and with all that cologne you just poured on, you probably smell like one of those guys who sells newspapers downtown."

"These are the only c-c-clothes I have." Rick walked through Stephanie into the bedroom, her form falling apart and reassembling like a cloud of bouncy gnats. "I d-don't have anything fancy. Why c-can't I wear what I always wear?"

Madge wrinkled her nose as if Rick had suggested he smear himself in cow dung. "Just because she likes you in your natural element doesn't mean she won't expect you to behave like a gentleman outside this cemetery. By the way, where are you taking her?"

Rick scratched his head. "I was thinking the D-Dandy Sandy."

"Oh, my God," Stephanie whined, sitting cross-legged on the bed. "You can't, like, take her to a dump like that."

"Is that place still around?" Madge asked. "In my day, it was rather nice."

"Your day was ages ago."

Madge pursed her lips, ignoring the insult. "I don't know why you insist on keeping it so hot in here, Rick," she grumbled as she wiped her glistening brow.

Hopping from the bed, Stephanie stood beside Madge. "He might as well take her to a truck stop diner."

"Actually—"

"Oh, my God, no."

Fanning herself with both hands now, Madge continued. "You need to take her somewhere classy, but first, we need to fix your attire. What have you got in the closet?"

Stephanie's muffled voice wafted from the sparse rack of clothes. "He's right. There's, like, nothing in here."

Madge tapped a finger against her chin. "I've got it. The Witherbee," she said, clasping her hands with a grin.

"Oh, The Witherbee!" Stephanie's faint voice cried from the closet. "Definitely take her there. She'll love it."

"He'll need a dinner jacket. And a hat." Madge misted into the closet, and the teen let out a surprised yelp as the women wrestled for space. Rick slid the door open, giving them light to see.

"See?" Stephanie said, brushing dust from her hot pink crop top as she escaped the crowded space. "He's got nothing but work clothes in there."

Giving up all hope of dressing himself, Rick plopped onto the bed and let them fight it out.

"He can't take her to The Witherbee if he doesn't have a dinner jacket," Madge protested as she exited the closet. Turning back to the wardrobe, she pointed with a squint. "Rick, dear, pull this out. I want a better look."

Reluctantly, he did as he was told and lay a jacket on the bed.

Stephanie leaned close. "Oh, my God, this is an undertaker's coat. He can't wear this."

"Well, there's nothing better in there. He can't walk out of here looking like some sort of lumberjack. And he still needs a hat."

"Damn right, he needs a hat." Herbert glowered from the doorway. "Gentlemen should always wear hats. Should never have stopped, I say."

"You were never a gentleman, Herb," Madge quipped.

Herbert scowled, his middle finger waving.

"Wait here." Madge suddenly flew up through the ceiling, and the rest waited motionless until her disembodied head popped from the plaster. "There's a trunk up here, and I think I saw something, but it's dark. Come up here, Rick."

A furtive glance at the clock slapped him with a violent jolt. "I don't have t-time for this. She'll b-be here any m-minute. Can't I just wear the j-j-jacket?"

"Get up here, now!"

Resigned, Rick climbed the rickety ladder. He emerged ten minutes later, holding a dusty top hat. "I'd look s-s-silly wearing this."

"Don't be ridiculous," Madge said, beaming. "Put the jacket on, and let's have a look."

Rick donned the top hat and coat and glared at his

reflection in the bathroom mirror. "I look like an under-taker c-c-cowboy."

"It'll do," Madge said, though the others didn't look so sure.

Overruled, Rick left the bathroom and collapsed into his chair. He'd been nervous before, but now he was downright terrified. He imagined Emily pulling up to the gate, dressed in an elegant gown, while he looked like a magician who'd just crawled out of his own grave. It hadn't even begun, and his first date was already turning disastrous.

Floating through the closed door, Taylor floated through the closed door, joining the uncomfortably quiet group.

"Whoa . . . who died?"

Outside, an argument broke out.

"He needs to lose the top hat," Stephanie said. "Taylor says no one wears top hats anymore unless they're at a Halloween party."

Unwilling to budge, Madge folded her arms. "He looks distinguished."

Rick remained silent as their voices blended into the background. His own voice—the one he'd carried from birth, that sometimes advised him well but usually didn't —pushed to the front, drowning out all else.

She won't like the restaurant.

She probably showered three times after that hug.

She won't show up.

You're a fool.

Over the drone of Stephanie's high-pitched whine, Rick had nearly convinced himself that Emily would never arrive and was probably laughing with her friends over the whole charade while he waited like an idiot beneath the full moon.

"What even is that?" Stephanie rolled her eyes. "Who-ever heard of a pashmina?"

"Dear, you can't tell me that pashminas went out of style between my time and yours. You would know if you saw one, and it would look perfect on Rick."

"Is it a hat?" Herbert said, chewing a pinkie nail. "I'm pretty sure it's a hat."

"I find it shocking that a man who claims to know everything about hats doesn't know that a pashmina is most certainly not a hat."

Herbert answered with a scowl and thrust of his bony hips. "I've got your pashmina right here."

Taylor stepped from behind the cottage wall, her hair glowing periwinkle in the low moonlight. "She's here."

Unaware of how many eyes were upon her, Emily climbed from her parked car. Something like a prom dress —puffy, shimmering material with rhinestones glued to the sleeves—swirled around her slender body. A tiara sat prominently on her head, and her hair hung loosely below her shoulders. Ruby red slippers sparkled as if Dorothy had clicked the heels herself.

"Oh man," Taylor said, "I think this is her first date, too."

Stephanie bounced on her feet. "This would be the perfect time to play Rick's song if he had one."

Rick gazed at beauty unmatched by any woman he'd ever seen, even in the old black-and-white movies. Everything else fell away as his captivating date glowed perfection.

"Rick, did you lock the gate?"

Madge's voice brought Rick back with a start. He *had* locked it. The gate, wide open during the day, was now tightly shut, the padlock wound through iron.

"I'll go unlock . . ." The words stuck in his throat as Emily gathered the folds of her dress, grasped the metal bars, and climbed the gate. Landing unsteadily on the other side, she spotted Rick, then raised a hand and a smile.

"Dear God," Madge whispered with a hand to her lips.

Approaching on shaky leg-sticks, Rick met Emily at the comment box. He couldn't keep from staring at her graceful gown and the plastic tiara atop her head. A shiver curled down his spine as she lightly touched his arm, and her eyes moved from his top hat to his boots. She smiled, the corners of her eyes crinkling.

Like Frank's used to.

"You look nice. Like an old-time banker."

"Thanks. I bury people in this coat."

A collective groan went up behind him.

"Oh. It doesn't look dirty."

"I don't usually wear it in the graves."

Sighing, Madge shook her head. "If they weren't so equally matched, I'd say this was already a disaster."

"Tell her she looks nice too!" Stephanie called.

"Uh, you look nice. Sparkly."

Emily glanced down. "I feel overdressed."

"No, it's great." He was unsure what to say next. "You can take it off if you want."

Emily's cheeks flushed as moisture collected at Rick's

armpits. He was blowing it. Here she was dressed like a glamorous movie star, and he'd just suggested she undress.

"You climbed that gate real nice," he said, scratching the back of his head. "I didn't see your underwear or anything."

Herbert cackled as the remaining residents shifted. Rick wished they'd go away, or at least hide, so he didn't have to witness their cringes.

"Train wreck," Madge groaned, "absolute train wreck."

Emily's flush grew scarlet. "Thank you."

"For all that's good in this world, please get her out of here," Madge begged. "I can't watch this any longer."

Rick extended a hand, and when Emily took it, his body tingled. "Are you, uh, ready to go?"

"Ready."

Releasing her hand, Rick fished in his pocket for his keys. Confused, he held them out.

Emily glanced down awkwardly. "Thank you, but maybe you should drive."

"Right." Leaving her alone on the path, Rick turned on his heel, and Emily hesitated before scrambling after him.

Herbert crooked his fedora with a finger. "He'll be lucky to get to the ballpark, let alone first base."

As Rick opened the passenger door to the hearse, he thought he detected a bit of horror. "Sorry, it's my work vehicle," he apologized, wishing he'd chosen the truck instead. Yet, the hearse was more comfortable, and he'd polished it to a high shine that afternoon.

"It's okay," Emily said, regaining her composure. "I've never been in a limo before." Climbing in, she clasped her hands in her lap. The bottom of her dress lay limp on the gravel, and Rick slammed the door onto it.

"Rick . . ." Stephanie called, but Madge lay a hand on her arm.

"Leave it, dear. Just . . . leave it."

AS THEY WERE LED PAST TABLES COVERED IN EXPENSIVE white linens, Rick felt horribly out of place. Diners peered over menus, none dressed as oddly as he.

Exposed below the knee, Emily tugged at her torn dress. Strips of thick, shiny material hung in greasy clumps while she smiled nervously.

After passing a half-dozen empty tables, they stopped at a small table in a darkened corner next to the kitchen doors. "Your server will be right with you," the maître d said while his eyes narrowed at Emily's bare legs.

Though tucked away, Rick felt exposed, as if being seated at the worst table only served to spotlight how much they didn't belong. "Excuse m-m-me, is there a q-quieter s-s-spot?"

"I'd rather stay here," Emily said, glancing between the other diners and the fan-shaped napkin floating out of her glass. "If you don't mind."

She was right. Neither of them would be at ease in a more conspicuous spot. "Th-Thank you, we're f-f-fine."

"Very well." Expressionless, the maître d took his leave.

A thousand forks were laid before Rick. What was he supposed to do with them? While he stared at the silverware, Emily examined the drapery, and a wall grew between them.

"So . . . do you come here a lot?"

"I've never been anywhere this fancy." Rick wasn't sure if he should have admitted that, but the words were out.

"Me neither. I've been to the Dandy Sandy, though. Grandfather used to take me there when he was . . . they have good breadsticks."

Rick's heart leaped—for once, his instinct had been right. "I wanted to take you there! They said it wasn't fancy enough for a first date."

"They?"

Too late to take the words back, Rick froze. The admission had tumbled out, and the giddiness he'd felt only a moment ago tumbled with it. *Think!* But his brain had shut down.

A tall, willowy man arrived, holding out two menus, and Rick breathed a sigh, hoping he'd evaded an uncomfortable explanation. He didn't want to lie to her, not as they were just getting started.

Not ever.

"Shall I bring you some wine while you decide?"

"Oh, uh, I'll j-j-just have w-w-w . . ." Without warning, Rick's tongue locked. He couldn't say it. Panic crept in, a hyperawareness that if he didn't calm down, coherent speech would soon be impossible. *Water, water, water . . .*

"W . . . W . . ."

Shifting uncomfortably, the waiter stared as beads of sweat broke out on Rick's forehead. Fists tightened, teeth clenched. *Just say it. Water. Water . . .*

"W—"

"Do you have chocolate milk?" Emily—calm, relaxed, and smiling—flashed a polite uptick at the corners of her mouth.

No. Please no. Rick had seen that look a thousand times before—the pity smile. School bullies were one thing. Rude people were another. But the worst—the absolute worst—were those who viewed Rick as if he were some sort of wretched blemish on an otherwise perfect society. How insanely stupid he had been. It was as if he'd been drugged, floating these past few weeks in a fog, making poor decisions under the influence of a handful of nosy dead people. What *had* he been thinking? He hadn't been looking for a relationship. Aside from Frank, Rick had never felt the need for one good friend. He'd been born, placed in a box marked "damaged," and left to fend for himself. After having spent a lifetime embracing his destiny, he'd thrown it all away to go on a date with a beautiful girl who apparently had her own problems to have ever considered dating him.

He needed to get as far away from this restaurant as possible.

"C-C-Can—"

"My apologies, Madame, but we do not serve chocolate milk." The waiter's lip curled into something like a snarl, his emphasis on the word *chocolate* distasteful.

Emily lowered her head. "I guess I'll just have water, too."

"Two waters," the waiter quipped through tight lips, turning toward the swinging doors.

"Sorry," she whispered, cheeks fiery red. "I wasn't thinking. Of course a fancy place like this wouldn't have chocolate milk."

The restaurant quieted as a swirl of tension surrounded the prom queen and the undertaker cowboy. Cocking his head, Rick examined Emily from every possible angle and tried to view himself from her perspective. But no matter how hard he tried, he couldn't see himself as she must.

Instead, he envisioned how she saw herself.

With a lifetime of embarrassment under his belt, it hadn't occurred to Rick that she'd have the same concerns. For the first time since he'd spied her from behind the shrubbery, he recognized the angst behind her down-trodden expression, the self-flogging at her own misstep. The waiter had embarrassed *her*, not Rick's inability to say one simple word.

Maybe they weren't so different after all.

He still wanted to be back in the cottage, only now with Emily at his side.

Straightening in a way his spine wasn't accustomed to, Rick called after the waiter. "You're sure there's n-no chocolate m-m-milk back there? A fancy place like this can't be out of chocolate m-milk."

The room hushed, and with a forced smile, the waiter returned. "We do serve hot chocolate. Would that do for Madame?"

Emily managed a smile, and ever so slightly, her shoulders relaxed. "Yes, that would be fine, thank you."

Rick's ego inflated as if he'd just rescued the damsel from a gang of big, bad outlaws in black hats. "Make it t-t-two," he added boldly, "and don't skimp on the whipped c-cream."

"Yes, sir," the waiter said before slipping away.

"Thank you, that was nice." Emily's smile was on the shaky side, and they both fell silent as the murmur in the room returned to normal. Distress tried to crawl back beneath Rick's skin, twisting through his gut. He wasn't one to make a scene, and he'd just made a darned good one. Maybe he should have let it go.

But when the waiter returned with two steaming hot chocolates, Emily's smile covered in a happy mess of whipped cream, Rick had no regrets. He'd make a thousand scenes for that smile.

And then a thousand more.

AS SOON AS HE OPENED THE MENU, HE KNEW HE WAS IN trouble.

Written in some foreign language, the dishes were incomprehensible. Worse, the exorbitant prices weren't. As Rick agonized over the print, the only category Rick recognized was *hors d'oeuvres*, and even those were difficult to understand.

Arriving with more hot chocolate, the waiter set the mugs down, rubbing his fingers as if they were filthy. "Are you ready to order?"

At a loss, Rick couldn't read whatever language this was. Italian? What if Emily asked for his help? He'd brought her here, after all. It wouldn't be out of the question for her to assume he could read Italian. Rick began to think he should go back to his original plan and head over to the Dandy Sandy.

"I would like the steak au poiver with pommes frites, along with your soup du jour, please."

What on earth had Emily ordered? Rick realized it didn't matter and seized the opportunity. "M-M-Make that t-two."

The waiter scurried away, and Rick gazed at Emily with awe. "I didn't know you spoke Italian."

"Oh, I don't, but I took three years of high school French."

He didn't understand what being able to speak French had to do with it, but he let it go.

They hit another awkward pause. Emily sipped hot chocolate, set her cup on the table amidst the clutter of emptied mugs, and lifted her chin.

"Did you grow up in town?" A fresh, creamy mustache coated her lip.

"Yes." Rick suddenly wanted—*needed*—to wipe the cream from her face. "I, uh, lived all over town. In a lot of places."

"Oh? How come?"

"I just moved around a lot."

With the subject clearly closed, the wall of silence rose higher. Rick ordered more hot chocolates, and the waiter called a busboy to clear the table before bringing their meals. Rick had been nervous about what they'd ordered, but now that he saw it, he was overcome with relief. "Hey! This is just steak and fries!"

The waiter stiffened. "Sir, you ordered steak au poiver with pommes frites."

Rick took in the sight. "Steak p-pulitzer with p-p-pong freeze. Right. Well, it looks g-great! You got any s-s-steak sauce?"

"And ketchup, please," Emily added.

As the waiter retreated with a look of utter horror, Rick took in the aroma. "Steak and fries! My favorite!"

PULLING UP TO THE GATE, RICK SHUT OFF THE HEARSE'S motor. He'd been dreading this moment since they'd left the restaurant. He was supposed to kiss her. In all the movies, romance novels, and TV shows, a kiss was the expected outcome.

He shook at the thought.

What if she'd hated the restaurant? What if she'd realized—as Stephanie frequently claimed—that he was little more than a silly dork? What if she ordered him to never speak to her again? A thousand possibilities raced as the cooling engine ticked in uncomfortable silence.

"I had a wonderful time, Rick. Thank you." Emily stared at her folded hands.

Should he kiss her now? NOW? "Sorry about your dress."

She tugged at the hem of her ruined gown. "It's okay. I'll turn it into curtains. I'm pretty good on a sewing machine."

Silence. Now? Seconds felt like hours, days, as Rick warred inwardly.

"I guess I should go," Emily whispered. "I don't want someone to drive by and think . . . you know."

The implication hung in the air as Rick's stomach rumbled ominously. If he didn't get to a bathroom immediately, the worst things would happen right there in the hearse. "I . . ." Time neither stopped nor raced as he struggled to remember what language he usually spoke, and his tongue swelled to a fat slab of meat. He was supposed to kiss her, carry her into the cottage, and ravage her until the sun rose.

Emily solved the dilemma herself with a softly planted kiss on the cheek, and Rick resisted the urge to stroke his own face. After climbing from the hearse, Emily leaned in through the open window. "Goodnight, Rick."

"Goodnight, Emily." Ah, that was it—English was his language. As she turned toward her Honda, an idea struck Rick. With one hand on his top hat, he leaned over the seat. "What's your favorite place in town?"

Emily hesitated only briefly before she turned. "The bookstore."

There went that idea. How could he take her on a date to a bookstore?

"Would you like to go there one of these nights after hours? It's nice when everyone's gone." She paused, a blush spreading, then added, "I can make sandwiches."

Rick could imagine them alone in her favorite place with no pretenses, no high-and-mighty waiters. *That could work.* "I would love to. When?"

"The store closes early on Sundays. We can leave after I visit Grandfather. I'll swing by around four?"

"Sunday it is, then." He tipped his top hat.

She opened the door and reached inside. "I almost forgot this." Grabbing her tiara, Emily smiled and closed the hearse door on her dress again. It tore as she walked, and by the time she reached her own car, her dress had been reduced to little more than a slip. With a wriggle of fingers, she climbed inside.

As Rick returned her wave, he held no doubt that he was the luckiest man alive.

16

THE BOOK AND NOOK

Rick moved through his chores in a daze as the previous night's events replayed on a loop—dinner, cheek-kiss, plans for more. Trudging to the old elm with his ax in hand, he stared at it for an age, forgetting why he'd gone. An hour passed while he filled a wheelbarrow with wood, then carefully stacked each log back into the woodshed. He grabbed his keys and ambled to the gate, still in his robe and slippers, perplexed when a group of teens whistled from a passing car.

His thoughts circled around Emily, Emily, Emily. She was in the quick movements of the barn swallows that swept the sky, in the ripples at the edge of Barlow Pond, in the layers of leaves he'd neglected to burn.

By noon, he admitted his uselessness and returned to the cottage. Slumped in his chair, he stared at the basket of apples—just one more thing that reminded him of Emily, Emily, Emily. How could he possibly wait another twenty-four hours for her arrival?

He was still in his chair as night fell. Lit by the last of a fire that had nearly burnt out, the cottage had grown dark. Hadn't he brought in the wood earlier? With one hand resting on his cheek, a ludicrous grin was plastered to his lips.

Deaf to the voices and blind to the wisps of smoke, Rick failed to notice as the residents arrived in the darkened room—staring, whispering.

"Uh, Rick?"

"Hmm?" Awareness crashed in. "What t-t-time is it?"

"It's time for the meeting," Madge answered with a sly grin.

"Oh. Why is it so d-dark?" Rick's bones creaked as he flipped on the light, the sudden glare burning his eyes. He shivered. *It must be thirty degrees in here.* How long had he sat motionless in the freezing room?

"Rick?"

"Yeah," he answered, disoriented as if he'd awoken in a strange place.

"Why don't you bring in the firewood before you freeze to death?"

"Huh? Oh, okay." Rubbing the back of his neck, Rick stumbled outside, and minutes later, the fire began to thaw the icy cottage. The warmth eased the fog behind his lids, and he became aware of their watchful eyes.

"What?"

Silence, and then . . .

"How did it go?"

"Did she like the restaurant?"

"Herbert thinks you gave it to her in the hearse, but we couldn't see anything. So, like, did you give it to her?"

Amused by some questions and downright appalled by others, Rick waited while they ran through a litany of curiosities, theories, and interrogations. There was no getting around it—he'd have to relay the date, yet he wasn't quite ready to give out all the details, superstitious that telling it would kill the magic.

Adjusting the colossal lacy bow atop her head, Stephanie considered Rick from beneath her lashes. "Oh, my God, did you know you poured an entire bag of dry cement mix in the flower bed by Old Lady Herman's grave? If she were still dead, she'd be turning in it right now."

"We gave you space," Madge added, "but enough is enough. Tell us about the restaurant. It was a good choice, right?"

"Did ya give it to her? Yeah, boy, I bet you did. Those hearses aren't just for dead bodies."

"Tell us everything," Stephanie begged.

"You don't have to tell us the sex part," Madge said.

"Yes, you do!" Stephanie cut in. "Especially the sex part!"

"For c-crying out loud, there was no s-s-s—" Rick stumbled. "None of that. It was only a first d-d-date." He recounted their dinner—even the peck on the cheek afterward. He nearly left that part out, but though he had no proof, he wasn't entirely sure they couldn't read his mind.

When he finished, Madge and Stephanie stared at one another, baffled. "How could you think it was an Italian restaurant?"

"So?" Stephanie asked. "Second date?"

Rick sighed. "Yes, there will b-be a second d-date. At the b-b-bookstore."

Silence blanketed the room. "The bookstore? Isn't that, like, a little low-key?"

"I think it's perfect. It is Emily's favorite place, after all."

"But won't it be weird with all those other people around?"

"We're g-g-going after hours," Rick answered, embarrassed at the innuendo.

"After hours, huh?" The old man stood with his back to the room, his arms wrapped around his body as they stroked his sides. "Emily, kiss me, my dear."

"Herb . . ."

"Come on, Emily," Herbert went on, "give us a smooch. No, not there. Lower—"

"Stop it, you old perv!" Taylor rose with flushed cheeks. "Emily isn't like that!"

Rick's eyes landed on the blue-haired resident. *How does she know what Emily's like?* She hadn't been here to hear Frank's tales of his granddaughter, hadn't lived for his stories as the others had. She'd never even met her.

Had she?

A log popped in the fire, and the thought sizzled to an ember. "Right," Rick said, struggling to return to the present. "D-Do we have any new b-business?"

For the remainder of the meeting, Rick fielded questions from the women. How was the food? What time would they go to the bookstore? What would he wear?

This time, he thought, *I'm wearing my flannel.*

As the chatter crept into the late hours, Taylor quietly slipped through the door into the black of night.

Sunday arrived, as did Emily for her regular visit. Rick fidgeted at the window, unsure if he should join her or leave her to make her visit in peace. Both options warred until her car pulled up, and at the sight of her, nothing could have kept Rick from her side. As he opened the door, he had to force himself to slow to a trot.

His gut sank as he realized the wind had blown the gate shut. Once again, Emily gathered her dress and kicked a leg over.

"No!" Rick called. "It's, uh, it's unlocked. Just swing it open."

Raising her chin in a smile, Emily climbed down, pushed through the gate, and ran to Rick, throwing her arms around his neck. This time, he didn't hesitate to return the sentiment. Then, remembering the others, he pulled away.

"I, uh, don't want them watching," he stammered, his arms tingling.

"Who?"

"Oh, uh . . . the people driving by."

Emily turned to the deserted road. "You're right. Shall we?"

"Should I wait for you here?"

"No, come with me, please." She reached for Rick's hand. "I'd like him to meet you."

Rick's nerves lit with a sudden spark. He hadn't thought of that. What *would* Frank think about Rick dating his beloved granddaughter? Frank had always said he wished Emily would find someone, but Rick wasn't sure Frank would approve of this particular someone. After taking Emily's outstretched hand, they strolled together toward Frank's plot. A nervous jitter shot through Rick as if he were meeting her actual, living grandfather. As if he didn't already know Frank and shared a thousand afternoons.

As if he hadn't said his own painful goodbye.

Glancing at his clothes, Rick worried he wasn't adequately dressed before it hit him that Frank wasn't only dead, he was gone.

Still.

Turning at a spot more familiar to Rick than Emily could ever know, she led the way to Frank's tombstone. In their shared silence, Rick had just enough time to hope she would keep her conversation with Frank in her head.

"Hello, Grandfather. I'd like you to meet Rick," she said, with a gentle squeeze of the hand and a tilt at the corners of her mouth. "My boyfriend."

Rick's heart skipped a beat. Was he really her boyfriend now? And didn't that make Emily his girl-friend? *I have a girlfriend.* He both loved and feared the sound of it. *Emily is my girlfriend.* He returned her squeeze.

"I'm happy and not lonely anymore. I wish you could be okay with my decision and come back."

Falling back to earth with a thud, Rick wished again that he could tell her the truth, to set her mind at ease, and let her be at peace. So much unwanted power he wielded.

"I'll be back on Wednesday. "I made you some apple butter, but I'm not leaving it here. I don't want to be a litterbug." With a guilty smile, she handed the small jar to Rick. "I'm ready."

"Right. Let's drop this off at the cottage."

Hand in hand, they walked beneath a darkening sky. At the cottage gate, the residents watched as Rick veered off the path and set the jar at the doorstep, leaving Emily temporarily alone at the comment box.

Stephanie skittered alongside him. "Like, seriously, you can bring her back here. We won't watch or anything."

"Uh-huh. You're nearly as b-bad as Herb."

"Hmm?" Emily asked from the path.

Rick would have to train himself to remember she wasn't one of them. "I said I wondered if you put any herbs in here."

"Just some allspice and nutmeg," she answered with a twist of her foot.

Leaving Stephanie at the door, Rick passed Madge and Herbert as one whispered "good luck" while the other proposed activities that made Rick blush—he hoped his face didn't reflect his embarrassment.

"I thought we could take my car this time if that's okay. Parking at the bookstore, well, you know, those spots are pretty small, and your limo . . ."

Rick hadn't been exactly thrilled about driving his date —no, his *girlfriend*—around town in a coffin-mover, either. "I think it's a great idea." Heading toward the gate, he spotted Taylor atop her tombstone as she sat.

Watching Emily.

As the Honda backed onto Main Street, the residents waved, and Rick had to hold his arm down to keep from waving back.

This was going to be a lot harder than he'd thought.

EMILY'S CAR SPUTTERED TO A JERKY STOP, AND RICK made a mental note to check the timing belt. The thought was oddly thrilling. *That's a pretty boyfriend-like thing to do. Maybe I should lift weights in front of her, too.*

A dim light shone from the store window. Not a soul was out, the streets abandoned. A light sprinkle fell as Emily popped the trunk, and together they carried a mountain of supplies inside. The familiar smell of aged paper dusted Rick. There were no promotional displays, no tables piled high with the hot book of the week, and no Starbucks in the corner. It felt authentic—somehow more real. He followed Emily to a large, open area where overstuffed chairs and oriental rugs surrounded a stone fireplace. Books—both old and new—swallowed every available space, and Rick regretted that he'd never ventured here before. Had he known what a treasure the bookstore was . . . well, maybe. The Book and Nook wasn't always empty of shoppers.

Emily spread a blanket over the rug and unpacked a virtual buffet. There were sandwiches, pies, cakes, and an untold number of chocolate milk bottles. A bucket of fried chicken was flanked by a cheeseburger from the Dandy Sandy, alongside six boxes of Junior Mints, a single turkey leg, and—of course—fresh apples. With little room left for either to sit, Emily frowned. "I might have overdone it."

Rick grabbed the lone turkey leg and stuffed it into his mouth. "No way, I'm starving."

Emily's brows furrowed. "Oh no, I forgot the silverware!" As she anxiously chewed the tip of a finger—not a nail, but her actual finger—Rick realized how at ease he felt. Gone was the usual worry over how he would inevitably screw things up, and he felt oddly . . . himself.

No. Better than himself.

"I don't mind eating with my hands. Some of it comes

with its own handle." Grinning through a mouthful of turkey, Rick waved the bone in the air, and after a moment of lip-biting, Emily's shoulders loosened, and she dug into her bag.

"I have something for you." She pulled out a handkerchief emblazoned with rhinestones, the edges piped with intricate stitching. She bit down again on her lip, holding the kerchief out. "I made it from my dress. What was left, anyway."

Turning the delicate cloth over, Rick inspected every detail. She'd even stitched her initials onto the back. He'd never owned a hanky before, and he was sure that the rhinestones would shred his nose. This was too lovely, too *Emily,* to fill with . . . well, to use. The very idea felt wrong. "Thank you." Tucking it into his front pocket, Rick patted the lump, yet its placement felt wrong. He tucked it into the neckline of his shirt instead.

Emily's lashes fluttered, and Rick's skin melted. "It looks fancy there, like a lobster bib."

They ate in comfortable silence, with enough food to feed the entire group of residents if they were alive to enjoy it. After downing half the bucket of chicken, Rick rubbed a hand over his protruding belly, calculating how much he'd pay for this later.

Emily hugged her knees to her chest. "I made too much. Would you like to take it home? Maybe for tomorrow's lunch?"

And tomorrow's tomorrow. "Thank you, I would."

Emily gathered the dishes in the darkened store while her dress swished in perfect circles. She flicked a switch, flames roared to life, and she sat with a smile. "It's gas. Wouldn't be smart to have a real fire in here."

Once again, silence reigned, and Rick fell deep into himself, trying to grasp the reality of it all. Only a month ago, he'd been quietly grieving the loss of a friend. He missed Frank; more than Rick thought he could miss another person, and now here he was, sitting on a picnic blanket in an empty bookstore with Frank's granddaughter. How had it all happened? He'd never subscribed to the idea of divine intervention, but it felt as close to fate as any other crazy idea. It was no more insane than spending his days talking to dead people.

What was crazy? What was sane?

Desperate to hear Emily's musical voice, Rick broke the silence. "Did you also grow up here in town?"

"I did," she said, seemingly equally relieved to breach the quiet. "I lived in the same house all my life. I spent a lot of time at Grandfather's house after my father died, though." Her smile faltered, and the lilt in her voice deflated. Silence enveloped them once again.

Switching gears, Rick asked, "Where did you go to high school?"

"Jonsrud High. You?"

"Same. It's a small town." Rick wondered what Emily would have thought of him back then—if she'd have given him even a second glance. He snuck a peek at her profile as she stared into the fire and decided she wouldn't have. Which group would she have fallen into? Spying the thin line of freckles tiptoeing across her upturned nose, he knew. She would have had her group of loyal friends, holdovers from grade school. Having likely belonged to the smart clubs—debate, chess, maybe even written for the school paper—she would have earned top grades and probably scored valedictorian. He wouldn't say she'd have been one of the most popular girls in school—he doubted she'd have been part of the typical cheerleader crowd—but she would have been well-liked. Her senior yearbook was likely filled with sentiments like, *see you in college!* and *I'll miss you, Em!* What would it be like to have sailed through those four years with little or no scars, unlike himself, marked and broken for life?

"Did you enjoy high school?" Leaning back, Rick prepared to hear tales of her adventures, the awkward teenage years sliding past her.

Too slowly, she faced him. "They were the worst years of my life." Flat. Emotionless. Nearly mournful.

No. Not nearly.

He sat up. "Why?"

Emily shrugged with the same faraway look that Taylor sometimes held while perched on her gravestone. "I was invisible."

Rick blanched. How could she have been invisible, this woman he felt pulled toward? Who outshone the sun with her very presence? He couldn't be the first person drawn to her.

"I have an older brother who was pretty popular. He's outgoing and boisterous, always the center of a crowd. He left somewhat of a legacy, and then I came along—quiet and shy—the exact opposite. So instead of trying to figure out why we were so different, people pretended I didn't exist. It was like that all through school. She laughed, a skittish, hollow sound that mimicked her sad smile. "That's pretty much how it stayed. Until I met you."

Guilt nudged Rick for having judged her so quickly. He didn't need to do the math to realize that *until I met you* translated to a lifetime of alone, alone, alone.

Like him.

"It's ironic, considering you spend so much time alone in that cottage. Maybe that's why I feel like you understand me."

Rick's mind reeled. For thirty years, he'd watched as other people somehow figured out the secret to living, who could make friends or at least avoid having a target on their backs. He'd always been a loner, long before it had evolved into personal preference. Yet, here was this beautiful creature—quirky, yes, but in the most charming way —who had lived the same life, walked the same paths, her shadow, like his, never mingling with another. It was like discovering a secret twin, and Rick wondered just how much more they had in common.

"Didn't you have a best friend? Most people have at least one, even if they suck."

"Yes," she answered. "Grandfather."

No wonder she was so upset that Frank had seemingly abandoned her.

"How about you? Have you always had a stutter?"

Breathing stopped, blood raced. Pinpricks of surprise stabbed. She'd simply said it, just came right out with it like it was nothing. As if Rick's stutter wasn't at the forefront of who he was. So much that it had to be ignored like a pimple too large to be acknowledged. Her head tilted, waiting for an answer he'd never been asked to give. People didn't just come out and ask about his stutter. It was Rick before Rick, the thing people noticed before all else.

But maybe his stutter wasn't who he was—perhaps it was only a tagalong in his life, a non-thing. Just a fact. Not *him*.

Not to her, anyway.

Rick felt compelled to lay his cards on the proverbial table. She'd opened up, and he owed her something in return. "The stutter made me pretty darned visible, especially to the bullies."

She twisted to face him, and as she removed her sweater, exposing the white camisole underneath, Rick wondered if her arms ever saw sunlight. They seemed untouched as if her very skin moved in darkness.

"What happened?"

He wondered if he should bother. He'd be exposing his weakness—that he was no fighter but a loser who'd spent a lifetime cowering. In movies, girls didn't go for the weakling. They went for the muscles. But she had, after all, just taken the same risk.

"I grew up in foster care. I never knew my father. My mother died before I was old enough to remember her."

He felt her intense gaze, her breath coming in short, quick bursts, and she whispered an airy, "Oh."

"Foster kids tend to get picked on more than anyone else, and the stutter made it worse. I was shoved, punched, and called a retard. They poured milk in my lunch and put glue on my chair. They tripped me in the hall, and once, a kid tried to drown me." As he spoke, Rick felt the punches, the kicks, and the arm-pinches so intensely that he nearly forgot she was there, lost in the swirl of memory. "It got worse in high school. A group of boys decided I was their personal punching bag. The things they did during those four years . . . well, I don't care to talk about most of them."

The old familiar embarrassment tried to creep up. He forced it down as Emily unexpectedly pressed her lips against his fingers before curling up in his lap. That should have sent him into a panic. Instead, it felt like she belonged there, nuzzling her hair against his chest. Content to stay forever, Rick ran his fingers through her hair, amazed at the thrill as her curls parted like butter.

"I like your stutter," she whispered. "It's cute."

Where had she been his entire life?

"Rick?"

"Em."

"Were you the one who buried him?"

He wasn't surprised she'd asked, only that it had taken this long. "Yes."

"Oh," she said, nearly a murmur. "I wish you had known him. He would have liked you."

Once again, Rick felt pressed into silence.

"There's an apple orchard behind Grandfather's house. I think it used to belong to some old farm, but the area got built up. Subdivisions came in, and the farm was long gone. But for some reason, the orchard stayed, and the neighborhood grew around it.

"We returned every year and picked apples. Buckets of them. Grandfather loved apples. He had an apple press in his basement, and we made apple cider, applesauce, apple butter . . . apple everything. My mother hated apples. My brother, too. Truthfully, by the time Christmas came every year, even I was a little tired of them." She laughed; soft, feathery notes, like a wind chime in the flutter of a breeze. "Now, when I smell apples, I can picture him clearly, like he's still right here.

"After he died, I spent a lot of time in the orchard— remembering Grandfather and enjoying the quiet. It's an odd place, that orchard. It's like it exists in a world all its own, and I'd sit on the grass and sometimes fall asleep. My mother was angry at first, saying, 'Let him go. He's dead.' After a while, she stopped bothering. I could feel him there—in the house, the orchard, all the places he used to be. I really felt him. I never really got the sense that he was gone. Until recently."

Rick bit his lip.

"Just over a month ago, I was in my room, not even thinking about him. All of a sudden, the room smelled like a thousand apples. It was stronger than when we worked the apple press—like someone had poured concentrated apple juice over everything. Then the curtains fluttered, and I felt—I know this might sound crazy—but I felt a hand on my shoulder. Just a gentle touch. Later, there was a red mark in the shape of a handprint.

"And ever since, he's been gone. Because of this job." After a pause, she added, "But just look at this place. I'm so happy here."

With her back pressed against his chest, Rick listened to her relaxed breathing even as his muscles tensed. The timing confirmed everything. Six weeks ago, Frank had walked out of the cemetery for the first and last time. "I'm sure he would have wanted you to do what made you happy. He wouldn't want you to be miserable."

"I just don't understand why he would leave." Her voice broke as she grabbed a napkin and dabbed at her eyes. "I know it must seem silly. I'm sure you, of all people, don't believe in ghosts."

Agonized, Rick came close to spilling everything. An uncharacteristic bitterness toward Frank—the man Rick, too, had loved—seeped beneath his skin. If only she knew the truth . . . "Emily—"

"It's okay," she interrupted. "It's sill. I know it is."

"It's not silly. He was important to you." If only Rick could let her know just how much they shared.

After a shift in the air, they drifted away from the deep end and talked about their hobbies, favorite books, and movies they both enjoyed. They had so much in common that even their differences seemed only to solidify their commonalities. In the ease of the old bookstore, Rick lost himself in her words. In the warmth of the fire. In himself.

He lost himself so thoroughly, in fact, that he failed to notice that for the first time in thirty years, Rick Holliday had spoken for hours without a single stutter.

ONCE AGAIN, RICK AND EMILY SAT AT THE CEMETERY gates in awkward silence. He nervously patted the lump in his shirt pocket where he'd tucked the rhinestone-emblazoned handkerchief and resisted the urge to wipe his brow.

Surely he should kiss her.

Clearly, the idea was preposterous.

Did everyone feel this way in the moments preceding a first kiss? According to the movies, they didn't. First kisses just seemed to happen naturally, with violin music and sparkly lights that came out of nowhere. *Just do it. It's probably no big deal for her. I bet she's had a hundred kisses.* Yet even in his imaginings, he knew that was likely untrue. The idea that Emily could also be eagerly awaiting her own first kiss filled him with the added pressure to get it right.

He spotted the others waiting at the cottage door as if anticipating an obscene play. With the strain of expectation too overwhelming, Rick decided it wasn't the night for first kisses. With a heavy heart, he climbed from her car.

Emily tilted her head out the window. "What's *your* favorite place?"

The question required zero thought. "Right here."

She paused, then offered, "How about we dinner in your cottage? I'll cook. Does Friday at six o'clock work for you?"

Something in Rick's brain ruptured, causing him to speak ridiculous words. He sauntered to her car window like an old rancher approaching lost city folk. As his mind detached from rational thought, he leaned into the window. "No," he said and watched her shoulders slump, then added, "try Friday at six-thirty, and I'll be the one cooking."

"Oh!" she beamed. "I would love that. I didn't know you cooked."

Neither did I.

"Great! I'll see you then." He was so thrown by this turn of events that he thrust his hand forward in a handshake. Confused, Emily took his hand, and Rick pumped it twice.

As he floated toward the cottage, one thought reverberated:

I hope she has a strong stomach.

17

FRANK'S APPLES

"You're doing it wrong. Do it the way I said."

"I am, but it won't f-f-fit."

"Push harder."

With a grunt, he pushed, yet no matter how hard he tried, it wouldn't go in. "I think it's c-crooked."

"It's not crooked. Jiggle it a little."

Gripping it tightly with both hands, he pushed again, and this time, it went in. "It's oozy. Is it r-r-rotten?"

"It's supposed to ooze."

"How d-d-do I get it out?"

"Scrape it with a butter knife."

Rick scraped the edge of the garlic press, and a mound of garlic seeped from the tiny holes, sizzling as he tapped it into the pan.

"Now pour the sauce in." Red spots splattered the stove, counter, and wall, and for the umpteenth time, Madge shook her head. "Why on earth did you volunteer to cook?"

"I d-d-don't know!" Rick yelled, flustered at his own

incompetence. Madge had promised to walk him through an allegedly easy spaghetti meal. Yet he soon discovered that nothing involving Rick and a stove was easy. He'd spilled an entire package of noodles on the floor and cut his finger dicing tomatoes. At least the sauce was red.

"Stir it!"

Sauce bubbled, painting the wall. Stirring quickly, Rick swore under his breath.

At precisely six-thirty, a knock came on the door, and Rick and Madge exchanged panicked expressions.

"Don't worry," Madge said, sounding unquestionably worried. "Take the noodles off the stove in eight minutes, drain the water, and serve. It'll be great." Her pursed lips and fanning hand suggested nothing would be great, but before Rick could say a word to stop her, she disappeared in a puff.

After removing the apron, he looked at his shirt—covered in tomato sauce—as another knock sounded. Rick ran a hand through strings of sweat-soaked hair and shuffled to the door.

Framed like a painting, Emily stood in the open doorway, and Rick's worries floated into the abyss. Throwing her free arm around his neck, she laid her lips on his cheek, and even after she pulled away, the soft memory of her touch remained. "May I?" she asked, nodding toward the interior.

"Yes, sorry," he mumbled, stepping aside.

"Oh, Rick, it's beautiful. It's the coziest room I've ever seen. The fireplace is huge. How old is this cottage?"

"It was built by Frances Barlow sometime in the mid-1800s." As he closed the door, Rick hoped he sounded casual rather than how he felt—teetering on the edge of madness. He studied Emily's face while her eyes roamed over every detail of his painfully private world. She was the first Liver to cross the threshold. Even Sandy Barlow, his mysterious employer, hadn't returned in a decade. Rick tried to imagine how the mismatch of a century and a half of other people's tastes must look to Emily's eyes. She likely attributed every rug, lamp, and painting to him, though, in truth, he'd added almost nothing to the décor. Yet it *was* very him as if the cottage and its contents had only waited for him to claim it.

"Are these your books?" She grabbed a hardcover from a teetering stack.

"Uh, yeah." Shifting uncomfortably, Rick watched as Emily flipped through the pages of *What in the Hell is the Cat Looking at—Fifty Tales of the Supernatural.*

She ran a finger along spines with titles such as *Parenting Tips for the Rebellious Poltergeist in Your Home* and *The Seven Stages of Grief—When Your Ghost Moves Out.* "It's funny—a cemetery caretaker reading about ghosts."

"What's in the bag?" he asked, desperate to divert her from his incriminating collection.

"Oh!" She pulled out a half-gallon of chocolate milk, her face painted with a happy grin. "Our favorite."

Our favorite. "I'll get some glasses." *Ours.* Rick sang the word in his head as he turned toward the kitchen. "Would you care to sit down?" Too formal.

"Thank you." Too polite.

He noticed that she sat not in a chair but on one of the couches. Stephanie had claimed that Emily's seating choice would demonstrate how "open" Emily was to how far things would go. But with untold witnesses, Rick knew precisely how far things would go—and how far they wouldn't. His heart skipped a beat at the thought while he poured two glasses, then anxiously sat on the opposite end of the couch. Feeling like a squatter in Stephanie's usual spot, Rick resisted the urge to twirl his hair as they made small talk about the weather, the bookstore, and the upcoming holidays.

Seemingly from nowhere, Emily asked where Rick would spend Christmas.

"Right here, where I've spent the last ten years."

Emily fell silent.

In a sudden panic, Rick sprang from the couch. "Uh, wait right here." He scrambled into the kitchen, the pungent odor of burnt pasta hanging in the air. With a peek into the smoking pot, his heart plummeted—nothing remained but a charred mess of burnt noodle-sticks. He might be the first person in history to have actually burned water. *Who serves spaghetti without noodles?*

"Dammit."

"What's wrong?" Emily called from the living room.

"Nothing!" Rick answered with a wobble, wishing for once that Madge would pop in unannounced and order him around. Maybe the meal wasn't a total loss. He poked at the blackened noodles with a pair of tongs—they were hard as a rock. Now what? He couldn't feed her rock-hard spaghetti with . . . oh no.

He lifted the lid on the sauce, and as he turned off the stove, his gut felt as hard as the blackened pasta. Where in the hell was Madge when he needed her—

"Rick?"

As Emily stood in the doorway, Rick knew there was

no covering it up now. "We, uh, might have to figure something else out for dinner."

"Maybe it can be saved." With one look into the pots, Emily cocked her head. "What do you have in the freezer?"

A shamefully high stack of TV dinners and a bag of frozen burritos stared blatantly back at her. "Meatloaf! My favorite!" Emily ushered Rick from his own kitchen, and he was so relieved to relinquish the responsibility that he gladly retreated. After stoking the fire, he quietly tucked the incriminating books into the bedroom.

Twenty minutes later, Emily set the table with placemats and cloth napkins Rick hadn't even known he owned. The dining room was instantly transformed. With added butter and sour cream, the warmed dinners looked nearly good enough for even the Witherbee crowd. While they dined, they compared their favorite classic movies. Emily liked the black and white romances, while Rick preferred a good old-fashioned Western. Hours flashed by—time had a funny way of slipping around Emily.

She started on the dishes while Rick tried in vain to scrape the cemented noodles from the pot. They talked while they worked in a seamless, natural stream. Working alongside Emily in what was essentially Rick's bachelor pad should have felt awkward. Instead, it felt as if she belonged there—that even the cottage felt more at ease in her presence.

After fishing a deck of cards from a drawer, they settled in while Emily wiped the floor with Rick in Rummy. As the night wore on, he glanced nervously at the clock, wishing she didn't have to go home.

Ever.

"These apples smell amazing," Emily said, leaning toward the fragrant basket. "Where did you get them?"

"There's an apple orchard behind Barlow Pond," Rick answered absently, trying to form a set of clubs. "I picked them at the end of September. They still seem good, though."

Emily plucked one from the basket and examined it. "They remind me of the apples that grew behind Grandfather's house."

Rick spotted a possible straight. "I'm pretty sure they're the same variety. Frank and I used to spend entire afternoons over there. He said it reminded him of home."

"Oh, did you know Grandfather before he died?"

"No, after. He used to say . . ." As the last syllable fell from Rick's lips, an odd sensation of disconnect raced as he relived the glaring declaration. He hoped she'd somehow missed it.

She hadn't.

"After . . ." Nearly a whisper. "*After* he died?"

"I . . ." Later, a thousand reasonable inventions swirled; Frank, a buddy from an old job. Frank, a friend from school. Frank, the sod delivery guy. Any Frank but hers. But, when it mattered, Rick's mind shut down.

Emily's brows furrowed and her face became painted in hurt. "You're mocking me."

Fantasy Rick, Thinking Rick, Better Rick, could have said, *I have so much to tell you*, but Actual Rick could only open and close his mouth like a fish out of water.

"You read my letters, and you're making fun of me. I thought . . ." The chair crashed as she rushed toward the door.

Rick's paralysis broke, and he hurried after her. "Emily, w-w-wait, I c-c-can explain."

As she snatched her coat, Emily slumped, and Rick hated the way she stared with her head cocked to one side as if she were trying to decide if she knew him from somewhere. "I need to go," she said as the light slipped from her eyes.

Panic, hard and furious, momentarily threw him, along with an odd fluttering in his chest. How could he possibly begin to explain? What words would make the truth sound reasonable and not the ramblings of a mad graveyard caretaker? "P-P-Please, listen to me," he begged without conviction. *Please.* "F-F-Frank . . ."

A worried Madge materialized. "What happened?"

Rick found his voice at the wrong moment. "J-Just what I need," he said, rubbing his forehead. "I should have known y-y-you wouldn't be able to s-s-stay away."

"What?" Emily stepped back, aghast.

"N-Not you." Rick climbed deeper into an ever-widening hole.

"Who are you talking to, then?" Glancing around apprehensively, Emily unknowingly pointed a finger directly at Madge. "Grandfather, I suppose?"

Rick blurted the truth, despite Madge's warnings and even his own gut. "I'm t-t-talking to Madge. She's standing next t-to you. You c-can't see her because she's d-d-dead." Hearing the stutter in his words, Rick sank even lower and gave in to his chair. He remembered those first days after he arrived at Serenity Grove. It hadn't been easy to accept the ghosts that spoke to him, followed him, and demanded his attention while his rational mind pretended they weren't there. He'd laughed the voices away and ignored their forms as they materialized and disappeared and kept right on proving their existence. And still, even he'd resisted.

How could he make Emily believe in people she could never lay eyes on, voices she could never hear?

He could see the wheels turning, her mind deciding. "I can't tell if you're insulting me or if you're crazy."

"N-Neither."

Everything—every speck of dust, every grain of wood in the cottage—stilled with her. Emily, the woman who believed wholeheartedly that her dead grandfather still existed—still *was*, in some form—held the truth of Rick Holliday within her grasp.

It occurred to him that in rejecting his truth, she'd be denying her own, and he decided to try swinging the cards in his favor. "The t-t-truth is that I can see and talk to the d-d-dead. At least those who've b-b-been buried here. Madge is one of them. F-Frank was another. That feeling that Frank was with you all those years . . . that was real, Em."

One by one, the others appeared. The women gathered around Emily while Herbert remained expressionless in the corner. Forming a semi-circle, Madge, Stephanie, and Taylor hovered near enough to warm her skin, had they any warmth to give.

Emily's gaze held a wariness—worse, a caution. "I see." Her voice trailed away, her words coated in a mixture of sympathy and discomfort that Rick knew well. More than that, she seemed on edge now, as if she'd just found herself locked in a room with someone two cards short of a full deck. "And they talk to you, these ghosts?" Her hand slid behind her back as she patted the door in search of the knob.

Rick's gut took a dive.

"I know how it s-s-sounds." The quake in his voice frustrated him, yet he forced himself onward. "I d-d-didn't believe it m-m-myself at first either, but yes, they t-talk to me and . . . Em, please don't."

A harsh wind blew through the open door, and Emily turned one last time. "I wish I could believe you. Maybe you're laughing at me, or maybe you really do think . . ." With a breath deeper than Rick thought humanly possible, she turned to face the cold, bitter night. "This is just too much."

"Emily . . ." A shudder sliced her name on his lips, and with it came such an overwhelming sense of helplessness, of utter loss, that it hurt to breathe.

"I'm sorry." Then, with a hesitation that gave him a brief sting of hope, she bit her lip.

"I hope you find happiness, Rick."

Their eyes met before she turned and closed the door with a hollow *click*.

Seconds stretched in the silence that followed until the muffled sound of her car speeding away crashed into his heart.

18

SAY HELLO TO THE GANG

Taylor had asked a question shortly after her arrival that, at the time, Rick had found difficult to answer.

But why can't you send messages to our families? Why can't you ask them questions for us?

It doesn't work that way, dear.

Taylor had spun, her sapphire hair flying. *But why? Am I the only one here who sees how cruel it is to leave people with questions he could easily answer?*

Rick had held his tongue, wanting the answer to that question himself. Why couldn't a person with his ability give people the closure they desperately needed?

Madge sighed. *It's complicated—*

It's not, though. Not when you really think about it. Taylor's lips had tightened.

The morning after the disastrous dinner, and with the closing of the door still echoing, Rick understood.

Sleep had come in fits, and when the sun finally rose after that long night, Rick abandoned all hope for rest and crawled out of bed. Cold encased the tiny house. He half-heartedly stoked a fire yet felt none of its warmth. Shuffling through the cottage, he barely registered the chill that jolted his bones. For once, he felt stifled within the walls that had hidden him from the world so well.

He needed to get out.

Plunging into the frost, he scurried to the comment box, unable to diminish his rising hope. With a trembling hand, he reached inside—empty. Hope melted into despair as gray skies mirrored his loss. The trees had lost color overnight, and the few remaining leaves had turned a dull, rotten brown. Passing tombstone after tombstone, he saw only symbols of death. Serenity Grove now represented endings, finality. Life had been banished from this place—as was the nature of graveyards.

As was the nature of Rick.

Pushing Emily from his mind was as impossible as drowning oneself. Too tired to fight himself, Rick wallowed. He should have been more careful. He could have said or done a thousand things once the blunder had been made. Instead, he'd stammered like the fool he was, unable to do more than to stare with horror as she'd walked out of his life, thinking him crazy, cruel—and he'd done nothing to defend himself.

Lost in the mire of his self-flagellating thoughts, Rick found himself standing over Frank's grave with no memory of how he'd gotten there. Unable to hold back a bitter smile, he grunted.

Of course. All paths led to the man whose bones lay six feet beneath the frozen earth. Frank had been a kind man, a wise man, a man who surely would have wanted better for his beloved Em. Why had Rick let himself believe he was good enough for her?

The idea occurred that he might actually be crazy. Could he really see and speak to the dead, or was it all in his head? His sight wavered as he sank to his knees, the icy ground sending a shock through his bones. He brushed the tombstone of the greatest man he'd ever known.

He did not know how long he wept.

———

FOR THREE DAYS, RICK SULKED.

At times, he nearly convinced himself that he'd never been enchanted by Emily in the first place, that he'd been happy floating through life solo. He'd always been a man of simplicity, and she had only complicated things.

Invariably, he drifted back into his gloomy thoughts. He'd had a shot at something good, and now that he'd had a taste, he found it impossible to envision even a second without her. She'd stumbled into his world, bringing light, and now that it had been extinguished, the darkness sank to a new depth. That the others avoided him only solidified the growing knowledge that he, alone, was to blame.

The rumble in his stomach made him nauseous. The idea of nourishment seemed preposterous. His freezer was filled with the same dinner they'd shared, and the thought of replicating even a moment from that night filled him with a kind of panicked madness. With each passing minute, Emily felt further away, as if she'd driven away from the cemetery and kept on going.

The wind shifted, closing in on him like chilly walls, and

the bitter cold bit through his skin—even the thickest coat couldn't warm him. Was this what love was? Pain, sorrow, regret? Or was this what remained when love broke you?

Echoes of her final words bounced in his head. *I hope you find happiness, Rick.*

With the bitter knowledge that there was no foreseeable solution, his face fell into his hands. As night closed on another day, the darkness deepened in his heart.

DRUMBEATS, FROM FAR AWAY.

One eye opened, then the other. More drumbeats. Rick bolted from the chair as he recognized the sound.

Someone was knocking.

"He's waking up! He can still catch her!"

Rick's head spun in time to see Madge and Stephanie race in from the bedroom. "What's g-going on?" His sleeping brain fully awakened, readying him for escape.

"She's here! Answer the door!" Stephanie turned in a circle, shifting her weight from one foot to another.

"Who . . ." And then, "Emily?"

"Oh, my God."

Rick rushed to the window, momentarily blinded by daylight. Blonde hair swayed as Emily trudged back toward the gate, the sight lighting a fire inside Rick so intense that a pain shot down his arm.

On the path, Taylor waved her arms, screeching, "Stop!"

Emily trudged on, her head low.

"Rick! Get out here!"

His sense returned like a slap, and he threw open the

door. "Em." Her name croaked off of his tongue as his throat tightened. Forcing air into his lungs, he tried again. "Em!"

She stopped. Turned. Not a word was spoken. Not in this world, not in the Next. Time, a funny thing already, wound in another direction, doubled back on itself, and sped onward. Emily scrutinized him. Was she searching for the truth? Or was she trying to peer beneath the man she thought she knew, only to find a madman? *Was* he a madman? He'd questioned it a hundred times.

"I . . ." Her jaw slackened, and whatever she was struggling to say died. She seemed at war with herself, a condition Rick understood more than most.

Seeing Emily on familiar ground, an odd, uncharacteristic calmness washed over him. "I'll answer all your questions. Can you come inside?"

Hesitation. Which side was winning? She could leave forever, never step foot within the cemetery walls again. Or she could hear him out. What he would say was still a mystery, even to Rick, but a shot was all he could ask for.

"Alright."

For the first time in days, Rick smiled.

EMILY REMAINED CLOSE TO THE DOOR CLINGING TO HER bag as if she'd strayed too close to a purse-snatcher. The sight sent a fresh wave of nausea over Rick. She'd undoubtedly come to say goodbye. The idea that she'd been prepared to give him another chance had been a fool's dream. His breath came in panting bursts as the residents gathered close. Keeping them away would have been impossible, not only because he couldn't physically push them out the door but because his fate seemed every bit as important to them as it did to him.

Thud.

Emily's bag dropped to the floor, and she rushed to him, throwing herself into his arms. Gripping him tight, she sobbed into his shoulder. "I tried not to believe that you could talk to him. But he really was there all those years, wasn't he? Just like I knew he was." Her body heaved as she wept, and after a long moment, she pulled back. "Is he here now? In this room with us?" Her eyes wavered with promise as she scanned the cottage interior.

Realization dawned. Rick could let her go on believing Frank was still here. Hell, he knew Frank well enough to emulate what Frank would have said. Rick, or Frank —*Frick*—could tell her how proud he'd been and instantly wipe away her sadness. Frick held the power to fix everything. Rick saw with perfect clarity the two of them enjoying a lazy afternoon on the banks of Barlow Pond, *talking* to Frank. Emily would be happy again, and they could live their lives right here, never leaving the comfort of the graveyard.

If you were still alive, would you want to be summoned here?

No, I guess I wouldn't.

Madge's words echoed, jolting Rick's nerves like a spark of lightning, and, with a sinking gut, he knew that he couldn't sentence Emily to that fate.

And so, Rick Holliday, a man who'd been discarded by the living and left to a lifetime of fending for himself, set his own desires aside for the first time to right a horrible wrong.

Ever so gently, he pulled back from Emily's sweet embrace. Searching her eyes, so full of want, he dreaded his own words. "Frank isn't here anymore."

Confusion swept in, and Rick wished he'd driven past the Caretaker Wanted sign that day to whatever else life had in store for him. Too much power was crushing for a man so inadequate.

"But . . ." She disconnected from his arms as if he'd slapped her. "You said you could talk to him—"

"I did. When Frank was here. But he's gone, Emily. I can talk to the ones who are still here, but no one stays forever."

With her back resting against the door, she slumped and buried her face in her hands. "I don't understand." Her muffled whisper felt like a blade against his skin. She refused to meet his eyes, and it gutted him. "Is this all a sick game?"

"Rick," Taylor said, stepping between them, "I can help."

And then he saw it.

Taylor pulled the Mr. Microphone from behind her back and swung it. "Don't ask what I had to do to get it."

———

"ARE YOU SURE YOU DON'T WANT ONE OF US TO DO IT?" Madge asked. "You're so soft-spoken."

Taylor clutched the nerf-topped microphone, her expression vacillating between terrified and hesitant before finally turning to resolve. "I can be heard. I know I can."

Emily followed Rick's gaze to the seemingly empty

space between them. "What are you staring at?" A simple question with so many complicated answers.

Rick took a tentative step. "If you want to end this now, you can leave, and I won't bother you when you visit Frank. He's gone, Emily, but there are others here. If there's any part of you that wants to give this . . . give *us* a chance, let me prove it." Taking her hands, he allowed himself a pinprick of hope when she didn't pull away.

Madge wiped a hand across her brow. "So hot in here—"

Emily's gaze wavered, her inner struggle evident.

"She's thinking about it." Stephanie moved close to Emily's ear. "Please, say yes."

Stronger than ever, the aroma of apples arose so abruptly powerful that the scent nearly knocked Rick off balance, and Emily stumbled back with a blink. That odd sense of something else at work emanated, and Rick hoped that, for once, things would work in his favor.

Emily gently pulled her hands away. "Okay, prove it."

He should have been relieved. Instead, Rick felt as if he'd just decided to storm the castle with a butter knife.

"Oh, my God, plug your ears, Rick."

Rick reached for the coatrack and fished a pair of earplugs from his jacket as Taylor held the machine to Emily's ear, bringing the microphone to her lips.

"I'm ready."

Rick pushed the earplugs in as the others scurried to the kitchen. "There's only one resident with us now. She's our most recent. Her name is Taylor."

Emily took an unsteady step back. "Taylor Jenkins? The girl who died in that terrible accident a few weeks ago?"

Before Rick could answer, Taylor flicked the switch on the microphone. Then, inching close, she took a breath.

"I BROKE MRS. CLAUSSEN'S CHAIR IN THE FIFTH GRADE, AND YOU TOOK THE BLAME."

Emily stumbled further back, and her hands flew to her mouth.

Rick turned, more than a bit alarmed. "Wait. Do you know each other?"

Taylor's cobalt hair flitted around the soft curvature of her face. "I INVITED YOU TO MY TWELFTH BIRTHDAY PARTY, AND YOU NEVER SHOWED UP."

Emily's head swiveled. Though Rick knew she couldn't see Taylor, Emily unknowingly stared directly at her. "I never . . . you never invited me—"

"I WENT TO YOUR HOUSE, AND SOME OLDER BOY SAID HE WAS GOING TO GIVE YOU THE INVITATION."

"I never . . . he never gave me anything!" Emily's hands moved toward Taylor's voice, exploring the air. "I never got an invitation. My brother must have . . . Rick, is this really happening?"

Rick couldn't decide if he should be angry, relieved, or both. Why had Taylor not mentioned this before? "Emily, I honestly don't know what's going on. Taylor, why don't you put down the mic for a second. Your screaming is giving me a headache, and I'm just about worn out."

"Screaming? I just hear whispering."

Emily seemed rooted to the spot, the bewilderment on her face mirroring his own. After a moment, Rick grasped her hand and haltingly moved her away from the door. Her outstretched hands groped the air as if she were walking a plank blindfolded. She half-bent at the couch, then stopped with a wince. "I'm not going to sit on her, am I?"

"You're fine. Taylor's on the other couch."

Emily lowered, checking behind her while she glanced nervously around as if expecting her dead friend to pop out and yell *surprise*! "Taylor?" Emily's voice wavered as she turned to Rick. "Is she still here?"

"She is."

Emily's lip quivered as a single tear rolled. "Taylor, I was so sorry to hear what had happened. I can't believe . . . Rick, I don't know what to say."

Still unsure where this was going, Rick waited for Emily to settle her nerves. Her next response would tell him everything. She could blindly accept this new reality or think of a thousand ways this was all some sort of trickery.

"So . . . Grandfather isn't here?" Emily asked.

Rick hadn't expected *that*. He cleared his throat. "He was, but not now."

She wrung her hands. "What happened to him? Did he leave? Because of me?" Her voice cracked on the last word. How long had it been since she'd blinked?

Everything he'd wished he could tell her was now a possibility. He no longer had to hide the truth as he watched her writhe in grief. Yet the truth would also dash her hope. Her grandfather was gone. Forever. The bitter irony of it made Rick grimace. "He moved on. From here to the Next."

"I thought once you were . . . you know . . . *that* was moving on."

So does everyone.

"When a person dies, they come here, or wherever

they're buried, and they wait to be sent to the afterlife. That's what happened with Frank. He moved on six, maybe seven weeks ago."

Emily stared into the fire. Rick didn't know if that was a sign of shock, but it didn't seem good. "I don't understand. Where is that? I thought this was the afterlife. I mean, the cemetery . . ." Drifting, drifting, her voice petered out like a receding wave.

Rick retook her hand and gently turned her face to him. She seemed so far away—too far. All that mattered was bringing her back, centering her to him. "There's a lot we don't understand. What I can tell you is that Frank was glad that you quit the library. I'd say he was pretty relieved. He knew you weren't happy there. He was so very proud of you, Emily."

"I . . . never told you about the library." She blinked, and Rick released a breath he didn't know he'd been holding. "Grandfather really said that?"

"Yes."

Emily's eyes darted furiously. "How many gh . . . people live in here?"

"They don't live here, not in the cottage, but they visit. There are four altogether."

Madge tentatively stepped into the room. "TELL HER HELLO FROM US, DEAR!"

"Oh, my God, tell her I said hi, too! HI EMILY!" Waving with both hands, Stephanie bounced on her toes.

"Uh, Madge and Stephanie say hello."

Emily looked at the ceiling, the fireplace, and the door. "Where is everyone? Why can't I hear them like I heard Taylor?"

Rick wanted this to go slower, to feed her information

in smaller doses. "Taylor was using a special instrument. Without it, you can't hear them."

"What kind of instrument?"

He hesitated. "It's . . . a tricked-out Mr. Microphone." He'd never had to say it out loud before.

"You mean those things from those old seventies commercials? Like a karaoke machine?"

"Sort of."

"Well, that's . . . wait." She peeked around the room. "Tell me again, Rick. Who's in the room with us? I want to know."

"We have Taylor, Madge, and Stephanie. Herbert is . . . I don't know where Herbert is."

"He's otherwise occupied," Madge said with an impish grin.

Emily stood, then immediately sat back down. "I'm afraid of running into someone."

Rick turned to the others. "Can everyone sit?" The residents scrambled to their usual places, except Stephanie, who took Rick's chair. "Everyone's out of the way now."

As Emily paced at the fire, Madge tucked her feet under while Taylor scrunched on a couch. "I have so many questions, but first, I need to say something." She turned from the fire. "I'm so happy to meet all of you. I can feel . . . *something*. I'm not sure what it is. It's not like how it was with Grandfather. It's more subtle."

Rick surveyed every inch of her, the way she stood statue-like, the curve at the corners of her mouth. It all seemed too easy. But was it? After all, this wasn't her first rodeo with the dead. In his way, Frank had prepared Emily for this first real confirmation that it hadn't all been the fanciful imaginings of a girl in mourning. "Sit down, Em, please." Rick patted the cushion beside him as an idea suddenly flashed. "I want to run you through an intake."

For the next several hours, Rick kept a steady stream of words flowing, stopping only to answer her occasional questions. Emily's eyes gradually became less wide, her breathing slowed, and blinking no longer seemed to be an issue.

Ah, dammit.

"We're gonna see some action tonight!" Herbert said as he swung from the chandelier. He looked around at the packed room. "You're all perverts. I knew it."

"Sit down and shut the hell up, Herb!" Madge stunned them all into silence. "I won't have our Emily spoken of in such a vile manner."

Our Emily.

Without another word, Herbert dropped and scurried to the corner.

"Rick, you look so tired."

The sun disappeared behind the western hills, and he stifled a yawn. Barely able to hold his eyes open, a weak smile was all he could offer. "I am."

Emily planted a kiss on his cheek before turning to the room. "I'd like to talk to you all tomorrow if it's alright."

"TELL EMILY WE WOULD LOVE THAT, DEAR!"

"Oh, my God, stop yelling. She's not deaf, just alive."

"And Taylor, I wish . . . I just wish I could hug you," Emily said.

Taylor turned to the window, her shoulders drooping.

"Can you walk me to my car?" As Emily gathered her coat and bag, she waved to the seemingly empty room. All but Herbert enthusiastically returned the gesture. Emily and Rick plunged into the cold night, and the shock roused him as if the past few hours had merely been a dream. He gladly took her hand when she offered it, squeezing hard.

At the gate, she wrapped her arms around him. "I'm sorry I didn't believe you."

Pulling back, Rick took in the sight of her. Her mouth was drawn, her eyes puffy and heavy-lidded. "Emily, I'm still trying to fathom that you *do* believe me."

She frowned. "Can you forgive me?"

He kissed her cheek. "There's nothing to forgive," he said, pulling away as he glanced toward the cottage. "By the way, they're outside watching us now."

Even though her exhaustion was evident, she managed a smile. "I don't care."

And the prom queen and the undertaker cowboy held one another as the first snowflake fell.

19

SEAN MCFADDEN DAY

Rick slept little, his mind refusing to wind down. What if Emily had come to her senses in the night and realized how ridiculous it had all been? He couldn't shake the recurring feeling that it had all been too easy, that she'd been remarkably accepting.

With no clue why, Rick raced to the door and found Emily waiting at the comment box, waving, the tips of her fingers caressing the air.

She came back.

"Are you rested? I have so many questions." Her smile warmed Rick like a flame as she entwined her wrists at his neck. "We could walk through the cemetery if you'd like."

Rick lifted his gaze to the Oregon sky, where clouds darkened the horizon. "How about we go inside, and I'll get the fire going?"

Emily wrapped her hand around his. "Let's get warmed up."

Rick built up the fire while Emily found two champagne flutes in the kitchen and filled them with chocolate milk. Rick joined her on the couch as her gaze flitted around the empty room.

"It feels kind of weird to do anything here, knowing . . . you know."

"Try taking a shower in this place."

Emily shuddered. "I guess you don't have any real privacy, do you?"

He laughed. "Not for a long time."

She curled against his shoulder while he threw an arm over hers, and the two of them lay quietly, warming one another. After a while, Emily broke the silence. "I feel bad."

Rick felt the sudden tension in her shoulders. "About what?"

"Taylor. She tried to be my friend, and I missed it. She must have thought I was snubbing her all those years."

Rick pulled back. "Is that what you wanted to talk about?"

"That, and some other things. I couldn't sleep. This whole thing is still pretty confusing."

"What we need is some lunch. I can't talk about dead people on an empty stomach. How about we try to rustle something up?"

"Sounds great," Emily said casually enough, though he couldn't help noticing her darting eyes.

"I'll tell you when someone shows up."

Her smile softened. "Thank you."

Together they perused the cupboards, which Rick had thought bare, but Emily spotted a dozen recipes in the making. He led her to the cellar, where she gathered jars of preserves, canned meats, and bags of flour. After hauling their supplies upstairs to the kitchen, Emily firmly ushered

Rick from the kitchen. Settling in at the table with the basket of still-fresh apples before him, Rick watched contentedly as Emily worked.

"Can you always see them?" Emily beat an egg into a bowl. "I mean, can they make themselves invisible?"

Rick watched her body glide beneath her long skirt. "As far as I know, they can't, but they don't tell me everything." Recalling Madge's recent remark about his dressing habits, he shuddered.

"Like what?" she asked.

"I don't know much about the other place they go. Heck, they can't even seem to agree on which direction it is." As the fire warmed, he followed her soft, measured steps. He watched her face stiffen with focus before melting into satisfaction as she placed a buttered pan on the stove. *I could get used to this.*

"And the only people that can be . . . I think you called them residents?"

"Yup."

"The only residents are people who were buried here at Serenity Grove? So, wherever they're buried, they stay there until they go to whatever's Next?"

"That's right." Rick took in the aroma of melting butter. "And caretakers. We have a special spot."

Falling quiet, Emily stirred the butter. After an apparent struggle, she asked, "But what happens to people that don't get buried anywhere?"

"What do you mean?"

"What about people who fall off mountains, get lost in caves, or die in plane crashes? The ones who never get buried?" Concern fogged her face. "Do they just wander the scene of their death until they go where Grandfather went?"

Rick had no answer for that. What *did* happen to people who just disappeared? The thought of becoming a forever wandering soul brought a hand to his chest.

"I can help with that, dear," Madge said, poking her head in from the bedroom.

Rick sighed. "Madge wants to come in. Well, she's already here."

"Hi, Madge!" Emily called from the kitchen. "How are you today?"

Madge's face broke into a gleeful smile. "I'm good, thank you, dear!" She took a seat beside Rick. "Oh, Rick, I do just love her."

"I know you do, and really, you c-can stop yelling." Rick covered his ears, smiling comically while he translated. "What's on your m-mind, Madge?"

Madge leaned close. "About the unburied ones. I don't want our poor Emily walking around with morbid questions like that unanswered."

Seemingly unbothered by Rick's one-way conversation, Emily carried two plates of fried eggs and sautéed apples to the table. "Where can I sit?"

"Do you mind sitting next to Madge so I can see you both without breaking my neck?"

"Of course." Emily sat where Rick pointed and dug in while he turned his attention to their ghostly visitor.

Madge painted a picture of a place where the unburied souls went, a place Rick found too complex to imagine, even with Madge's vivid descriptions of soft, whispering rivers, ever-blue skies, and a perpetually orange sun. Time was determined by wounds, both physical and otherwise.

The more healing needed, the longer they remained among the green valleys and flower-filled meadows. Animals roamed this mystical place, moving from one soul to the next, giving comfort and draining sorrow from the over-wrought.

Rick wondered aloud how Madge knew, with such clarity, that such a place existed. A gray smile coated her lips. "Some people are sent there for healing before rejoining their bodies." She would say no more, so Rick did his best to relay the story.

Emily swallowed hard and rose. "Excuse me," she said as she rushed to the bathroom.

Rick groaned. He should have lightened up the descriptions and left out some details. He'd had ten years to get used to the idea of a life after death, and Madge's truth had shaken even him a bit. They waited in silence until Emily returned, dabbing at her eyes.

"Rick, tell her I'm sorry. I didn't mean to upset her."

Before he could, Emily spoke. "Thank you so much, Madge. It's beautiful." A smile brightened her face as she sat. "Don't you see, Rick? It's the Garden of Eden."

He stared, stunned. "Is it t-t-true, Madge? Is it really the Garden of Eden?"

"Let's just say that there's some truth in everything," she answered, dispirited.

Madge answered Emily's never-ending stream of questions. Though on some subjects, she gave only vague answers. Rick kept a close eye as he translated, relieved that much of it seemed to put Emily at ease. Rick wondered if she were a religious person. Did the information conflict with or cement her ideas of life after death? Rick had never attended a church service or cracked open a Bible from any faith. For the first time, he found himself questioning his own preconceived notions. It seemed that the living world had it both incredibly wrong and remarkably right.

From the other side of the door, a throat cleared. "Uh, hey."

Rick cautiously opened the door, surprised to find Taylor standing in the rain.

"Are you guys . . . um, busy?" Taylor peered into the cottage with an odd timidity. "I didn't want to, you know, intrude."

Embarrassed, Rick moved aside. "Em, Taylor's here."

"Oh, Taylor! Come sit with me. I have so much to ask you." Emily flew to the couch and patted the cushion beside her.

Taylor hesitantly joined her. "Rick, can you, you know, translate for us?"

"I've been d-d-doing it all afternoon."

Emily's face twisted in grief. "I'm so sorry about what happened."

"Thanks, it's not so bad now."

Through Rick, the two women who'd missed their first chance at friendship made up for lost time. They relived memories of their school days, recalling shared yet separate experiences with the same teachers from the same lonely outer view. It seemed Taylor had been yet another unseen member of the Outcast Club of Hood Valley. Her revelations shamed Rick. Why didn't he know her? Why hadn't he taken the time?

Why didn't he know any of them?

"So, you really didn't get my invitation?"

"I asked my brother last night, and he said he couldn't

remember anyone bringing one. But that was ten years ago." Emily sat straighter. "But we can still have a party! We can have one right here, can't we, Rick?"

"We already have one coming up," Madge said, scurrying in from the dining room. "Sean McFadden Day is fast approaching. Goodness, things have been so crazy I forgot all about it. I have so much planning to do."

Emily turned to Rick. "What's going on? You're quiet, and your head keeps turning."

"It seems you've been invited to participate in some festivities. I'll explain later. Right now, I'd like some alone time with my g-girl." He gently shooed the reluctant dead from the cottage.

After they'd all gone, Rick joined Emily on the couch.

"I like your friends, but it's nice when it's just us." She covered his hand with her own.

His desire for privacy turned to anxiety. Surely he was supposed to kiss Emily *now*—should probably have kissed her ages ago. Yet he found himself wishing for an interruption. Even an appearance by the lamp-humping Herbert would be a relief. The thought that Herbert could save Rick from a simple kiss sent his already overworked brain into a tailspin. *Just kiss her. They do it in movies all the time. Close your eyes, lean forward, and—*

"How do you know we're really alone, though?" Emily's smooth, lyrical words squashed Rick's near-bravery and gave him the out he'd been looking for.

"I don't." He meant it.

She squeezed his hand and smiled. "Then we should . . . shouldn't . . . I don't know . . ." Her body language affirmed that Rick might not have been the only one adding dates and subtracting first kisses.

Perhaps he wasn't alone in feeling like they'd just lucked into an eleventh-hour reprieve.

OVER THE WEEK THAT FOLLOWED, EMILY MADE NIGHTLY visits to the cemetery. Rick led her to Barlow Pond, through the sweet, sharp pine grove, and stood quietly with her at the precipice above the valley floor. As he guided her to each resident's grave, she spoke to their tombstones. "I know you're not here, but it's the only representation I have of you." Emily relayed how much she looked forward to meeting each of them one day.

Rick kept to himself the glimpses he caught of the residents hovering behind trees, watching, listening.

Some days, the residents walked with them. On other days, they were left in peace. In the hours without her, Rick felt lost. He was unsure what to do or how to exist in her glaring absence. A decade of routine blew away with the breeze as he wandered the cottage, obsessively checking clocks and counting down the hours to Emily's next visit—to the next time he could breathe. His heart hurt, and an unfamiliar tightness in his chest brought on helpless moans. The only solution was to go to bed early to hurry the arrival of the next day.

Rick wasn't the only soul disrupted by her absence. For the residents, Emily had become a vital connection with the living world that Rick, in his quiet maleness, couldn't provide. Even the cemetery seemed to deflate when she climbed into her car each night and drove away.

One chilly afternoon, Rick and Emily strolled the gravel path toward Frank's grave. Having fallen into a repetitive pattern, Rick hadn't realized she'd stopped until he was yanked back.

"What's wrong?"

With a strange mixture of relief and finality, she smiled. "He's not here. I have him in my heart, and that's where I look now when I miss him."

Although Rick knew that in some way, Emily would probably always grieve for Frank, at least now she was at peace. That night, as he put out the last of the fire and laid his head on his favorite pillow, he began to see that Emily was fast becoming more than just his girl. She wasn't merely a woman with whom he spent pleasant afternoons. He could deny it no longer.

Rick was falling in love.

———

THE RESIDENTS WERE IN HIGH SPIRITS—SO TO SPEAK. According to the others, Madge had locked herself in her kitchen, creating dishes no one could enjoy. Stephanie covered her grave in waves of pink, purple and white crepe and strung Christmas lights around the perimeter. Taylor tied limp balloons to her tombstone, complaining that no one had thought to die with a helium tank in their possession. Herbert swung from the dead elm that gave his resting place a sufficiently un-robbable air and sang an ear-splitting rendition of the official song of Sean McFadden Day: *Mine Eyes Have Been Closed to My Body.*

Emily arrived with enough decorations to open her own party supply store, the trunk of her car filled with shopping bags and four boxes marked *party decor.* Rick helped unload the car, and Emily fell immediately to work.

She hauled out an endless array of streamers, signs, and favors, reminding him of the time he'd gone to the circus, and the stereotypical forty clowns had climbed from a Volkswagen. A large, hand-painted banner read, "HAPPY SEAN MCFADDEN DAY!" She'd even drawn green shamrocks, the Irish flag, and a symbol Rick didn't recognize.

"What's this?"

"It's the McFadden family crest. I googled it." She winked, and it was all Rick could do not to sweep her into his arms, watchers be damned. "Do you think they'll mind that I brought all this stuff? I know you said they decorate too, but I can't see what they put up, and I want to feel like I'm celebrating along with them. By the way, you haven't told me who Sean McFadden is. I'm dyin . . . er, curious to hear the story."

Rick smiled. "All in good time. To tell you the truth, it's a bit morbid, and I'm not exactly comfortable with the whole thing."

Emily raised a brow. "Now you've really got my interest."

The next hour was a flurry of activity. Racing through the cemetery, Emily decorated paths and added decor to every resident's resting place except Herbert's.

"Trust me," Rick warned, "he doesn't want anyone near his grave."

"Quiet, jackass," Herbert muttered from a nearby oak. "If that young lady did a little dance for me, maybe I wouldn't mind." Cackling, Herbert humped the air, and Rick ushered Emily back to the main path, overcome with an irrational desire to cover her eyes.

The night was bitterly cold, and Rick draped one

blanket over Emily's shoulders while laying another on a small stretch of grass. She opened the picnic basket. "Tell me now, Rick. Please?"

The festivities began with an old Irish tune only Rick could hear, and an odd sense of aloneness swept in as he realized Emily would be left out. While he described the music, he suddenly wanted—*needed*—to share this part of his world.

Far wiser than he, Emily lifted her cell phone, hit a button, and transformed the mood with Celtic music.

"You think of everything." He planted a firm peck on her cheek, then wondered what would happen if he moved his lips just a little to the left . . .

"Now, tell me about Sean McFadden, and don't you dare leave out a single gory detail."

Kiss-crisis averted, Rick leaned back on his elbows. "Sean McFadden invented a casket lining that prevents the newly dead from . . . uh . . . peeking into their own coffins. Apparently, it's difficult to resist, and when their bodies are still decomposing—"

"Say no more. Goodness." Emily shuddered, pulling the blanket tight around her.

"I told you it was morbid."

Emily's gaze lingered on the trees. "No, not when you think about it. No one thinks about them after they're gone. No wonder they celebrate him."

After stuffing themselves with sandwiches, pies, and chocolate milk, they joined the celebration. Emily danced the perimeter of each grave, careful not to step on the grass that covered the residents' bones. Rick danced, too, inventing his own moves. He stepped back occasionally, claiming the need to catch his breath. In truth, he just wanted to watch her. The residents danced alongside the Livers, Madge tapping her feet while Stephanie twirled, snapped, and swiveled her hips. Even Taylor mimicked Emily's movements, her laughter echoing in the chilly night air.

As a full moon lit the sky, Emily grabbed Rick's hands. "Let's visit Herbert. We can't leave him out—"

Rick shook his head. "He won't want us there. Least of all me." And yet, she pulled him along, and as they rounded the elm, the old man shrieked with rage.

"What the hell, Rick? Can't a man dance on his own grave in peace? Why aren't you patrolling the grounds? I'll tell you something, you little shit, at the next meeting . . ." His weathered, crackly voice trailed off as Emily pressed a button on her phone. She played not the Irish tunes that had been the night's theme but a mournful Elvis love song. Herbert stopped in his tracks. Emily began a slow waltz, golden hair caught in the moonlight as her long skirt swished. Humming along, she swept her arms from side to side, gliding in the dark.

"Rick," Herbert whispered, his voice suddenly rough, "ask her how she knew."

"Knew what?"

"Just ask her, jackass."

Rick did.

Emily whirled and continued her slow, mournful dance. "I looked up Herbert's obit. It mentioned this song."

Rick glanced up in time to see Herbert's purposeful approach. Though he knew Herbert couldn't touch her, just seeing him walk that way put Rick's hackles on end. As Emily twirled, Herbert moved to the center of his plot, and the warning in Rick's heart gave way to amazement.

There was no mistaking it—a single tear trickled down the old man's hardened cheek.

"I danced to this song on my wedding day," Herbert breathed, watching as Emily swirled around his tombstone. "Edith. My Edith."

Rick was dumbstruck. Heck, he hadn't even known Herbert had been married, always assuming the old man's bachelorhood; he'd never said otherwise.

"Listen, punk. I'm gonna ask you something, and you better not say a word to anyone."

"I promise," Rick said, with complete honesty, as Emily made a second round.

"Can you . . . can you ask her to dance with me?" Refusing eye contact, Herbert seemed abashed at his own request.

Rick was so touched that he immediately complied.

Emily stopped, her expression serious. "I would be honored." She extended a hand, palm up, toward the long-dead man. After a pause, Herbert's hand passed through hers, yet she moved forward as if pulled. Her arms rose, awaiting her partner. "I believe the gentleman leads." After a quick warning glare in Rick's direction, Herbert put his hands to hers. They moved in unison like two living, breathing people. One hand hovered against her hip while the other appeared to grasp hers. They were so well coordinated, Herbert matching Emily's movements so precisely, that Rick had difficulty comprehending that they weren't touching.

Herbert, the man who seemed hell-bent on making everyone miserable, who floated through death as if he'd never had an ounce of humanity, began to hum. He moved like Gene Kelly as the moonlight illuminated his frail body. For the first time, Rick looked at his nemesis with something close to awe.

At the song's conclusion, Emily bowed to her invisible partner. "Thank you for the dance. Happy Sean McFadden Day." She pressed a button on her phone. "I've got the song on auto-repeat. I'll be back later to pick it up."

The music began again, and Emily joined Rick at the path. "I could use a rest." A wisp of blonde hair fell, and she absently tucked it behind her ear. Rick found himself leaning forward. The moment was *now*.

". . .the kid would have done it for two . . ." Herbert whispered as he swayed, his arms lifted as if he still had a partner.

Or remembered another.

This is his moment, not ours. Rick pulled back, an action far more difficult than he'd expected, and wrapped his girl's hand in his.

They turned toward the path, leaving Herbert alone with the memory of someone gone but not forgotten.

———

"Was he happy?"

Rick scooted across the blanket. "I don't know if there's a proper word to describe it, but yes, I'd say he was happy."

Emily brought her hands together. "I wasn't sure about him based on what you told me, but I'm glad." She briskly slid her hands over her skin as the night air grew colder.

Rick's stomach flopped. For once, it wasn't anxiety that sent fire coursing through his veins, lighting his blood to a boil. This time, it was certainty.

Decisiveness.

As if he were witnessing the actions of some other caretaker in some other cemetery, Rick reached out, and his hand looked somehow disembodied. The hand—*his* hand—touched Emily's shoulder and gently pulled her close. He felt her breath on his lips, soft and warm, like a butterfly's flutter, while her eyes, so blue they matched the spring sky, met his. Locked in each other's gaze, neither moved, neither spoke. He paused to cement this final moment before everything would inevitably change, and, capturing the memory, he filed it away before a single word pushed forward.

Now.

He'd always wondered why people closed their eyes, but now, as his lips met hers, he couldn't have kept them open if he'd tried. Emily inhaled sharply before pressing her lips into his. Had she been waiting, warring with herself as he had? It didn't matter now. All that mattered was this touch, this night. He ran his hands through her soft, silky hair and moaned. A momentary tremble gave way to ease. Why didn't people talk about kissing the way they gushed over other things? He could do this forever.

Pulling back, he rested his forehead on hers and said something he never thought he'd hear from his own lips. "I love you."

She said nothing, and instantly, he knew he'd overstepped. She didn't share the sentiment. How could she? She barely knew him. He wished he could take the words back. He shouldn't—

"I love you too, Rick." She placed a cold hand against his cheek. "I think I loved you from the moment I saw you hiding behind those bushes."

Rick was surprised by his own laugh, and he lifted her chin. "Do you, uh, need to go home tonight? This party will be going on for a while."

Emily left him no time to regret his words. She smiled, grabbed his hands, and said, "I could have a sleepover if that's what you're asking." She bit her lip.

He stood. "I'm asking."

Emily slid her arms around his neck and kissed him so deeply that it ached.

Not knowing he would do it until he did, Rick gathered her into his arms and carried her into the cottage. Inside, he set her gently on her feet and closed the door as Irish music filled the night.

20

THANKS, BUT NO THANKS

They spent the day in the cottage, neither willing nor able to leave the other's side as a storm crashed against the house. Emily made breakfast while Rick cleaned; he could do *that* much. She flipped through his collection of Bob Hope movies while Rick kept the fire stoked. Engrossed in one another, they spent an hour simply staring out the window as the pines groaned and swayed—tumultuous outside, calm inside. No residents disturbed them, leaving the Livers in peace.

Movies had taught Rick that relationships were about trouble and heartache. About trips to the mall, fabric stores, and art galleries. Not to mention the fights, the tears, and forced to wear pressed khakis. He'd thought it was about losing himself to another person, giving up who he was, and spending his life being told when to speak, where to stand, and what to think. But as he ran his fingers through Emily's hair, he realized he'd missed out on living entirely. Sean McFadden Day had marked the end of one life, and overnight he'd begun living in a world without loneliness or despair. Only weeks before, the residents under his care had been all the human contact he'd needed —and even they had been more than he'd wanted.

Emily suddenly grabbed his hands, breaching the quiet. "I'd like you to come over for Christmas dinner. I want you to meet my mom and brother, and I want them to get to know you now that we've . . . you know."

Rick's throat squeezed, and sweat coated his palms. Frank had been kind enough and had probably cared for Rick. But the rest of her family? Her mother and brother wouldn't see him the way Emily did. To them, Rick would be little more than a lowly caretaker who hadn't figured out how to dress non-homelessy. He had nothing to offer and couldn't hold a proper conversation. And regardless of Emily's feelings for him, they'd see him as he was—not good enough for her.

Even as her hands twisted in waiting, he knew he could never agree. Rick wanted to be with Emily on his terms, in his world. There existed between them an unspoken agreement, and here she was, trying to drag him from his comfort zone.

Nope.

He prepared to refuse this beautiful creature who wanted to share her life the same way he'd begun to share his.

Thanks, but no thanks.

Echoes of thirty years of solitude, some of them self-imposed, most not, dug beneath his skin. No, absolutely not. There was no way he would meet her family. She would be upset, but she'd get over it, eventually.

Rick prepared to let her down in the easiest way possible.

"Th-Th-Thank you. What t-time should I b-b-be there?"

———

HE AWOKE DISORIENTED. WHAT TIME WAS IT? WHAT DAY was it? Snow gathered at the windows as tiny flakes swirled. The fire had long gone out, and the cottage was clutched in an icy chill. Rick glanced at the open book in his lap—*Ghosts and the Women Who Love Them; Ten Steps to Building a Better Relationship with the Spirit in Your Home*. Tossing it aside, he ran a hand through his hair. Rick shuffled across the rug with aching bones and thought back to the evening news. They'd predicted a white Christmas, and he needed to get to the woodshed before the snow piled too high.

Christmas. Oh, God.

Bile crawled up his throat. Forcing it down, he placed a hand on the knob.

I'm meeting her family today.

"Rick!"

He whipped his hand away as if the doorknob were on fire. Why was Emily here already? Wasn't he supposed to meet her at her house? He wasn't prepared! With a long, broken breath, he cautiously opened the door.

"Merry Christmas!" Stephanie, Taylor, and Madge stood in the doorway, each sporting a tacky Christmas sweater. Stephanie pointed to a wobbly pair of foam antlers on her head. "Oh, my God, can you believe I found these just sitting in the closet? Is Em here? Taylor and I wrote her a Christmas poem." Craning her neck, she peered inside.

"She's n-n-not here. G-G-Go away." Rick slammed the door and ran a shaky hand over his queasy stomach.

"Hey!" Stephanie muffled voice called. "Why'd you do that?"

Grumbling, Rick opened the door again. "S-Sorry. Merry C-C-Christmas. C-C-Come in."

Balancing a tray of cookies, Madge pursed her lips. "I must say, you do seem prickly today, dear. We thought we'd celebrate with you and our dear Emily. Unless you'd rather we left you two alone."

"He doesn't look like he's much in the mood to celebrate," Taylor ventured as the three women drifted inside.

"Oh, my God, you guys aren't, like, fighting, are you?" Stephanie's antlers waved in the low light as she brought a hand to her chest. "Don't tell me you broke up. Oh, my God, oh, my God—"

Rick grunted. "It's n-n-nothing like that." He was exhausted. Since Emily's invitation, he'd paced, foregone food, and avoided the shower. One scenario after another played out in his mind, all ending in inevitable disaster. He'd even spent an evening practicing the exercises an over-enthusiastic school counselor had once forced on him, standing at the mirror for hours, repeating one simple phrase.

"Hello. P-Pleased to m-meet you. Hello. P-P-Pleased to m-m-meet you. H-H-Hello . . ."

D-D-Dammit.

Closing his eyes, he'd tried a breathing technique he'd read about, laying a hand on his stomach while inhaling from his diaphragm. He took slow, deep breaths, in and out, until his breathing calmed. "H-Hello. I'm p-p-p . . .

I'm p-p-p . . . ugh." Flinging his toothbrush across the bathroom, he'd stomped to his chair, spent.

Now, Rick felt as unprepared as if he were about to model the latest fashions at a nudist colony.

"What is it?" Madge adopted an air of concern, and she wasn't alone. They all showed the same worry.

Even as the thought formed, Rick's head swam with the idiocy of what he was about to say.

"I th-think I n-n-need your help."

21

P-P-PLEASED TO M-M-MEET YOU

Rick's truck wheezed to a stop in front of Emily's house with a mechanical gasp. In one hand, he held a crumpled paper, and in the other, the steering wheel in a death grip. He'd focused so hard on keeping his shaking to a minimum that he'd nearly run off the road and taken out the town Christmas tree.

The residents had scurried through his closet, pointing to the same staggering array of worn flannels and wrinkled jeans. They shouted orders to "Hold this up!" and "Oh, my God, this isn't the sixties!" They'd argued over colors, patterns, and cuts.

Just when Rick thought he couldn't take another minute, Taylor appeared.

"You guys have been dead way too long to dress him. I'm taking over." She unceremoniously ushered the remaining dead from the room. Twenty minutes later, Rick emerged in jeans and a muted gray sweater Taylor had found in a box headed for Goodwill, along with an old can of black shoe polish. While he fretted over how the day would go. Surely it would end in nothing less than absolute disaster. Rick shone his work boots to an acceptable level of cleanish.

Madge brought her hands to her lips. "He forgot to put on a tie . . ."

"Men don't wear ties anymore. Besides, he hasn't got one."

"But he could run to the st—"

"No tie," Taylor said, solidly crossing her arms.

Now, here he was outside of Emily's house, dressed as if he'd crawled from a donation box—which wasn't entirely inaccurate. On rubbery legs, Rick's looked between the house and the paper in his hand, the address barely discernible through the smudged ink. Emily's parked Honda assured him he was at the right place, but something felt wrong. He was sure he'd never been here, yet the three-story Victorian looked familiar. In dire need of a fresh coat of paint, the once white trim was entirely gone in places, exposing bare wood. Two large walnut trees framed the path, their roots lifting cracked bricks. He shook away the déjà vu, rattled. No wonder the house felt so ominous; he was about to be reduced to a fool within its walls.

He could turn around, feign illness or injury, and hightail it back to the cottage. He ran through a list of ghostly predicaments that would sound legitimate. Emily would say, *Oh, Rick, you simply must attend to that immediately. Fly, my love . . .*

Right. And what emergency would he invent at New Year's, Easter, or the Fourth of July? How many gatherings could he squirm out of? Worse, what if she decided to bring her family to Serenity Grove? They all had a common reason to visit. How long would he be able to avoid them?

He ran a hand through his hair with a groan, aware he'd just ruined the styling Taylor had walked him through.

Oh well. This is me, like it or not.

Rick cocked his head. Where had that come from? He'd never thought such a thing before. Yet, somehow, it felt right. This was him, and there was little he could do to change it at this late stage. Emily liked—no, loved him. Wasn't that all that mattered?

Rick took a step toward the door, and when he didn't die from it, he took another. They were baby steps, but they were miles apart in a lifetime of Rickness. As he crossed the derelict porch, he spotted a broken swing hung at a precarious angle. *I should fix that.* Despite himself, he couldn't hide the smile. *So boyfriendy.*

He knocked only once before the door flew open, and Emily wrapped her arms around his neck, holding on as if he were a buoy in a flood. "I'm so happy you're here, CT."

Returning the embrace, he kept her afloat while she shook. Was she crying? Gently, he pulled back, breaking Emily's grasp. "What's wrong?"

Though her eyes were moist, there were no tears. Instead, there was something else. Rick thought back to the memory of Emily's invitation, biting her lip as she'd awaited his reply. He remembered her warbly voice in the bookstore as she'd relived how invisible she'd been. How she'd had no friends, no sleepovers, no parties.

"Am I the first guest you've invited over?"

Fumbling with her hands, she chewed her lip as only she could. "Y-Y-Yes."

Had she stuttered? He couldn't hold back the chuckle that rose.

"I'm nervous, too." Had he *not* stuttered? He reached out, intending to caress her cheek, but his fingers diverted to her lips. He lifted one side while the other remained drooped. He lifted the right side, and this time, the rest of her came with it. "It'll be okay."

Her smile remained, and he realized, somewhat awestruck, that taking care of someone else made him forget his troubles. He felt an instant yet crushing kinship with Madge. His nerves calmed, and peacefulness took over. All that mattered now was Emily.

"Okay, y-y-yes, it'll be o-okay." She wiped a tear and laughed, music in his core. "My stutter is w-worse than yours."

Rick squeezed her hand. "I could teach you some exercises for that."

With an exhale, Emily turned. "All I need, I have right here."

Together they walked through the door, and by the time the sun set on that Christmas day, nothing would be the same.

IT WAS THE MOST DEPRESSING ROOM RICK HAD EVER stepped into.

Dark wasn't the right word. The house was cloaked like a mausoleum, with shades drawn tight across every window. A single lamp had been lit, creating more shadow than light, while faded rugs and obscure paintings hid in the dimness. A dusty piano sat in one corner, covered in framed photos, and from Rick's vantage point, he saw that nearly all were of a woman and boy, both dark-haired and tall. *Her brother, then.* None showcased a blonde girl or woman. Peering through the bleakness, Rick scoured the room for evidence of Emily's existence. On the opposite wall hung a lavish painting framed in gold. The portrait flaunted the same two people, mother and son, she sitting proud and he behind with a hand resting upon her shoulder.

But there was no Emily.

The woman who had raced through the cemetery, sprinkling decor, streamers, and balloons, seemed like a ghost in her own home. No tree had been decorated, and no garland adorned the mantel. Christmas had forgotten this house.

And the house had forgotten her.

A thought began to echo. *God, I want to take her away from this.* Rick wanted nothing more than to rescue her, to spirit Emily away from this place of unwelcome. He would take her home to the cottage and the residents who loved her as he did. His jaw set as he clenched his hands, so overcome with a mixture of love and hate it made his head swim.

Emily's profile was little more than a shadow in the engulfing darkness. Her eyes were fixed on the staircase— perhaps waiting for *them* to come down. She tucked a strand of hair behind her ear, a move so natural that it propelled Rick to determination.

She's coming home with me. Tonight. His breath halted, stunned, not by the idea but by the absolute certainty of it. Nothing made more sense, not the sun in the sky or the moon at night.

A shuffle from upstairs caused Emily to jump. She waved in the direction of the couch, her body in the room but her spirit elsewhere. "Please, have a seat. I'll be back with Mom."

"Right."

Haltingly, Emily climbed the stairs, and more than he ever had, Rick looked forward to tomorrow.

And tomorrow's tomorrow.

———

"I CAN DO IT MYSELF. LEAVE ME ALONE." A WOMAN'S voice, deep and raspy, bellowed. Breaking glass followed the thud of a body hitting the floor. Footsteps rushed. A door opened. Feet shuffled.

"Let me help—"

"Get your hands off of me. I told you I'm fine."

Two shadows moved down the staircase. First, Emily, her face choked in worry. She smiled, looking about as happy as a funeral procession. A tall woman with dark, mussed hair followed, descending with a white-knuckled grip on the railing. A robe was tied lazily around her midsection. She stumbled, and Rick held his breath as she caught herself and made the journey to the bottom.

A tension-filled smile cracked Emily's face. "Mom, I'd like you to meet Rick. My boyfriend."

The woman's pursed gaze roamed from Rick's face to his shoes and back again. She shuffled forward with carefully measured steps.

Rick held out his hand as his nightmare sprang to life. "P-P-Pleased t-t-to meet you, Mrs. B-B-B . . . B-B-Bennett."

Scowling, she thrust her hand forward, looking away as Rick pumped it twice. The sour smell of alcohol was overwhelming. Teetering on brittle legs, she leaned too far back. Rick worried she might fall before she flailed and returned somewhat upright.

"So." She stopped there. Nothing else, just *so*.

Rick wondered if he should speak.

"You're the grave-digger who's been bedding my daughter."

Well. Rick could think of no response to *that*.

Emily tugged at her hair, running her fingers through it as if trying to keep the strands from flying away. "Sit down, Mom, while I get dinner ready."

Mrs. Bennett swung her head so quickly that this time, she did lose her balance, stumbling back and nearly slamming into a dusty curio cabinet. Instinctively, Rick rushed forward and grabbed her by the arm, and with a disgusted glare, Mrs. Bennett wrenched from his grip. "Don't touch me. I don't need . . ." She trailed off, and once again, Rick got a whiff of the strong booze that seemed to seep from her pores; it was all he could do to keep from covering his mouth.

As she stumbled toward the couch, Rick stepped out of her path. She fished a cigarette from her pocket with shaky hands. After several attempts, she finally lit it.

Emily's already overwrought smile twisted her face into something from a horror film. "I could use a hand in the kitchen."

He would have jumped from a third-story window if it had meant escaping the reeking woman on the couch. "Right."

Ever-smiling, Emily fell to work, opening cabinets and

pulling out pots and pans. She opened the fridge, closed it, then opened it again. Grinning insanely, she inspected the ceiling. "I can't remember what I . . . what I was going to . . ." Her voice trailed off, and she fell silent before finally bursting into sobs.

Rick crossed the kitchen in two long strides. "It's okay. I'll help however I can. You don't have to do this alone."

Her shoulders heaved, and after a long while, she managed to pull away. "I really thought she'd be alright. She promised."

Rick tried his best to smile. "I once lived in a foster home where the dad had that problem. I've dealt with this before."

Emily blinked. "Oh, Rick. I just wanted to give you a nice Christmas. I wouldn't have brought you here if I'd known—"

"As long as I'm with you, that's all that matters. To be honest, it was you I came to see. I have a bit of a crush on you." Fluttering his lashes bashfully, he feigned an exaggerated *look how shy I am* grin.

Her warbling laugh lightened the gloom. "Well, if you really want to help, there's a ham that needs to go in the oven."

"Ma'am, yes, ma'am!" With a flourish, Rick saluted, clicked his heels, and marched to the fridge. Before long, they fell into the same natural pattern they had at the cottage. Emily gave instructions, and Rick followed. She whirled through the kitchen on lighter feet, grabbing bowls and serving spoons.

"Table's set. Ready to eat?"

Rick brushed a hand across her cheek. "I'd eat a horse if you cooked it." He planted a kiss, and she melted.

"You ruined the surprise," she whispered, her face buried in his shoulder. "I was saving the horse for dessert."

Now. I can't wait until after dinner. Hell, I don't think I could stomach dinner.

"Em—"

A door opened. Slammed. Footfalls on the floor.

Emily paled. "My brother's here."

For once, Rick's nerves didn't shatter, and his heart didn't skip a beat. He'd survived the awkward meeting with her mother, and encountering her brother couldn't possibly be worse. With each passing second, a grain of hope swelled to the size of a cantaloupe. He could do this. He would survive.

Following her into the living room, Rick found Emily's two remaining relatives side-by-side in a living replica of the dozens of photos around the room. Her brother's head was shaved into a buzz cut, and a white sleeveless tee peeked from under a letterman jacket covered in athletic awards that Rick knew—*knew*—he'd never earned.

He knew it because he'd been there the day her brother had swiped the jacket from the kid who had, before shoving him into the mud as he laughed. Aside from the beer gut that now oozed over his belt, he hadn't changed a bit.

Donny crooked his head like a dog, and a slow, stupid grin spread over his face.

"Well, if it ain't Stutter Boy."

EMILY'S EYES FLITTED FROM ONE MAN TO THE OTHER AS Rick stared into Donny's dark eyes, so different from

Emily's blue. Though her brother's hair was dark brown, everything else about him was Emily to a T. They had the same nose, jawline, and mouth.

How did I miss that? And suddenly, The truth he'd passed off as déjà vu or as the overworked nerves of a man prone to nervousness slammed into him. It was so apparent that he couldn't believe he'd dismissed it. Of course the house had seemed familiar. Though he'd never before stepped inside, he'd spent his childhood avoiding it, walking blocks out of his way to keep from passing by.

"Do you know each other?" Emily's voice was rimmed with a heightened edge. "And why did you call him that, Donny?"

Her brother settled into one of the dining chairs, throwing back a casual arm. "We knew each other." Donny eyed Rick with the same smile Rick remembered from grade school and the same smirk he'd carried through high school.

And when Rick looked into those dark eyes, they held the same maniacal grin they had on the day he'd died.

22

STUTTER BOY

When the last day of school arrived, no one was more relieved than Rick. The fourth grade had finally come to a tired end, and summer meant escape from Donny and his half-witted bootlickers. Fifth grade hovered so far in the future it barely registered.

Donny had it in for him. All year, he'd tripped Rick, pulled his hair, and hocked loogies into his food. Rick had grown so distrustful of his lunch tray that he'd lost eight pounds.

On the first morning of summer break, Rick ran the entire seven blocks to the pool. The first to arrive, he stripped to his swim trunks and raced for the water, falling more than diving into the cold, quiet void. For an hour, he was alone. Every other kid in town was sleeping in, taking advantage of the blessed absence of caffeine-deprived teachers. Wading beyond the shallow end, Rick floated beneath the summer sun. Sounds became muffled, distant. He knew already that when others arrived, he'd head to the library, maybe even check out that *Narnia* book his teacher had mentioned. For now, he would enjoy the isolation, the muted quiet, the serene peacefulness only an empty pool on a warm summer day could grant.

A shadow appeared, and everything turned dark as Rick was plunged beneath the surface. He gasped for air but pulled in water instead. Arms flailing, he tried desperately to swim upward, but something held him in place. His lungs burned, and his vision muddied as the shadow floated away. The pressure on Rick's chest suddenly lessened.

When Rick broke through the surface, he tried to take a breath, only barking out a mixture of mucus and pool water. Instinct took over as his lungs worked to expel the crushing fluid. Disoriented, he dog-paddled toward the pool's edge, and when he could finally take in a full breath, it only made him cough harder.

As he came within an arm's reach of the edge, a voice set his nerves aflame.

"Well, if it ain't Stutter Boy."

There was no need to look; Rick knew that voice like his own. He kicked harder. If he could just make it to that edge . . .

He was yanked backward and took in more water. Rick kicked weakly, but Donny was at least a foot taller and ten times stronger. The edge receded, and Donny spun Rick with ease, bringing them face to face. Cocking his head like a dog, a slow grin crawled onto Donny's fat lips. "You shouldn't swim alone. It's not safe."

Donny pushed Rick back under. Rick fought, gulping water, and in a moment of mad clarity, he wondered where the lifeguard was. The pool grew dark. His arms flailed once, twice, and then the world drifted away.

At the tender age of ten, Rick Holliday, otherwise known as Stutter Boy, passed from this world to the Next.

———

AT FIRST, THERE WAS ONLY BLACKNESS.

His lungs no longer burned, but his head felt funny. *Woozy* wasn't quite the right word either. He floated, not in water now, but in darkness. Fear fled like a wisp of smoke, and a foreign yet comforting warmth wrapped him in an embrace.

A pinprick of light emerged ahead, like the last light from an old TV. The brighter the light shone, the more serene he became. As the illumination approached, Rick wept. The glow seemed to come from galaxies away, yet he somehow knew it traveled at an incredible speed. He sobbed with overwhelming ecstasy—surely such joy had never existed—and he prayed it would never end. Wherever he was, he'd be just fine staying right here for all eternity.

The light transformed into a window to another world, and a woman's voice called from the other side.

Rick, why are you here?

Rick, yes. That was his name. Had he forgotten? How long had he been in this darkness, in this light? Then, in a flash, he remembered everything. His name was Rick, and his mother was . . . Helen? Yes, Helen, and he remembered her face from another life. When she'd sung.

Hush little baby, don't say a word,
Mama's gonna buy you a mockingbird . . .

She'd grown older, a little more worn. And still, she'd sung.

And if that mockingbird won't sing,
Mama's gonna buy you a diamond ring . . .

He remembered a hospital room, the shades drawn, as she lay in the light of the open doorway. Still, she'd sung.

And if that diamond ring turns to brass,
Mama's gonna buy you a looking glass . . .

She'd beckoned with the twist of a finger. Climbing onto the bed, he'd curled his small body next to hers and listened to her heart—weak, feeble—as he fell into slumber.

A nurse had tried to awaken him and pull him from his mother, but it hadn't been the nurse who'd stirred him.

His mother had quieted, and her heart beat no more.

Now, in this tunnel of both light and dark, she reached for Rick, her hand pushing through the window, and he reached out in response. And then . . .

. . . he was pulled back with a jerk. The light shrank. Another hard yank and the blaze became a pinprick. One final pull and the illumination vanished altogether. Though his lungs burned, he shivered. He was cold, so cold. His eyes fluttered open to brightness. It hurt too much to look, so he closed them again. Hurried voices shouted orders. Machines blared. Someone jumped on his chest until he thought his ribs would shatter. He risked opening his eyes again and saw a man in a white coat pressing furiously on his chest with a closed fist. Someone said, "He's coming to."

Rick spent ten days in the hospital. His foster mother visited him once, along with his caseworker, and after that, no one. For a while, he vividly remembered the light that was his mother, and he kept closing his eyes, trying to go back. Over time, the vividness turned to a faded remembrance until the memory left him for good.

A nurse told him he'd nearly drowned in the pool that day, but he was lucky—*so lucky*—that an older boy had dragged him to the surface.

"Wh-What was his n-n-name?" Rick asked, still hoarse, but he feared he already knew the answer.

"What was that, hon?"

"His n-name. The b-b-boy who pulled me out of the w-water."

"Oh. I think it was Danny. No . . ."

"D-Donny." Rick's heart sank.

"That's right. I'm sure you'll want to thank him once you're back home. He saved your life."

Rick stared out the window. After a while, he closed his eyes and tried to see *her*, but the only face behind his lids was Donny's.

23

BY THE LIGHT OF A STREETLAMP

The memory of twenty years past stung fresh.

Rick's tormenter leaned casually back. He'd remained unchanged; physically and in the shit-eating grin he'd carried through all those years.

Tormentor. Murderer.

Tormentor. Murderer.

"Are you having a fit? Say something, Stutter Boy." Donny's black eyes honed in, dug so deeply beneath Rick's skin that he instinctively wanted to run. His murderer's mouth tilted into a sneer, and just like that, Rick knew he'd been bested. Just as he always had.

"Rick?"

Hearing his name on Emily's lips, Rick shook his head, unable to fathom how he hadn't seen it before. The siblings' features morphed—yin and yang, black and white, up and down—different but so very much alike.

"How do you know each other?" Emily asked, her voice so far away she may as well have whispered it from a dream.

"We went to school together, didn't we, Stutter Boy?" Donny advanced a step.

Visions of busy school hallways and deserted restrooms flooded Rick. No longer was he the caretaker, the conductor of meetings, an arbitrator for the dead. In a snap, the Rick of Now was replaced with the Rick of Then —the vulnerable boy he always would be. What a fool he'd been to think he could be more than the quivering, fearful mess he was at his core.

"Stop it, Donny," a strange, beautiful woman said, utterly without conviction. "Don't call him that."

"Aw, come on, Emmie, he knows I'm just playing. We used to play like this all the time." Another step. Donny's eyes danced.

Emily's mother stumbled toward the stairs. "I'm not hungry. Feed yourselves."

Rick finally found his feet, and as he grabbed the door-knob, he heard Donny's rough voice behind him.

"You shouldn't go out there alone. It's not safe."

Plunging into the cold, Rick realized his coat was still inside, but going back was the last thing he would do. As his feet pounded the wooden porch steps, Emily followed. "Where are you going?"

Rick's inner voice screamed. *Please, just leave me alone.* Never again would he touch her porcelain skin, never brush against her lips with his own. Those were things a man did. As in a play, Rick had merely been playing the part of Man With Shovel. Now that the facade had been dropped, Emily would see Rick as he truly was: a weak, forever-boy. Fear and humiliation, fresh and oh-so-familiar, propelled him faster.

"Rick, stop. Please."

He hit the sidewalk and fished through his pocket, and for one heart-stopping moment, he feared his keys were in his jacket inside the house. Then his fingers curled around metal. Ignoring Emily's calls, Rick jammed his key in the truck's lock.

"Rick," she begged, catching up, "please don't let them get to you. We can go somewhere else and have our own dinner. I shouldn't have invited you here."

He ceased fumbling with the key and whirled. "Did you know?"

"Know what?"

He had to get away, to escape Emily's sad, bleeding-heart eyes. Perhaps that was what had drawn her to him in the first place. Maybe she was one of those man-fixers, a woman who set their sights on someone who needed a life makeover, a transformation—someone to mold. The idea struck him so hard, followed by such certainty that his blood began to boil.

This is me, like it or not. A humorless chuckle fell.

Had she really thought she could just waltz into his perfectly manicured world and turn it upside-down? Rick had been happy, truly happy before Emily had come along. A lazy afternoon and a few kisses had brought little more than angst and bitterness.

His laugh, cold and harsh, sounded distant. "Who d-d-do you th-think gave me that n-n-name?" *Stutter Boy.* Always, always the boy who stuttered.

"Sometimes Donny can be blunt, but he's not a bad person—"

"He k-killed me, Em."

Pity again. Emily's voice softened as if she were

speaking to someone too stupid to understand. "He didn't
kill you, Rick. You're standing right h—"

"He drowned m-me. It's why I can t-talk to *them*." He
looked so deep into her eyes that it hurt. He needed her to
be on his side, to believe—to see her brother for who he
was. "That's the w-worst of it, b-b-but he t-tormented me,
Em. For years."

Wheels turned as she mulled over his words. "I believe
that you think he somehow . . . I know he wouldn't do
what you're saying. Maybe you're confused." She groped
at her neck.

Rick's stomach dropped a thousand miles while his
brain misfired. "Maybe I am, Emily. M-M-Maybe I have
b-been all along." He climbed into the truck, and the crank
of the engine turning over brought home the finality of it
all. He hesitated before throwing the gear into drive, then
turned onto the street.

He left her standing by the light of a street lamp, shivering in the cold as a single snowflake fluttered.

———

As he drove, Rick tried to empty his mind. Of her,
of Donny, of the whole damn mess. Halfway to the
cemetery, the snow began to fall hard and thick, yet he
barely noticed. Donny's face had etched itself permanently onto Rick's retinas—that smug, arrogant, stupid
grin that had haunted him for years. The hands that
pushed him under the water. The voice that still called
him Stutter Boy.

And then, Donny's face superimposed with Emily's. A
woman so pure that she found it unfathomable that her

brother capable of such monstrous things. Unfathomable or unwilling.

And Frank. In five years, he'd never mentioned a grandson. Why? Rick raced through every ugly twist. Who knew? Who didn't know? Why had the truth been kept from him all this time? With the passing of each block, Rick resisted the urge to double back. He wanted to apologize. Another block and his anger flamed anew. *She* should be the sorry one.

After parking haphazardly at the gate, Rick stomped toward the cottage, pausing at the comment box. What did he expect? An envelope marked 'CT'? Yet he couldn't resist lifting the lid. Disappointment unleashed into his chest at the sight of the empty box. Allowing the top to slam shut, he walked inside.

He didn't bother turning on the lights. It was better this way. The darkness matched the well in his heart.

RICK WOKE IN HIS CHAIR. HIS BODY ACHED, AND HIS LIDS felt puffy. He slipped on his boots and reached for his jacket before remembering he'd left it at Emily's, then plunged into the cold wearing only a flannel and jeans. The snow had stopped falling sometime in the night, though at least four inches had piled up. The wet slush of dripping water made his ears ring. He opened the gate and walked back to the cottage, passing the comment box without so much as a glance.

Anger, humiliation, and indignation glued Rick to his chair. He added the occasional log to the fire, more from habit than warmth. He told himself he was relieved to have

Emily ushered from his life. Intrusions and future holidays were a worry no more. He was now free to spend them as he always had—alone, with the occasional wandering spirit thrown in for good measure. As he congratulated himself for having gotten out early, he ignored his increasing nausea and mindlessly nibbled at half a tuna sandwich before throwing the rest in the garbage. He was probably getting that twenty-four-hour flu the paper said was going around. It certainly had nothing to do with Emily.

Rick comforted himself with repeated assurances that he was happy now. Fulfilled now. Content now. He spent another fitful night in his chair. The third day repeated on a loop, and his twenty-four-hour flu only worsened, though the thermometer claimed his temperature was normal. Occasionally, he caught glimpses of movement. But, like Emily, the residents had disappeared from his life. It had been days since he'd heard the happily chirping teen, the mother of the world, or the old man. Even Taylor seemed to have abandoned her own tombstone.

On day four, something flitted in his peripheral vision.

"Get out!" he barked.

Nothing moved, nothing changed. He wasn't sure there'd even been anyone there.

For the remainder of the days leading to the New Year, Rick was as close to comatose as a man could be. Eating sparingly, he took to sleeping on the couch when he could no longer stand the chair. He picked up books and stared at the covers. He was little more than a body with a beating heart.

Finally, his anger subsided, the shame boiled down, and Rick reached the bottom of his emotional well.

NEW YEAR'S EVE ARRIVED—JUST ANOTHER DAY. WITH his caretaker duties forgotten, Rick hadn't walked the grounds, nor had he bothered to open the gate, an oversight that caused Herbert to pop his head into the fireplace, hiss a string of swear words, and pop out again before Rick could register the old man's presence. He woke earlier than usual, though he hadn't fallen asleep until well after midnight. Rest was impossible for more than two or three hours at a time without waking in the sweat of faded dreams.

An odd shuffling at the door sprang him to attention, and Rick bolted from the couch.

"Rick? Can we come through?"

Unsettling disappointment lay him back down. "Leave me alone."

Stephanie and Madge invited themselves through the closed door, both taking in the sight of the disastrous living room. Madge perched on a chair arm while Stephanie claimed the opposite couch.

"Why d-doesn't anyone around here l-l-listen to me?"

"We've left you alone for nearly a week now. It's about time you stopped pouting and talked to us."

Rick sat up, letting the thin blanket slip to the floor. "Just leave m-me alone. Jesus, is there some law that says just because I c-can talk to you, I'm required to? I never asked for any of th-this."

Stephanie's voice quivered. "But we're your friends—"

"I never asked f-for your friendship," Rick grumbled, pulling the blanket to his chin. He'd been born cursed, and there was no spell, antidote, or cure for his innate Rick-ness. All he could do now was live out the remainder of his days and try to stay out of his own way. How pitiful he was—even the dead had more fulfilling lives than he. A lifetime of pity from others couldn't match the ache he felt for himself. Now that the anger had dissipated, he couldn't hide the truth of what really made up Rick Holliday.

Loser.

Coward.

Stutter Boy.

"I never asked f-f-for any of it."

Madge shuffled to the window, her heavy feet scraping the wood floor. Laying a hand on the sill, lowered her head and moaned.

"You know about Donny."

Rick tried to work out Madge's expression—knowl-edge and sympathy with a bit of the-jig-is-up thrown in. Familiar anger shot to the surface. It was true, then—everyone was in on the ruse. Yes, they'd all had a hand in pulling the wool over his eyes, and like a fool, he'd gone along with all of it.

"What d-did you say?"

Madge blinked but didn't avert her gaze. "We wondered when you'd find out."

His heartbeat punched him in the face. "You all knew?"

"Just Madge and me," Stephanie whispered.

How oblivious had he been? He rose on unsteady legs. "G-G-Get out of m-my house."

"Rick, listen. We—"

"You kn-kn-knew." If he didn't sit, he would collapse.

But sitting was impossible, so he paced, slicing his finger-nails into his palms. "Emily knew, t-t-too."

Such a fool.

"She didn't know. It's not what you think—"

"Nothing is ever what I th-th-think." But, quick as a butterfly, the fight left him. Self-pity won out, and with a sigh, Rick sat, his cheek in one hand.

Madge struggled, wringing her hands. Finally, after a deep breath, she spoke.

"It was the month before Frank left, and I was having a bad day."

24

THE BEST LAID PLANS

S tephanie and Frank sat surrounded by ripening fruit in the old apple grove while Madge unleashed a torrent.

"The first year, they came every Sunday. I sat in the tree over my grave and listened. It was like I was still alive —like I still mattered." She wrung her apron. "One Sunday, they didn't come. I was sure there'd been an accident, that someone was in the hospital, and for a week, I went crazy with worry. The following Sunday, my daughter came but not my sons. They'd gotten busy with work, school, and a long list of other things. She said she'd try to make it the following week.

"It didn't slip past me that she said *try*. I think I knew, even then, that it was the end. You hear it from other residents, but I guess I thought my family would be different. Before I knew it, they were only showing up on Christmas and Mother's Day, and even that only lasted a couple of years." She turned toward the valley. "It's been twenty-eight years since anyone's come."

Frank patted her knee while Stephanie fished in her pocket for a handkerchief. The group fell silent while a falcon rose over the valley floor before diving toward the earth. Dancing, falling.

"I know it's silly. I've been dead for decades. Why would they keep visiting a corpse that's long rotted? I don't even know if they're still alive. My children would be in their fifties now." She lowered her head.

"It's harder for us to move on than it is for them," Frank said, his voice gravelly yet gentle. He strolled to the plateau, where the land disappeared into the canyon. "Did I ever tell you I have a grandson?"

The women exchanged a glance. "No."

"Nasty boy. Nothing like his sister. He was always a bit out of control, but after my son died, he turned rotten to the core."

"Like, why didn't you ever tell us?"

"I was ashamed. It's partly my fault. There was always something about that boy—he and his mother both. Something about her always struck me wrong. Her drinking problem aside, she was never affectionate toward my son. When Donny came along, it was as if she'd forgotten my son was ever there." Frank gazed over the lowland, watching the falcon rise into the sky, its talons visible even from this distance. "My son died on the inside long before he breathed his last breath.

"Em was young when her father got sick, and his illness took him so quickly that she never had a chance to remember him. Once he was gone, her mother turned her attention to the boy, and Emily was left to fend for herself. I took her under my wing and became the father figure she'd lost. I tried to do the same with Donny, but he wouldn't have it. Before long, Donny decided I wasn't welcome anymore, and the mother allowed him to impose his will in the house. He was barely ten when he puffed out his chest, crossed his pudgy little arms, and stared at me like he was ten feet tall. He told me I had to leave, that he was in charge now.

"It wasn't my way to take orders from a child, but Emily needed me, and I knew if I fought, they'd find a way to keep us apart. So I stayed away, and as the years went on and the boy got older, he just got meaner and nastier. Puberty hit him like a closed fist. I should have given him a good, hard spanking the instant he tried to assert himself. But you know what they say about should-haves and would-haves. By the time I realized my mistake, there was no turning him around. Truth be told, I'm not sure there ever was a chance—he had too much of his mother in him—but maybe I could have lessened the damage, molded him into something a little less spoiled.

"After my son died, it was Emily that kept me going. Without her . . . well, I don't know if I would have made it. She was strong—more than even she realized—and never allowed herself to be influenced by those two. And after I died, in the five years I've been here, I've spent most of my time thinking about her, sending her messages. Emily has felt my presence so much that she's been unable to move on.

"When we don't let go, they can't either." He faced the women with a weak smile. "I think it's time I let my granddaughter go."

A WEEK PASSED, AND MADGE AND STEPHANIE FOUND Frank in the apple orchard sitting on a pile of leaves—the first hint of autumn gathered around him. His face was distant and pained.

"What's wrong? Is it Emily?"

"I popped in on my grandson. I don't know why; I just found myself there. I flipped through his memories—wasn't the slightest bit guilty about it—until I found one that stopped me cold." He remained fixed on a distant point. "It was more than just seeing—I *felt* it. I never want to experience that again."

They waited while he blinked away looming tears, and walked to the canyon edge. "Rick's near-death experience, the attempted drowning, and the boy responsible . . ."

Stephanie tilted her head. "What?"

Madge laid a hand on Stephanie's arm. "Dear God, it was Donny, wasn't it?"

Frank turned and spoke the words that would alter the lives of two people, for better or worse. In his eyes lived guilt, but in the purse of his lips, resolve.

"I have to save them both."

"FRANK HAD TO LET EMILY GO, SO SHE COULD MOVE ON," Madge finished as her words echoed in the crackling fire.

Rick couldn't contain his anger.

"S-S-So he left her, with those . . . I can't even call them f-f-family." He was incredulous that Frank would abandon the one person who'd needed him most, throwing her to the wolves. "How c-could he?"

"Oh, my God, are you really that dumb? Do you really think he left her alone? Like, it's so obvious."

Rick was seething now. "He w-w-was all she had! You s-saw the s-s-state she was in when she f-first showed up. Frank j-just left her wondering, thinking she'd d-done something wrong." Emily's words floated back. The sorrow, the tears she'd shed that night in the bookstore as she'd spoken of Frank's final contact. Memory boiled him, burned him, made him wish Frank were still alive if for no other reason than to clock him.

"Emily didn't d-d-deserve that."

Madge stepped forward, beseeching. "Don't you see? He didn't abandon her, Rick. He led her here." She knelt before him as the fire crackled.

"He led her to you."

———

IT ALL BEGAN TO MAKE A SLOW, PAINFUL SENSE. RICK needed to repeat Madge's words, if only to make them click.

"Frank saw D-D-Donny drown me. From D-Donny's m-memory." His words sounded distant, like the residents' voices when they moved between worlds.

Rick's mind reeled, the missing pieces still drifting. "B-But, he left her. His final contact was so—"

"Ambiguous?" Madge cut in. "Yes, it would have to be, wouldn't it, dear? He'd always been with her. Until that night, she'd never needed to visit his grave, and when Frank left, Emily went to the one place his spirit might linger, as he'd known so well she would."

Rick braced for her next words.

"He forced her to come looking for him. Where she would find *you*."

Click.

Rick's ears filled with white noise. Frank had meant for her to find him. *Him*. Rick Holliday. Stutter Boy. A bitter taste coated his tongue. He really had been a fool.

"Oh, my God, he loved you like a son. He said it, like, all the time."

"Why d-didn't he tell me?" Rick glanced between the two women. "Why didn't *you* t-t-tell me? I could have done . . . I don't know, something."

Madge knelt. "You would have done what you've always done, and Frank saw something hidden that even you couldn't see. He expected you to find it. But with how you've reacted, I think Frank may have overestimated you."

The slight stung, but Rick couldn't deny she was right. He was the same weakling he'd always been, and Emily's love had done nothing to strengthen him. Frank had used his last contact to help them both, and Rick had let him down. Hell, he'd let everyone down.

The sweet aroma of apples seeped into every pore, lingered on his senses, and he shot to his feet. "I've been s-stupid."

"Like, so stupid."

"You've been a jackass, just like I always said you were," Herbert cackled, swinging from the chandelier with his middle finger flailing.

Rick stared, and then a long, slow laugh cracked the air like a whip. "I'll be d-damned if you're not, right, Herb." He grabbed his keys and headed for the door.

Taylor stood outside as if in waiting. "You should take the truck. That hearse is morbid."

He should have known they'd all be here. Maybe Emily had been right. Maybe they were able to make themselves invisible after all.

Maybe Emily had been right about a lot of things.

25

ON THE EVE OF A NEW YEAR

The truck died in the slow, sputtery way that old trucks do. Emily's house—and Donny's—beckoned and warned at once. Rick felt a bit sputtery himself.

Danger and love resided within those walls. Yet his newfound determination was so fierce that he cursed his feet for not moving fast enough. Never again would he hide from the Donnys of the world. Never again would he doubt the woman he loved.

Approaching the wide porch, Rick's cheeks stretched. Each footfall was driven by foreign resolve. Still, it did little to squash the rising panic as he rapped on the door. Any one of them could answer, and two of the three possibilities could be disastrous—not the best odds. But he would stand his ground, come what may.

This is me, like it or not.

His nerves sprang to life as he ground his boots into the porch, stiffened by the noise of his shuffling steps. But

. . .

Come what may, come what may.

He couldn't deny the relief at the sight of Emily's mussed blonde hair. That perfect row of freckles across her nose. Blue eyes sparkling with life even as they drooped with exhaustion. His soul took a deep, gathering breath. "Can we talk?"

She allowed a pinprick of a smile. "Oh, yes, Rick."

"YOU'RE SURE YOU DON'T WANT TO BRING MORE?" HE asked as they stood in her sparsely decorated room.

She shook her head. "This room—this house—never really felt like my own. Your cottage is my home now."

"Well then, let's get you home."

An hour later, on the eve of a new year, they arrived at the cemetery, Rick in his truck and Emily following in her Honda. In the bed of the pickup, an ancient trunk that had once belonged to Frank rattled, and in the backseat of Emily's Honda were two packed bags and a box of her most treasured books.

Rick groaned as they pulled up to the gate and cranked the window down. "Wait here while I move the hearse."

While Emily waited at the gate, Rick maneuvered the hearse behind the cottage and parked his truck beside the comment box. *Every morning, from here on out, her car will be here.* With a grin, he glanced toward the gate, where Emily was rummaging through her books.

"I found the perfect book for you at the Book and Nook the other day," she called as her fingers sifted. "I know you think those ghost stories are silly, but this one—"

A clunk of metal and a loud pop sliced through the air. Emily's fingers paused in the cold, crisp breeze. Her head flinched, her brows tucked down, and she spoke her final words.

"Do you smell apples?"

A SCREAM BROUGHT RICK AROUND IN TIME TO SEE IT ALL in brutal slow motion.

A delivery truck hopped the curb, riding the sidewalk before slamming into the side of Emily's car. The blue Honda slid sideways toward the gate, and Emily had enough time to turn before she was struck.

The keys slipped from Rick's fingers with a metallic clang. He raced to the gate, his legs swimming through water, his childhood nightmare of running against an unseen force coming to life. Reaching for the padlock, he realized his keys lay behind him. He hopped the gate, landing at an angle that wrenched his ankle, but he forced the twist to bear his weight and skidded to Emily's side.

Spots danced in his vision. Blackness nearly overtook him, and he had to steady himself against the wrecked Honda.

Later, but not now.

Emily lay on the frosty ground, her hair splayed while the car's front tire rested on her chest. A slow trickle of blood spilled from her mouth. Her blue eyes stared wide and unblinking as the sun peeked from behind a cloud. Her face had paled as if she'd been plunged into white powder.

"E-Emily?"

Her lids fluttered, though she didn't seem to register his voice.

Soundlessly—breathlessly—her lips parted, and Rick realized with terror that she couldn't breathe.

"Hang on, j-j-just hang on." He grabbed the car's bumper and tried to lift it, but it had been wedged into the fence. He pulled with unknown strength, yet even that wasn't enough—he only succeeded in loosening the bumper from the frame. With increasing panic, he lowered it, afraid it would fall apart in his hands and crush her. He quickly returned to Emily's side. Her mouth opened and closed, opened and closed, even as her lips turned an alarming shade of blue.

"Listen to m-m-me," Rick whispered, his voice dangerously unsteady. "I love you m-more than anyone or anything in this world. I'm so sorry, Emily. This is all m-m-my fault."

She lifted a shaky hand to his lips, a simple action that seemed to require more strength than even Rick had to give. Grasping her hand, he pressed her warmth to his cheek. "S-Stay with me, Em. I can't live without you. I honestly c-c-can't." He wanted to say more, but words failed him.

Two distinct crowds had gathered—one on the street and one behind the gate. The residents huddled together, their hands pressed against the invisible force that kept them from the living world. Stephanie screamed—a blood-curdling sound that caused several in the crowd to glance around. Taylor spoke not a word, and Herbert kicked the gravel.

Madge took a tentative step forward. "Rick, please tell us she's alright."

Dismayed at the sudden rush of time, Rick shrieked. "S-S-Somebody help her! P-Please!"

A woman in yoga pants sobbed while a group of men worked to pull the delivery driver from the wreckage. "P-P-Please!" Rick heard the crack in his voice, desperate to be heard, to be noticed for once.

In the background, a distant siren warbled, excruciatingly distant, as Emily's chest hitched, resting longer between futile gasps for breath.

"H-H-Help is c-c-coming." Rick's words mingled with his sobs. He gripped her hand so tightly that he worried he might hurt her, yet even in his grief, it was clear she felt nothing. Later, when his memory taunted him, that was what would tear him apart the most. "Just a little longer, Em. I love you. Stay with me, p-p-please."

It took ten minutes and a group of volunteers to lift the car. Rick stayed close while paramedics performed CPR, and from a million miles away, someone whispered, *already gone.* Refusing to release her hand in the ambulance, Rick followed as Emily was rushed through the glass doors. The nurses' steps seemed slow, and he willed them to move faster, leaving Emily's side only when they wheeled her into a room and someone gently but firmly led him to a waiting area.

"Let the doctors do their job."

Rick stole a glance at Emily as plastic tubes were swiftly connected to machines. The doors swung shut, and then, she was closed away from him.

It might have been an hour, it might have been a day. Time halted as Rick slumped in a hard, plastic chair. Somewhere, a TV quietly droned. It was all he could do to keep from bolting into Emily's room. They needed to know she wasn't just any patient. She was different, important, Emily. Her face swirled, and his brain broke in two, reducing him to little more than a man in fearful waiting. He prayed. Bargained. Made appeals to whoever may be listening. He asked the universe to take pity not on him but on the woman who'd done nothing to deserve the cards life had dealt her. He promised to go far, far away if that's what they wanted—he pledged never to leave her side if that appeased them more.

Two doctors pushed through the swinging doors—too slow. Their words were a jumble of sounds; Rick no longer recognized speech. One asked if he were a family member, and he absently responded, "B-B-Brother." Someone opened the door to her room, spoke more gibberish, then drifted into oblivion.

Emily lay awkwardly on a bed made of metal, her head tilted to one side as a thick, transparent tube snaked from her lips. Even as Rick approached, he prayed, promised, begged. A wall of machines beeped as he gripped her limp hand, and when he finally found his voice, Rick unleashed a never-ending stream of soft, desperate pleas.

"Just come b-back, okay, Em? Don't . . . please don't l-l-leave me here alone." He smothered her lifeless palm with soft kisses that begged for life.

And then, a nearby machine changed its rhythm, and its beeps became erratic missteps. Rick buried his face in Emily's abdomen, unable to stop the audible account of the end from penetrating his ears. Doctors rushed in, carts fell into place, and time crawled as Rick remained in an uncomprehending haze. Where was her drunken mother or her godforsaken brother? Hope rose and fell until the beeps were replaced by one long, maddening tone that no one raced to mend.

No.

People stood solemnly by as her breathing ceased. *No.* He searched a face that now seemed oddly to belong to someone else—a mask, a cheap imitation of the woman who'd once worn it.

No.

A nurse entered, and hope rose. Em could be fixed. She *would* be fixed. Why was everyone moving so slowly? Rick raced around the bulky metal-framed bed to the Life Machine and pointed. "P-P-Please. M-M-Make it work again." He tapped the machine as if to relay an important message to someone who didn't speak his language. "It s-s-stopped. H-H-Help her."

Help me.

The nurse averted her gaze from the sobbing man tap-tap-tapping on the EKG as a white line solidly and resolutely claimed his Em. "Let me call the social wo—"

"I don't need a fucking shrink!" Time was wasting away while this ridiculous nurse failed to recognize the urgency of it all. Dropping to his knees, Rick wrenched Emily's still-warm hand through the metal rail, proof she wasn't gone, never gone. Encasing her lifeless hand with his own, he breathed life onto her skin to keep hers from escaping. "I t-take it b-b-back. I take everything b-b-back."

"Sir . . ."

"No," he whispered, the word small and insignificant.

The sobs came then, and he thought they wouldn't stop if he lived to be a thousand.

26

GONE

His feet moved—an automatic reflex. It mattered not where he went, only that he walked. Snow fell in swirls, prompting a dim awareness that he should be cold, yet Rick felt nothing.

There *was* nothing.

Hours earlier—or perhaps days—a guard had gently escorted him through the hospital's glass doors as they slid open with a *hushhh* and a vague sense of swarming cold.

Gone.

"Let me call someone to take you home." A pastor, a nurse, and a hundred others had offered the same, and Rick had responded only with silence. Where did he live? Did he have a family member who could pick him up? A friend, perhaps? A dim memory surfaced of a shocked staff member after Rick had muttered, "All m-my f-f-friends are g-g-ghosts."

After that, his immediate thought was *Emily*. But . . .

Gone.

Cars passed as if the world still moved. Wind gusted as

if there were still a reason. He breathed as if there were still a need to take air. His thoughts shifted from the moments before the crash to the moments after.

I need to find her, tell her I'm sorry.

But.

She's gone. *Gone? Impossible. I need to get to the cottage.*

But. *Where is she?*

Gone.

A SHELL OF RICK'S FORMER SELF RETURNED TO THE cemetery with no memory of how he'd gotten there. Staring at the gate, he couldn't release the image of her standing there, her hair lifting, falling in the breeze.

Do you smell apples? Her head turned.

Rick shuffled toward the bent iron, walking mindlessly over shards of broken glass. *This is where she took her last breath.* He fell to his knees, brushing the snow aside where spots of her blood sprinkled the concrete.

. . . smell apples? Turn . . .

Rick examined the blood. A tickle in his mind preceded outright refusal. *Rust, it's only rust.* Relieved, he released a breath. A mad chuckle spiraled into the night as he lowered his weary body onto all that remained of her.

After an age, someone called his name. "Rick." A distant voice. "Come inside. Please."

He returned to darkness, shutting out the voice.

After a while, Rick's eyes opened to a white world. He saw a gate of twisted metal and a car bumper in the shrubs. None of it was real—the scene from earlier, the ghosts who wandered through his life, the blood—rust, only rust —beneath him. They were the imaginings of a madman. A laugh rang out before freezing to the concrete, and he casually concluded that he must be crazy. People didn't talk to ghosts. People died and went away forever.

And ever.

A twinge of pain stabbed as he tried to connect this thought to Emily. Rick shook his head violently, scraping his cheek on the concrete.

No.

"Rick, please." Another voice. "Let us help."

"Go away. You're not real." He closed his eyes, yet the voices went on. And on. And on. They murmured senseless syllables, these voices in his head. He tightened his eyes until spots swarmed. Emily danced there, too, her body swiveling as her dress floated the way it had the night of the party. The night he'd loved her, and, for whatever reason, she'd loved him back.

"At least come inside so you can sleep in your bed."

Emily, her hair spread on the ground, trying to breathe, trying to speak . . .

Do you smell apples?

Sobbing. A woman.

Rick peeled his face from the frozen ground. A blue-haired girl leaned against the broken gate, her shoulders heaving, and a stranger in an apron patted her arm, speaking softly.

Why is that girl crying?

Images rushed in, quick and cruel. Emily's eyes, her voice, her gasps for breath. Her lifeless body. A man in scrubs wheeling her away, shrouding her face forever.

Suddenly, Rick began to shiver. His body stiffened as

he tried to pull himself up but couldn't. He crawled to the gnarled gate, snow sliding from his back as his hands curled into stumps. He grabbed hold of the metal; the residents stepped back.

Taylor met his gaze as her sobs quieted. She hurt; he could see it. She'd lost a friend, and she hurt. Pulling himself up on numb legs, Rick tried to take a step and caught a glimpse of Madge's watery eyes. Then Stephanie appeared, her chin quivering. They mourned Emily. They were real, and they wept. The simple truth of it—their loss mirroring his own—crippled him. Falling again to his knees, with one hand clutching the cold, crushed metal, Rick began to sob.

"Help m-m-me."

They rushed to his side, encircling him. Taylor tried to touch him, but her hands flowed through, and she cursed herself for still being dead. Rick's sobs intensified, melting into wails.

Madge's face contorted as she leaned close. "Rick, dear, can you walk?"

He could only shake his head.

"That's alright," she whispered, soft, soothing. "We'll get there together."

His sobs refused to quit, so he nodded.

And so, side by side, through the snow and the pain of a world collapsed, they crawled.

27

EIGHTY HOURS

Rick's eyes fluttered open. His back screamed. Once he'd made it inside, he hadn't been able to go further than the rug at the fire, where he'd collapsed into a fitful sleep.

Emily's gone.

His stomach churned while needles of pain sliced through his core. Closing his eyes, he forced sleep, and another hour passed. *Emily's gone.* He returned to oblivion.

When he awoke, he wandered the cottage like a ghostly vessel. Drifting from room to room, he counted the hours Emily had been gone. He tried to comprehend how she'd been alive, breathing and laughing only thirty, forty, fifty hours before. Panic arose when he couldn't remember the last time he'd felt her hand warm and soft on his skin, and it so grieved him that he had to steady himself against a wall.

At sixty hours, he curled into a corner and wept until he had no more tears. At seventy, he ate half a frozen dinner, and at seventy hours and nineteen minutes, he retched. At seventy-one hours, he fell into a nightmarish sleep on the kitchen floor, waking in sweat as dawn shattered the night. With creaking bones, he tried to place the unfamiliar cottage. A pillow lay just out of reach, fallen from the couch where he'd slept since Christmas—the day of the fight when he'd pushed Emily aside and punished her for having been born into the wrong family.

A decade of routine whispered—raking, trimming, righting upside-down flower pots. But what was it all for? It seemed ridiculous to go about those trivial tasks that served nothing and no one. After a while, he'd lose his job along with his perfect, solitary cottage. What did it matter? He'd be homeless. So what? He'd remain here until he was put on the street like garbage. Until then, he'd go back to bed, sleep if he could, and stare at the walls if he couldn't.

Come what may, come what may.

At eighty hours, Rick limped into the bathroom. Something told him he was supposed to change his clothes and open the gate. He ran a toothbrush over his teeth and combed his fingers through greasy hair. He didn't know why, only that it seemed like he should. He shuffled, too exhausted to take full steps.

In the bedroom, he was met by six staring eyes. Madge sat on his unmade bed, Stephanie rested on the floor holding her knees to her chest, and Taylor ventured a weak smile from atop the dresser.

Pity. Concern. Sadness. They offered all of those things and none of them. Rick moved past the residents to the living room, where he lit and stoked the fire. Why was the cottage so cold? Dropping into his chair, he waited for warmth.

After a time, they settled on the couches—watching

him, watching the fire. If they were expecting some action. Too bad—he could do no more. His mind was blank, his thinker broken.

Madge braved the first contact. "We're all so sorry. We know how much you loved her. We loved her, too."

Sorry. The word echoed. What a silly concept with too many meanings. Rick had heard other mourners say it as he'd lowered their loved ones into the dirt. That was what he was now—a mourner.

A truth tried to reveal itself before slipping from his grasp.

"Rick, dear, I know this is hard, but . . ." Madge struggled, and again, Rick tried to reach for the thing that would tear him apart. Something—there was something he was forgetting. "You'll need to prepare. It's already been three days . . ."

It hit him so hard that it actually knocked his head back. He grabbed his chest, gasping.

No, no, no. I can't do that.

And yet the very nature of his job cemented the morbid reality of it. He lunged from his chair and paced at the fire, resting a hand against his forehead. "I can't b-b-b . . ." The word refused to emerge, crawling back down his throat.

The very idea churned his stomach—digging Emily's grave, lowering her casket into the earth, throwing shovels of dirt onto her body. He was struck by the callousness of life. Whoever or whatever controlled everything seemed to have chosen him as the eternal butt of every joke. Life gave and took. And took. And took. Then it slapped him in the face with his own loss. *Look what you did,* life whispered, as it ground his nose into the shattered remains of his pathetic existence. *Now . . . sit in it.*

"I know it's not fair. There are no words to express how unfair it is. But Emily has a place here, and no one else can do it."

"No." He shook his head wildly. They couldn't seriously expect him to perform such a grim task. The very idea brought on a fresh wave of anger.

"G-G-Get out!" he bellowed, raising his fists to his temples as he slid down the wall and rocked on the floor. Like a child, he covered his ears.

"Rick—"

"I s-said get out! Ungh . . ." It was all so unfathomable. Unthinkable. "Get out, get out, get ou—"

A sudden whoosh of air sliced through his skull like a cold knife. Though there was no pain, something told him it should have hurt. *Would* have hurt. Pulling his hands from his ears, he opened one eye.

With one hand wavering, Herbert glared at the mess that was Rick and whipped a hand forward again. Though it disappeared into mist, the effect was the same.

Rick's skin crawled. The ghostly remnants of Herbert's phantom blow coated his face, teeth, and tongue like dust. "D-Did you just s-slap me?"

"Oh, my God, Herb, I can't believe you just did th—"

"I pity that girl," Herbert seethed, crossing his arms over his chest.

"Herb, that's quite enough." Madge's voice shook. "I think you should lea—"

"She's gonna show up in a few days," Herbert went on, ignoring them, "and her little shit of a boyfriend is gonna be lying here, crying and whining about how life isn't fair. Boo-hoo, I never get what I want."

Madge stepped forward. "Herb, get away from him."

Undeterred, Herbert continued sifting through the man-puddle on the floor. "Are you just gonna leave her in limbo? Maybe hope someone else magically comes along and does your job for you?"

He leaned close, his face inches away, and Rick cringed.

"Are you gonna run away from this, like you run away from everything else?" Herbert straightened. "How's that worked out for you so far, punk?"

The fire crackled while snow tapped at the windows. Rick wanted to scream, to banish Herbert from the cottage and spit at his ghostly form.

And then Herbert's eyes softened, and once again, Rick caught a glimpse of the man beneath the mask. The other Herbert stepped forward, the Herbert who'd danced on that cold night, and the sight was both wondrous and terrible.

Herbert covered his heart as if in salute to the flag. Though it was probably his imagination, Rick could almost feel the man's breath tickle his ear. "Don't fail her when she needs you the most. You'll pay for it longer than you think."

With that, every wrong turn replayed and beat Rick with invisible fists. He'd spent his life searching for one hiding place after another. His childhood had been nothing more than a series of events that had seemed out of his control, yet he'd never fought back. Not once had he stood his ground, met blow with blow. He'd only halfheartedly done the exercises to improve his speech, convinced they would do no good. After hiding away in the cemetery, he'd created a life where he could shelter himself in obscurity.

Then Emily had come along, and he'd congratulated himself for having stepped from his comfort zone when all he'd done was drag her into the muck. He'd brought her into his lonely world rather than take a single step into hers.

Herbert was right. *Damn.*

Rick unfurled his limbs from the cold floor. Lists, errands, and things to do whipped him. He'd wasted so much time wallowing that the clock now raced as he grew determined not to founder. "Has the paper come yet?"

Herbert smirked.

"It's at the gate. We, like, tried to read the front page, but it's rolled up so tight . . ."

With a lifetime of missteps behind him, Rick stood straighter than he had in days. He strutted to the door with renewed purpose. "I only n-need to see one thing, and it's not on the f-front page." He opened the door, determined to get it right this time.

"We have some p-planning to do."

———————

As Rick unfolded the paper, his breath halted at the front-page photo that barely hid the body beneath Emily's Honda. Yet they'd missed something crucial—painful. Just beyond the car's twisted backside, her arm lay on the pavement, palm up, with a small, thin bracelet visible.

"Rick . . ."

"It's alr-right." He tore his gaze away and flipped through the thin pages, knowing precisely where to look. It was his job to know.

He skimmed passed colorless photos of men and women who'd lived full lives, raised children to adulthood, and belonged to all the clubs associated with people who'd lived long enough to have finished everything. Here was Margaret, there was Jay. Rick lingered over their faces, not quite ready to see the face he sought. And then . . .

Emily. His girl. Her hair was shorter—did they not have a more recent photo? This one had to be at least ten years old. Her lips held the bare trace of a forced smile, and even in her picture, she looked forgotten.

"Read it, please," Taylor said quietly.

Rick cleared his throat, unsure if he could.

———

Emily Bennett (1996 - 2019)

Emily Lorraine Bennett passed away on Dec 31st (see article page 1). She was 23.

Born in Hood Valley to John and Deborah Bennett, she graduated from Jonsrud HS and went on to attend Portland State University. She worked briefly at the Hood Valley Library and most recently managed the Book and Nook.

She is survived by her mother, Deborah, and her brother Donald.

A private funeral will be held on Sunday at Twin Oaks Gardens. In lieu of flowers, the family is accepting monetary donations in Emily's name at Hood Valley Bank.

———

HER ENTIRE LIFE HAD BEEN SUMMARIZED IN FOUR SHORT paragraphs. The casual, terse outline of Emily's existence had so thrown Rick that he'd missed the most crucial part.

"Why are they burying her across town, away from Frank? Is her father buried over there?"

"They cremated him. Frank said they scattered his ashes in the river." Madge stared at the open page. "It makes no sense."

The fog parted, and Rick saw the ugly truth. "I know why. They're k-k-keeping her from me. This is D-D-Donny's doing."

Taylor paced at the fire. "I can't believe Donny would go through that much trouble just to, I don't know, stick it to you."

"Rick might be right. Neither had been fond of Frank. And Donny clearly hasn't changed." Madge turned to Rick. "As crazy as it sounds, this might be some sick revenge."

That Donny hated him was not up for debate; there was a lifetime of loathing between them. But Emily—who, despite her family's best efforts, had grown into a person so opposite, so removed from them—had become the target of their hatred.

"No, not m-m-me. It's *her* they're angry w-with." Rage shook Rick so violently that he thought he might implode. "They're not getting away with this. D-Donny has bullied me—Emily—for the last time."

Rick grabbed his keys.

"What are you going to do?"

The answer came before his brain registered it, but when he spoke, he knew it was right.

"I'm bringing Emily home."

28

BETTER LATE THAN NEVER

Though two cars were parked in the driveway—Emily's Honda glaringly missing—the house looked empty. With the curtains closed tight and no sign of activity inside, it was as if even the house was drowned in Emily's absence.

I have to do this. For Em.

Rick had repeated the mantra a hundred times on the drive over. *I have to do this. I have to do this.* Hope had led him there—that he could reason with Emily's mother and that, for once, he wouldn't fail.

"Em," he whispered, lifting his knuckles to the door, "if there's anything you can do, I sure could use the help."

Knock. Knock. Knock.

A shuffle and the fumbling lock broke the mournful silence. Mrs. Bennett—in the same robe from the Christmas dinner that never was—reeked as she swayed in the doorway. Now that he could see her in the light of day, Rick couldn't help noticing that she shared Emily's nose, upturned and thin, though without the row of freckles he'd found so endearing.

"Who're you?" Her head rolled back as her eyes flitted in and out of focus. "Paper said to donate to the bank." She moved to shut the door.

No. It won't end like this.

"Miss . . . Mrs. B-Bennett, my n-name is Rick. We m-m-met last week. On Christmas?" He shifted nervously.

Mrs. Bennett drifted back, steadying herself as she gripped the door frame, and a mad chorus began in Rick's head. *Weebles wobble, but they don't fall down. Weebles wobble* . . . Shaking the tune away, he fought to regain his focus.

"Who?"

Rick's foot pinched against the door frame, loosening, squeezing. When had he stuck his foot inside? He pulled back during a loosening pulse. "I'm. . . I was Emily's b-b-boyfriend."

"What does he want?" a familiar voice cawed. Donny stepped forward, and mother and son stood together in an eerie imitation of the portraits inside. "Go inside, Mom. I've got this."

Something close to a grunt tumbled from Mrs. Bennett's lips as she shuffled into the darkened house. Rick's heart thump-thump-thumped as he locked eyes with the boy-turned-man who'd once held him beneath the water, laughing.

Laughing as he'd died.

Run. Go back to the cemetery. This was a stupid idea. Did you really think you'd convince these people to do the right thing? Rick calculated the number of steps to the truck. If he took the stairs two at a time and had his keys ready, he just might make it.

And then, the faint aroma of apples drifted in as if on a current. A calmness cleansed Rick, and the hairs on his arms settled flat. A soft whisper—words he couldn't make out—hushed. His knees straightened, his back stiffened, and he planted his feet firmly onto the porch.

Fearlessness had never been a Rick Holliday trait, had never been a word anyone would have used to describe him. Which was why he didn't recognize it when it made its first appearance. Whatever it was, he liked it. "Don't do this to her," he said, bold, brassy. "Bury her with her g-grandfather. You know that's where she'd want to be."

Donny snickered, turning toward the interior. "What did I tell you, Mom? It's just like I said." Turning back, his eyes danced. "I knew he was a pervert."

A grunt barked from inside the house.

"You're a real sicko, you know that?" The door widened, and Donny stepped onto the porch. "I told Mom all about guys like you."

Rick stood his ground, fighting the urge to run from his lifelong adversary. The sharp scent of apples stayed him.

Another step. Donny sniffed, lifting his nose as if he smelled something rotten. "Guys like you are sick. Up here." He tapped a pudgy finger to his temple. "I know why you want my sister in your playground. I know what you'd like to do to her." His finger came down and landed squarely in the center of Rick's chest. "You're a nectarine. A filthy, rotten nectarine. That's why you like to dig graves. So you can get your sick rocks off."

Nectarine? What . . . Rick was so thrown that his fear withdrew in a rush. A thick, echoing laugh roared suddenly, and as he held his stomach, Rick realized it had come from him.

Donny blinked and took a half-step back. "What are you laughing at, freak?"

Nectarine! Trying desperately to gather his composure, Rick caught his breath as tears welled, and he swiped a hand across his cheeks. "You, D-Donny, I'm laughing at you." It felt good to laugh again, to find hilarity amid grief, and to see Donny for what he really was—nothing more than a failed childhood bully.

Regaining his sobriety, Rick met Donny's stare. "The word is necrophiliac, and if anyone's sick, it's you for keeping Emily from Frank. Do the right thing. For her."

A hateful smile widened Donny's already large face. "It ain't happening, Stutter Boy."

Rick's stomach churned as he realized the futility of his mission. There was no reasoning with people like Donny, who were consumed with a lifetime of hatred and drunk on the power of squashing others. Doing the right thing was beyond him.

Rick turned toward the street in defeat. He could always visit Emily across town and get on as the caretaker when a spot opened up. But the others—she'd be lost to them forever, and even though Frank was gone, it would break Emily to be apart from what remained. As Rick descended the steps, he imagined her arrival in a strange cemetery, the mourners gone, her casket covered in fresh dirt. Lost, alone—

"That's what I thought."

Rick's foot hovered over the last step, and he turned.

Resting lazily against the door frame, Donny bared his teeth. "You're just like her—weak. I tried to tell her not to hang around retards like you. All I did at the pool that day was try to take out the trash. But she wouldn't listen. She always had a soft spot for—"

Rick hadn't known he could move so fast.

Lucky for him, neither did Donny.

Like a bullet, Rick's fist shot out and landed in the crook of Donny's nose with a sickening crunch. Pulling back, he looked at his hand as if it were some foreign object magically attached to the end of his arm. He splayed his fingers open, then closed them again. Adrenaline rushed, and joy flooded in unlike any he'd known.

I want to do that again. And he did. Twice.

Contrary to what Rick had been led to believe, payback wasn't a bitch—it was exhilarating. Payback was a long time coming, and he savored the solidity of skin-on-skin, knuckle-to-nose. A stream of blood poured from Donny's snout. A nose that now looked alarmingly askew.

That's a lot of blood.

"You punched me! You freaking punched me, you retard!" Donny's voice rose with a nasal whine, and Rick fought the laugh that bubbled up his throat. "Mom! The retard hit me! Shit, I'm bleeding!" Donny stared wide-eyed while he cowered in the doorway. "Why'd you do that?"

Rick felt incredible, dizzy with exhilaration, and his knuckles throbbed with the most satisfying hurt in the world. He wanted to do it again, to pummel Donny into the ground and keep going. He could—the way Donny cringed proved that.

Emily's face floated before him, reminding Rick why he'd come. His fist loosened. If he couldn't convince Donny to cooperate, Rick would have to find another way.

Overcome with sudden weariness, he knew he may have ended thirty years of misery with a couple well-deserved punches, but he'd lost the real fight. Emily would be buried in the wrong place, and there was nothing Rick could do to stop it.

Returning to his truck, Rick barely registered Donny's blubbering cries for his mother as a thought occurred.

"You were right about one thing," Rick called over his shoulder. "I *am* just like her."

At least there was one thing to smile about.

———

"WELL, THAT SETTLES THAT, DOESN'T IT?" A MOROSE gathering of the formerly living hovered near the fire. "They're never going to bury Emily here now. Rick pretty much ensured that when he punched Donny. Justified, but it's put us in quite a pickle."

"Better late than never," Taylor said as she slumped into the couch."He should have done more than punch him. Donny murdered him, after all."

"You can always visit her. She's not, like, gone forever." Stephanie's wan smile revealed that even she knew it was a weak attempt.

The adrenaline had worn off hours ago, leaving Rick with sickening knowledge. In two days, Emily would be buried across town, separated forever from the people who loved her the most. "I'd l-like some alone time. I need s-s-sleep."

One by one, they quietly disappeared. Only Madge hung back. "He would never have agreed to bring her here even if you hadn't broken his nose." She tried a wavering smile before she, too, quietly disappeared.

Rick shuffled to the bedroom and piled the blankets back onto the bed, and a single thought haunted him as he fell into an uneasy slumber.

I failed her.

29

DIGGERS

"**W**ake up, you little shit!"

Flipping on the bedside lamp, Rick tried to adjust his eyes as Herbert straddled his chest. Though he felt no weight, the sight was disturbing enough. "Herb, w-w-what the hell—"

"They're digging me up! I told you they would!"

Sliding from beneath the old man, Rick scrambled out of bed. "What are you t-t-talking about?"

"What I've always been talking about, shithead! Grave robbers!" Herbert screeched, hopping in place. "They're out there right now! Go get 'em!"

Stephanie dashed into the room, breathless. "He's right, Rick. There's, like, two of them out there, digging. Oh, my God . . ."

Needing no further proof, Rick snatched a flannel. "They're actually d-digging?"

"They snuck in ten minutes ago." Madge gave Rick a sympathetic glance. "The gate . . ."

Rick groaned. *Of course.* The broken gate that, in his

grief, he'd neglected to repair. Something reached inside his chest and squeezed. This was all he needed. His feet slid on the wood floor as he raced into the living room and jammed his boots on.

"Be careful." Taylor peered out the window. "They're big guys, and they have that shovel."

"D-Don't worry. They'll take off as soon as they s-see m-m-me." Rubbing a hand against his chest, Rick grabbed the fireplace poker and turned to Herbert. "I guess I owe you an apology—"

"Stop your yapping and get out there!"

Poker in hand, Rick raced out the door and prepared to defend an old man's grave.

RICK'S HEART KNOCKED AGAINST HIS RIBCAGE AS HE raced toward the back stretch. Darkness reigned; clouds had invaded, blocking out the sliver of a new moon. Hearing voices, he stopped and, with horror, recognized the *shhhp* of a shovel breaking earth. As he rounded the corner, he spotted the diggers—two boys, and from the looks of them, not yet out of high school. One dug while the other held a camp light, shivering. A prank, then— probably a dare. That they'd chosen this particular grave to desecrate was likely mere chance.

It had to be.

"Hold it steady," Shovel-Boy hissed.

"I can't help it," Light-Boy said through chattering teeth. "It's effing cold out here."

Rick stepped from behind the tree he'd intended to chop down a thousand years ago amidst Herbert's belly-aching—protests which now seemed ludicrously foreshad-owed. "Hey, there! What are you d-doing?"

Two heads shot up. "Shit, Cody . . ." Light-Boy dropped the lamp into the hole, which made him now simply Boy. "Run!"

The vandals took off toward the gate, diving behind the row of bushes near Frank's grave. One cried out as he crashed into the hidden bench.

"Get up, Cody!"

Rick gave chase, nearly running into Shovel-Boy, who swore and sprinted around the hedge back toward the gate.

"Man, don't leave me here with this psycho!" Boy yelled, scrambling to follow.

Leading with the poker, Rick raced after them. It was difficult. He struggled for breath, the squeezing in his chest intensifying as the muscles around his ticker tightened. As he tore around the mangled azalea, he slid on gravel, nearly toppling Frank's tombstone.

The others appeared, and Herbert fled in the opposite direction. "My body better be intact!"

Wedging himself through the broken gate, Rick caught his flannel on one of the bars. A patch of fabric flapped in the breeze. He spied the boys up Main Street before they skirted into the alley behind the old Revenue Hotel. He didn't need to catch them—they'd likely never return. Still, Rick's feet carried him beyond the gate into the dark, abandoned street. Caught up in the horror of the last few days—hell, of a lifetime—Rick was propelled by new determination. Giving up now was an impossibility. For once, he was not about to allow someone else to win the fight.

He ran on for another block before stopping. With his

palms on his knees, he doubled over. He rubbed his chest to ease the increasing ache as his suddenly puny lungs struggled.

The street lamps grew dimmer, casting vague shadows on the pavement. Struggling for breath, Rick took several steps toward the sidewalk. Someone had wrapped an enormous rubber band around his chest, and he clutched his shoulder as it radiated pain. His left arm turned numb as his fingers moved a thousand miles away. The lights dimmed further, and the shadows disappeared.

A rainbow of stars flashed, and the last thing Rick Holliday did was reach out and try to grab one.

30

MOURNERS

The women stood at the gate, craning to catch a glimpse of either Rick or the diggers.

"I wish Herb would stop already. I can't, like, hear anything through all that."

"I still can't believe he turned out to be right."

Herbert's anguished wails filled the air while the others waited. As the hours wore on, the women grew uneasy, and even Herbert, after he'd finally ceased his howling, joined them to stare beyond the gate into the land of the living. The night grew quiet, with not a car or a Liver to be seen, and when the sun eventually rose, none had moved from the mangled iron.

"I told him a thousand times, but he didn't listen. No one ever listens. I warned that little shit—"

"Herb, dear, shut up. Someone's coming."

The residents shuffled aside as an old pickup pulled up to the twisted gate, followed by a police cruiser. An elderly man climbed down from the truck, then turned to the officers. "Can't open the gate. Delivery truck hit it th' other day. You probably heard." The officers squeezed through the opening and followed the old man into the cemetery.

"Who's that?" Taylor asked.

Madge watched the three men trudge toward the cottage. "It's Sandy Barlow."

Taylor frowned. "The guy who hired Rick?"

Madge could only nod.

"Like, what's he doing here?"

"I've only seen him one other time," Madge whispered. As the rest stood near the broken gate, Madge followed the three Livers in slow, halting steps.

"After the last caretaker died."

FOUR LONG-DEAD SPIRITS FLOATED INTO THE COTTAGE AND huddled together. Stephanie and Taylor held one another, sobbing quietly while Madge slid down the wall and settled in a heap. Even Herbert stood with his hands solemnly clasped, shaking his head.

At the coffee table, Sandy Barlow glanced through Rick's book collection. "It's a darn shame. He was still pretty young. Never expect to have a heart attack at thirty." He grabbed an apple and inspected it before gingerly returning the fruit to the basket. "It'll be damn hard to replace him."

An officer emerged from the bedroom, clutching a small notebook. "I just got off the phone with dispatch. He's got no next of kin, and there's no one to claim the body. We'll have to transport him to the state cemetery."

Madge brought a hand to her mouth. "No! They can't just send him to some anonymous place . . ."

The elderly man who'd been awaiting Rick on the fateful day he'd turned his truck around, who'd shaken his hand knowing nothing happened by chance, turned. Though he spoke to the officer, Sandy Barlow's gaze locked on Madge in a strange embrace.

"No need. All of my caretakers have a place right here."

THE RESIDENTS REMAINED INSIDE LONG AFTER THE LIVERS had gone, and the cottage grew dark and cold. There was no Rick to stoke the fire, no Rick to turn on the lamps. He wasn't there to listen to their complaints, read comment cards, or worry over flowers. Rick was so entirely not there that his absence was everywhere.

Madge gazed out the window, watching the rain fall in sheets while Stephanie and Taylor brooded on the couch, their hands clasped together in grief. Herbert slumped in a corner chair, staring at the darkening walls.

"I guess we should get ready. Rick will be here in a couple of days." Madge said somberly. "This won't be easy."

"Oh, my God, they'll never be together now. Rick will be here, and tomorrow, Emily will be across town. It's not fair."

"I know, dear. Those two never had anyone but each other. And now . . . he's going to be a mess for a while."

"Tell me about it," Taylor said, swiping a hand across her cheek. "That first day is a bitch."

WHEN A GOOSE WALKS ON YOUR GRAVE

The cottage lightened as the clouds broke, allowing a stream of sunshine through. Though no living being inhabited the dwelling, four dead souls had taken up residence overnight, mourning their growing losses. Sunlight washed the dusty floor, an unwelcome guest piercing the darkness they'd cocooned themselves in.

Taylor had spent the night cursing the cruelties of both life and death. A friend lost, found, and then lost again, Emily would now be elsewhere, while Taylor remained forever alone. Emily would have understood her world and known the people she'd known. She would have known that Yahoo wasn't the name of a chocolate soda. "Yahoo. Not Yoohoo." She realized she'd said it aloud only when Stephanie jerked her head up. Taylor had anticipated a thousand questions, yet the teen merely turned back to the wall.

Madge spoke weakly, her apron limp in her hands. "At

least we won't have to make space in the closet. Rick won't be bringing a lot of knick-knacks—"

"Stop!" Herbert tilted his head like a curious dog as his face transformed from puzzled to exhilarated. "Oh!"

"What is it now, Herb?"

"Seriously, can't you just let us—"

"Oh, boy!" Releasing his grip on the chandelier, Herbert crashed to the floor. He gathered his limbs and snapped his bones back into place. "A goose is walking on my grave!"

Madge rushed to the old man's side and shook his shoulders. "Are you sure?"

"Of course I'm sure, woman!" Flinging her away, Herbert raced to the door.

"What's happening?"

"There's no time, dear," Madge answered, following the old man. "Come along."

As Herbert reached the cottage path, a single word shrieked through the wind.

"Travis!"

———

THEY REACHED THE GAPING HOLE OF HERBERT'S GRAVE TO find the old man dancing, two middle fingers pointed toward the sky as he jigged and kicked, clapped, and stomped. Herbert's exposed casket lay in a pool of mud and crumpled leaves, and the roots from the old elm had wound around the cheap pine that encased his bones in a macabre embrace.

"What in the heck is that?"

Atop Herbert's pine box, a large goose strutted, its feet pattering atop the askew coffin as it waddled.

"What's in its mouth?" Taylor pointed, breathless, at a bound roll of papyrus in the bird's beak.

"Herb got his papers." Madge backed against the elm.

"But what's it doing there? And how did Herb know?"

The old man danced, skirting the edges of his open grave, and spat on the ground with a cackle.

"Like, you've heard that phrase about a goose walking over your grave?"

"Yeah . . ."

Stephanie's expression suggested the answer was obvious, nodding toward the coffin. "Well . . . duh."

Herbert hopped into the hole and snatched the papyrus. The goose promptly flew away as Herbert opened the scroll. He read quietly, his eyes moving over the yellowed parchment before it disintegrated. "It's here! It's finally here!" he yelled, followed by a string of vile words. With a lunatic grin, he scurried to the elm and performed unspeakable acts against its dry, rough bark.

"Would someone please tell me what's going on?"

Sweeping her hands over her arms, Madge glared at the old man as he thrust his hips against the dead tree. "Herb is moving on."

"That's right, I am!" the old codger shouted, wrapping his legs around the elm. "Travis is finally going to get what's coming to him!"

"Herb, please . . ." Madge begged, throwing her hands over Stephanie's ears.

Slipping from Madge's grasp, Stephanie plopped onto the deadened grass. "Well, goodbye then, Herb. I can't say it's been, like, nice knowing you all these years."

Taylor settled beside the teen. "So, you're leaving, then? In twenty-four hours?"

"Hell no, I ain't waiting. I'm out of here." Tucking his thumbs behind his suspenders, Herbert turned toward the gate. "Travis, you little shit, here I come!" With one final sneer at the three who would remain, he flipped them the bird and leaped onto the path.

"It's always odd to see someone you've spent so much time with just walk right through," Madge said wistfully over Herbert's fading laughter.

"At least Rick will be happy. Or, like, happier, I guess."

The man who'd caused Rick so much grief and filled his days with endless complaints and unsolvable problems flew through the gate and shouted one final sentiment before plunging into traffic.

"So long, assholes!"

Two days later, the last remaining residents stood beside the gate as the hearse rolled in.

32

NEXT

The soul that was once Rick Holliday swirled through obsidian. With no body to limit him, he felt nothing and everything. He was sense and being, a singular entity and every man. He was Rick who once was and Rick who would become yet again.

He met a familiar woman from another life, who'd once held him, rocked him, and died with him at her side. After singing a hauntingly familiar lullaby from times gone by, she told him a great many things, and Rick felt at peace. In the vacuum of time, he remained with her for a thousand years and grew to love her again.

And then . . . light.

It's time for you to go.

He protested, denying the light and begging to remain. She told him that their time had come to an end, but they would see each other in the . . . he'd never heard the word, but knew the meaning just the same. The woman who had once been Helen and called herself Mother held him, kissed his cheek, and turned Rick toward the light. Faltering, he took a step and looked back.

She was gone.

The dust that had once been his body pushed forward into brilliance. Floating for millennia, he became memory, emotion, love. And then the darkness shifted. Gray replaced black, and his body once again took form. In a tunnel that pulsed with each step, the light grew stronger. The brightness took shape, and a door appeared—small, larger, largest. As he lingered before it, there was no question, no fear, no decision to make. He would walk through because his essence knew the door was truth. Life.

Next.

In the moment before Rick returned to his earthly self, knowledge besieged him. He knew where everything had begun and when it would end. He knew the history of humankind, earth, and beyond—the Before, the Next, and the After. He understood the meaning of life, death, and being.

Finding his voice, he whispered, "Oh." It was all so undeniably clear.

As he stepped through, the light abated along with his newfound knowledge. Blue and white swirled as his vision narrowed. Raising a hand, Rick stroked his face, suddenly so very *there*. The blue morphed into sky and the white into clouds, and he was gifted with sight once again. A falcon screeched—sound. He caressed his ears, tasted the air, and felt the breeze on his arms.

Once again, Rick Holliday was.

THOUGH SOLID, HIS BODY SEEMED ODDLY LIGHT, NEARLY weightless, and Rick half-expected to float into the abyss. His limbs appeared the same, yet his body was new, without the limitations, aches, and pains he'd suffered in the Before. He inhaled, exhaled, and inhaled again. Did he even have lungs anymore? He could have inhaled forever. Gone was the persistent shoulder pain he'd carried since childhood. There was no hunger, no tiredness, and no nagging backache. Colors swam into view. Purples and pinks and . . . dear God, what color was that? The air sparkled with something sort of blue, kind of purple, and yet not quite either. He scanned the valley. Everything seemed more robust, more there, somehow, as if someone had sharpened the contrast in his vision.

Turning from the canyon, he found his tombstone. Rather than the usual slab of unmarked granite, Rick's marker was engraved with his name, birth date, and, he mused, the date of his death. Stepping aside, he noticed the freshly laid sod. Had there been a funeral? Not likely. He strangely found that he didn't care.

So. He was a resident now.

Stepping toward the wooded path that led into the heart of the cemetery, Rick stopped. Turned. Cocked his head. His curiosity was too strong to resist. He raced back to his grave and pressed against the loose sod until the ground gave way, and he plunged into the earth. His arms swam, moving through soil until his head slammed into something cold and metal. He reached forward, touched it, and tried to push through, but it was solid. Arms flailing backward, he pedaled until light and air warmed him once again.

He laughed. "Thank you, Sean McFadden, my Irish champion."

A QUICK GLANCE TOWARD THE SKY REVEALED IT WAS LATE afternoon. Strolling the tree-lined path from the caretaker's grove, Rick was distracted by the spring in his step. Each footfall felt light and bouncy as if the soles of his feet had been infused with helium. He could walk forever without getting winded. As his arms sliced effortlessly through pines, a laugh rose so childlike that anyone crossing his path would have thought him mad.

Emerging from the trees, his breath ceased. The sight before him was entirely unexpected. Tiny globes of colorful light swarmed the air, dancing and rising before swooping toward the earth. A sphere swam to his upturned palm, rolling, expanding, and diminishing, filling Rick with unexpected solace. What were they? Living beings or drops of spiritual dust? Dazzling, delicate whispers trailed the orbs as they returned to the sky.

Rick stopped at the hedge that bordered Frank's grave and felt the first bitter stab of sorrow. Emily's face pierced his mind, and her smile jabbed his heart. How long would he mourn her? How long would she be alone? His step faltered, and he was suddenly weak in the knees. The torment he would forever endure settled in, burrowing beneath his skin.

The gate—from where *she* had first entered his life— had been replaced, a shiny new padlock hanging from its bars. Memories clawed, choking him with a reopened wound that would never heal. Though his body felt renewed, his spirit had tagged along with him into his new existence.

There were other kinds of pain.

Approaching the comment box—the point of their first contact—he tried to lift the lid, yet his hand fell through. Again, he reached out—again, he fell onto empty space.

Emily, I'm so very sorry. For everything.

With a gash in his soul, Rick thought of the others, bound to this life for decades. How long would this age last for him? How many lifetimes would he be forced to endure without her?

As the cottage came into view, he planted his feet on the path he'd meticulously maintained for the final ten years of Life Number One. He hesitated as a new realization swept over him.

The cottage was his no more.

HE KNEW HE SHOULD GO INSIDE. IT WAS NEXT. A NEW caretaker would likely have moved in by now, cleared Rick's belongings, and hid them away in the dusty attic. Would his books still be stacked on the coffee table? His chair waiting near the fire? He felt an unexpected affinity for Serge, his predecessor. Had Serge mentioned walking into his cottage that first time, his possessions boxed up like so much insignificant rubbish? Had Rick missed the telling of Serge's home scrubbed of all proof that he'd ever been there?

So easy it was to rid the traces of a man from his earthly life.

He could remain outside, let the others find him. Heck,

unless some miracle had occurred in the last few days, Rick at least knew where to find Taylor. He had no clue how to move to the other side; someone would have to teach him. That, apparently, was not knowledge included in the Next. A heavy sigh rushed as he reluctantly accepted his fate.

The time had come for Next.

He stepped forward, expecting to crash into the door so thoroughly that he nearly fell forward as he passed through, bracing against an impact that never came.

Relief swelled as he spotted his chair in its usual spot, his books stacked on the coffee table, and the sweet scent of apples still permeating the air. Rick knew his sense of smell would disappear over time, so he filled his lungs with the aroma while he still could.

His cottage—*the* cottage—was not empty.

Huddled together, the residents radiated timidity. Madge appeared wary, while Stephanie and Taylor looked downright terrified.

How bad had he been?

As they seemingly prepared for an outburst, Rick realized he loved them all. They'd been a part of him all along, and now it was time to truly belong to them.

"What's wrong? Never seen a dead guy before?"

A pause, and then, chaos.

They raced to surround him. Warmth radiated from their bodies, and he felt their breath on his skin. It hadn't occurred to him that these things could be felt on the other side. *His* side, now.

"Rick, can I, like, hug you?"

That they could touch him now had never entered his mind, either. In the Before, he'd avoided touch, lived a life of disconnect, detached from human camaraderie. But in the Next, he could handle it. No. He longed for it. He spread his arms wide. "Come here."

Exploding into giggles, Stephanie threw herself at Rick, her arms locked around his neck, and she squeezed so hard that his very breath escaped him. Her body had more substance than any object he'd touched Before. It was as if the last thirty years had been just a warm-up to the real thing. Here in the Next, touch was absolute.

"Don't hog him, dear. Some of us have waited a long time for this, you know."

They each took a turn, hugging, touching, and grasping his hands. They ran their fingers through his hair, clapped him on the back, and entwined their arms with his. Never could Rick have imagined that the power of touch could be so brilliantly healing. He was lifted, consoled, soothed. Worry fled, and sorrow vanished.

Speckles of the colorful globes swam into view, and Rick knew then what they were, realizing with awe that it was more than just an emotion, an idea. It had substance, and though unseen in life, it was there, none-theless.

Love had a form, and it was beautiful.

Gently, Madge swept a stray hair from his forehead. "I've wanted to do that for ages," she said, her chin quivering.

Her face came to him then. As the globes multiplied, surrounding him, Rick silently admitted the secret hope he'd held—that somehow she'd made it. Her absence screamed. Yet the globes made complete forlornness impossible.

Someone else was missing. "Where's Herb?" They all

spoke at once, and Rick couldn't hide his shock upon learning that Herb, of all people, had received his papers.

"All of our theories have gone out the window. Herb was the last person I'd have thought ready to move on."

With a sober expression, Taylor stepped forward. "I can't tell you how happy we are that you're here. How happy we all are."

Rick smiled weakly while his heart twisted. *Here come the condolences*. Yet he felt ready, prepared. He would get through this. "I guess I'll need some time to get used t—"

"We're all happy you're here, dear," Madge interrupted.

"Yes, Taylor said that."

"Like, *all* of us."

Something deep inside, some profound part of Rick, stirred. Love. Acceptance. Hope.

And once again, Rick Holliday very nearly knew . . . something.

A peripheral movement turned his gaze toward the bedroom door. His heart thumped twice and stopped. His throat tightened, his knees weakened, and he fell to them.

"Hello, Rick."

Emily. Her golden hair. Her freckle-lined nose. Her smile. There.

Here.

Next, indeed.

33

THE HAUNTING OF TRAVIS FIELDS

He ran.

For more than two decades, Herbert had tested the barrier. Bracing against the expected impact, he prepared to bounce back as he always had. But this time, he sailed through the open gate to freedom.

Racing alongside traffic, he entertained no thoughts of what was to come in the Next. He'd expected to be at the cemetery for decades. Maybe centuries. With no valuable lessons learned and no progress in his soul, there had been no desire to move on to whatever the afterlife had in store for him. Travis had been Herbert's single focus since the day the heart attack had taken him. He'd never expected robbers to actually dig him up; that had been as much a surprise to Herbert as anyone. His only concern over the years had been that Travis might die before he could exact his revenge.

He hurled his body through a sedan. Strapped into a car seat, a small girl jolted, her round eyes fixed on the stranger.

"Mooooom! There's a man!"

Tapping her fingers along to the radio, the girl's mother absently answered, "No yelling when Mommy's driving, sweetie."

Herbert chuckled—not unkindly—as the girl gaped. "You've got a great future as a caretaker, kid." Racing back into traffic, he felt exhilarated. It would be a long jog, but he'd waited twenty-one years for this—he could wait a bit longer. Turning onto the highway toward downtown Portland, he sprinted alongside the stream of cars.

At least two people spotted him. A woman pointed as she drove past, her mouth a round *O*, and nearly ran her car into the ditch. A young man driving a VW van painted with massive, garish daisies rolled down his window and called, "Right on, old dude!" He threw a peace sign, and Herbert reciprocated with a well-practiced middle finger.

So much had changed in the decades since his death. Formerly lush farmland had been covered with a sprawling business park, and the feed store was now a boxy, ugly apartment complex surrounded by acres of pavement. Even the Christmas tree farm he and Edith had visited year after year had been cleared to make room for an automatic car wash. Nostalgia flooded in, and Herbert's eyes moistened for the first time in an age. But he had a job to do, so he shook the memories away and ran on.

It took nearly four hours to get to the building where he'd died. At least *that* still looked the same. The street-level diner was still there, and the same cook worked behind the counter, though his temples were now speckled with gray. Entering the building, Herbert headed straight for the stairs. Solidity worked differently at the cemetery— there was no way he would chance the elevator only to fall through the earth. He wasn't entirely sure there wasn't a Hell to sink to. He ran down a single level, landing at a door:

MAILROOM
SECURE PERSONNEL ONLY

After allowing a moment to revel in a dream about to be realized, Herbert floated through steel.

That he recognized no one didn't surprise him. What did, however, was that the mailroom was now sparsely staffed. The few scattered employees couldn't have been older than Taylor, staring at computers and tapping on pictures. Several shuffled around the room, zombie-like, with small, flat calculators in their hands. They seemed oblivious to the people around them as they mindlessly touched screens. Other than the placement of the windows and an antique metal desk in the corner, the mail room bore little resemblance to the place where Herbert had taken his final living breath.

No matter. He wasn't here to gawk.

Herbert glided by a young man and woman, their eyes glued to screens. The woman—blonde and buxom—had some sort of round, hollow object embedded in her earlobe. She stared stupidly at Herbert, her lips slightly parted.

"Hey, you can't, like, be here and stuff." She sounded so much like Stephanie that Herbert half-expected her to twirl her hair. There was no way he could know how close he was to the truth—that she was the niece Stephanie hadn't lived long enough to meet.

Sporting a t-shirt that read, *I pooped today!* the young

man beside her asked, "Dude, who're you talking to?" He looked through the ghost, unseeing.

The dead man walked on, making his way to a door adorned with a plaque:

TRAVIS FIELDS
MANAGER

His heart raced, and saliva coated his tongue. This was it. After all these years of waiting, planning, and biding his time, he was finally here.

"Seriously, you, like, don't see him? He's right there, dork."

Herbert zoned the voices out, and as he floated through the door, he lost his breath. Slack-jawed, he stared at the man who'd taken his life—mocked him, humiliated him. The man who'd forced him to deliver tampons as the rest had snickered behind his back.

The man who'd aged. Badly.

In his mind, Herbert had preserved Travis as the young, vibrant pissant he'd been on his final day. With the same slight build, expensive suits, and perfectly styled hair. Herbert certainly hadn't imagined Travis would have turned into . . . this. At least a hundred pounds heavier, fat oozed over Travis' belt while folds gathered beneath his chin. Aside from a few stray wisps, much of his hair was gone, and he seemed to have developed a grotesque skin condition that covered his face with red, scaly blotches. A legion of bottles littered the desk—migraine pills, heart-burn pills, and a bottle of Pepto-Bismol so large that Herbert couldn't fathom that it came in that size.

While Travis stared blankly at a screen, Herbert

inspected a family photo that included the now-fat Travis, an obese wife, and two enormous, pimply-faced kids.

None smiled.

Curiously absent were the crayon drawings, watercolor handprints, and crappy macaroni art kids brought home from school. Aside from the depressing photo, no evidence existed of Travis's chubby offspring. Nothing in the room registered pride, dignity, or a family Travis couldn't wait to get home to.

Ignoring his growing unease, Herbert stepped out of Travis' line of sight—not that he would be seen until Herbert addressed him. He mentally ran over the words he'd perfected over two decades to ruin him, terrify him, and, hopefully, make him piss his khakis. Travis would be permanently altered after this, forever looking over his shoulder. Herbert had come up with a few one-liners to ensure *that*. He readied himself for the ride of his death. This was going to be grand. Epic. It was all he could do to keep from giggling like a schoolgirl.

Stepping forward, he parted his lips, took a deep breath, and . . . closed his mouth.

Taking inventory, Herbert counted seven bottles of medicine—store-bought and prescription. Leaning close, Herbert poked at the pin on Travis's tie. Here was something! A gift from the big boys upstairs, maybe an executive club. Squinting, he read the tiny lettering.

RF.

Familiarity jogged. Herbert had seen this pin years ago. *RF*—did it stand for an organization? An award?

And then, he knew. They were initials. *RF—Robert Fields*. Travis' father.

So what? It meant nothing that Travis wore his father's

pin. So, he'd never earned his own five, ten, or twenty-year badges. Who cared? It was no big deal.

And yet . . . it was.

Herbert seated himself opposite his nemesis and examined every inch of Travis' blotchy face and fat, plump skin. With a sinking gut, he knew there was nothing he could do that Travis hadn't already done to himself.

Time itself had avenged him.

Unaware of his ghostly visitor, Travis's lids drifted shut, his chin fell forward, and he began to snore.

Herbert had seen enough.

With more disappointment than he thought possible, he slipped from the room. Shuffling back through the office, he passed the woman who'd told him he couldn't, like, be here and stuff. This time, Herbert's presence went unnoticed. She and her deskmate were embroiled in an argument about something called genital piercings. He didn't want to know; he moved through the door.

Outside, with twenty hours before the Next in front of him, Herbert tried to think of what to do. Leaning against a magazine rack, he picked his teeth with a yellowed fingernail. He'd made no alternate plans. It had always been about ruining Travis, and now the asshole himself had beat him to the punch. Dazed people passed with their heads down as they stared at calculators. Even if Herbert were a Liver, he would probably have still gone unremarked. Why was everyone so attached to calculators nowadays? Calculators that looked a lot like the one Emily had brought that night when she'd played that song, and they had danced.

A smile broke his lips apart, the pieces fell together, and Herbert knew how to spend his final hours.

He ran.

HERBERT PERCHED ON THE SILL OF THE OPEN BEDROOM window. The boy looked just as Herbert had pictured—overweight, buzz cut, and wearing a filthy t-shirt that failed to cover a hairy, blubbery stomach. The only thing that threw Herbert was that half of the boy's face was covered in bandages.

Herbert smiled. *Way to go, Rick. Looks like you got him good.*

At a makeshift desk—a plank of wood balanced over two milk crates—Frank's grandson ogled photos of women in various stages of undress while his fat fingers reached out to the screen. An odd grunt bubbled up his throat.

That was enough for Herbert.

"Hey, dickhead."

Donny turned toward the closed door. "Go away, Mom. I'm busy." Turning back to the screen, he traced a nude woman's body with a greasy finger.

"Over here, dumbass."

This time, Donny turned toward the window. His dark eyes widened as his face drained of color.

Herbert smiled. Yes, this. This was what he'd waited the entirety of his death for.

"Grandpa?"

Grandpa? This idiot thinks I'm Frank? Herbert was astounded, insulted that he'd wasted his final contact on some serial masturbater who couldn't tell the difference between his own grandfather and a perfect stranger.

But . . . this might just work.

"Yes, you little . . . get your hands where I can see them."

Both arms shot in the air as if at gunpoint. "Don't hurt me, Grandpa! I didn't do nothin'.'"

"Listen to me, you pussy on a cracker." Now Herbert was in it, going for the ride, getting his due. But he felt an urgency. He needed to get this done. More than that, he needed to get this *right*. Herbert waved his arms to make himself more imposing. He'd heard you were supposed to do that if a bear ever crossed your path, and this fat idiot looked enough like a bear for Herbert to give it a try. "Bury my granddaughter at Serenity Grove, not some shitty no-name cemetery across town."

Donny made a gagging noise as a line of drool fell in a thin stream.

"Pull yourself together, asshole."

Donny shook his head. "No, no, no . . ." The high whine made Herbert want to plug his ears. He took a step closer, then stopped; better to keep a distance. Donny might be a fool, but there was no need to test it.

"Stop your blubbering and promise you'll bury Emily with me." He inched back into the shadows.

Donny only continued sobbing. "No, no, n—"

"If you don't shut up, I'll shove my fist so far up your ass you'll be shitting my fingernails for a week." Now *that* felt nice. It was a line he'd prepared for Travis, but he enjoyed using it on Donny even more.

A snot bubble grew and shrank with each breath Donny took, and he looked at Herbert-Frank with such complete horror that Herbert actually felt giddy.

"But . . . we already . . . paid for the other—"

"Do I look like I give a shit? I'll bury you there myself

if you don't do what I say." He jabbed a fist upward, a visual reminder of what would happen if Donny didn't comply.

Donny got the picture.

With a shriek, he scrambled backward, falling from his chair, and covered the seat of his pants with pudgy hands. "I will, I promise! Just don't . . . don't do that, Grandpa!" Loud wails bounced off the walls, and Herbert worried the mother would come in and ruin everything.

Time to wrap this up.

"Shut up. Now, I need you to say it, or God help me, this fist is going where the sun don't shine. Say it."

"I'll . . . I'll make sure Emmie gets buried at Ser . . . Ser . . ."

"Serenity Grove, jackass."

"Serbenity Graves. I promise. Just don't . . ." Gripping his ass, Donny wailed louder as he rocked.

Herbert felt . . . he wasn't sure what he felt, but he liked it. It was like he was the world's oldest Boy Scout earning his Eagle badge. Cautiously remaining in the shadows, Herbert took one menacing step toward the cowering heap of flesh rocking and rolling on the floor. When Donny screamed, Herbert knew he had him.

"Bury my granddaughter with me, and I'll never return. If you don't . . ." Climbing back onto the windowsill, he shook his clenched fist one final time to drive the point home.

"I promise, I swear," Donny whimpered.

In a sudden moment of clarity, Herbert knew then that nothing happened by chance. This moment—this deed— was why he'd been chosen for the Next.

It was time to move on.

Herbert swung his legs out of the open window and allowed them to dangle. He hadn't felt this good in decades—not since his wedding day.

As he dropped onto the lawn below, the cantankerous old man known to some as Herbert, to most as Herb, and to one as Frank tucked his thumbs behind his suspenders and headed down the darkened street. He cast no shadow as he moved along the deserted road.

He could feel it—the Next was near. *I'm a little late, but Edith, I'm coming home.*

In a wisp of smoke, Herbert was gone from this life and entered the Next.

34

THE RESIDENT

I n all the years that the residents had spoken of their common room, Rick could never have imagined its true splendor. With thirty-foot ceilings, the walls were inlaid with gold tiles, and a grand piano in the corner was surrounded by thick velvet curtains. Along one wall, floor-to-ceiling windows looked onto an English garden and purple mountains beyond. Chaise lounges, plush sofas, and not one but three stone fireplaces gave the room a warm yet sweeping aura of opulence.

The place was anything but common.

"This room is amazing," Emily said, awestruck, as she glanced around.

Rick was dumbfounded. *Why did they spend so much time in the cemetery bothering me when they could have been here?*

Clutching a glass of champagne, Madge joined them. "It's beautiful, isn't it? Stephanie decorated it."

The teen shrugged bashfully. "Whatever. I, like, read it in a book once."

"Everyone over here, please," Madge called as she moved to the center of the dance floor and raised her glass. "I'd like to propose a toast to Emily, our newest resident. We thought we'd never see you again, and we're not quite sure what happened, but I know I speak for everyone when I say we're all delighted that you've joined our family. We couldn't have wished for a better addition."

Emily's hands smoothed over long strands of golden hair as a blush washed her porcelain skin, and she shook her head in silent, humble protest.

Taylor rested a hand on Emily's arm. "Honestly, it would be better if you weren't here, but . . ." Her voice trailed off with a smile, and Emily grasped her hand.

"Oh, my God, I'd take you over that nasty old Herb any day." Stephanie twirled a finger around a lock of hair. "Things are gonna be way more fun now."

"To Emily," Madge said, and in unison, the residents drank. Champagne splashed to the floor.

"Ew," Stephanie whined as she pulled off a shoe and poured liquid onto the floor. "Couldn't we have just raised our glasses? Grody." Moving toward the corner, she dropped the needle onto an album, and Debbie Gibson's young voice echoed in the expansive room. "Looove, it's only a dreeeam . . ."

". . . as any d-d-dream may s-s-seem . . ."

Knowing that it was bound to happen when you heard anything forty thousand times, Rick laughed.

Emily pulled a small pink envelope from her bag. Taylor's name was scribbled across the front in an awkward slant. "I have something for you."

"What's . . . oh, wow, this can't be . . ." Taylor ran a finger across the childlike handwriting.

"I looked everywhere," Emily said, "and finally found it on a shelf in Donny's closet."

Taylor opened the envelope, reached inside, and pulled out a small card.

A birthday invitation.

Emily grinned. "We should have another party to make up for the one we lost."

"I can't believe you found it." Taylor thrust her arms around Emily's neck, then pulled back, laughing. "Let's hope someone left some Hello Kitty decorations in that closet. Madge says that thing goes on forever."

THE PARTY WAS STILL GOING STRONG IN THE LATE HOURS. Holding tight to her Boo, Emily joined Taylor near the piano, and the two of them made headway on the friendship they'd been denied in their living years.

Madge hovered in a darkened corner, and when her eyes met Rick's, she beckoned with a crooked finger. Making his way across the large room, his curiosity burned as he noted a hand hidden behind her back.

"Did you know that Frank was a bit of an artist?" she asked when he halted at her side.

"He mentioned it once but said he'd used up the last of his charcoal."

"Yes." She brought her hand around. A worn sketchbook was gripped in her fingers. "He finished the last drawing the week before he moved on. I think you should see it."

Rick took the sketchbook as Madge joined the others on the far side of the room. He was awestruck as he flipped through sketches of the residents, the cemetery above, and even Benson. The details of each resident— even the soft shadows in their features—were rendered in astonishing detail. Rick knew that in Frank's living days, he'd been a veterinarian. Yet the drawings were so beautiful, so real, he could easily have had a second career as an artist.

As Rick reached the final drawing, his breath caught, and he fumbled with the sketchbook.

In the center, Rick's charcoal profile showed the slightest uptick of a smile as he sat in a rocking chair on an old rickety porch. At his side, Emily rocked in a matching chair as she reached a hand toward him. The tall grass seemed to sway in a breeze, and an ambling brook wandered from one side of the page to the other. The likeness was so accurate that Rick couldn't help the moan that escaped. He didn't need to count the perfect row of freckles across her nose to see how precisely detailed the drawing was. Rick ran a finger over the basket of apples drawn between them, so perfect a replica of the one in his cottage that he could almost smell their sweetness.

Then, his gaze roamed to the background, and his skin prickled. A skillfully drawn Herbert sat on a windowsill holding his fedora in one hand and, in the other, an outstretched apple. Yet it wasn't the apple or even Herbert, but the room he was drawn in that grabbed Rick's attention. Why did it look so familiar? As he peered closer, Rick realized that the room was a near-replica of Emily's bedroom. Yet it was different somehow, as if the furniture had been replaced. He certainly hadn't noticed that plank balanced on milk crates when he'd helped her pack her belongings.

Beneath that, the words, *Nothing is random.*

He couldn't fathom what the old codger had to do with anything. But before Rick could begin to work out the meaning, gathering voices caught his attention. As Taylor and Emily approached, Rick closed the sketchbook and slid it onto a nearby shelf.

"Did you know we're both Aquariuses?" Taylor asked, bumping her shoulder into Emily's. "Anyway, Emily said she wanted to hang out with you. I guess that's okay since we have, I don't know, the next forty or fifty years to catch up."

Emily locked arms with Taylor, a happy glow on her cheeks. A pink globe hovered above, casting a faint light onto Emily's blonde hair as she held her hand out—eerily reminiscent of the sketch.

Nothing is random.

"Are you ready to explore more of this place? Taylor says this is just the tip of the iceberg. Oh! And she says if we follow the map, we can see an actual iceberg!"

Taking Emily in his arms, Rick brushed his lips against her forehead. "If it's an iceberg my lady wants, an iceberg she shall get." They walked toward the glass doors, and just when Rick thought he couldn't love her more than he already did, he surprised himself.

35

THREE MONTHS LATER

S pring arrived early, and though it had been nearly seven months since her last living breath, Taylor could still feel a sliver of the sun's warmth on her bare arms. She still spent many a lonely afternoon atop her tombstone, watching traffic flow on the other side of the gate.

Old habits died hard, even in the Next.

It wasn't just her unwavering attachment to the living world. It was quieter up here—Stephanie was in the midst of her latest fit over the quilt Madge had pieced together, using, among other things, Stephanie's *Frankie Say Relax* t-shirt, and now, without a caretaker, there was no one to run the meetings where the two could fight it out in an orderly manner.

Mooney had visited once more since Taylor's burial. According to him, their parents couldn't bring themselves to come. She watched the cars zoom by, looking for the familiar vehicles of her family. She wondered—not for the first time—how much of the world beyond the gate had already changed.

She'd finally gone down—or up, or sideways—and unpacked. In an ironic twist, Emily's death had given Taylor renewed life as they shared tales of eerily similar childhoods. Both had lived in silence, hoping for notice, acceptance, or an outstretched hand. Both had swirled within the same ebb and flow and occupied the same quiet space, each unaware of the other's pain. In death, they shared mutual anguish, combining their experiences into one. It was nice to have someone who understood, who'd been there, done that.

Still, Taylor found it hard to let go of the world she was no longer part of, even as it rolled smoothly on without her. So, she sat, chin perpetually in hand, keeping watch over the living.

But, as Taylor was soon to discover, nothing was random.

A breeze caught strands of her sapphire hair as an unfamiliar car pulled up to the gate. Taylor lifted her head as a man climbed out.

He looks familiar.

She watched as the stranger limped through the gate, passing the *Caretaker Wanted* sign fluttering in the breeze. The man peered around, alternately reading tombstones and glancing at his phone. Nearly bald, his head reflected the sun. At least fifty pounds overweight, it somehow suited him; his pudgy cheeks gave his face a permanent smile. Something about the way he hobbled from one tombstone to the next, how he pulled his teeth over his lips as his hand slid gently over the lettering—made Taylor grin.

And in that moment, she nearly remembered . . . something. The image of a rolling peach flitted briefly before dissipating.

The man passed, and Taylor waved. Some habits were hard to break, while others were downright impossible.

"Hello, Liver."

She greeted every visitor this way—every delivery man, every jogger who darted by, unaware of her continued existence. She knew she should stop; it only brought on bouts of depression when they went along, oblivious to her thereness. Yet she was hooked—addicted to hope, desperate for the desire to be acknowledged. Worse than being dead, Taylor feared being forgotten. And so, she waved.

The stranger met her gaze and greeted her flourish with his own. "Oh. Hello there!" He turned, glanced from tombstone to tombstone, then back to his phone.

Taylor froze mid-wave. *Shit.* Scrambling down, she slipped on the grass, landing on her elbow. *Shit, shit!* She followed from a distance as he turned from the main path. From the bench hidden behind the hedge, Taylor peeked through the opening as the man stared at granite, freshly etched, and read the name aloud.

"Emily Lorraine Bennet." He sighed, slumped, and fell silent.

Shit!

Evaporating in a hurried wisp, Taylor returned moments later with the others. They gathered close, fighting for space at the hedge as the stranger stood motionless over Emily's grave. A minute passed, then two. The visitor brought a shaky hand to his face and swiped his cheek.

"Hello, Emily, my name is Charlie. I'm the one who . . . I'm the one . . ." His face turned skyward, his hands dropped to his sides, and a choking sob echoed. He ran a hand over her etched name. "I was driving the truck that day."

With a gasp, Emily brought a hand to her chest.

"It took a while to get here. I was in the hospital for a long time and had to learn to walk again." Charlie's voice broke, anguished, and his very breath exhaled pain. "After they told me what happened, all I could think about was getting here. To tell you how sorry I am."

From his coat pocket, he pulled a worn photo. His mouth twisted into a grimace. "I found this online. They told me in the hospital that my heart had stopped and that I was clinically dead. Only for a minute, but it feels like part of me never came back. Maybe some of me stayed there, on the other side, wherever that is." He placed Emily's photo at the base of her granite, crowned with the date of her final living breath.

"I wish there was something, anything that I could do . . ."

Emily looked to the rest, and they nodded.

"Anything . . ." The words stuck in Charlie's throat as the woman he mourned stepped from behind the hedge and stood before him.

"Actually, Charlie," Emily said with a smile, "there is something you can do."

———

THE CARETAKER'S BOOTS CRUNCHED THE GRAVEL AS HE walked toward the gate. The sun was warmer now; spring had settled in, pushing back the long, cold winter. He pulled the right gate closed, then the left, clashing them together before chaining the padlock.

He spotted something in the shrubbery. Leaning close, he grabbed the weathered *Caretaker Wanted* sign, folded it, and tucked it into his back pocket.

Leaves were already budding on the trees—he turned down his collar to allow the warm breeze to brush against his skin. The scent of pine sweetened the air as he passed the small grove that lined the path to his cottage.

A wooden box nailed to a little white fence with the word *Comments* printed in bold letters awaited him. Inside, he found several slips of paper and glanced at them briefly before shoving them into his pocket.

A black cat wound between his legs, and he bent to scratch between its ears. "Hey there, Benson. How's my boy today?" The cat scurried away, winding through tombstones into the sunshine beyond.

Straightening, he followed the gravel path to the cottage door. The key turned; the door swung open. Setting the papers on the table, he glanced at his watch—almost seven. As the fire crackled in the empty room, he stared blankly at the couches, recliners, and wooden chairs arranged in a semi-circle, with his chair at its head.

Voices wafted in while soft murmurs traveled over a vast chasm. The whispers grew louder, closing the distance between time and space. Shapes formed while the temperature dipped, and lights flickered as the chatter increased.

At the hearth, the fire wafted as if a wind had blown through. A basket of peaches rattled, and the wood floor creaked as if burdened with an unseen weight. Soft shadows appeared, then darkened, and the caretaker waited, allowing them to settle into their usual spots.

The silence was cut with a squeal. "Oh, my God, you guys. I finally figured out Rick's song." With her boom box balanced atop her shoulder, Stephanie hit the play button.

With a Little Help from My Friends echoed.

Rick Emily's hand, her Boo resting between them.

"Right," Charlie said as he leaned into the light, "let's get started."

PART II - BEFORE THE NEXT

In that single moment, I knew. Not nearly, not a faded thought. I knew. You can run from destiny, but eventually, it circles back around. One way or another, your fate meets you in the end.

36

TAYLOR

ONE WEEK BEFORE

I loved singing along to Evanescence in my car. That band understood me; they got me in a way no one else ever did. *Fallen* was the first CD I'd put in that old Civic, and it's still there. At least I think it's still there —it's probably crumpled to dust by now.

"Wake me up inside, wake me up inside . . . ugh."

The week before I died, I got stuck in the usual traffic snarl on the way home from the movie theater, where I'd been promoted to Big Shot Day Manager. That meant I got to oversee all two of the daytime employees, which was two more than were needed. No one spent an afternoon at the theater in a dinky town like Hood Valley, except for that one Star Wars kid—*he* was there all the time. My most crucial duty was to count popcorn kernels in that no-brainer job. No joke; once a week, I scooped unpopped kernels from the bottom of the kettle and counted how many hadn't popped. I guess I don't need to tell you how valuable Big Shot Day Managers are.

Traffic ground to a halt and I peered ahead—as usual, there was a bottleneck at one of the three lights in town. Over the summer, the city council had held a series of heated town hall meetings that had resulted in a stalemate. Some said another light would divert mountain tourists to the next town over—diverting their shopping dollars right along with them—while others said a fourth light would make Hood Valley appear too "citified." In the end, they couldn't even agree whether the issue should be on the ballot, so it was dropped, and there I sat, waiting for some idiot to make a left across two lanes of traffic.

The cars finally started to move again, and I pulled up to the Book and Nook, where the latest Laini Taylor book was waiting for me to snatch up. I loved her books so much that I'd recently dyed my hair that fabulous blue to match Karou's. How could I not obsess over Laini Taylor? We shared the same name, after all. I'd often found myself daydreaming of Karou, of sprouting wings and flying to the rooftops, wishing I could just lift up and soar away from it all. I liked Laini. She got me.

The bell over the door chimed as I entered the darkened bookstore. Covered in old rugs and comfortable chairs, the Book and Nook was so much better than those cookie-cutter stores that had sprung up all over Portland. I knew the store's layout as well as I knew my own house, and, precisely where the Laini Taylor books were shelved. I'd even worked at the store over the summer and probably would have remained until the day I died, but the cinema had offered me a hefty Big Shot Day Manager raise to return.

It was the first time I'd been back since I'd quit, and, curious to see who had replaced me, I peeked around the tall shelf with a copy of *Night of Cake and Puppets* held close. No one was manning the register, so I headed down another aisle until a peripheral movement caught my eye, and when I spotted her, I groaned.

You have got to be kidding me.

Her back was turned as she bent over a stack of books and ticked items off a list, and yet, even from my limited vantage point, I could tell she hadn't changed since high school. She still had that long, blonde hair, still wore a dress down to her ankles, and still covered it with a sweater that made her look like an old lady on her way to a bridge game.

Emily.

Before she became a Big Shot Librarian, Emily had worked at the Book and Nook, and I'd memorized her schedule, making sure to come in on her days off. When she left for the library, I spotted the Help Wanted sign in the window, and a part of me applied just to stick it to her by stepping into her old role—although a much deeper part had just wanted to spend my days in a world of books. Back in school, especially after the D-word happened, I'd felt a kinship toward her. She'd been quiet like me, shy like me. And she'd always seemed so lonely.

Like me.

The year of the Big Divorce, I'd needed a friend, and I took a chance and invited her to my birthday party, even hand-delivering the invitation to her older brother. Did she show up? Did she call? Did she apologize for skipping out on the most important birthday of my life?

She'd done none of those things, and the following

Monday at school she walked right by as if there wasn't this big, invisible, *Hello Kitty* party between us. Even the other outcast at school was too cool to be seen with me.

After that, things changed. *I* changed. Having given up on making friends, I transformed into the weirdest version of myself I could manage. I threw away every stitch of clothing that wasn't the blackest of black. At thirteen, I dyed my hair to match, and at fourteen, I pierced my nose. Since I was too young to go to a professional, I did it myself. Mom flipped when she saw it, infected and red, and rushed me to Doc Johnson's. They removed it, wasting all the pain I'd put myself through, but the day I turned eighteen, I got three of them all at once.

In the bookstore, I hid behind the wall and tucked my precious Laini Taylor away on a random shelf. I could always order it online. There was no way I was about to let *her* ring up my purchase, so I slipped out of the store, cursing the bell as it betrayed my presence.

Fuming over Emily's return to my one refuge in this godforsaken town, I walked to the grocery store, annoyed that I'd have to figure out her schedule again. I'd gotten used to going in whenever I liked. Stupid Emily.

The automatic doors slid open, and, lost in thought, I bumped into a man carrying a bag of groceries, and as fruit rolled in every direction, the strangest thing happened. He looked at me, right in the eyes. No one did that. Ever. I'd done a pretty good job of becoming invisible; I was like a living ghost. The man smiled in such a vulnerable way that I forgot my irritation and smiled back. I couldn't have stopped if I'd tried. He carried his plumpness in his face— like how some people, no matter how much weight they lose, always have inflated cheeks. That was this guy.

He's kinda cute.

He waved. "Oh! Hello there!" There we are, standing a foot apart, and the guy waves. As he bent to scoop up a wayward peach, I kind of felt . . . familiarity is the only word that comes close, though that's not it, either. Maybe it was that smile. It was jarring.

I was about to chase after a peach that had rolled to the cart return when another man appeared out of nowhere, scooped up the fruit and handed it over.

"Oh, hey! Thanks!" Plump Guy said.

"N-No p-p-problem," the other stammered, then quickly tucked his head down and hurried away.

Plump Guy looked back at me with that smile that I couldn't help returning, and I swear something clicked. I heard it, like an audible *snap*. I knew this guy, and yet, somewhere deep inside, I knew I'd never met him.

In that moment, I very nearly knew . . . something.

"Dude, move."

With the spell broken, Plump Guy's eyes focused, he turned to a grumpy-looking teen in the doorway, and the memory of something yet to happen vanished.

Twenty minutes later, I turned onto my quiet street in a sleepy, tree-lined neighborhood, with six cold Frappuccinos sitting in the passenger seat. Elms and oaks were in the beginning stages of autumn transformation, laden with leaves fading to pale shades of green and yellowed tips. Mom had kept the house after the Divorce, and even though I was twenty-two, I'd never seen a reason to move out. Mooney, on the other hand, couldn't wait to leave, escaping before the smoke cleared on his eighteenth birthday cake. Unlike him, I liked that house. Loved it, I guess. I'd grown up there, and after the Divorce, the house had been all that remained from our old life. Losing it would have meant losing everything.

Mooney always said I didn't like change. So did that stupid therapist my parents sent me to when Dad shacked up with that skank that became our first step-mother. Maybe they were right.

What's so great about change anyway?

I could always spot our house as soon as I passed the haunted one. Rumor had it that years ago, some crazy old man had lived there, and the creepy house had sat empty since he'd died. Mom said the house used to be the nicest on the block, but when the man's wife died, he changed, and the house just kind of fell apart the way they did when no one cared anymore. I hated passing it—those abandoned rockers on the porch gave me the shivers. But as soon as I marked the creepy house's broken steps, I only had to look up, and there was my sanctuary, our big house with the wraparound porch. I stepped on the gas.

After parking, I fished my phone from my purse. I didn't have one of those fancy iPhones; no one called me enough to justify the cost. Instead, I'd inherited Mom's old Blackberry, except it was purple, so I called it my Purpleberry. I liked that phone—outdated and forgotten, like me.

As the sun dipped beneath the horizon and the shadows crawled, I called my brother from the car. "Are you coming tonight?" Mom always made a big deal out of Halloween. She went all out, and I mean *all out*. She put lights around the porch, dragged inflatable ghosts to the lawn, and last year, she'd scored a fog machine. We hosted massive parties on Halloween night, a tradition she'd started when we were kids, and every year, she roped Mooney into helping out. There was too much for us girls to handle, she told him, claiming we needed a man's help. I thought it was just an excuse to get him to come home. Even Buster seemed to be forgetting him.

"Tell me you're not driving, Taylor."

Once. I texted in traffic *one time,* and Mooney never let me live it down, even though it was only for a second and I was watching the road the entire time. You would have thought I'd just stabbed Buster the way Mooney flipped. Ever since, he'd been on me about texting and driving, something I didn't even do. I wasn't stupid.

"I'm parked in front of Mom's, geez."

We'd been close, once. When the D-word flipped our world on its tail, Mom had been out of it, and for the first year, it was kind of just Mooney and me, a year that resulted in Mooney taking on the job of Big Shot Overprotective Brother—a role he still hadn't relinquished.

"You better come over, Mooney. Mom can't figure out the fog machine, and you know how she is with things that come with an electrical cord."

He sighed. He did that a lot, ever since he'd gotten that job at the insurance company. "Fine, I'll be there in a few," Mooney said as if he'd agreed to dispose of a body. "And don't text and drive. I don't want to go to your funeral."

"You wish." I tossed my phone into my bag.

Even now, I can't forgive myself for saying that.

———

THE HOUSE WAS QUIET, AND DECORATIONS WERE STREWN everywhere. Mom wouldn't start until we were all together —another tradition. For days, she'd brought in boxes from whatever closets she'd hidden them in, and now the floor was covered.

Tinker mewed from the windowsill. I picked her up and scratched behind her ears. Tinker had shown up several years before, and two days later, had given birth to a litter of kittens right on the front porch. We'd given most of the kittens away, except the one with the sleekest black fur. I'd felt, I don't know, like that kitten and I were meant to be together. But one morning, he disappeared, just as I'd worked up the nerve to ask Mom if I could keep him.

I dropped Tinker back onto the sill and peeked out the window as Mooney's Trans Am sped up the street. He wasn't usually a speeder—if anything, he was an annoyingly cautious driver. But everyone sped past that creepy house. A minute later, he barreled through the door, his hair tousled, and his shirt sleeves rolled up to his elbows, like one of those Wall Street guys that always look like they've had too much coffee. I had to stifle a laugh.

"Where's Mom?" he barked, grabbing a box marked 'Halloween Yard.' "I want to get this done."

"Put that down, Morton," Mom called, as she hefted a large box from the kitchen.

Moony hated being called by his given name. Who could blame him? He was named after some Great-Great-I-Don't-Even-Know-How-Great Grandfather that had died a gazillion years ago. Dad and I had always called him Mooney, but Mom—as you've probably already figured out—was a stickler for tradition.

"We need to have a talk." Mom always looked a little nervous—as if she was always expecting bad news—but, on that day, she walked with an added jitter. That weird sensation washed over me again, as if I almost knew something.

"It's been a long week," Mooney grumbled, "and I just want to get ho . . ."

I followed his gaze to the kitchen door.

"Hey kids," Dad said, and, just like that, the last ten, miserable years melted away.

DAD STOOD IN THE KITCHEN DOORWAY, AN ODD, STRAINED smile just touching the curvature of his lips as if his face was unsure what to do. I couldn't breathe. My brain flipped over and laid like a turtle, and even the air seemed to thicken.

Ten years before, Dad had walked out of the house and didn't come back. After that, Mom and Dad hadn't even been able to breathe the same air. At each of our graduations, they'd claimed opposite ends of the gym, and when we were younger, Mom would drop us off at Aunt Caty's, and Dad would pick us up an hour later. *An hour.* Just to be sure they didn't accidentally pass on the street.

Someone had died. Was dying. The apocalypse was here. A nuclear bomb was on its way to Hood Valley, and we were minutes from being written into history. There was no other explanation for Dad to be standing like that as if he'd been there all along, trying to smile and blowing it.

Mom looked from Dad to Mooney, then back to Dad. "Sit down, Mooney. Please." She never called him Mooney. Someone really *was* dying.

Dad widened his smile with such force that he resembled a badger trying to chew out of an iron clamp, while Mooney just sat on the couch and stared. Or rather, he shot daggers from his eyes. After the Divorce, Mooney and Dad's relationship fell apart when Dad married Kaden, a girl that looked about a minute older than me. They'd split up three years later, but Mooney never forgave him. After that, Mooney shut himself off from everyone, even me. He started hanging out at his friends' houses after school, walking in the door with seconds to spare before curfew. Christmas mornings became a flurry of opening gifts before he raced back to his room.

My gut dropped to the floor as a million thoughts tried to form, but all I knew was that something was wrong.

Really, really wrong.

"I guess you're both wondering why I'm here, huh?" I could tell Dad was trying to be casual; he actually leaned against the door frame and crossed his arms. *Just standing here like I always do,* his body said, while his face knew otherwise. He gave up and stood behind Mom, seated in her favorite chair. And then the unthinkable happened.

He rested his hand on her shoulder, and Mom . . . smiled.

What's going on?

"We need to have a talk," Mom repeated, her face pale and looking about two seconds from hurling right there on the rug.

"I don't want to hear anything he has to say." Mooney leaped to his feet and took three steps toward the door.

"Your mother and I are back together," Dad said. Just like that, as if it were nothing—crazy words and all.

Mom sat stiff, her face a mess of emotion while her brows furrowed and her mouth tried a faltering smile.

Halfway to the door, Mooney turned into a statue of skin. "You're what? Mom, what's he talking about?"

It had to be a joke. A Halloween prank. There was no way this was happening, no way our parents were getting back together.

"We've spent a lot of time talking and getting to know each other again." Mom's eyes flitted briefly to mine. "We're working things out, and we hope you two can be on board."

My turtle-brain tried to right itself again and failed. Mom and Dad. Together. Talking. Working things out. It wasn't that I didn't want to believe it, it's just that I couldn't allow myself to be open for that kind of a letdown. Still, I couldn't stop the images that flashed of our old life—the life Pre-D. The four of us at the lake, eating ham sandwiches with that sweet mustard Dad liked. The four of us trudging through the muck and mud at the Christmas tree farm for hours, searching for just the right tree. The four of us at the cinema watching the latest Disney film. The four of us, all over time. Slowly, the words sank in, my turtle brain finally flipped back, and...*bing*! It would be the four of us. Again.

Only, one of us wasn't having it.

"Mom, no." Mooney shook as his face burned red. "You're not seriously doing this, going back to *him*."

"Hey now, kid," Dad said, shifting into Parental mode.

Bad idea, Dad.

Mooney's gaze didn't falter, and his eyes bored into Mom. "He doesn't belong here. Not after everything he put us through." Mooney turned away with a snarl.

Mooney was crushing the first real chance for us to finally be a family again, and I wasn't about to take that sitting down. I flew from the couch. "Why won't you just listen? If this is what Mom wants, who are you to—"

"This isn't what Mom wants! It can't be. God, Taylor, have you forgotten what it was like when he left the first time? Do you really want to watch Mom go through that again?"

Even I had to admit, the D-word had been rough on Mom. Ten years later, she'd never so much as had coffee with another man. After Dad left, Mom was done. But even Dad had seemed alone, in his own way, after the D-word. Unlike Mom, he'd dated a string of women, eventually marrying—and divorcing—three of them. Dad had never really pulled it together either, and in their own ways, they'd both seemed to be trying to find their way back to each other.

"That won't happen again," Dad said, though he was hiding behind Mom when he said it.

Mooney laughed, a vicious, throaty sound. "Right, okay. Whatever. Hope you're happy, Mom," and before anyone could stop him, he was out the door, slamming it behind. The three of us stood immobile as Mooney's footsteps stomped down the steps, his engine roared to life, and his car raced away.

It all was happening so fast. I'd barely had time to register the fact that Mom and Dad were, well, Mom and Dad again, before Mooney had thrown a giant kink in it.

And then it really did hit me. *Mom and Dad are getting back together. Mom and Dad are . . . getting back together?*

Mom's face was drawn, and Dad looked as if Mooney had punched him in the gut. The words repeated on a loop, and I felt the start of a smile.

Mom and Dad are getting back together.

THREE DAYS BEFORE

I'd been waiting outside Mooney's apartment for hours. I looked at my watch for the hundredth time—nearly eleven. The first two hours, I'd waited in my car, leaving one voicemail after another until my back ached, so I moved to the tiny slab of concrete outside of Mooney's apartment door and was just nodding off when his loud Trans Am pulled up to the curb. Avoidance was practically Mooney's middle name. I could have predicted that he'd be MIA.

The past three days had been . . . odd. Dad was always at the house, and that morning, he was there at breakfast, smiling from the kitchen table while Mom stood at the stove. In a way, it was nice. No, it was great. Just like it had been in the Before Time, when we'd talked over breakfast while Mom cooked, always hovering somewhere nearby but never really there. For ten years, I'd thought of those mornings until it ached, and now, here we were again, sitting in the same chairs, in the same kitchen, eating the same bacon and eggs. The good old days had returned, and everything was right again in the world.

So why did it feel so wrong?

Mom stood at her usual spot at the stove in the same stance, with the same frying pan, wearing the same bathrobe. She even wore the same expressionless face. Before the D-word, Mom had looked like that a lot. I guess I'd forgotten, and the memory of her married gaze had slowly disappeared over time. It wasn't sadness, really—more like there was just no one home.

What do you expect? That after ten years, Mom and

Dad are just going to fall back in love with the snap of a finger? It takes time. This is weird for everyone.

And then it hit me. It was Mooney's fault the pieces hadn't effortlessly fallen back into place. Dad seemed fine, but it was clear that Mom needed, I don't know, Mooney's blessing, I suppose. I needed to make Mooney see what he was doing to them. To all of us.

Mooney halted halfway up the path. "What are you doing here?"

"Where have you been?" I stood, my back cracking. "You're acting like a baby, you know."

He shoved by with a snort and placed his key in the lock. "I'm a baby, huh? *I* am?"

"What's that supposed to mean?" I followed him inside.

"Just leave me alone, Taylor. Not everyone has to be on board with this." He tossed his keys on the coffee table and disappeared down the hall.

"On board with what?" I called, knowing precisely what he meant, but I wasn't about to sit back while Mooney ruined everything for the rest of us. "Oh, you mean, with Mom being happy again?"

He stepped from the bedroom. "Of course I want Mom to be happy. That's why I'm against this . . . this farce. He's going to do what he always does. Before you know it, we'll be calling some twenty-year-old bimbo 'Mom.'"

"Are you that stupid?" I was so furious I had to keep from slapping him. "Don't you see that's why he had all those failed relationships? He was trying to find Mom."

"Dad doesn't know what he wants."

There was no talking to Mooney when he was like this,

so I turned toward the door. "You're ruining this for her, you know."

My hand landed on the knob, and what Mooney said next stopped me.

Haunts me now.

"Ruining it for her, or for you?"

Something in the way he said it made me want to shrivel into a ball. I wanted Mom and Dad back together for their sakes, not mine. For *her*. It was all for Mom.

But . . . but.

"Bite me, Mort," I said and slammed the door.

ONE DAY BEFORE

The day before I died, I drove home in a stupor. The whole day had been a fog—I had to count the stupid kernels three times before I finally gave up and guessed.

Mom and Dad kept muddying my mind. I'd remember the good old days when we were a family, but then those memories would fall away, replaced by Mom's blank face, like a painting obscured behind a layer of lamp oil.

Had I remembered it wrong all those years?

As I pulled up to the house, I took in the lawn decorations, the streamers in the trees, and the fog machine pouring out low-lying clouds. My heart skipped a beat as I stared at Dad's car parked in the driveway as if it had every right. Why was its presence bothering me so much?

And then I saw it.

He'd parked in Mom's spot. She always—*always* —parked on the left, nearest the door. Now, her car was on the right, displaced.

It's a parking spot. It's not like he knocked her out of

line for the throne of freaking England. I laughed aloud at my insane overreaction. It was silly.

Wasn't it?

Though Dad's car was parked like some sort of declaration of ownership, Mooney's was glaringly missing. I opened the front door to a blast of *Monster Mash*. The usual guests were milling about; neighbors, relatives, Mom's co-workers. Streamers, pumpkins, and colorful leaves covered every inch of space. She'd even coated the carpet in orange glitter.

We'll be cleaning this mess up until Thanksgiving.

I pushed my way through the crowd, the loud conversation—and even louder costumes—giving me a claustrophobic sense of unease. Mom's parties were the highlight of the year, and even though I'd never really cared much for being in large groups, it made Mom happy, and that was good enough for me. It always took a while, but eventually, I could loosen up and almost start to enjoy myself. This time, however, the house crawled with an undercurrent of gloom that felt different, yet oddly familiar.

I had to get out of that room, so I stepped into the kitchen, and the sight that greeted me should have sent my heart soaring, should have filled me with glee. Instead, I was slammed with that weird despondency that I couldn't quite put my finger on.

The noise of the living room drifted away as Elvis purred, *I Can't Help Falling in Love with You* from the kitchen radio. Mom and Dad danced, his arm around her waist while she rested her head on his shoulder. And then he swung her around, and when I saw her face, I stopped breathing. She should have looked content, blissful. Maybe even a hint of a smile. That was what I was expecting, anyway.

Instead, she looked displaced, like her car on the wrong side of the driveway. It all came rushing back, the familiar sense of how it really used to be. The Before Time hadn't been sunshine and roses, it hadn't been two happy parents and a house bursting with laughter.

It had been this.

I quietly escaped to the couch and moped, a skill I'd honed during the ten years Mom and Dad had been apart while I'd wished for the literal song and dance that was now playing out in the kitchen. For a decade, I'd fantasized of returning to a life I'd invented, a childhood that had existed only in my reinvented memory.

Mr. Hancock, the loud guy from next door who was always the first to have one too many, attacked the Jell-O brain on the table while music blasted over the partygoers. Gran watched them from her usual spot in the corner, filing away bits of gossip to throw in Mom's face for the next twelve months.

And then, the single woman who'd recently moved across the street caught my eye. There was an old apple orchard in the neighborhood behind us, and every year, Mom dragged me over there to pick apples. As she always did for new neighbors, Mom had whipped up a batch of apple butter, packed a welcome basket, and left it on the woman's porch. But the neighbor had sent no thank-you note, given us no passing wave. She just pretended we weren't there.

So, what was she doing at Mom's party?

Aunt Caty tapped me on the shoulder, interrupting my thoughts. "Tell me that's not your father's car parked out there." Her face twisted into a grimace while one hand rested on her hip.

"Dad's in the kitchen with . . . oh, here they are."

The kitchen door opened, and as they entered the room, Mom blinked, and Dad glanced quickly away.

In a flash, Aunt Caty took two broad steps, grabbed Mom by the elbow, and ushered her back into the kitchen. I never liked to throw the "hate" word around—Mom said if you were going to use that word, you better mean it. Yet if I had to describe Aunt Caty's feelings for Dad in one word, well, that would be the one.

Dad sat in the chair that even Mooney and I never sat in because it was Mom's. There'd never been a 'This is Mom's Chair' sign, it just *was*, and seeing him there, I clenched my fists wondering how much more of Mom would be shuffled aside.

I snuck to the kitchen and opened the door a crack.

"This is a mistake. Think of everything he put you through. Not to mention the kids."

A pot rattled, feet shuffled.

"Let me set you up with Dave. He likes you, and I know you like him."

I poked my head in just far enough to watch as Mom shook her head, slowly, as if she barely had the strength to do even that.

"Why are you really doing this?"

Mom turned her back and fiddled with a bowl. "It's comfortable. I know him, I know his habits, his patterns. I always loved him, Caty."

"Comfort and familiarity are no reasons to restart a failed marriage. What about the infidelities, the lies, the control he had over you?"

More shuffling silence as Mom turned the bowl on the table, slowly, clockwise, and I wished I could see her face. "I've made my decision. We're going to the courthouse tomorrow to make it official."

Aunt Caty paled. "Paula, no."

Mom's hands flew to her face, and she broke into tears. Her back was bent as if she were carrying that ridiculous backpack from that *Wild* movie. Her sobs gutted me, and I broke a little then. "But Taylor is so happy now, Caty."

I flinched. *What*?

"The divorce changed her. It changed all of us, but it changed her the most. Do you know how hard it was to watch my beautiful, vibrant girl turn into—"

"Into you?"

Mom brought her hands down. "Yes, into me. She doesn't take chances, she doesn't make friends. She's so afraid of getting hurt that she's cut herself off from the world." She gasped a breath, letting it out in segments. "If I can fix this, I think she'll start to come out of her shell."

Aunt Caty shuffled around the table and laid a hand on Mom's shoulder. "Taylor is an adult now, Paula. Millions of kids come from broken homes. They deal with it, and Taylor will too. But it's up to her to do that. It's time you started living for you."

I couldn't listen to any more of it, couldn't stand another moment, and I quietly eased out of the doorway and slunk back into the living room.

Mr. Hancock was passed out on the couch, so I settled on the floor in the corner. The feeling that had crept over me the last few days was back, stronger than ever, like a blanket of bitterness. For ten years, I'd wanted Mom to be happy, assuming her happiness was dependent on Dad's return. But maybe Mooney had been right. Perhaps it was *my* happiness I cared about, no matter who had to pay the price.

The party began to wind down, and most of the guests stood in clusters—except for that strange woman from across the street. Alone in the center of the room, she danced, her arms wrapped around herself, sliding a hand to her thighs and back up again, bringing more than enough skirt along for the ride. *Dark Horse* played on the radio as her body circled, a radius of empty space surrounding her in a tantalizing aura.

Dad was watching her, too. Almost imperceptibly, he nodded with a smirk, a bond between them, an invisible draw.

I wanted to hurl.

Mom returned from the kitchen, Aunt Caty in tow with that stabby look she reserved for Dad. Like a zombie, Mom shuffled toward Dad, her eyes flitting between Dad and the neighbor, and her step faltered for a moment—a nanosecond, really—but she dragged herself forward, and when she reached Dad, she laid that same limp hand on his shoulder.

Dad started, his guilt betraying him. He rose from her chair—*her* chair, dammit—and said, "How about I get you a drink?"

Mom smiled. Was that even the right word? No. It wasn't a smile.

She yielded. "Yes, thank you." Surrender. Concede. Relent.

Oh, Mom.

I HAD TO GET OUT OF THERE, FAST. BUT BEFORE I COULD make my escape, Mom stopped me on the way to the stairs.

Shit.

"You're going upstairs already?"

"Too many cookies, I guess." I knew my face wouldn't give me away—real nausea boiled beneath the surface.

Mom brushed her hand along my hairline, something she'd always done when I was sick. "I'll come up later to check on you. Do you need Pepto?"

My eyes moved on their own to the center of the room. To her. To him. I felt the color drain from my face. "No, thanks, I just need to lay down."

She looked at me—hard and scrutinizing—searching for the truth in my lie. Suddenly, we were two women cut from the same cloth, cursed with the same ineptitudes, the same weaknesses. The question was; who had weakened who?

Without thought, I grabbed her, wrapped her in a hug, and held her close. Even now, I can still smell her hair, can feel her arms stiffen before she relaxed, and returned the embrace.

"What was that for?" A question, but not.

Not really.

I forced a laugh. "You know I get all wishy-washy when I'm sick."

She turned me around and gave me a gentle nudge toward the stairs. "You get under those covers, and I'll be up in a bit. Scoot."

If I'd known, I would have hugged her twice as hard, would have told her I loved her and spoken the words that remained unsaid. I would have dragged her into the kitchen like Aunt Caty did and told her I was okay.

If I'd known.

My LAST NIGHT ALIVE WAS A ROUGH ONE.

For a decade—too long, really—I had mourned the loss of my family, wished for a magical reunion that would make everyone happy again—make *me* happy again. I'd lived in a world of reinvented memories, a falsehood, a yearning to regain what had never been. I'd seen Mom's static, halted life after the Divorce as a sign that she wasn't whole without Dad and that no other man could ever fill his shoes. In reality, I realized, it was me who hadn't moved on, and I'd stopped Mom from living as she stayed behind with me, the two of us hiding from the Next.

At least my final words to her hadn't been a lie. I really did get sick, hurling into the toilet that joined my room with Mooney's empty one, unable to dispel the image of Dad leering at that woman. Mom came up twice during the night and rested her hand on my forehead while I pretended to sleep.

As dawn broke on my final day, I knew what I had to do.

FOUR HOURS BEFORE

I raced downstairs, breathless with decision. Once I'd made up my mind, I felt an urgency to hurry, hurry, hurry. Mom started work late on Wednesdays, so I knew exactly where to find her—sipping yesterday's coffee at the kitchen table.

Another painful clue of the life I'd led her to.

I burst through the door and found her . . . not there. A note had been tacked to the fridge by the magnet I'd made her for Christmas a decade earlier. Even though it was peeling and in dire need of a trip to the garbage can, she'd kept it.

Mom knew my thoughts on change.

Skidding on linoleum, I rushed to the fridge and ripped the paper from the magnet. Then, as a final gift to Mom, I tossed the magnet into the trash. "For us, Mom." I smiled as I unfolded the note.

Meet us at City Hall, 1pm. Huge surprise :) The added smiley face made it all the more gruesome.

I glanced at the clock—five past nine—and exhaled in relief. Still plenty of time. I scoured my bag and almost panicked before my fingers finally found my phone. Running through my contacts, I found Mom's cell number, dialed it, and listened as it went straight to voicemail. *Shit.* Mom had a frustrating habit of turning her phone off every time she got into the car, even just to go to the corner store. *You can't be distracted by something that's turned off,* she'd say. I used to roll my eyes at that.

Now . . . now.

I called Mooney with the same result and left a message—mostly swearing.

Shit, shit.

Racing to my room, I took the stairs by twos. Buster had curled up on my bed, stealing the warmth I'd left behind, and what I did next was the only action that resulted in no future regrets, no *if onlys*.

I wrapped my arms around my dog, kissed him on the nose, and whispered, "I love you."

I cling to that memory now, as I watch the grass grow over me.

Nine-thirty. Time enough for a shower.

Though I was filled with a welling panic, desperate to stop my parents from making the worst decision of their lives, at the same time, I was strangely calm. Everything was going to work out, and I damn well wanted to be clean when it did. After rushing through a shower, I was in my car by ten, yet the calmness I'd felt before was washed down the drain with the suds. Reminding myself that I had time, I tried to slow my breathing.

I had three hours to go half a mile.

The car roared to life, and I dialed Mom's office while the engine warmed up. The receptionist said Mom had taken a personal day. No, she hadn't left a forwarding number. Yes, I could leave a message. More panic as I threw the car into drive and left my house—my world— for the last time. Fifteen minutes later, I tapped my foot impatiently while a different receptionist dialed Mooney's desk. I listened as she left a message informing him that I was waiting in the lobby. She motioned for me to sit, but I opted to pace while I repeatedly checked my phone. Some-how, it was already eleven-fifteen. Why was time suddenly moving so fast? The receptionist gave me the stink eye when I asked her to try again.

Bitch, don't even.

"Your visitor is still here. Uh-huh. No problem." As

she pressed a button on her phone, I swear she sneered. "He's in a meeting. Would you like to leave a message, or did you want to continue to wait?"

Mooney was in no meeting. I quickly scrawled a note, tossed it at the bitch, and hurried out the door.

———

BACK IN MY CAR, I STARTED SECOND-GUESSING everything as the clock on the dash announced it was already eleven thirty-five. What had seemed like all the time in the world now felt like no time at all. That I had an hour and a half to drive through three measly lights should have put me at ease. But what if that wasn't long enough to talk Mom out of this ridiculous plan that had, only a day before, seemed to be the Best Idea Ever?

What if?

I reversed onto Main Street, nearly backing into a parked car. Tires squealed as I stomped the accelerator. Those three traffic lights were the only thing standing in my way, the barrier between a bad decision and a close call, and just my luck; lunch-hour traffic had begun.

One light behind, two to go.

God, how could I not have seen it? Ten years Mom had wasted, waiting for me to give her some signal that it was okay to move on, to live. Dad; he'd moved on. Was that so wrong? Mooney and I both had seen him as the enemy, but now I understood that my brother had only done what Mom couldn't. What *I* couldn't. He'd made a change, and maybe change wasn't so bad after all.

City Hall loomed ahead, and the irony of it all hit me as the light turned from red to green. I laughed; not any old laughter, but the crazy kind you hear in movies. I was about to snuff out my life's dream, to stop the event I thought I'd wanted for a decade.

And then, everything stopped.

ONE MINUTE BEFORE

One minute remained before the Next, and as my heart warmed with joy, the strangest thing happened. With my final sixty seconds ticking away, I heard a *click*, and a single thought permeated my being.

This is it.

I no longer felt part of myself. I saw me behind the wheel as if I were watching a movie, and I was the star. I *knew*. My life was winding down to the final moments, and in a disconnected way, I understood there was no stopping it. My last act had already been written, it needed only to play out. I'd heard stories of people who looked over their own bodies in hospital rooms, hovering high above after it was done.

No one tells you it happens *before*. That in that final minute, it's already over, and you can only watch, helpless.

Two lights behind, one to go.

My phone buzzed; Mooney's ring. I watched myself jump in my seat, pull my phone from my bag, and read the screen.

Where RU??? OMW to city hall. RU coming???

The final light turned green, and my car began to pass through the intersection.

Fifteen seconds.

I watched as my foot pressed on the gas and I picked up my phone. I screamed from above, *Don't! Put it down!*

Instead, the other me averted her eyes from the road, laughed at something on the screen, and typed her final message. Ten seconds.

OMG, I lol so hard I peed my pa—

My head hit the steering wheel, and in that final second, one word spilled from my lips.

"Mom . . ."

And then, I knew everything.

NEXT

I don't know how much time passed in the living world. Time, I've learned, changes. It stopped for me—it went on for everyone else.

I came to while Rick lowered my casket into the ground. My parents and Mooney stood at my grave, a sea of people around them, their faces still, broken. I tried to speak, to tell them I was here, to stop crying.

Mom, stop.

But, like in nightmares, nothing came out. I'd had my chance.

Mooney glared at Dad and stomped toward the gate, and I finally found my voice as I chased after him. "Mooney! Stop, I'm here! Did they get married? Tell me!"

But Mooney only walked on, his head hung low, and as he passed through the gate, I followed. And then I didn't. Something held me back, some force. I tried again and hit an invisible wall. *What the hell?* Again and again, I threw myself at the open space that trapped me within the walls of the cemetery until one final push sent me sprawling on the gravel. I was still laying there when Mom passed over me, with Dad close behind.

Cars roared to life, doors opened and closed. They were leaving, and I would be left here forever. After they'd all gone, I ran into the woods on the eastern edge of the property—I had to get as far away from my casket as possible—and screamed.

Eventually, night fell, and something happened.

My breath stopped, the sight unlike anything I'd ever seen. Tiny globes of colorful light swarmed the air, dancing, rising, then swooping toward the earth. A globe swam to me, and I lifted my palm where it settled, rolling on my skin, expanding and diminishing before rising toward the sky. I couldn't fathom whether they were living beings or orbs of spiritual dust. I only knew that they were dazzling, delicate whispers that filled me with comfort.

I turned, and the fluttering globes surrounded me as I spotted the cottage. I knew I had to go there, knew it was where I would begin the Next. I was propelled along, not entirely under my own power. The globes calmed, but they also pushed.

The time had come for the Next.

37

STEPHANIE

ONE DAY BEFORE - 1987

Oh my God, my best friend's party was going to be the bomb.

Tracy was throwing a totally gnarly bash for her eighteenth birthday. It wasn't fair that my parents wouldn't let me have one for stupid reasons like "grades" and "attitude." Whatever. At least they'd loosened the reigns enough to allow me to go to Tracy's. We were in her room trying on outfits, and I swear to God, I looked so rad. Tracy had the most righteous earring collection. I rummaged through her jewelry box and found a pair of tubular hoop earrings that totally went with the bow in my hair. Tracy worked in her dad's hardware store, and she was always at the mall buying earrings, and clothes, and all the stuff I couldn't afford. My dad had offered me a part-time job in his office, like, a thousand times, but I mean, come on. Who wants to stuff envelopes for eight hours on a Saturday?

She had the latest Debbie Gibson record, and we danced to "Only in My Dreams" while I pulled on a pair of fingerless lace gloves. Tracy was totally into Tiffany, something that I felt was wrong, wrong, wrong. Tiffany was just a Debbie wannabe, and she looked like one of those girls who would beat me up in the school hall if she had the chance. Whatever. Tracy was so lucky to have a record player in her room. At my house, Dad insisted that the record player stay in the living room so he and Mom could like, be aware of what my sisters and I were listening to. So totally bogus.

"Oh my God, no way are you wearing my Madonna skirt!" Tracy was always super dramatic about her clothes. Like, I would let her borrow my clothes—even my freaking Guess jeans—and I would never hound her, but she was such a stickler about hers. "I told you not to wear that around your cat. He always sheds on it."

"Take a chill pill. Patches can't help it." It bugged me when she dissed Patches, always accusing him of getting fur on everything as if he did it on purpose. Cassidy's cat had had a litter three years before, and the second I saw Patches I knew we belonged together. Mom threw a fit when I snuck him home, but eventually, she fell in love with him, too. It sucked that Cassidy's mom died not long after, but that only made Patches extra special. I mean, what would have happened if he'd been in that house with her when it happened? Like, he would have starved to death.

I threw on my denim jacket and admired my reflection —so rad. I looked just like Samantha from *Who's the Boss*. What was her name? Allison Midano? Something like that. She was so totally cool. As I scrutinized the jacket in the mirror, a thought occurred that totally creeped me out.

"You're not like, inviting Deborah, are you?" Oh my God, I hated Deborah. She was my mortal enemy and everything, and it wasn't just me, either. No one liked her ever since she did *that thing.*

"Oh my God, give it a rest, already." Tracy edged me out of the mirror and spun her skirt. "I feel sorry for her."

"How can you feel sorry for her of all people? She practically murdered Mrs. C."

Tracy kicked off her boots, tried on a pair of flats, and swiveled her body, viewing herself from every possible angle. "They said it was an accident."

"Gag me." Everyone knew it was no accident. Deborah was always, like, off her rocker. Like, there was something wrong with her noodle. She never had any girlfriends in grade school or junior high, and when we all moved on to high school, she totally hung out with the heavy metal crowd. You know, those guys who wore parachute pants and like, grew their hair long and banged their heads to Ozzy. Those guys always made me nervous. Deborah never came to the school dances, never participated in sports or any after-school stuff—not even Camp Fire, and *everyone* did Camp Fire. Any time we had to gather for some lame assembly, her shadow was barely visible in the corner where the lights were dimmest. She was weird from day freaking one.

I rolled my eyes. "I heard she's preggers. Again."

Tracy rolled hers right back. "She is so *not* preggers. Why do you even listen to that stuff?"

"I heard it from like, four different people, so it's practically confirmed."

It wasn't like it was totally out of the question. Deborah had gotten preggers a couple of years earlier and was probably already knocked up when she did that thing to Mrs. C, and now she had a fat, ugly little boy. Danny, or Donny, I think. Something like that. That sweet John Bennett was supposedly the father, and he like, *had* to marry her. Everyone felt so sorry for him.

"Just tell me you didn't invite her."

"Oh my God, I didn't invite her. Happy? Billy's coming, and even he didn't want her here."

My heart took a left turn at the mention of her brother. *Billy, Billy, oh my God, Billy.* I sang his name in my head, then quickly checked myself. I couldn't be like, obvious, even though I was so totally amped. I casually looked out the window, like I didn't even care or anything. "I thought Billy wasn't coming home until school was out." I wanted to pat myself on the back for how well I'd pulled off not caring at all that Billy was coming to the biggest party of the year.

As Tracy rummaged through her jewelry box with the little ballerina on top, I was grateful she wasn't able to see the goofy smile I couldn't wipe away.

Billy was such a dreamboat. He was hot when I first saw him, and he only grew more sizzling over the years. Some boys go through this super awkward stage in their teens when their faces break out, and their voices get all weird, and they sound like Peter Freaking Brady. Not Billy. His face remained smooth, and his voice just deepened one day without that awful wavering period, and he instantly became dreamier.

"Yeah, he's coming. I guess he finished early. It's different in college. Oh my God, I can't wait for college."

I leaned back on her bed and kicked my feet up, looking totally disinterested. At least I hoped so. Oh my God, Billy was *so* cute. Totally one hundred percent bodacious.

And older.

I saw him the first time in the first grade when he'd come to Parent's Night. There he was, looking hot with his dark, feathered hair, while their parents ogled over Tracy's macaroni art. I knew right then that we would marry and we'd have a hundred babies. He'd probably be a doctor, and I would throw Tupperware parties just like Mom. Over the years—when I wasn't grounded for something stupid —I'd hang out at their house every chance I got, and while Tracy and I did our homework, I'd watch her brother play that Atari thing, making this funky little orange guy jump up and down over this pyramid of colored blocks. If not for Billy, I'd have been a lot better at algebra.

I'd see him in the school halls, roughhousing with older boys and stealing older girls' Trapper Keepers and I'd melt a little. Then he'd notice me, wave and smile, and I'd melt entirely. When he moved on to junior high, the elementary school had suddenly seemed so . . . elementary. No longer did I bother to peek around every corner, or look for him at assemblies. He was just so not there. At least I could go over to Tracy's house and watch him play those video games or do his homework, or watch reruns of *Gilligan's Island,* always with an apple in his hand and his legs propped up on the coffee table. Sometimes I'd convince Tracy to scrap the homework and move to the couch. For some reason, he was totally into *I Dream of Jeannie,* and even though I hated that show—I mean, come on, why wouldn't Captain Nelson just let Jeannie do her magic, or whatever?—I sat through it just to be in the same breathing space with him.

Then Billy went off to college, and suddenly he was nowhere. He wasn't at school, wasn't at home, wasn't sitting on the floor helping a couple of plumbers rescue Princess Apricot, or whoever. His absence left a hole in my heart, and my world crumbled.

I never told Tracy that I cried every night for a month after Billy left for college. I never let it slip that I wrote our names together on the inside of my Pee-Chee circled by hearts. She never knew that I'd filled my diary with visions of our life together; a tiny house with a white picket fence and little kids running around and a mailbox with *The Murphy's* scrawled across it.

It wasn't just that I worried about Tracy's reaction to my crush. There were other complications. Billy's parents were super strict and uber-traditional. They were always trying to hook Billy up with some girl from their church, or the daughter of a family friend. Their parents expected that she and Billy would marry nice Catholic people and go on to have nice Catholic families and live nice Catholic lives. I was most certainly not Catholic. I came from practically the most Lutheran family in Hood Valley.

I came close to telling Tracy a million times. She was my best friend, and I felt terrible keeping my biggest secret from her. But the thing was, she never really complained about her parents' plans for her future. Like, she never fought it. It was just the expected outcome. So, what would she think about her best friend being head over heels in love with her brother?

On the day before the big party, though, something happened. Something *clicked*, and I decided I was going to do it. Maybe it was the panic of knowing Billy was away at college, meeting all sorts of fancy, smart college girls. Maybe it was the heat of time running out. Even now, all these years and lifetimes later, I still don't know what made me spill the secret I'd kept bottled inside. It was like I was setting my Jeannie free.

We moved to her vanity—one more thing that made me so jealous. I was the one who'd always wished for a vanity in my room, a pretty white one with roses painted around the mirror. But when Tracy had asked her parents, they'd just gone out and bought her one. I mean, okay, so she'd had to work extra hours at her dad's store for a month. Still—she'd practically stolen my idea.

"I have something to tell you." I brushed a rainbow of blue eyeshadow over her lid. "Pinkie-swear you won't get mad."

"How can I pinkie-swear when I don't know what it is?" Tracy craned her neck, peering into the mirror. "Did you like, murder Deborah and dump her body in the woods or something?"

"You wish." Now that I was ready to spill it after all those years, I was suddenly not ready at all. I bit my lip. "I'm in love."

She pulled back and gave me a long, hard stare. "Oh my God, with who?"

My tongue grew a hundred times its usual size, suddenly sapped of moisture. I could lie, say I was in love with John Bennett. He was cute. But he was married to that awful Deborah. Maybe Stephen, that boy from Band who played the trumpet. But that wouldn't work either. He was a terrible trumpet player, and if there was one thing

Tracy knew about me, it was that I hated bad trumpet playing.

"Billy." I just said it, just let his name spill from my lips. I stopped breathing. Like, I've been dead now for more than thirty years, and I still catch myself doing it, and I don't even *need* to breathe anymore.

Tracy's jaw slacked, and her lips took an upward turn. "For reals, who is it?"

"I *am* for reals. It's Billy."

The smile disintegrated. "Nu-uh."

"Yuh-huh."

She sashayed to the window, her skirts swirling, and she just stood there all quiet. I'd known she wouldn't jump for joy or anything, but I hadn't expected her to say nothing at all. Maybe she hated me. Maybe she was happy for me. Her silence could've meant anything.

She turned, so slowly, and stared from beneath her dark lashes. "It's not a good idea. You know that."

I went from holding my breath to nearly panting. It wasn't like I hadn't seen *that* coming. It was why I'd waited so long. Yet worrying about it and living it were two different things. "Why not?" I already knew the answer.

"For one thing, you're not Catholic."

"So? Like, don't have a cow. Chill out, already."

Tracy made a guttural noise that sounded like someone had punched the air from her. "What do you mean '*So*'? Have you met my parents? If you haven't noticed, they're pretty much set on him marrying like, not a Lutheran girl." She put her hands on her hips. "A *German* Lutheran girl, no less."

"I didn't say I was going to marry him. *God.*" Why

was she fighting me so hard? Like, so what if her parents didn't approve? I did lots of things my parents didn't approve of. "Am I not good enough for him or something?"

Why did I keep asking questions I didn't want the answers to?

"Stephy . . ."

"Whatever. I gotta book." I grabbed my Strawberry Shortcake backpack—the one with Custard's little paws resting on the ladder—and headed for the door.

"Stephy, stop."

I stopped but refused to face her.

"It's not a good idea. You're just . . . not Catholic, and that's a big deal. You've always known that."

That was what it came down to, really. Our religions had always been the one difference between Tracy and me, and her parents' rules were unbreakable. I didn't get it, I never had. Like, who obeyed their parents so unflinchingly? We were older now, practically adults, and the faster I raced toward adulthood, the more I realized my parents knew nothing about me. They'd forgotten teenage struggles, the pressure of fitting in, and they overreacted to everything. Couldn't they understand that music was just music, and fashion was just fashion and that the world hadn't hatched some diabolical plan to ruin me?

The thing that drove me crazy was that Tracy defended my parents—*my* parents. When they grounded me for sneaking out of my window after bedtime to grab a pop at the corner store, she took their side. *You shouldn't have snuck out. Just stop breaking the rules.* Sometimes it felt like Tracy was like a second mom.

But as much as I hated it, I knew she was right. Her

parents were die-hard traditionalists. Why couldn't they just get with the times? Diana Ross had married that funny-looking white guy. If she could do that, why couldn't Billy and I grab a stupid burger at the Dandy Sandy?

I jumped when she laid a hand on my shoulder and turned me to face her. "You're still coming, right?"

I couldn't stay mad. It wasn't Tracy's fault that her parents were old-fashioned. "Yeah, I'm coming."

"Good. Bring that new Prince album. Lisa Sullivan said it's totally rad."

"Sure."

Heading home, I threw on my Walkman and let Belinda Carlilse's sultry voice wash over me. For reals, the Go-Go's had The Beat. I decided to cut through Mr. C's backyard. I shouldn't have—he was nutso, even though it wasn't his fault he'd gone bonkers after Mrs. C died when Deborah did *that thing*. The kids at school were starting to whisper that his house was haunted—the weeds had taken over the grass, and the paint had peeled away in ugly chunks. Even I was beginning to get creeped out. But it was so much shorter than going all the way around, and besides, he hadn't mowed in years.

How much did he really care anymore?

TWO HOURS BEFORE

"How did you get here so fast?" Tracy asked. "We like, just got off the phone."

"Dad dropped me off," I lied, and followed her into the kitchen, where empty bottles of Hi-C littered the counter. As she grabbed a stack of Styrofoam cups, she went into full-on Mother Mode. "You shouldn't cut through his yard. He's crazy."

How did she always know? "He's not crazy. He's just . . ." I could think of no other word that fit him. He *was* kind of crazy now, and it was all that stupid Deborah's fault. "Don't flip about it."

I could tell from the way her face scrunched up like a deflated basketball that she was about to lay one of her lectures on me, but the doorbell saved me.

"Oh my God. How do I look?"

Her dark hair was teased so high there had to be an entire can of Aqua Net holding it in place. I could never get mine more than three measly inches off my head. "Bitchin'."

She smiled and bounced from the kitchen.

An hour later, the party was in full swing. People were rocking out to that new Michael Jackson song, and guys were sneaking up behind girls whispering, "I'm bad, shamone." I didn't know what a shamone was, but if Billy whispered it to me, I would just die.

I hid in a darkened corner and sipped punch. I'd heard that someone had spiked it with some hardcore peach California Coolers, but it didn't taste spiked to me. Not to brag, but I was no stranger to alcohol. Dad used to let me sip his Near Beer, which I'm pretty sure had a *lot* of alcohol in it. I must have developed a high tolerance; I never felt woozy or anything.

I'd promised myself I'd put on a brave face for Tracy; I didn't want to bum out her party, but as the action ramped up, I couldn't help thinking back to our conversation from the day before.

And then, as if he'd read my mind, Billy was there. I

hadn't even seen him enter, and I'd had my eyes glued to the door all night. One moment, there was this empty space in the room, and the next moment, he filled it. Oh my God, he looked so much older, so much more mature. And he had muscles now. When had he cultivated that hot bod? He'd cropped his jet-black hair short, almost military style. I'd liked his loose hair, nearly to his shoulders, but this was so. Much. Better. My heart skipped forty beats, and when his gaze met mine, I think I smiled, but I was so nervous that there's a good chance I may have grimaced.

And then, oh my God—he started toward me. I turned in a circle—I still don't know why—and began looking for something on the floor. I tried to appear cool, nonchalant. *I could care less that you're coming over to me,* I hoped my eyes said.

But I so totally cared and was so totally *not* cool.

Billy came within ten steps when Tracy swooped in from nowhere, grabbed his arm, and pulled him into a huddle. Her face was stern—almost angry. He rolled his eyes, and I could tell they were arguing. As I stood in the corner, he glanced at me. Oh my God, they were talking about me, and Tracy was telling him everything. She probably even knew about the Pee-Chee in my locker. I wanted to die.

Someone put that new U2 album on the record player, and "With or Without You" began to play—a weird, almost mournful song that brought down the mood of the entire room. The lights dimmed, and people began slow dancing.

Was that the crux of their argument? With or without *me*?

They hugged, Billy left for the kitchen, and Tracy

slowly walked to my corner. I remained silent while she looked like she was trying to figure out how to say something. There was no way to read her face. Like, it could have been anything she was trying to work up the nerve to say.

"So," she said.

I waited as she looked at the wall, the chair—*Billy's* chair—at everything that wasn't me.

So.

Finally, she spoke, and my knees weakened just a little.

"I need to tell you something." She crumbled as if someone had let the air out of her. "He likes you, too. For like, ever, I guess."

What?

"Yesterday, when you said you liked him, I wasn't surprised. We had that conversation already at Christmas, except it was Billy saying it then." She looked away, guilty.

What???

I didn't want to know the answer, but I had to ask. "You told him the same thing you said to me, didn't you?"

She only stood there, fiddling with her skirt. "Billy is transferring to Portland State in the fall so he can like, date you and stuff, and I guess Mom and Dad are okay with it."

Too much information muddied my brain. "He's transferring . . . to the university a half hour from here?" Then the bigger statement hit me. "Your parents are okay with it? Like, how would you even know that? Unless . . ."

Oh my God, he'd talked to them, too.

"I guess they finally realized that there are like, no other Catholics in this town, and Dad said that if Billy had to date a townie, it might as well be someone they already considered a daughter."

A daughter . . . like, I couldn't even.

But I slowly began to realize that his parents weren't the problem. Tracy—*my best friend*—was. Shock was replaced by anger. It had been Tracy who couldn't accept Billy and me together. My best friend in the whole wide world, the person I'd rarely spent more than a day without, aside from that time her parents took her to Disneyland—was responsible for keeping me from the love of my life.

"How could y—"

"I'm sorry, Stephy. It's like . . . when you grow up thinking one way, it's hard to start thinking any other way. I was wrong."

My mind reeled with a thousand questions. Her parents had accepted it all too easily. Or had they? It had always been Tracy who'd insisted that they were the strict, unbending parents with a singular focus. Had it all been a lie? I wanted to be angry. I wanted to shout and stomp my feet and ruin Tracy's party.

But this weird feeling rushed, and suddenly I loved her more than I thought possible. My anger drifted away, and a calmness washed over me. Madge says it's the Next's way of making sure we don't head into it with unnecessary baggage. I like to think she's right.

Tracy looked over my shoulder, then awkwardly walked away, and I knew he was behind me. I felt it, like a breeze, and heard it, like how ambient sound suddenly grows hollow in the presence of another, and I turned to face my lifetime crush.

"So, like . . ." He scratched his head while his face

twisted. "It would be fresh if we went to the Dandy Sandy together." Oh my God, he was nervous. *Billy*. Nervous!

"For sure, that would be choice." So smooth, as if I went to the Dandy Sandy all the time with all the boys. "I'm totally down."

"Righteous. Let me like, get my coat. Or, you know, whatever." He nearly tripped on his own feet as he swiveled toward the closet.

"Wicked. I'll chill in your car."

"Rock on," he said and stumbled away.

My whole life was coming together, and I pinched myself to be sure I wasn't dreaming, just like they did on TV. And when I winced from the pain, I smiled.

THIRTY MINUTES BEFORE

Oh my God, the garage was freezing. Shivering, I hurried to the car and climbed through the passenger side, my breath forming a vapor.

It all started to sink in. I was going to the Dandy Sandy with Billy. *Billy*. Not that guy from homeroom, that dumb old pizza-faced Freddie Perkins, who had invited me once to have a soda. A soda! As if we were living in olden times.

Fifteen minutes later, I started to get nervous. Why was Billy taking so long? Maybe Tracy had changed her mind. Maybe Billy had changed *his* mind. My fingers were frozen, and I cupped my hands and breathed warm air to lessen the chill.

That's when I noticed the keys sitting in the ignition.

"Radical." I leaned toward the driver's side, turned the key, and the car roared to life.

And in that single moment, I very nearly knew . . . something.

The radio kicked on, and Lisa Lisa belted out, "Head to Toe." I sang along while I turned up the heat.

"I think I love you from head to toe, I know." I checked my makeup in the mirror and touched up my lip gloss with *Kissable Baby Lips*. As the heater kicked on and I leaned my head back, I hoped I looked more kissable and not at all like a baby. *Here today, gone tomorrow.* Oh my God, I loved Lisa Lisa. She like, totally got me. I sang it along with her.

"Here today, gone tomorrow."

NEXT

When I was little, I went through a phase when I realized I wasn't going to live forever, and I totally obsessed over it. How would I die? Would it hurt? Would I be old or young?

It never occurred to me that it would end up being embarrassingly stupid.

I caught my eyes drooping. Where was Billy? My head felt a little woozy, and that old Elvis song came on the radio just as I was drifting off.

"Cuz I can't help falling in love with you . . ."

Billy and I were finally going to be together. How many girls got the chance to live out their dream of true love? A dream that, for me, had clung to the edges of my life for as long as I could remember. So lucky . . .

"Darling, so it goes, some things are meant to be . . ."

The strangest thing happened then. I heard a *click*, and a single thought filled my being.

This is it.

Oh my God, I *knew*. My life was winding down to its final moments.

Hovering above the car, yet somehow able to see inside, I watched my head nod. I screamed from above, *"Don't fall asleep! Get out of the car!"*

Instead, I closed my eyes. Ten seconds.

In that final second, one word spilled from my lips.

"Billy . . ."

And then, I like, knew everything.

I DON'T KNOW HOW MUCH TIME PASSED IN THE LIVING world. Time like, depends on where you exist. It stopped for me, and it went on for everyone else.

I came to as Serge lowered my casket into the ground. My parents were standing above me with Tracy and Billy on either side, surrounded by a sea of people—kids from school, cousins, people I didn't even know. Even Mr. C was there, though why, I still don't know.

I tried to speak, to tell them I was there. Stop crying.

Billy, stop.

Nothing came out. Just like in those dreams when you try to scream, I like, couldn't say a word.

When the pastor stopped talking, Billy put an arm around Tracy. "Why was she even in Dad's car, Trace? I waited outside forever."

Oh my God. I died in the wrong freaking car.

One by one, they passed through the gate, and I followed. And then I didn't. Something held me back, some force. I tried again, hit a wall. *Oh my God, what the flip?* Again, and again, I threw myself at the invisible forcefield that trapped me within the cemetery until one final push sent me sprawling onto gravel.

Cars roared to life, doors opened and closed. They were leaving me behind forever. So, I climbed the tallest tree within shouting distance of the gate and screamed.

Eventually, night fell, and something happened.

The sight, unlike anything I'd ever seen, stopped my breath. One of those weird globes swam to me. I lifted my palm, and it like, settled on my hand, rolling on my skin before lifting off toward the sky. Oh my God, I couldn't fathom what they were. I only knew they were the coolest, most amazing things ever.

I turned, and the fluttering globes surrounded me as I spotted the cottage. I knew I had to go there, that it was where the Next would begin. I walked passed the comment box and toward the cottage door.

The time had totally come for the Next.

38

MADGE

ONE YEAR BEFORE - 1984

In 1984, doctor's offices were dreadful places. I never understood why they were decorated with cheap, plastic chairs that were in no way made for waiting, painted in shocking oranges and dark olives. There was always at least one clown painting, and the carpet had clearly been a steal.

Do they still decorate them like bus stations, dear?

"Mr. Dillard?"

A snippy-looking thing wearing a skirt far too short for her long legs led us down the narrow hallway. I didn't want to make that walk. Instead, I wanted to race back home, make Marty that chicken parmesan he loved so much, and bring him a dozen boxes of Twinkies. We shouldn't have been in that narrow hallway on a journey that would change everything.

She led us to an empty office and left us to figure out on our own if we should sit or stand. The short hike already had Marty huffing and puffing.

"Sit down, dear," I said.

Fifteen minutes later, Dr. Warner entered the room, his eyes glued to a chart. I didn't even think he realized we were there, from the look of surprise when he saw us across the desk. "Mister . . ."

An awkward moment passed. "Dillard. Marty Dillard," I said, vexed.

"Yes." That was all he said. No apology for the wait, or for forgetting who we were.

For holding Marty's future in his hands.

Marty had finished chemotherapy three months before, and we were about to find out if it had worked. Or took. Or whatever it was they said to wives that meant their husbands weren't going to drown in their own lungs. Dr. Warner removed his glasses and pinched the bridge of his nose. I wished I knew how to read that man. Doctors seemed to have a natural poker face, keeping the rest of us from deciphering what was going on behind their eyes. "Mr. Dillard, I'm afraid the cancer has spread to the lymph nodes."

I waited for the magic words. All doctors had the magic words, the ones that began with the most magical of all words—*but*. Except there was no *but*, and Dr. Warner only stared silently.

"What's the next step?" I peered at the doctor, still trying to determine the truth behind his unreadable features.

I should have been watching Marty. *He* knew.

"There is no next step. Is that right, doc?" He squeezed my hand, and I looked at Marty, really looked at him. It was funny. He'd been underfoot for three long months while I cared for him, emptied buckets of his vomit, and pressed cold compresses to his forehead. But only in that office did I really look at him for the first time since he'd gotten ill.

He was dying. It was written all over his face, and somehow, I'd missed it.

Dr. Warner pushed his glasses back, folded his hands, and rested them on the desk—rich mahogany with an expensive-looking blotter. Italian leather, I guessed. I studied every item, every grain of wood on that desk—anything to avoid what came next.

"I'm very sorry, Mr. Dillard." It's a strange feeling to discover that even the doctor has lost hope. Eventually, it angers you. But when you first hear it, it's just odd.

"How long?" Marty's face was stoic, brave, as if he were asking how long before the leftover turkey went bad.

"Anywhere from a few weeks to a year, Mr. Dillard. It's hard to—"

"How *long*?" Marty leaned forward. He was like that, dear. Ambiguity was a quality he despised.

Dr. Warner removed his glasses again, and I was beginning to learn at least that much about him—he didn't like to see clearly when he dispensed bad news. "I would say two months. Maybe three." He turned to me. "Now is the time for keeping him comfortable, tying up loose ends."

Glasses: on.

And then, as if a transaction were complete, a deal made, as if there were no further use for the Dillards, we were dismissed. It's strangely final when a doctor ushers you from his office for the last time—with his glasses on.

It didn't escape my notice that no one escorted us back to the waiting room. The whole lot had washed their hands of us. There was no need to show us out, no time for a gentle pat on the back or a comforting word. It was as if Marty were a car that had been declared totaled, and now we were headed for the crusher. The hall had grown narrower, the exit a million miles away. I didn't want Marty to reach that door. Help was here, but we were leaving it, walking away, abandoning hope, and once we crossed the threshold, it would be a death march. Marty held the door open for me as he'd held all my doors for the past twenty years, and when I walked through, my Marty truly began to die.

As we passed through the waiting room, the TV droned on about the weather in a way that felt obscene. A man sat in one of those uncomfortable plastic chairs, his fingers gripped tightly around the fedora in his lap. I knew him from somewhere.

"Hello, Mr. C," Marty said.

Of course. Mr. Casper was one of the favorite teachers at Hood Valley Elementary. Both of my boys had him—he'd send their report cards home with encouraging notes scribbled on the back, even though my boys had a problem turning in homework. I'd met his wife once—lovely woman. Our cat, Sylvester, came from a litter they'd had a few years back, and Mrs. Casper had seemed to think Sylvester would be the perfect name for a male cat. She would have been right, had Sylvester not surprised us all and turned out to be a girl.

But in the case of Sylvester—and as it ended up with

my Marty—I suppose there were some things that I didn't want to see too clearly.

SIX MONTHS BEFORE

I know that most people abhor hospitals, but I loved them. My friend Thelma worked at Hood Valley Hospital, and before things had gotten worse for Marty, I'd meet her in the cafeteria every week, where we talked about our favorite afternoon story, *Hope's Hospital.* I hadn't seen her since Marty had gotten sick, but then again, I hadn't seen a lot of people during those long months. After we walked through those waiting room doors, I hated hospitals. Not just the one in our tiny town, but every last one. They were where people like my Marty went when no one else knew what to do with them.

The doctor had said three months—Marty lasted six. I know it's awful to say, but those extra three months were no blessing. I should have been grateful to have more time with him, to be at his side, to comfort him. But nothing could ease Marty's suffering. The pills didn't work, and the special diets only made him bloated. Rather than a blessing, the added time was a curse.

The children and I surrounded his bedside at the end. Even now, I'd like to believe he knew we were there, but I think the cold, hard truth is that he didn't. He hadn't spoken a word for three days, and that morning, when I couldn't wake him for his cocktail of pills, I called that new emergency line, 911. It was the only time I used it— the day my Marty died. Marty always said that 911 number was just a fad, that people wouldn't trust a centralized system for emergencies.

Do they still use it, dear?

The boys sat on Marty's left while Cassidy and I flanked his right as "American Pie" wafted in from the nurses' station. Marty loved that song—he said it had hidden meanings. I wondered if he could hear it, or if his pain was too loud.

A machine blared, slicing into my core, and a nurse walked in, held a stethoscope to his chest, and calmly walked back out. I wondered why she didn't run. I'd seen enough episodes of *Hope's Hospital* to know that when a machine made a sound like that, nurses were supposed to run, so her neutral gait—that casual stroll in and out— made me question the impact of the siren. Maybe the machine had malfunctioned. Surely her steps would have had more urgency otherwise. But another instrument began to blare, then another.

This time, it wasn't a nurse who came in but a chaplain.

It took an hour—a long, slow, torturous hour. With each sounding alarm, a faceless person strode in, shut it off, and left. The boys cried silently while Cassidy wailed. That this was happening was unfathomable. It wasn't some stranger, some distant relative lying there with tubes snaking out of every orifice. It was my Marty. In twenty years, I hadn't spent a single day without him, had never slept alone in our marital bed. He was late for dinner once, but that was only because the Pontiac had gotten a flat.

I don't remember the moment when it happened because it didn't seem like a single moment, but a series of them. There was no instance when I looked at Marty and knew. It snuck up on me like a thief. He was still very much Marty when the chaplain left the room, and when a nurse asked if we needed a ride home. I peered at her, trying desperately to comprehend what she was asking of me. "We'll stay here, thank you, dear." How dare she suggest that we leave Marty's side for even a moment.

She blinked, and something in her eyes changed.

And then I knew. Yes, dear, I knew.

THREE MONTHS BEFORE

Dark clouds covered the sun and that mist that Hood Valley is known for rolled in. As if the house weren't already empty enough, Marty's absence somehow filled the spaces in every corner.

I'd just given the last kitten away. Sylvester had birthed another litter just over a month before. We really had thought she was a boy when we named her. I was particularly attached to those little guys, as I was sure Sylvester had gotten pregnant on the day of Marty's passing. I'd counted back, calculating with that ten-key machine Marty had kept in his office, and the days lined up. It was as if those kittens were Marty reincarnated. I know it sounds crazy, but I couldn't deny the numbers.

Cassidy's friend had come by that morning to pick up the final one—a beautiful black-and-white kitten that she named Patches on the spot. That dear girl was so happy, so enchanted by him, and she picked up the kitten and held him close to her chest.

In that single moment, I very nearly knew . . . something.

I watched from the window as she disappeared into the fog.

In the three months that followed Marty's death, I was

unsettled. Not in the grand, sweeping way you would expect, but in the little things. My house felt wrong, somehow, as if it belonged to someone else. The kitchen, where I'd spent the best twenty years of my life, felt overtaken, changed, altered. I no longer knew every nook and cranny like the back of my hand. I couldn't remember where I kept the flour—I spent twenty minutes looking for it, only to find it in the same cupboard where it had always been—and I let a pot boil out its water, scorching the bottom. Thank God Marty's mother was no longer alive to see *that*.

The house was quiet—too quiet, and it wasn't just due to Marty's absence. Ron had returned to college, and Martin had just up and left a week after Marty's funeral, muttering something about a road trip. And Cassidy—my sweet, dear Cassidy—announced she was moving in with her boyfriend. At seventeen. What purpose did I have? I had no children to care for and no husband to look after. Even my friends had stopped calling. It was as if a sign had been hung around my neck, spelling out the word *quarantine*.

I knew women who were getting jobs, building careers. One woman on our street didn't even have a husband, yet she owned a house and drove her own car. Women were finding independence, living their own lives, dreaming their own dreams. I suppose you wouldn't understand, but I liked my life exactly the way it was—or had been. I'd gotten all the fulfillment I needed by looking after the needs of others. I never understood those women liberation folks. I still don't.

But I hadn't planned for what would happen when I was no longer needed. Of course, I knew the children would one day grow up and fly the coop, and somewhere deep down, I knew there was a chance that Marty would be the first to go—he'd been a lifelong smoker, after all—but I just hadn't planned for it all to happen so simultaneously. Though I was still relatively young, I suddenly felt as if time had sped up. I felt sixty, seventy, eighty-years-old, and it didn't take long before I lacked my usual pep. But then, I no longer had a use for all that energy.

In a matter of months, my world had gone from the chaos of a houseful of people to the drudgery of a house too large for just a cat and a middle-aged woman in the beginning stages of menopause.

Once a week, I left the house for a quick trip into town and loaded a cart with aluminum trays of frozen food, and with each trip, the wine I threw in got cheaper. I began keeping a bottle under the couch so I wouldn't miss a second of *Hope's Hospital*—the one thing I looked forward to every day. Oh my, I loved that Faith Kane. So sassy, so strong, so everything I wasn't and never could be. She had no husband or children, and yet, she was happy. Well, not then. Her lover had just fallen off a cliff, and all indications were that he'd died, but you never really knew with the daytime stories.

And then, one dark, cloudy day, the front door opened unexpectedly, and Cassidy stood in the doorway. I hoped my face wasn't red. My face tended to grow a permanent blush when I drank. But I was also going through The Change, and even in the dead of winter, the house felt like an oven.

"Mr. C quit. Can you believe it?" As Cassidy strolled toward the couch, I worried that she'd be able to smell the booze. Then again, I hadn't showered since . . . I wasn't sure. Hopefully, she wouldn't notice. She stopped at the basket where we kept the mail and began sorting through the overflowing pile. "I bet it's because of what happened to Mrs. C, and everyone knows that bitch Deborah is to blame."

"Language, dear."

She snorted, and though she'd turned her back, I felt her typical grimace. I knew my Cassidy.

"Anyway, everyone's talking about it. Some people are saying he went schizo or something."

I wriggled to ensure she wouldn't spot the bottle beneath the cushion. "Goodness, dear. I'm sure Mr. Casper isn't crazy, he's probably just trying to cope. He did just lose his wife, after all. Such a lovely woman. Wasn't she a teacher, too?" I hoped my jittery nerves didn't show.

"Everyone loved her. And mom, that awful Deborah is preggers. Can you believe it?"

"She can't possibly be pregnant. She's only a teenager —she's practically a baby herself."

"Everyone's talking about it."

I couldn't say I was shocked, not really. Deborah had always been different. When they were much younger, the kids and I had spent many a summer afternoon at the park, and Deborah never joined in with the play, choosing instead to hover on the sidelines, watching. I know it's not a nice thing to say, but dear, something was off with that one.

I hoped Mr. Casper would be okay. I truly did. He'd always been such a kind, gentle soul.

Cassidy left abruptly. At least her departure *seemed* awfully sudden. To tell the truth, I don't remember. My memories got a bit foggy after the first bottle.

My attention drifted back to the TV, and when Faith took a drink, I joined her.

ONE MONTH BEFORE

As "Unchained Melody" played on the kitchen radio, an odd thought surprised me.

I wasn't entirely sure I was alive anymore.

I checked my pulse—strong. I brought a palm to my lips and exhaled—warm. All indications were that I was still very much alive.

But I felt quite the opposite.

I'd awoken that morning with an ominous feeling that something was different, that something had changed overnight. My head ached—the most reliable clue that I was, in fact, alive—and I pulled a bottle from my night-stand drawer. I could no longer crawl out of bed without a drink, and I lay back while the alcohol worked its magic. I wasn't an alcoholic, dear, though I know it may seem that way. I had always enjoyed a nice glass of red wine with dinner, sometimes even at lunch with my girlfriends at the Dandy Sandy. And every Thanksgiving morning after I put the turkey in the oven, I rewarded myself with a mimosa. Sure, my drinking had increased a little since Marty's death. But who could blame me?

I checked my reflection in the bathroom mirror—pale skin, lifeless eyes. I sure looked dead. I lifted the lid from the toilet tank and pulled out a bottle of Mad Dog—horrible tasting stuff, but it gave a quick result.

Back downstairs, I peeked out the window. Before Marty had died, it had been my habit to pull back the curtains first thing every morning, announcing a fresh, new day. Now, the curtains remained closed, the daylight far too painful for my increasingly sensitive eyes.

The girl who'd taken Patches was passing by with that friend of hers. What were they now, fifteen? Sixteen? Likely the same age that I had met my Marty, the only boy I'd ever dated, the only man I'd ever kissed, and the only man I'd never been with . . . if you get my meaning. Marty was all I'd ever needed. I watched with a strange sadness as the girls passed the house and headed toward the high school. To be young again. So full of hope, the future still far ahead. Had the girl who'd taken Patches already met her Marty, or was he still in her morrow? Time was a funny thing. You could never see forward, but you were forever cursed with the ability to see what had already come to pass.

I was jolted from my thoughts as a noise sounded from upstairs, like a heavy object being pushed across the room. I glanced to the couch—Sylvester was sleeping, twitching with dreams of the chase in the movement of her paws. Taking the steps one by one, I wasn't scared exactly, but I still hadn't gotten used to being alone. Having gone straight from my father's house to my marital home, there had always been someone else around, until now.

I didn't remember closing the bedroom door. Before, when Marty was sleeping off the oceans of medication they'd had him on, I would close the door to give him as much quiet as possible, but I hadn't shut it in months. There'd been no reason. I'd probably closed it out of habit. That's what I told myself until I heard shuffling on the other side. Barely ten minutes had passed since I'd gone downstairs. I supposed someone could have broken in during that time, so I gathered my courage, smoothed out my apron—when had I put that on?—and turned the knob.

The room was empty, and the bed was unmade since there no longer seemed a reason to make it. The dresser drawers were closed, aside from the nightstand, where that bottle of Mad Dog peeked out. That the room appeared ransacked meant nothing—I hadn't tidied up in months. The light beside the rocking chair was on. *That* was odd. I hadn't turned that light on since the beginning of Marty's sickness. When he could still sit upright, he'd liked to sit in his chair and read by the lamp. When he became too ill even for that, the light went off and had remained off—until now. I knew I couldn't have turned it on—the brightness would have been too glaring. When had my eyes become so sensitive? I turned to leave.

Movement in my peripheral vision set my body rigid, my breath coming in short bursts, and I turned toward the rocker.

As if saddled with a sudden weight, Marty's chair slowly rocked.

I found my breath, my muscles relaxed, and something *clicked.* Overwhelming calm descended, with a lightness I hadn't felt since Marty had fallen ill. I stared at his chair. Not our chair, *his* chair. Scuffed and battered, Marty had lugged the rickety old thing home from a yard sale in the first year of our marriage, and it became the subject of our first real argument.

"Marty Dillard, you take that thing right back where you found it." I'd crossed my arms over my apron, determined to keep the eyesore out of my house.

"I can fix it," he'd said, with that smile that gave him a boyish charm. "It's not that bad, Madge."

"Not that bad?" I circled the chair and laid my hand on one of the armrests, which promptly fell off. "Dear, this is kindling."

He wrangled it into the garage and spent the afternoon pulling it apart, and I popped my head in every so often to groan at the pile of wood and nails on the floor.

"I hope you're going to clean this mess up before my parents arrive." I was already a nervous wreck. We'd planned to announce my pregnancy, the timing of which was uncomfortably close to our wedding date. Marty hadn't so much as laid a hand on me until our wedding night, and good thing, too—that first time was all it took.

"They won't be coming in the garage." He buried his nose in a manual on woodworking. "It'll be fine."

I left in a huff, sure that my husband didn't love me, that he'd set out to embarrass me, and that my house would soon be filled with all manner of broken furniture that he'd never be able to repair. But within a week, that chair shone, polished to a deep cherry, and the arm re-attached.

"It still creaks," I said, wrinkling my nose at the sound.

His face lit with a grin. "I like it."

For nineteen years, the chair held a prominent place in the living room. Only Marty ever sat in it. Not once did he announce it as his, and not once did I ever have to tell the children.

We all just knew.

"Marty?"

The rocker quickened before it stilled, the way it used to when Marty got up.

Marty.

I DON'T KNOW WHAT WOKE ME—THE CREAK, OR THE LIGHT —and I sat up slowly, holding my pounding head in my hands.

Marty's chair rocked, forward and back, illuminated by the lamp.

"Marty?"

The rocker slowed to a stop, and I fell back into a fitful sleep.

OVER THE FOLLOWING WEEKS, MARTY BECAME A FIXTURE around the house once again. I know you might not believe it, dear, but he was there. I felt him—that undeniably Marty-like energy filled my days with his presence, and our bedroom was no longer the lonesome reminder of everything I'd lost.

I moved the TV upstairs, nearly dropping it down the steps. Taylor and Emily say that TVs are much lighter now, but in those days, they were the weight of a mini-refrigerator. It took more than an hour to push it up the carpeted steps and into my bedroom.

Our bedroom.

It would have been easier to move the rocker downstairs. But the mere thought of touching it, displacing Marty . . . dear, I couldn't even entertain the idea.

My Marty had come home.

ONE WEEK BEFORE

Marty and I were in the bedroom, he rocking in his chair and me laying in the bed, the bedspread tucked to my chin. It was sweltering hot, but I'd found that until that first swig of Mad Dog kicked in, the air seemed to almost hurt when it touched my bare skin.

I sat up, the covers falling around my middle. *Hope's Hospital* was on. When had I turned on the TV? I craned my neck toward the screen.

It couldn't be. It just couldn't.

Mona was dead? No! Faith collapsed in a heap, the telephone receiver still in her hand, and the screen faded as the credits rolled. Mona had been a fixture on *Hope's Hospital* since its debut. Mona *was* the show. How could they do this?

I flew from the bed, ignoring the pounding inside my skull, raced downstairs, and tore open the front door, nearly tripping on the stack of newspapers clumped around the welcome mat. How long had it been since I'd brought the paper inside? I scooped them up and dumped them on the living room floor. It took ten minutes to find that day's paper, and when I did, my heart sank as my worst fear was realized.

It was Friday, and I'd have to wait until Monday for the next episode of *Hope's Hospital*.

The show had become my only connection to the world beyond my bedroom door. My children were gone, and my friends had all but disappeared—Thelma hadn't called in months. My husband was dead. I was as invested in the lives of Faith and Mona as I had once been in my neighbors'.

And dear, I just couldn't take yet another person dying on me.

I spent the weekend in a swirl of alcohol and sleep. Marty rocked on, his chair the only other being—living or otherwise—in my closed-off world.

Monday afternoon arrived with a screech from the alarm. Maybe Mona wasn't dead. Perhaps it was a case of mistaken identity or an as-of-yet undiscovered evil twin. When it came to the daytime stories, anything was possible. I slammed the alarm button, the rocker stilled, and after one quick swallow, I stumbled to the TV. I turned the knob and waited for the screen to warm up as I climbed back into bed.

As the episode wore on, it became clear this was no case of mistaken identity, no evil twin. Faith stood at Mona's hospital bedside, much as I had done six months earlier, and held her mother's hand as I'd held Marty's. She cried as I had, begged and pleaded as I had. It was as if I were watching my own story play out on the small screen.

I was three sheets to the wind by the end. I usually tried to stagger my drinks, but on that awful day, I just couldn't. The bottle was nearly empty when Faith spoke aloud to Mona's empty apartment.

I can't live without you, mother. She took a drink from a bottle eerily similar to the one in my own hand. *I won't.*

The credits rolled, the music played, and Marty began to rock.

And then, with the clarity of a bolt of lightning, I knew what I had to do.

NEXT

It wasn't waking on the floor that had brought me to. I'd fallen out of bed several times over that week.

It was Marty.

Rocking gently, his chair was in motion, the lamp illuminating the dark. I peeked at the curtains—no light crept in. I'd broken the alarm clock, but I could tell that dawn was still hours away.

The chair stopped suddenly as if a hand had stilled it.

"I know, Marty. Today."

For the first time in days, I stumbled downstairs. An odor soured the air, like old milk that had been left out, and the couch was askew. A vague memory of running into it the week before tried to surface, and I shook the image away. It didn't matter.

Nothing else mattered.

Hope's Hospital had sent me riding an emotional roller coaster as Faith made her rounds through the town of Pineview, tying up loose ends and saying obscure goodbyes. She'd made a decision and was going to carry it out, a decision that made sense to me. Faith couldn't possibly go on without Mona. Maybe the show was making room for new, younger characters. Who knew? I only knew that Mona was gone and now Faith was about to be gone too.

And like Faith, I accepted that I couldn't go on without my Marty. Not here, on this plane anyway. Marty was somewhere, and part of him was here, but the rest of him . . .

I shuffled to the kitchen, flipped on the light, and realized it didn't hurt. My head wasn't pounding. I held my hands out—for once, they didn't shake. For the first time in who knew how long, I felt wonderful. Digging through the fridge, I found a single egg and released it into a bowl of cold water. When it sank to the bottom, I knew it was still good, and then laughed at the irony. Did it matter if the egg had gone bad? I likely wouldn't be around long enough to feel the effects if it had. As the egg sizzled, I hummed along to the radio. Marty liked his eggs sunny-side up with toast to dip into the yolk. I'd never cared for it myself, but on that day, I ate it Marty's way.

After wiping down the counters, I moved to the sink, where maggots swam in the standing dishwater. How long had it been since I'd left the dishes to soak? I scooped the grub out of the sink, tossed the rag out the back door, and scrubbed the dishes.

I showered; my goodness did that ever feel good! Returning to the bedroom, I headed for the small secretary in the corner that we'd inherited when Marty's mother had passed. I relished the idea that I'd be writing my letters on it, and as I pulled a sheet of stationery from the drawer, the rocker began again, moving forward, moving back.

"I know, Marty. I'm working on it."

The rocker stopped, and I wrote my letters. Folding the last sheet, I tucked it into an envelope and brought the top down on the secretary, closing it for the final time. I laid the letters on my bed as Marty began to rock once again.

A swallow of the last of the Mad Dog brought the rocker to a stop.

For the next three hours, I scrubbed, straightened, and laundered, racing through my chores as I once had, back when it had mattered. By noon, the house sparkled—every room, every stitch of clothing, and every dish. I tossed away the perishables and emptied the trash three times. I filled Sylvester's bowl with his favorite food and left enough water for a week, hoping it would be enough. Just in case, I left the flap of the pet door open.

Pen and notebook in hand, I made the slow walk through the house. Of all my tasks that day, that took the longest. For each item, I wrote a name on a sheet of paper and taped tags to lamps, jewelry, and even the last of the laundry detergent. I wanted no fighting, no wondering what I would have wanted. Everything would be handled, everything settled.

And then, I made my final trip to town and bought two bottles of the best wine I could afford.

———

THE ROCKER BEGAN AS SOON AS I ENTERED THE BEDROOM, and I set the wine on the nightstand. From a high closet shelf, I brought down the glasses we'd toasted with on our wedding day. The rocking sped up. I fished my wedding dress from a box, scribbled Cassidy's name on a sheet of paper, and lay my wedding dress—Cassidy's dress now—on the bed, and the rocker went so wild that I felt the movement of it in my feet.

"I know, Marty. I know." I only had one remaining task. Returning to the nightstand, I opened the bottles and filled both glasses, setting one beside his chair, and Marty rocked furiously.

He was there, dear.

On the radio, that lovely song by that poor man who'd died eight years before began to play. Hadn't he died of an overdose? Had it been accidental? I wasn't so sure.

'Cuz I can't help falling in love with you . . .

Opening the first bottle of pills, I poured a handful into my palm. Funny little things, those pills. They could have been aspirin or arsenic. They all looked the same, yet some could save, and some could kill. Cupping my hand to my mouth, I let the pills spill onto my tongue. After nearly choking on the first handful, I realized I'd have to take smaller handfuls or else . . . well, that was silly now, wasn't it?

In the end, three handfuls were all I could muster, my head already spinning. I drank the remaining wine in one gulp, swiped a hand across my mouth, and lay back on the freshly made bed. By then, the rocker was going so fast that it banged against the wall. One of the boys would have to fix the hole it was bound to leave.

"I know, Marty. I'm almost there."

As I closed my eyes, I heard the chair crash to the floor. And then there was silence.

With sixty seconds to go, I heard a *click*, and a single thought permeated my being.

This is it.

I knew. My life was winding down to the final moments. In a disconnected way, I knew there was no stopping it. I couldn't change direction. My last act had already been written, it needed only to play out.

Suddenly, I needed to stop it, to reverse course. I watched myself from above, floating over my own bed, and screamed. *Throw it up! Don't die, this is wrong!* Instead, I listened as my breathing deepened and slowed. With only seconds remaining in my first life, I knew I'd made a mistake. Marty wouldn't have wanted this. And the children . . . *My God, the children.* What had I done?

"Marty . . ."

And then, dear, I knew everything.

———————

I CAME TO AS MY CASKET WAS LOWERED INTO THE GROUND. My children stood at my grave, Thelma next to them, their faces still and broken. I tried to speak, to tell them I was here. *Stop crying.*

Oh, my dears, stop.

Cassidy stared blankly at my coffin, and Ron shoved his hands into his front pockets in the same way I'd always told him not to. But Martin, my youngest, was the worst. His arms were folded over his chest, his gaze wandering from the trees to the cottage in the background. He wasn't sad, wasn't sorrowful.

He was angry. All of them. Angry with me.

Our pastor stopped talking, folded his bible, and my mourners—of whom there were surprisingly few—began to walk away. Except for the children. Cars roared to life, doors opened and closed, yet my children—the three most important people in my life—remained standing over my grave.

"You know," Martin said, expressionless, "she never returned my calls. I called her once a week, left messages on that machine Dad bought before he died, and she never returned them."

It wasn't true! But a memory crept in. Martin *had* left a few messages, and I'd meant to call back, but . . .

But.

"So, she didn't return your calls. So what? At least she didn't miss your college graduation."

That couldn't be right. Ron was only in his third year.

Or was it his forth? Something *had* come in the mail a few months earlier, a wide, square envelope that felt stiff, as if there were a card inside.

Or perhaps an invitation.

Cassidy grimaced in that way of hers. "At least we know what was important to her. I got the Christmas star. What did you guys get?" She laughed—a harsh sound that came from deep in her throat.

No! I'd wanted to make things easier, but all I'd done was reduce the worth of my children to a few boxes of Christmas decorations and a near-empty box of Tide. And then it hit me—the letters. Surely the letters would make everything clear.

"What did your letter say?" Cassidy asked as if sensing my own question.

"Same drivel as yours, and Ron's." Martin shoved his hands in his pockets like his brother. "I read them all."

Drivel? How could he say that?

Cassidy turned. "My favorite was the part about how we shouldn't be sad because she would be with Dad now. We should be . . . what was the word she used?"

Martin answered, though I already knew. "She said we should be comforted knowing they were together."

Ron kicked at a clump of dirt left behind on the grass near the hole I'd been lowered into. "Don't you feel comforted now? Mom and Dad are together! It doesn't matter that she left us behind, but hey, they're together. That's all that matters, right?"

And that's when I knew the harsh reality of my mistake. All that time, I'd thought my children no longer needed me, when in truth, they'd needed me more than ever, and I'd abandoned them, long before I died.

They passed through the gate, and I followed. And then I didn't. Something held me back, some force. I tried climbing over, tried digging a hole underneath. All I ever got was a broken fingernail that never grew back.

Eventually, night fell, and something happened.

Tiny globes of colorful light swarmed the air, dancing, rising, then swooping toward the earth. A globe swam to me, and I lifted my palm as it settled in my hand, rolling on my skin, expanding and diminishing before lifting off toward the sky. And I knew then my other mistake.

Marty hadn't been calling me to join him. He'd been trying to stop me from it.

When I saw the cottage, I knew I had to go there, knew it was where I would begin the Next. I was propelled along, not entirely under my own power.

Dear, the time had come for the Next.

39

HERBERT

FORTY YEARS BEFORE - 1958

I scanned the quiet group of nine- and ten-year-olds, searching for just the right one.

"Who volunteers to write the multiplication table for twelve?" I waited, unsure if anyone would step up until finally, a girl in pigtails shyly rose a hand.

"I knew there was at least one brave soul here. Come on up, Mary."

Rising from her seat, the timid girl walked with stiff arms and grabbed a piece of chalk from the tray with a questioning look.

Glancing at the board, I resisted the urge to slap a hand to my head and quickly swiped an eraser across the blackboard, obliterating a row of fractions. "Go ahead, Mary." I gave her a smile that she seemed in desperate need of.

Her eyes softened, she turned to the blackboard, and before long, numbers began to fill the space. *12, 24, 36, 48*

. . . Her hand hovered, and she tucked her bottom lip under her teeth.

So that the others wouldn't hear, I leaned in close. "Try sixty."

Her eyes lit up like the sun, and she smiled, exposing a missing front tooth before turning back, continuing even after a hundred and eight. Sometimes kids needed a push, a boost of confidence to shine. They didn't teach that in college in those days—I'd discovered it on my own.

Whispered giggles issued from the back of the room as I spied a folded note pass from one girl to another, and all eyes turned to the back row as I walked the aisle. "Hand it over, please, Miss Brookings." Hesitantly, she held up the note, and I unfolded it.

Mary loves Mr. C was scrawled beneath a crude drawing of two stick figures kissing—or planting corn. Whoever had drawn it would not likely be moving onto art school. Both girls appeared as terrified as if I'd read it aloud, so I gave them each a stern look, folded the note, and tucked it into my pocket.

"Girls, there's a time and place for doing homework. Right now, I'd like you to focus on the board." As I headed back toward the blackboard, I heard the unmistakeable exhale of relief behind me.

"Mr. C, should I keep going?" Mary had worked her way up to three hundred and sixty, white scrawls of chalk sliding at a downward angle as the board was nearly filled, and the bell rang, saving me the embarrassment of having to tell her to stop.

"You did a fine job, Mary," I said, as she hurried to her desk to gather her coat and lunch pail.

As the rest of the children filtered into the hall, I

stopped the note-passers. "I trust there won't be any more of that in class?"

"Yes, sir. I mean, no, sir. Sorry, sir." They scurried from the room, and I gathered my papers into my briefcase and headed toward the teacher's lounge. I loved children and was happy to finally be teaching, but that didn't mean I didn't look forward to that mid-day break. I entered the lounge, and as the door closed, the noise of hundreds of school children became blessedly muffled.

"Well, if it isn't Mr. Charming." Dan Clark, one of the fifth-grade teachers, waved me over to his table. I joined him with a raised brow, wondering when the ribbing would finally stop. "Oh, come on. All the girls are calling you that. At first, it was Prince Charming, but I'll be darned if someone didn't decide that it wasn't respectful enough, so now it's Mr. Charming."

I shook my head with an embarrassed groan.

"You should be flattered," Dan said, bits of bread floating in his beard. "My first year, they called me Mr. Dark." He ran a hand through a thick, black mane. "I'm sure it was the hair."

Desperate to change the subject, I unwrapped my sandwich from the newspaper I'd folded it into and took a hungry bite. "How's it going with the dance?"

As Dan launched into a lengthy list of complaints about the decorations, inappropriate music, and teachers unwilling to volunteer, I allowed my mind to drift. It wasn't right that the girls called me *Mr. Charming.* That was the kind of thing that got a grown man sent to the principal's office—fast. A teacher didn't gain respect from his students with a nickname like that—

"What do you say, Herbert?"

I looked up, jolted from my thoughts. "Sorry, what was that? And please, call me Herb."

"I asked if you'd be up for chaperoning the dance. As the only single man here . . ." Dan waved a hand at me as if that explained why I was made for chaperoning.

I was only surprised it had taken this long for someone to ask.

"Happy to, Dan."

———

THE BEST INFORMATION REGARDING THE STAFF OFTEN CAME from the students—and the latest rumor was that a new teacher was on the way. But as the week had worn on, a new teacher was the last thing on my mind. Though I'd willingly accepted the chaperone job, as the night of the dance grew closer, I found myself wishing I'd turned it down. It wasn't so much the dance, but Margaret, who'd been giving me looks and making not-so-subtle remarks in the teacher's lounge. Over the weeks, there had been several similar interactions. Aside from my—I thought—apparent disinterest, there was the added complication that Margaret was married. The last thing I needed was an angry husband showing up in the middle of class to teach *me* a lesson. According to the gossip mill, her marriage had been on the rocks from day one, and she'd been on the hunt the moment the honeymoon ended. The idea that I was the prey she'd set her sights on had caused more than a few sleepless nights.

"I heard you're chaperoning, Herbert," she said as she cozied up to my shoulder in the lounge.

"Yes, ma'am. And please, call me Herb."

"Lucky me. I'll be there, too." She winked a smile, and before she sashayed into the hall with a purposefully swing in her hips, she added, "Save the first dance for me, Herbert."

I found myself hoping that the rumors of a new teacher were true and that it was a man—a young, single man.

FORTY MINUTES LATE, I SLIPPED INTO THE GYMNASIUM. Filled with timid children, girls huddled in tight groups while boys shoved each other into walls to prove their manhood. The streamers, balloons, and banners hovering over two hundred anxious pre-teens gave the gymnasium the ambiance of a colorful wake rather than a dance.

The guilt I felt at being late was quickly drowned out by the soulful voice of Bobby Darin belting out that new song I'd heard everywhere that year, "Mack The Knife." Growing up on the farm, my brother Albert and I had cut all the rugs. I was Gene Kelly, and he was Fred Astaire. As a teacher, I'd even considered using dance as a tool to teach the kids math. Somewhere along the line, someone had decided girls weren't natural mathematicians, and the lie had stuck. Now, the country was filled with girls convinced they were already bad at something they weren't even encouraged to try.

The power of dance could've changed that.

Margaret spotted me, and before I had a chance to duck into a corner, she was already on her way, swinging her hips like a cha-cha dancer. "Herbert," she breathed, reeking of Old Fitzgerald, the same cheap whiskey my father had once kept beneath the floorboards, "you made it. I'm thrilled."

"Please, it's Herb." I glanced around the darkened gymnasium, hoping for a skirmish to break up or some improper behavior to correct. Unfortunately, there was nothing but halos all around, no matter how hard I looked.

"I believe you promised me a dance." She batted her eyes in an over-dramatic way that only teenagers and drunk women were capable of, as her hand slid up my arm. I had promised her no such thing, and she knew it. Her teeth, I noticed, were smeared with lipstick when she opened her maw to smile in a way that should have warmed me, yet only made me want to cringe.

And then, just when it seemed that I wouldn't be able to get out of our eventual dance, rescue arrived.

———

THE NEW TEACHER WAS MOST CERTAINLY NOT A MAN.

She was beautiful, even more dazzling than that Marilyn Monroe everyone was going on about. Though it was popular in those days for the ladies to wear their hair in short, tight curls, she'd swept hers into a loose bun, allowing long, blonde wisps to fall around her shoulders. The new teacher stood no more than five feet tall—a foot shorter than my six-foot frame—yet she didn't allow vanity to prevail, wearing flat saddle shoes as if she were on her way to the local sock hop.

I loved her the instant I laid eyes on her. And the first time she laid eyes on me, she pursed her lips and walked right by without a second glance.

"How about it?" Margaret's raspy voice pierced my ears, the smell of alcohol wafting like cheap perfume.

"Hmm?" Whatever question Margaret had been awaiting an answer for had slipped into the ether. It was impossible to look away from the mysterious new woman —as impossible as if someone had asked me to ignore gravity and float into the blue sky. As she lingered at a nearby table stained with sugary punch and frosting, I was sure she was listening. Her head was cocked, a wisp of blonde dangling, and she fiddled with a stack of those newfangled Styrofoam cups as if they were the most exciting things she'd ever encountered.

A hand slid down my arm again, and I nearly jumped out of my skin. Margaret grabbed my wrist like a vice and yanked me toward the dance floor, my heart racing while my shirt dampened with sweat. Helpless to stop it from happening, she pulled me along, and I saw my reputation die in a flash.

And then an angelic voice filled my head so entirely that I thought I'd imagined it—until I spotted the new teacher blocking Margaret's path, and her eyes were pinned to mine. "There you are, I've been looking everywhere."

Time halted as Margaret glared at the smiling woman who stood in her way, with eyes so blue they were nearly violet like Elizabeth Taylor's. They burrowed into my soul.

"You promised me the first dance, remember? Oh, I'm so sorry, Miss . . ."

It seemed that Margaret would refuse to answer as she dug her nails into my skin, her grip on my wrist was so wrenching that the pain was immense. I twisted from her hold, and Margaret's gaze swiveled to her now-empty hand. Gritting her teeth, she spat, "It's *Missus* Greene, and we were about—"

"Mrs. Greene, that's right. We haven't been formally introduced, though I did meet *Mr.* Greene earlier this week at the bank. Lovely man, your husband." The strangely captivating woman let loose a smile so full she could have had a successful career in used car sales.

At the not-so-subtle reminder that she was a married woman, Margaret straightened, brushed her hands over her pleats, and said, "I'll be sure to tell him you said so." Her eyes narrowed to slits.

My knees weakened just a little when the younger woman turned to me. "Ready? You did promise." Her gaze widened.

Now, I was not a simple man. I'd always prided myself on my ability to read people. Still—it took a moment to gather her meaning, but when I did, I grabbed hold. "Yes, I believe I did." I turned to Margaret. "I hope you don't mind."

Margaret lifted her chin and painted on a smile. "Not at all." She hobbled away on heels far too high, and I breathed a sigh of relief.

As if my neck were on a spring, I swung back to my rescuer. "Thank you. I wasn't sure how I was going to get out of that."

She cocked her head, questioning. "You still have to dance with me, you know. She's watching."

And kids, my heart fluttered. I struggled to regain some semblance of manhood and cleared my throat. "Well, I certainly can't dance with you if I don't know your name." I brought a finger to my lips and turned my eyes toward the ceiling. "I'd say by the way you saved me from that brute, you must be the Lone Ranger."

She gave no response, as if she were trying to figure me out, and let me tell you, I've thought about that moment more in both lifetimes than you'll ever know. She could have walked away, and my life would have taken a different course entirely. Instead, she softened. Only for a moment, you understand, but that moment defined me. "Miss Cline," she said, extending a hand.

I could not have stopped smiling if my life had depended upon it. "Mr. Casper. But please, call me Herb. Shall we?"

"A Teenager in Love" poured from the speakers, a ridiculous song for two grown chaperones to dance to, but nonetheless, I wrapped my hands around hers, and we fell into sync as if a lifetime of dances were already behind us. She was surprisingly good. As our bodies twisted a respectable two feet apart, her eyes flitted toward the corner. "Mrs. Greene seems to have set her sights on Principal Iverson. Poor man." As I tried to count the specks in her eyes, it wouldn't have mattered to me if the principal were swinging from a chandelier.

When I was young, I believed that life was a series of random events, that we were thrust into an already flowing tide and bumped around like flotsam. Maybe we would land on a beach, or perhaps we would float until the end of time. We went where the waves took us and adjusted accordingly. I believed that wholeheartedly until the night of the dance. Miss Cline could have simply watched the embarrassing scene play out and allowed Margaret to pull me and my reputation—which already teetered on the edge —into oblivion. Most would have done precisely that.

The very idea makes my heart hurt.

The song ended and "Runaround Sue" began to play. "I guess we're safe now." I stepped back and bowed low, though releasing Miss Cline's hands was one of the hardest things I'd ever had to do.

"Think nothing of it." She refused to meet my gaze, her eyes moving in an odd circle around me. "You're a terrible dancer, by the way."

"Excuse me?"

"It's nothing personal." A smile began to form before she crushed it back. "You stepped on me twice."

Bullshit. "Wait here."

Part of me was fired up; I was Gene Kelly, dammit, and I wasn't about to allow her to accuse me of anything less. And yet, another part was giddy; Herb Casper had never been one to walk away from a challenge. Leaving her standing alone in the middle of the gymnasium, I whispered to the boy operating the record player, and he flipped through a crate of albums. When my eye landed on the right one, I shot him a thumbs up and sauntered back to Miss Cline, her hands resting on her hips.

"Your name, please?"

She looked taken aback. "Miss Cline. I told you that."

"Your first name."

"Oh." She blushed. "Edith."

I smiled. "Well, Edith, prepare to have your berries razzed." Groans echoed around the gymnasium as The Jitterbug began to play. Only oldsters jitterbugged, but I happened to be good at it. If he hadn't been shipped off to our Aunt Betsy after our mother died, Albert could have attested to that. My feet whirled as hers remained still while one hand remained on her hip.

And then she smiled; a genuine grin that made the world sigh. "Herbert Casper, you have met your match." She grabbed my arm, slid to my side, and jitterbugged me right into the atmosphere. Our bodies jittered, they bugged, they came together and fell apart in perfect synchronistic form. Kids gathered, clapping and stomping. It was a scene straight from that Christmas movie, the one with that hot tamale, Donna Reed. We ebbed and flowed, apart and together, until we moved seemingly by a force that wasn't our own, and when the song ended, the applause that greeted us was otherworldly.

I pulled her into a bow, and when I peeked in the direction of the punchbowl, Principal Iverson shook his head with a grin.

"We shouldn't have done that." Edith straightened her dress and tucked a fallen hair behind an ear as the fury died down and the students resumed their awkward dances.

"You can't deny that the kids loved it."

The smile waned, and she stiffened once again, thrusting her hand to me in a decidedly professional manner. "Thank you, Mr. Casper, for not stepping on my toes. That time, anyway."

"It's Herb."

"Yes, Herb. Well." And just like that, our moment was over as she turned, blending in with the crowd.

In that single moment, I knew. Not nearly, not a faded thought. I *knew*. You can run from destiny, but eventually, it circles back around. One way or another, your fate meets you in the end.

At the punch table, Edith stood as stiff while she scanned the room, her eyes moving from right to left until they had nowhere to land but on mine. Turning her neck as if to break contact, she remained fixed on me. Our eyes spoke, longed, danced the way our bodies had, and though she did not know it, I'd already wrapped my heart in a bow with her name on it.

———————

TWO HOURS LATER, THE DANCE FINALLY BEGAN TO WIND down. While half of the kids had been picked up by worried mothers, the other half lingered in corners. I only needed to wait for the kid manning the record player to give me my cue.

"Folks, this is the last dance, so grab your partners. This one is for teachers only."

Elvis began to croon, "I Can't Help Falling in Love with You," and, taking the most momentous risk of my life, I approached Edith at the punch table.

Oh, God, oh no.

Margaret swam into view, her body swaying as if she'd been lying in wait, her lips crinkling into an off-center smile as she lifted her hand to me.

I was not a cruel man. In the end, I became a crass, foul-mouthed fool, but never cruel.

Aside from that night.

With a nod, I strolled right on by, and the pained look on Margaret's face is still imprinted on my memory, all these lifetimes away from that warm September evening.

At the punch table, words failed me. I could do little more than hold my head up as I floated toward Edith. *Save me,* I mouthed.

Edith rolled her eyes, a quirk I came to love like many

others over the years. Over time, I learned that the eye-roll meant we'd struck a deal. God, I loved that woman. Still do. All these universes later.

She accepted my outstretched hand, and we moved back to the dance floor. As I wrapped my arms around her, I knew I would marry her. How long it would take to convince her, I didn't yet know.

Luckily, not long.

I took in the scent of her hair—some sort of lavender scent that she would keep hidden for decades. After she died, I scoured the town grocer searching the shelves, opening bottles for a whiff, desperate to find the shampoo that made her hair smell like that. A month after I buried her, I found a near-empty bottle of lemon verbena on a high closet shelf with a note attached:

You keep asking how I get that lavender scent in my hair. Well, here it is, and I put it on my neck, not my hair. How you could think this was lavender, I'll never know.

It was dated May 1st, 1967. She'd planted the note, waited nearly twenty years for me to find it . . . and died waiting.

In the gymnasium, I lost myself in that hair, and when the song ended, and the lights came up, it was as if someone had shut out the magic. Suddenly, I hated those lights.

"I watched you slip a fiver to the record-player kid." With a gotcha look, Edith turned and strutted toward the pile of coats. "You paid too much. He would've done it for two."

"How do you know?" I called, embarrassed to have

been caught. "Five dollars is pretty cheap—" A song blared then, cutting off my words.

"Here's a special request to play us out." The kid leaned away from the mic, looked at me, and shrugged, and I couldn't hold back laughter as that Elvis kid told me, on Edith's behalf, that I was nothing but a hound dog. She grabbed her coat and purse and didn't bother looking back before walking out of the gym.

Sassy from day one. That was my Edith.

THIRTY-NINE YEARS BEFORE - 1959

We had a simple ceremony at city hall with a small reception in the school gymnasium. Principal Iverson quietly let the janitor go early and opened a side door for Edith and I, along with several other teachers, and we danced to what would be our song, the one where that young Memphis boy with the gyrating hips couldn't help falling in love.

On our wedding night, we continued the dance alone in the living room of that first small house, the one with the forgotten apple orchard behind it, while Elvis crooned from the record player. Occasionally over the years, once we could afford more luxurious living, I offered to take her on a real honeymoon—to the Grand Canyon, or maybe even Mount Rushmore—and every time, she had the same answer.

"Why do you insist on replacing the best night of my life, Herb Casper?"

We lived in that house for a year, until one night, we came home to find a fireman standing in the smoldering ruins of our kitchen. We lost everything, but as Edith was good at pointing out, we didn't have much to lose. "Everything we need, we have right here," she'd said, and wrapped her hand around mine. As always, my Edith was right. The insurance company gave us five thousand dollars—about four thousand more than that run-down shack was worth—and we bought a three-story house in the Summerfield neighborhood, with wide steps leading to a front porch big enough for a couple of rockers.

"This is where we'll sit when the children are asleep," she'd whispered. Girls, boys, it didn't matter, as long as there were plenty. I saw it as clearly as she did and signed the papers without hesitation. "It's going to be awfully quiet until we start filling this place up," I said after we moved our two remaining unscorched boxes inside.

Later, that porch would shine, but on that first night, it was rickety and old and in dire need of repair. As the sun slowly set in the west, a gentle breeze moved in the tall grass as water trickled from an ambling brook. With a creak, she settled into the empty rocker, her hand took mine, and our fingers intertwined. Our rockers swayed forward and back, and her smile made the world explode. "One day," she said, "you'll wish we'd bought a bigger one."

It was the only time when Edith turned out to be wrong.

WE TRIED EVERYTHING, AND I MEAN *EVERYTHING*.

A neighbor had convinced Edith that yams increased the fertility of some tribe of African women, so she ate yams until her skin turned yellow. Her lady-doctor told her to lay on her back after—you know—and raise her legs in the air. That only gave her headaches. And then came the six months of grapefruit. Edith ate grapefruit in the morning, guzzled grapefruit juice in the afternoon, and rubbed it on her skin at night. I'll admit she smelled darned good for that first week, but by the end, the smell of grapefruit only made me nauseous.

We didn't have any of the fancy, expensive treatments back then. What we had was hope, Elvis, and grapefruit. And, in our case, those just weren't enough. My Edith was born to be a mother. She taught a roomful of seven-year-olds for six hours a day, and still, it pained her watching them walk out after the final bell. At home, she knitted blankets from her rocker on the porch and pieced squares of fabric into elaborate quilts by the fire. Sometimes, I wished I hadn't let her talk me into that big house. It only served as a constant reminder of how many people were missing.

But Edith was not one to brood over such things. She never cried over the children who never were, didn't let her smile so much as falter each time we got the call that the rabbit didn't die. That woman kept a brave face even when we were forced to accept that children were not in our future. I know it killed her, every childless year that passed, but, she was strong—stronger than the old codger who married her. And each time we got the news she didn't want to hear, she made my favorite meatloaf, the one with the pineapple chunks on top, and we spent the evening dancing at the fire to our favorite tune, the one that perfectly expressed how much I could never have helped falling in love with her.

TWENTY YEARS BEFORE - 1978

Twenty years is a long time to remember something like it was yesterday. That dance, the first time I smelled lavender that turned out to be lemon, the songs our future selves bonded over while we swayed to voices that now are all long dead. Time, they say, is a funny thing. It doesn't move the way Livers think it does. Time is more like those video cassettes of *Hope's Hospital* that Edith used to watch in the evenings. You can rewind it, view it over and over, but you know that what you're watching was once in the present—in the Now.

In the Next, time takes on a different meaning. It doesn't stop exactly, because it never was. When you cross to the other side, you realize that time is but an illusion, little more than a manner of marking events. Life is merely a series of cliffhangers, though someone, somewhere, knows how it will all end.

The night I met Edith, twenty years seemed a lifetime, an unfathomable measurement of breathing, living, and existing. Yet, when I rewind the cassette of my life's events, it all happened in the blink of an eye. During those twenty years, I taught two of Madge's children, Tracy Murphy, and a young girl named Helen who later gave birth to a son who would die protecting my grave.

We are all connected.

Edith and I were never blessed with children to fill the rooms of our large house. She used to joke that we should have bought a shack and that the irony would have guaranteed a large brood. But we'd gotten cocky and bought a relative mansion, ensuring not a clutch of laughing children, but unused space. Edith also used to say that God had blessed us not merely with a houseful, but with hundreds. We taught them reading, writing and 'rithmetic and we'd loved them as our own while we watched them grow—some into people we were proud of, some into less. But though she tried to hide it, there came to be an undercurrent of regret just beneath the surface. As a couple, we'd never bothered to see which one of us had the problem. Edith said it didn't matter, and that in the end, it was a cross we both bore.

In all those years, I kept only one secret from her, and in the fall of 1978, I arranged for a substitute teacher for the day.

"I don't understand why you have to go all the way to Portland," Edith said as she gathered graded papers. "Why can't Dr. Hannigan see you?"

"Some new test they want me to take, and Dr. Hannigan doesn't have the equipment. You know how it is in this town. It takes forever to catch up."

She pecked me on the cheek. "Well, don't go running off with some young nurse. I hear those Portland girls are loose."

"You know I can't promise that. Look at me." I waved a hand over my scrawny body and pointed to my already thinning hair.

The truth was, I was headed to Portland because small towns have big ears, and on the morning of our twentieth wedding anniversary, the results arrived in the mail, confirming my worst fears—it was me. I was the problem. I'd failed my Edith, hadn't been able to give her the children she'd longed for. She gave me twenty years of companionship, and all she'd asked for in return was the fulfillment of a single wish.

The least I could do was remove the burden of failure from her shoulders, and I offered to take her to The Witherbee for our anniversary dinner. Something nice. Something special.

"The Witherbee is too pretentious, not to mention expensive. And besides, you love the breadsticks at the Dandy Sandy."

"Not exactly what I'd call a place fit for a twentieth-anniversary dinner." What I really wanted to say, I couldn't. *I want to take you to the best place in town because somehow that will help to make up for all I've stolen from you.* How would I ever tell her? How could I ask her to spend another twenty years with a thief?

Not wanting a fuss, we hadn't mentioned our anniversary to the other teachers. But, we were naive to think that no one would have figured it out. We had, after all, met and fallen in love in that very building. When the lunch bell rang, we met at the teacher's lounge and found it locked. I should have known something was amiss then. "Great. I guess we're eating with the kids," I grumbled, and as we headed toward the cafeteria, I failed to read Edith's amused expression.

In the middle of the lunch hour, Principal Iverson walked onstage, grabbed the mic, and the room quieted almost immediately. "A special couple is celebrating their twentieth wedding anniversary today," he said, as his eyes landed on our table.

And that song, the one we'd danced to the night we met, and again on the night we'd married—the one I danced to on my grave with that lovely Emily, who looked so much like my Edith—began to play.

"Come on up here, you two."

Students rose in applause as we walked, embarrassed, to the stage. I peeked to the area beyond the curtain and spied one of my former students, John Bennett, working the record player. I offered my hands, Edith took them, and we began our swirl around the stage. I really couldn't have helped falling in love with her. I held her close, closed my eyes, and floated within that scent of lavender that wasn't. I was lost in her.

I still am.

"I should have slipped the kid a fiver to play that other song we danced to the night we met."

Have you ever *felt* someone smile?

"Five is too much. The Bennett boy would have done it for two."

"And, just how would you know?"

She remained silent as the song wound down, the kids began to clap once again, and I took a step toward the short stairs that led off the stage.

But my Edith didn't budge.

The Bennett boy lifted the record from the turntable, put another in its place, and "Hound Dog" roared. He glanced at me, shrugged, and gave me a thumbs up.

That was my Edith, in a nutshell.

THAT NIGHT, AS WE PREPARED FOR BED, I DECIDED TO KEEP the test results to myself. Though the truth would release her of the guilt I knew she must have carried, I wasn't sure how much of an anniversary gift that knowledge would be. Another day—the next, perhaps. As we climbed into bed, pecked one another goodnight, and rolled to our sides, I heard the click of the bedside lamp, and through my closed lids, I knew the room had darkened. I listened for Edith's telltale breathing with envy that she could fall asleep at the drop of a hat, while I laid awake each night struggling for respite.

But that night, her breathing remained quiet, shallow. "Herb."

Don't say it. Don't . . .

"I'm happy, with or without children."

I opened my eyes and stared at the curtains fluttering in the open window. "You read the results."

I felt her shift as she rested a hand on my bare shoulder. "Herb—"

"No, Edith." I couldn't think, couldn't process that she knew. That I was going to tell her eventually meant nothing. All that mattered was that she knew that I was to blame for all that empty space around us.

She quieted, and I felt the bed sheets rustle as she lay back down, and it was another hour before her breathing changed.

Guilt, you should know, follows you through every lifetime.

FOURTEEN YEARS BEFORE - 1984

Our twenty-fifth wedding anniversary was going to be the hugest blowout in the history of Hood Valley. I'd planned it all year, and Herb Casper was no party planner. I didn't like parties and had never felt comfortable in crowds. At least not groups where the average age was older than ten. Edith, on the other hand, lived for them. No party was too large, no room too crowded.

She could talk for hours—no one could tell a story better than my Edith—effortlessly turning strangers into friends. I could often find her in a corner, nodding, while someone poured their heart out. People gravitated toward her, found a kinship. Edith was like that.

We'd never hosted a party of our own—she'd never even suggested it, never wanted to put me in a position she knew I'd be uncomfortable in. So our twenty-fifth wedding anniversary would've been the biggest surprise of her life.

Principal Iverson had arranged a parent-teacher conference after school, tying Edith up long enough to give me time to decorate our house. Somehow, word got out, and half of my students came knocking on the door ten minutes after I arrived home, begging to help. And as the children raced through the house, I saw what could have been. Some sat at the kitchen table cutting paper into ribbons, while others chased one another through the yard, hanging streamers here and there, covering our beautiful, lively oaks in pinks and blues. Feet pounded against the stairs. Shoes echoed on the long wooden planks of the front porch.

In bittersweet clarity, I saw what I had denied my Edith.

I lived my first life under the misconception that the moment I died, I'd be granted the knowledge of things past, present and future—that I would know who'd killed JFK, whether the world was round or flat, or if life was predetermined or a random series of events. It's true that you learn truths—those and many more. But the most gut-wrenching truth you learn is that you already knew most of it. The punishment dealt by death is the inability to keep your eyes shut to your own crimes.

As Taylor's future mother hovered close to Taylor's future father, I turned from the truth and passed out a dozen paper hats.

The phone rang, and I raced to it, shushing the children. "Casper residence," I said, while dozens of sets of ears listened.

"She just left my office," Principal Iverson said. "I'm on my way now."

I hung up without saying goodbye and turned to the children. "Mrs. Casper is on her way," and without another word, they gathered coats, plastic lunchboxes, and backpacks and headed toward the door.

"Hold it just one minute, kids. You don't think I'm going to let you leave before the party's even gotten started, do you?"

All of those young, wide eyes settled on me, and a boy who would become one of the first casualties of Desert Storm spoke up. "Do you have more jobs for us?"

I laughed. "No more jobs. You're all invited to stay. We can call your mothers after Mrs. Casper arrives. Now go and hide!"

Squeals of excitement flew as the children scrambled, squeezing behind chairs and into closets. One even slid under the rug, leaving a noticeable lump on the floor.

It was a five-minute drive from the school. I looked at my watch—Edith would be halfway home by now. As I stood at the window, my nerves jolted as the principal flew around the corner and raced toward our house. I glanced up the street—Edith's car was nowhere to be seen. When the principal reached the steps, he took them by twos, and he was neither a young nor a slim man. "I parked around the corner," he panted, looking for a hiding spot. His eyes landed on the corner, and he raced to it. "Move over, kids."

Time passed, and the children became restless. Principal Iverson twisted from behind the chair and hobbled to the window. "Did she have errands to run after school?"

"Not that I know of." I couldn't lift my sinking gut. Edith always came straight home. In twenty-five years, she'd never been late. We ran our errands together, shopped together, gathered craft supplies for the kids together. Something was wrong.

By five o'clock, she was an hour late. Most of the children had to get home, and I watched, that sinking ship in my gut dropping lower, as, one by one, they left.

Principal Iverson lay a gentle hand on my shoulder. "I'm going to drive over to the school." I glanced away from the window long enough to see the worry behind his eyes. "Everything's fine, Herb. She probably ran out of gas and is waiting for someone to swing by. You know how women are."

I knew how women were. But I also knew how Edith was. She topped off her tank every three days whether it needed it or not, and if she had run out of gas, she wouldn't have waited for rescue. She'd have made the walk home in fifteen minutes, tops.

Principal Iverson threw on his coat and was headed for the door when a police car pulled in front of the house. I recognized the man who climbed out of the cruiser; he'd been a student twelve years earlier. Good kid, a bit on the portly side, hailing from one of the few Catholic families in a predominantly Lutheran town. He went on to have two children, and his boy would go on to be the caretaker who would replace Rick. Charlie came after my time, and it was a good thing, too—his father would undoubtedly have been the one to finally recognize me, and that would have ruined everything.

For the remainder of my life, I blocked out the memory of the policeman making that long, slow walk up the flower-lined path that led to our door. By sheer will, I forgot the words he said to me, the sorrow of it all, and wiped the images of the remaining guests' gasps, groans, and one *Dear God* from my mind. Now, those images, those sounds, are with me. Death allows you to forget nothing. I know there's a reason, though it escapes me.

Principal Iverson drove me to the hospital in silence, and sat with me while a doctor explained her injuries, patted my back as they rolled her into surgery. I never forgot *that*. Some hours later, after the principal had gone home with the promise to return in the morning, the officer approached me in the waiting room, his hat gripped in his hand.

"Can I sit, Mr. C?"

"Please, call me Herb." On automatic pilot by then, I directed him to the empty chair next to me.

The Martin kid—I know he wasn't a kid anymore, but they always remained kids to me—sat gingerly and faced me.

"Sorry. You'll always be Mr. C to me."

I guessed it went both ways, then.

"We know what caused her vehicle to veer off the road. There'll be a report in the morning, but I wanted you to know first before anything got out. Mrs. C had a lot of friends here at the hospital, and, you know, loose tongues . . ."

My brain focused on the word *had*. She *had* a lot of friends. Much as I liked the Martin kid, I wanted to punch him square in the jaw then for writing off my Edith before her time.

"A girl walked in front of her car, and witnesses say that Mrs. C tried to avoid hitting her. That's when she hit the pole."

A kid in the road. Irony is cruel. "What girl?"

"Her name's Deborah Bennett. Fifteen, Caucasian, lives over on—"

"I know where she lives." I knew Deborah.

And I had known her mother, Margaret, too.

When Deborah ended up in Edith's first-grade class, she was as shy as they came. Stephanie and Madge would tell you that Deborah had always been odd. But the other funny thing about time is that it enables you to rewrite history. In truth, Deborah was little more than a lost soul in need of a friend. That her mother was a drunkard only made things worse.

I could say a thousand things about my Edith, but if I could only settle on the one that I loved most, it would have been her ability to see past facades to the real person hidden under the cloaks they invented. Whether they were troubled kids or troubled parents, she saw below the surface to the potential beneath. Edith had tried everything, but in the end, she couldn't reach the girl, who'd distanced herself from the world. As we followed her path through the school over the years, Deborah became more withdrawn, and by the time she entered middle school, there were already rumors that she'd followed in her mother's destructive path.

I had to know.

"Was she . . . had the girl been drinking?"

Officer Martin, who would always be a kid to me, lowered his head and slowly nodded.

———

THE FOLLOWING MORNING, I SPOTTED THE DILLARDS walking through the lobby like a couple of zombies. When the wife looked at me, I knew she'd be dead inside of a year. Don't ask me how I knew. The words just scrawled themselves on my brain and stuck there, and when I read about her suicide later, I was so far gone that all I could do was toss the paper aside and wonder, of the two of us, which had made the wiser decision.

———

HALF OF HOOD VALLEY SHOWED UP FOR EDITH'S funeral. Students, former students, friends, neighbors, teachers. Some smothered me with pity while others gave mumbled condolences. A man I was sure I'd never met told me he'd lost his wife three years before and insisted that he knew how I felt. It was all I could do to keep from laughing in his face.

No one could possibly have known how I felt.

A surprising number of people asked to speak. Two girls told of the Christmas cards Edith had sent year after year to each of her former students, a fact I was ashamed to admit I hadn't known. A young college man told how she'd kept his artwork on her classroom wall for years after he'd moved on. I knew the drawing—a firetruck—it hung on the wall behind her desk. I could have told him it was there still, but words were beyond my capability. When the machine that had given Edith breath pumped for the final time, I ceased to speak. Instead, I walked from the hospital without a word and refused to make arrangements for her funeral. Principal Iverson sat at my kitchen table and made every necessary call, arranged every preparation, while I rocked on the porch staring at the house across the street, at the grass, at my aging hands. Without her, I was capable of nothing, and so I checked out.

After a month's leave, the first words I spoke were, "I resign." I didn't know I was going to do it until that first day back, but I should have seen it coming. The school was our second home, the students our children. Edith was everywhere. I even smelled that lemon verbena, the scent clawing at me from the inside. The best of her lingered in that school.

And then, a year after I buried her, I got a call from Serenity Grove, and the nightmare of all nightmares hurled into my life, something that no sound man can ever recover from.

"I'm not sure how to say it, Mr. Casper, but we had some trouble with vandals, and it looks like they did some damage to your wife's plot." He went on, saying something about graffiti, what he was doing to repair the damage, and assured me that it would be good as new.

I said nothing, staring at the kitchen sink while he spoke. And then he said something that brought me out of my haze like a slap.

"I should tell you that they did some . . . digging."

Silence on both ends. It must have been a full minute before I gathered the ability to speak.

"Are you telling me that someone dug up my wife?"

He cleared his throat. "The body is intact."

My mind spun out of control, out of my head, out of this world. "You need to stop pussyfooting around and tell me what they did to my wife, you little shit." Before that moment, I'd never spoken such vile words to another person. It was as if someone else' voice had taken over my own. After listening to the caretaker apologize for what felt like an eternity, I threw the phone across the kitchen, grabbed my keys, and drove to the cemetery, ignoring every stop sign and both traffic lights on the way, and marched straight to her grave, where a blue tarp had been tented.

I bent, walked under, and lost my breath.

Dirt was splayed in clumps, her tombstone askew. Rain filled misshapen holes, and then, I saw the unthinkable. Her casket had been pried open, and crowbar marks etched the side. Taking a step closer, I dropped to my knees. Though darkness exuded from within, I saw it immediately. I couldn't *not* see it. I remembered pointing to it when Principal Iverson had asked which dress Edith would want to be buried in, and I'd chosen that one because she'd liked the frilly lace at the sleeves.

It was the lace I saw, and though I didn't see her hand or the bones that would have remained, the lace was all it took. My wife's dead hand was somewhere. Right. There. When I tried to run, I tripped over my own feet and fell, my face splattering in the mud. I lifted my head and saw the caretaker—the one before Serge—his eyes wide with horror.

And it was that look, those eyes, that killed Herb Casper for good. His eyes reflected what was in my own soul, and when I saw the proof of it, I could exist no longer. Herb Casper, otherwise known as Mr. C, sometimes known as Mister Charming fell away, and Herbert took his place. A shell clamped around my heart, hard, like walnut, impossible to pry open without just the right tool. Humanity was lost—if ever it had existed, if ever it had been anything more than a pipe dream.

My weathered cross claims the year of my death to be 1998. The actual year was 1985, and I died as I rose from the mud beside my wife's desecrated corpse. Rick liked to laugh off my concerns of grave robbers as if they were something that happened only in cheaply made B movies, but the truth fed the shell over my heart.

Had Rick bothered to read my intake, he would have learned that my wife—my Edith—was buried on the other side of that dead elm. It was never my grave that I so desperately needed him to protect.

Without so much as a glance at the caretaker, I walked toward the gate, and as I passed, the newly born Herbert Casper spoke his first words.

"You should be patrolling the grounds at night, jackass."

NEXT

You've heard the story of my death, so I don't need to go into that. An old man had a heart attack and died—nothing extraordinary there. It's what happened after that may interest you.

It shouldn't come as a surprise that my funeral was a pretty low-key affair. Principal Iverson was my only mourner, and even he had nothing to say. Yet he'd shown up, watched as my body was lowered into the ground, and hobbled away on a cane. He must have been the only person who still remembered there had once been a man behind the crass thing I became in the years that followed Edith's death.

I watched him pass through the gate, but I didn't bother trying to follow. I knew that the gate served to seal me within a punishment I was destined to suffer for eternity.

Eventually, night fell. And something happened.

Tiny globes of colorful light swarmed the air, dancing, rising, then swooping toward the earth. A globe swam to me. I lifted my palm to the air, and it settled in my hand, rolling on my skin, expanding and diminishing, before lifting off toward the sky. I knew it was her, my Edith, comforting me one final time with delicate whispers that filled me with awe, comfort.

I turned, fluttering globes surrounded me, and I saw the cottage. I knew I had to go there, where I would begin the Next. But there was something I had to do first.

Though I hadn't visited in over a decade, I knew where she was. I walked right on by the cottage, beyond Barlow Pond, and into the small wood behind, and on the opposite side of a dying elm, I came to Edith's grave. Weeds crawled the sides of her forgotten tombstone. Flowers donned the surrounding graves, but hers had been left bare. Seeing how I'd abandoned her, my heart twisted. I knelt before her headstone, placed a hand on the faded granite, and knew that she was gone. I was in the Next, and my Edith had traveled on without me.

For the first time in fourteen years, I cried. Pain gushed in waves, and I thought I'd die all over again from the agony. The globes tried to surround me, but I pushed them away, screamed at them to leave me, take me, leave me, take me. Time, I've said before, exists only in your world. I can't tell you how long I cried, screamed, and resisted the love that tried to crawl inside.

I know now that I will be trapped behind these iron bars for the rest of eternity, and that I'll probably never have the chance to finally stick it to Travis. I also know that life really is a series of random events and that the only purpose of living is to just try to stay out of your own way. To believe otherwise would mean that my Edith was taken intentionally, and that is just too much for this old man to think about.

As I sit here in this darkened cottage, the clouds break, allowing a stream of sunshine through. Unsure what else to do after hearing the news of Rick's untimely death, we've taken up residence, mourning our growing losses. Morning sunlight washes the dusty floor, an unwelcome guest piercing the darkness we've cocooned ourselves in. He'll never know it, but I loved Rick like the son I so desperately wanted. And as troublesome, miserable, and vulgar as I have been, if there were some way I could bring his Emily here, I would do it without hesitation. No one should be left on their own in the Next—

What's this? It can't be . . . but it is! A goose is walking on my grave.

The globes surround me, but they also push, and as I fly through the gate, I know that the time has come for the Next.

40

BENSON

I need to find the man. His smell is inside, and the one they call Buster smells it too, but Dog knows the scent is meant for me, so he stays. I cannot see the man's face, but that doesn't matter. It's his smell that I need to follow. It was faint in the house with Dog, but it's stronger out here, like an arrow pointing the way. Like bitter flesh, I can taste it.

His scent arrived an hour ago in Human time, and now I know everything. I am the last in a long line. We have been with the Humans from the beginning, connecting with them. Sometimes we seek them out—other times we are brought to them by other Humans who do not know they are a small part of our journey.

Nothing is random, nothing is by chance.

The man's scent is momentarily hidden from me. I wait, knowing he has not gone on to the Next—*that* has its own scent. His smell mingles with another's, and his odor grows strong. He is agitated—three dots swim before me, and I know now that the dots are his frustration. I will see the dots many times before the end. After a while, the other scent disappears, and the smell of calmness cloaks me as the darkness fades. My Human is alone now. He thinks he is happiest when he is alone. I follow, sniffing the pleasant scent—even better than the herb the Humans give us. There is nothing like the scent of our Human.

The Humans seem unaware of their role, and of ours. They believe their lives are random, chance events. They do not see the role we each play, and I know that is how it should be, though this is confusing to me.

They do not understand that the Humans they love are on their own paths and that they cannot alter the course of another by merely wishing for it.

Taylor does not know that she cannot be held responsible for her mother's decisions. And that her father and brother are bonded now as they speak together at high schools warning teens of the dangers of texting and driving.

Stephanie does not know that her untimely death affected others in ways that go beyond her and that Billy would go on to start an organization to educate grief counselors on treating surviving family members of carbon monoxide poisoning. He named it Overcoming Monoxide Grief, or, OMG.

Madge does not know that many years after taking her own life, as her daughter Cassidy left the Dandy Sandy one cold, foggy night, she took a left instead of a right and spotted a man as he prepared to jump to his death from the Barlow Bridge. The despair Madge's suicide had caused propelled Cassidy to pull over and prevent the stranger from committing the same mistake. Two days later, with Emily's photo in hand, Charlie was finally able to visit her grave and release the guilt he'd held for having been behind the wheel on the fateful day that ended her life.

Each of us is chosen long before our time.

The sky is darkening, and I can see the gates ahead. Sensing my beginning, I hurry. As I watch from outside the gate, my Human carries boxes from a truck, and I know that he is just beginning his own journey behind these walls. He is different from others—his Human talk is fragmented, but he does not see that his crippled speech serves him. He carries death—from his Human mother as well as the taste of his own—and is drawn to it like a moth to a flame, as it has brought him here.

Nothing is random.

I glance behind, knowing that once I pass through, I will not leave this place again until the end. There is no sadness in this; it is part of my Knowing, my path, and I grieve for nothing. My Human exits the cottage, and I move toward him. His scent strengthens, builds, and overwhelms me. We are bonded now, though he will not know this for a long time. I rub my body against him, both to grab his attention and to begin our path. Touch is always the beginning. He kneels and scratches behind my ears.

"Hey there, b-boy, where'd you come from? Go on now, time to get home. It's darn near d-dark."

As it began, his words close the circle.

Scattering toward the wood, I seek my new home where I will remain behind these gates.

But there is one job that remains.

I catch the scent of the other's grave. Though he is a good man, he hides it well. His suffering has soured him, but that, too, will be for the higher good. Lifting a leg, I mark his spot; there is no greater show of respect for the man who will lead us all to the end. The globes appear as they do for those of us who can see them. Colors, bright and beautiful, surround me, and I am at peace. I settle at the base of the great elm that overlooks the grave of the one they once called Herb.

Darkness falls, and I am ready for the Next.

THE END

Windy Prasert lived most of her life in the Pacific Northwest and even spent one very impoverished year on the island of Maui. After raising two kids to adulthood without the need for probation officers, she focused her attention on writing.

As a full-fledged, official grown-up (her driver license confirms this), Windy enjoys a good book that can whisk her into another world, another life, another's trials and heartache. She's a sucker for a happy ending and a good laugh. When she's not immersed in a book, she can be found making homemade apple butter and binge-watching Clifford the Big Red Dog.

Obsessed with all things Elvis, Windy hopes one day to reside at Graceland in a pink Cadillac. She currently lives in Texas with her husband and two cats.

WindyPrasert.com

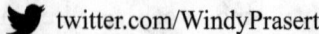
twitter.com/WindyPrasert

instagram.com/WindyPrasert

goodreads.com/windy_prasert

SIGN UP FOR MY NEWSLETTER TO RECEIVE A BONUS STORY!

"STAMPED OUT"

It's 1975, and Madge can almost taste victory: she's competing for the unofficial title of Housewife of the Year, and has nearly collected enough S&H Green Stamps to buy the punchbowl that will prove her domestic superiority once and for all. Never again will the ladies of the Wednesday Afternoon Women's Auxiliary League put her last on the neighborhood phone tree.

But when the latest catalog comes out, a brand new prize upends the playing field completely. If only Madge can get her hands on the first 12-inch color TV on her block, she'll secure her reign indefinitely.

In her mad dash to collect the stamps she needs, Madge transforms from the Happy Housewife of Hood Valley into a frantic, soap-opera-obsessed stamp collector who will do anything short of breaking the law—and maybe even that—to get her hands on the ultimate prize.

Visit WindyPrasert.com and subscribe to my newsletter for your free bonus story!